A RAKE LIKE YOU

BECKY MICHAELS

For Georgia
Thank you for always being the best listener
Fergie and Fanny Forever

Prologue

❧❦❧

London, England
June 1810

LOUISA STRICKLAND DASHED down the front steps of Lady Ramsbury's Park Street mansion without much thought. As it turned out, rational thoughts were hard to come by when one was angry, confused, *and* upset, especially when one was feeling all those things simultaneously. Although she could hear Charles Finch's frantic shouts coming from behind her, she did not stop, despite having no idea where exactly she was going. She only knew she needed to get away from Charles as soon as possible.

"Louisa!" he yelled.

She looked over her shoulder to find him no less than ten paces behind her. Turning forward, Louisa muttered an unladylike oath under her breath, one that her stepmother would have rightfully scolded her for using.

Home, she decided. That was where she was going.

Louisa quickened her pace, passing brick town house after brick town house with long, purposeful strides. Hopefully no one was peeking out their windows, watching her. That was the last thing Louisa needed: a headline in one of tomorrow's scandal sheets that read *VISCOUNT D— AND MISS S— QUARREL ON THE LAST NIGHT OF THE SEASON. NO ENGAGEMENT IN SIGHT!*

Louisa took a right on Green Street. Only a few more yards, and she would be home. She reveled in the idea of slamming the door in Charles's face just before he could catch her. Such a conclusion to their time together might do him some good. Some men needed a woman or two to slam a door in their face.

But then Louisa felt his gloved fingers wrap around the crook of her elbow. Without hesitation, she spun around and slapped the viscount clear across the face. The sound echoed like a clap of thunder on a rapidly cooling summer night.

"Unhand me!" she cried.

Charles let go of her. Somewhere, a dog barked, probably startled by the sudden loud noise reverberating through the streets. Louisa was rather startled herself. She hadn't realized she had it in her.

Louisa stared down at Charles, his face presently turned to the side, cradling a cheek marked by an angry red handprint. He cursed, turning to face her. She remained expressionless, doing her best to ignore the way her palm stung. She had never slapped anyone before and hadn't expected to injure herself in the process.

"What the hell was that for?" Charles asked angrily, still holding his hand to his cheek.

Louisa's nostrils flared. How could he ask such a thing after what she'd seen?

"Surely you do not expect me to remain celibate through such a long charade!" he exclaimed when she didn't answer.

Celibate? Charade? Louisa winced at the words. So he hadn't gone to bed alone every night, thinking of her as she thought of him before she went to sleep. Why would he? It *was* all a charade, just as he said. That was what she wanted, after all.

Then why, she wondered, did it hurt so much? She stood in front of him, hands clenched into fists at her side. Inwardly, she told herself not to cry. Of all people, Charles Finch would not see Louisa Strickland cry.

"No, I did not," she said, her unaffected tone nothing but a façade. "But I did expect you not to embarrass me in front of the entire ton. Now I will inevitably be poor Miss Strickland, the girl who would have been a viscountess had she not caught her intended in the library doing unspeakable things with the entertainment for the evening."

Charles looked away from her, closing his eyes and bringing a thumb and forefinger to his temple. He let out a deep sigh, then turned to look at her, his blue gaze capturing her mirror one. There was something deeply endearing about Charles's boyish good looks, and she softened toward him against her better judgment.

But then she promptly squared her shoulders. She would not forgive Charles—not this time.

"I did not *mean* for you—or anyone—to catch us." He paused for a moment, reaching for her hand, the one that had just slapped him. He ran his thumb over her knuckles, his soft touch making her freeze. "I highly doubt anyone noticed we were missing from the party aside from you, so terrified to be alone for five minutes."

Louisa inhaled sharply, her anger flaring. They both knew she didn't particularly enjoy social occasions, but there was no reason to bring it up now and insult her. *Do* not *try to blame this on me, Viscount Drake*, she thought.

Charles started again. "If you hadn't followed me—"

She snatched her hand away from his. Unable to contain herself any longer, she began to shout at him.

"Whatever *you* were doing appeared to be something you wanted to do for much longer than five minutes. I am surprised you could pull yourself together long enough to chase after me like a madman! Why didn't you just let me go?"

Louisa's eyes drifted toward the crotch of his breeches. When she looked back up at his face, she was sure she was flushing, and Charles was shaking his head. "You are jealous, that's what you are," he said, quietly laughing as he wagged a finger at her.

She folded her arms across her chest, throwing her head back to avoid his accusing gaze. "I am *not* jealous," she said. He did not look like he believed her.

Instead, he smiled at her as if she'd just told a great joke, but the only farce was the affection Louisa and Charles pretended to have for one another in public.

It was a ruse Louisa took part in to avoid any *real* attachments or potential proposals that season, having no desire to marry despite what society demanded of her. Charles Finch was her annoying neighbor and former childhood friend; they had grown apart as they grew older. Why he agreed to help her, she had no idea, but that didn't matter now. The party at Lady Ramsbury's was the last rout of the season. The Stricklands would return to Kent tomorrow, and Charles would stay on in London doing what rakes like him typically did in town: drinking, gambling, and whoring every evening, presumably in that order.

"It's true," Louisa continued, resisting the urge to slap him again, though still desperate to erase the smile from his face.

Those smiles were what had addled her brain in the first place, causing her to run when she saw him with the opera singer bent over the red settee in the library. Those smiles had tricked her into believing he felt something for her when he hadn't at all.

Louisa wished she had laughed when she saw them. She should have laughed when their gazes briefly met while Charles thrust into the woman from behind. That would have shown just how ridiculous Louisa believed him to be. After all, she really wasn't jealous. She certainly didn't wonder what it would have been like to be the opera singer that evening.

"I pity the women who fall for your charms," she said, ignoring those intrusive thoughts inside her head. "You are nothing but a degenerate, destined to spoil your father's name and waste his fortune. I appreciate the help you have given me over the past few months, but I am through with you now. Let us return to being indifferent neighbors. Good night, Viscount Drake."

Louisa turned quickly, dashing the last few yards down the sidewalk to the house her father had rented for the season. Mr. Strickland was a wealthy gentleman, but he owned no property in London. Like his daughter, he much preferred the comforts of Strickland Manor, their estate in Kent. But Mrs. Strickland, Louisa's stepmother, convinced her husband that his eldest daughter must have a season in town, no matter how much Louisa protested. In the end, his wife's wishes won out over his daughter's.

"Louisa!"

She stopped halfway up the front steps, slowly turning to face Charles, who remained standing below her on the sidewalk. The glow of the lamp beside the front door illuminated those aforementioned boyish good looks, causing her heartbeat to falter. A splattering of light freckles marked the bridge of his nose, and his dark hair formed thick, unruly curls on top of his head.

"If you are not jealous, then why are you angry with me?" he asked, slowly climbing the stairs, a frown playing at his lips. He stopped on the step beneath Louisa, their heads nearly level with one another now. She could smell the brandy on him.

"I am not angry with you," she quickly countered, growing nervous. She did not want him to press her anymore on the topic of jealously, so Louisa shook her head instead, forcing a smile. "I am only tired and ready to go home. You know how I hate it here. Now, if you'll excuse me, I would like to—"

Charles grabbed hold of her hand as she turned, causing her head to snap back in his direction. Their lips were mere inches apart now, her hand still resting in his. His eyes drifted downward, and she was somehow out of breath, though she remained utterly still.

"You claim you wish to be nothing more than indifferent neighbors, but why can't we part ways as friends? We have grown close during this season, have we not?"

She narrowed her eyes at him. "Friends?" she asked. What business did she and Charles Finch have being friends? They had completely different interests and goals in life.

"Friends," he repeated, their faces still mere inches apart. "I know you are curious about what Miss Coppola and I were doing together. I see it in your eyes. I could return to Kent as well, you know, and show you—"

Louisa did not hesitate. She slapped him again, this time across the other cheek, so they had matching red handprints. "You are the worst sort of rogue, Charles Finch," she hissed. "I would never be interested in a rake like you."

Retreating into the house, Louisa heard his laugh on the other side of the door. She closed her eyes, resting her head against it. In the darkness of the entry hall, silent tears dampened her cheeks. She angrily wiped them away, noting a light emitting from one of the rooms down the corridor.

Papa's study. Louisa went to the mirror in the entry hall, inspecting her eyes. She wanted no evidence of tears when she visited her father. Slowly, she walked to the room, where she found him in his armchair, his legs propped up on a stool. He wore his spectacles, and a thick tome rested on his lap. Louisa stood in the doorway, smiling at him. She would have preferred to stay home from Lady Ramsbury's party as well, but there were different set of rules for young ladies and seasoned gentlemen like her father, much to her chagrin.

Louisa cleared her throat, and Mr. Strickland looked up from his book. He smiled. "Louisa! You are home early."

"I grew tired and quietly snuck away before Mrs. Strickland could notice," she said, coming to stand beside him and bending over to press a kiss to his temple as she rested her hands on his shoulders.

Mr. Strickland furrowed his brow. "Did Lord Drake not propose?" he asked. "I would have thought you would be out until dawn celebrating."

Louisa tried to feign sadness. Surprisingly, it wasn't all that hard. Although she had never wanted to become engaged, Charles had disappointed her in other ways, ways she would never be able to explain—at least not to her father. "Unfortunately, Lord Drake did not come up to scratch this evening."

Her father's frown deepened. "Is that why you look so upset?" He immediately shook his head. "Do not give up hope, Louisa. There is still time. He may return to Kent for the summer and call on you at Strickland Manor."

Louisa hoped not, but she didn't dare say that aloud. She had to pretend that she was permanently wretched so that her stepmother wouldn't try to force any other suitors upon her in the future. But in truth, Louisa still needed some distance between her and the viscount to focus on her true desires: one day running Strickland Manor by herself.

Everyone thought her father was odd for naming Louisa as his sole heiress instead of his nearest male relative. But the entailment of the estate ended with Mr. Strickland, so now he could do whatever he damn well pleased with it, thank you very much—or at least that was what he always told anyone who ever questioned him. And Louisa was happy with his decision, for it meant she would achieve total independence, unlike most of the women she knew.

"I wouldn't plan on it, Papa," she told him bitterly. "You know how the viscount loves being in town. I suppose it was my mistake to pursue someone so young. Drake is not ready to settle down."

Her father made a sound of annoyance. "Then he should not have led you on to believe that—"

"It is fine, Papa," Louisa insisted, hoping to end the conversation. Perhaps her show of heartbreak was too convincing. "I am sure I will recover once I return to the country. I have been craving the fresh air for a while now, and I am willing to bet you have been feeling the same way."

Her father grunted his agreement. Then his eyes became bright, as if he had just gotten a splendid idea. "Perhaps we might invite Cousin William to say with us this summer. You enjoy his company, don't you?"

Louisa's face immediately fell. "Not particularly."

"Louisa!" her father exclaimed, his eyes widening.

She only shrugged in response. Cousin William was Father's nearest male relative, the one they said *should* inherit Strickland Manor. They were distant cousins, sharing the same great-great-grandfather. Periodically, he would come to Strickland and attempt to woo her, but Louisa found him terribly uninteresting. Besides, he only wanted her for the estate, and there was nothing worse than a man who only wanted a woman for her inheritance.

Forcing herself to smile slightly, Louisa bent down to kiss her father on the temple once more. "I apologize, Papa. I am only tired. Perhaps Cousin William might come some other time when I am not so worn out after such an eventful season in town."

Her father nodded, and they bid each other good night.

Later, sleep eluded Louisa in her bedroom, where she tossed and turned at least half the night, her mind still too wrapped up with thoughts of Charles Finch. Louisa supposed that was her punishment for making a deal with the devil.

CHARLES FINCH, Viscount Drake, heir to the Earl of Bolton, stood on the steps outside Louisa Strickland's green door, laughing to himself. He had enjoyed tormenting Miss Strickland since they were children, but at one-and-twenty, she had become much more than a rough-hewn young girl with long, awkward limbs and flaming red hair. Now teasing her felt much more dangerous, but unfortunately for him, he couldn't help himself anyway.

He hadn't been joking about his earlier proposition, though Charles would never admit it to anyone. It was much easier to let Louisa—as well as himself—assume that he was, hence why he continued to laugh to himself, albeit somewhat sadly now, while returning to his aunt's party, his hands stuffed into the pockets of his breeches. But Charles could not fret for long, knowing if he'd confessed to only using the opera singer to rid himself of his desire for Louisa, the response would have been much the same. She would never have believed him.

Charles sighed, his forced laughter fading as he turned back down Park Street. He brought a hand to his chest as he walked, wondering how such an awful feeling had come to rest there. The past few months had just been a game he and Louisa had played to trick their families and the ton —hadn't it?

She didn't want to marry. Neither did Charles—not yet, anyway. He supposed he would eventually, as was his duty, but at present, he shuddered anytime his mother or father mentioned heirs or spares. Their so-called attachment was the perfect distraction from their true motives: using each other to avoid *actual* engagements, especially on her part. At three-and-twenty, Charles would have years before any real pressure to settle down began. Louisa was not so lucky.

Most women weren't.

They'd always planned to go their separate ways at the end, but Charles never expected their subterfuge to end so poorly. He came to a stop on the sidewalk and looked over his shoulder, wringing his hands at his chest. Perhaps he ought to go back and apologize. No. He'd only feel worse. When he faced forward again, he closed his eyes, picturing a naked Miss Coppola beneath him. That should have been a distraction enough, but soon Miss Coppola had red hair and much longer, shapelier limbs.

Charles immediately opened his eyes, moving forward once more, quickening his pace toward his aunt's Park Street mansion. He didn't need Louisa, and whatever lust he may have felt for her after spending nearly every day with her for three months would subside given time. If Charles could have any woman he wanted, why should he settle for a blue-stocking whose only goal in life was running her father's estate after he died?

The answer was that he shouldn't, so he returned to his aunt's ballroom with a smile on his face, feeling as though someone had just lifted an enormous weight off his shoulders. He looked around the room, admiring the bevy of young, attractive women his aunt had invited that evening. Now he could dance with any one of them without fearing Louisa's censure over what such actions might do to their public image as a supposed couple.

But before he could approach any of them, Mrs. Strickland appeared at his side, a concerned look on her face. The woman was only ten years older than her stepdaughter Louisa, her face still vacant of any deep wrinkles. His other neighbor and friend, the Duke of Rutley, had pointed out Mrs. Strickland's attractiveness on more than one occasion— as did every other male who learned Charles was courting Louisa.

Pretending to court, that is. And no longer pretending anymore, thank God. She was more trouble than she was worth.

Charles beamed at Mrs. Strickland as if he hadn't just chased her stepdaughter through the streets of Mayfair after she found him with his breeches down and his cock inside another woman.

"Are you enjoying yourself, Mrs. Strickland?" he asked. Despite his jovial tone, the woman's look of concern only grew, but he ignored it, looking out onto the ballroom of twirling dancers. "Quite the crush, don't you think?"

"Indeed," Mrs. Strickland replied, pursing her lips. "Have you seen my daughter, Lord Drake? The last I saw her, she said she was going to look for you."

His lips twitched, fighting an even broader smile forming on his face. Louisa always hated when her father's wife referred to her as her daughter. Louisa would make a point of correcting her whenever she did, saying she was Mrs. Strickland's *step*daughter, as if the idea of actually being related to the woman was bloodcurdling. Despite all that, Charles was sure Mrs. Strickland loved Louisa, even if Louisa did not always reciprocate her stepmother's feelings.

"I did see Miss Strickland," he admitted, nodding. "She said she was tired, so I offered her my carriage to take home. She happily accepted, and I reckon she is already in bed as we speak, eager to return to Kent tomorrow morning."

Mrs. Strickland regarded him as if she knew he was lying, but how could that be? He was sure no one had seen him chase after Louisa into the street. Everyone had been in the ballroom at the back of the house—except for Miss Coppola, of course, who he'd left half naked in his aunt's library.

Charles searched for her now across the crowded ballroom. Perhaps she would enjoy a second rendezvous at his private apartments later than evening. Such tempting thoughts were interrupted by Mrs. Strickland, who cleared her throat beside him.

"Did you speak of anything else while you were alone, my lord?"

Louisa's stepmother looked up at him with such hopeful eyes that it almost upset him to crush her hopes for an engagement between him and Louisa. His palms even became sweaty under the woman's critical gaze. If he told her his courtship of her stepdaughter was nothing but a ruse, he imagined it would be something akin to stepping on a defenseless field mouse.

"We did speak of something else," Charles began, nodding. Mrs. Strickland leaned in closer, her eyes wide. He tilted his head to the side as he regarded the woman, releasing a sad sigh from his lips for dramatic effect.

"What was it?" Mrs. Strickland asked, leaning closer yet. Charles wouldn't have been surprised if she grabbed hold of his jacket and began shaking him. He looked away, sighing again.

"I suggested that I return to Kent tomorrow as well so that we may continue our acquaintance, but she was not interested."

Charles turned back to Mrs. Strickland, his face the picture of hurt. She looked as if she was trying not to scream. "Not interested?" she repeated.

As Charles sadly nodded, Mrs. Strickland shook her head. "I apologize, my lord. I do not know what's come over her. Perhaps she was only tired and didn't mean it. Yes, that can be the only explanation. I will have her write you first thing tomorrow morning and explain herself."

Charles realized then his grave miscalculation. He'd blamed the end of their courtship on Louisa instead of himself. Mrs. Strickland would be furious with her, and Louisa, in turn, would be even angrier with him.

"There's no need," Charles said quickly, growing panicked. He shook his head. "I am sure the decision was entirely mutual. In fact, I'm relieved she does not want me there."

Now Mrs. Strickland stiffened. She looked down, pulling a fan from the velvet reticule hanging around her wrist. "You are *relieved*?" she asked.

Charles grimaced. Could he not just say the right thing for once? "I only mean that I am still young, and Louisa understands that, and—"

"That's enough, Lord Drake," Mrs. Strickland snapped, her face turning red as she rapidly wafted her fan in front of herself. Charles turned red as well, immediately realizing the impropriety of calling Louisa by her Christian name. He looked around the room, hoping neither his mother nor father were near.

"I will take my leave, then. Give your aunt my regards. Perhaps we will return next season, but most likely not." The woman snapped her fan shut, and Charles nearly jumped. "I will have a terrible time convincing Mr. Strickland to fund another season after *this* disaster. It will be my fault for encouraging her to chase after a viscount, after all."

"Mrs. Strickland—"

The woman held up a single gloved hand, effectively silencing him. He supposed it was better that way. The truth would have only disappointed her more, and Louisa would have killed him if he admitted to their ruse over the past three months.

"Good night, my lord."

Mrs. Strickland turned on her heel, leaving him to stare after her, wondering again if he had made a grave mistake. Louisa Strickland would undoubtedly be plotting his murder by morning.

Charles suddenly felt a large hand on his shoulder, and when he turned, his friend Robert, the Duke of Rutley, was standing behind him, his dark brow arched at him. "What was that regarding?" he asked.

"Miss Strickland," Charles replied casually, trying to appear uninterested so Rutley would stop asking questions. But the duke continued.

"What happened?"

Charles sighed. "Our courtship came to an end this evening."

The duke snickered. "No surprises there. I saw you run off with the opera singer earlier this evening. I gather everyone else did as well."

It was a good thing Louisa didn't have a brother, and that her father was much too eccentric to ever challenge Charles to a duel. But Charles did not wish to think upon her any longer. "Shall we visit the cardroom?"

Rutley shot him a skeptical look, which Charles ignored. He grabbed a glass of champagne from a footman's nearby tray, only half listening as Rutley spoke. "You have already lost a thousand pounds at cards this week."

"Come on," Charles said, taking a swig of champagne. "I am sure I will make it all back this evening." He clapped his friend across the shoulder. "I can feel my luck changing as we speak."

But he did not make any money back that evening, nor the evening after that. He lost money every night until he was in so much debt that he was sure Louisa or her stepmother had somehow cursed him that evening. But the entire ton knew that the only curse Charles Finch suffered from was stupidity, and it would be another seven years before he broke it.

Chapter One

London, England
May 1816

CHARLES FINCH WOKE like he did most days, with a distinct pounding in his head from an excess of drinking the evening before. Except lately, he did not limit his drinking to evenings. A bottle of brandy was the first thing he reached for most mornings, even before the bellpull beside his bed that he used to summon his valet.

But this morning, he recalled the promise he'd made to himself last night at the club while surrounded by old friends, plentiful liquor, and cheap whores. Charles meant for last night to be the final hurrah before he gave that all up, as there was no use denying it anymore. His life was in shambles, and he had to do something, especially after his past plans to fix things had failed so tremendously it could almost be considered comical.

With few options for moving forward, sobering up was his

only choice left. How else could he begin to clean up the mess he'd caused?

Remaining prone beneath soft linen bedclothes, he reached for the bellpull, tugging it downward. His muscles ached, and his joints creaked with every movement. Charles wondered if he had always felt so old or if he only noticed the total weight of his nine-and-twenty years on this planet now that he had decided to swear off liquor.

When his valet, Mr. Gibbs, finally appeared, the man—a middle-aged fellow with round, ruddy cheeks and a thick neck—seemed out of breath when he opened the door, appearing at Charles's bedside panting. Charles turned, propping himself up on his elbows. The bed linens pooled around his waist, revealing his bare chest.

"What's the matter with you?" he asked, squinting at Gibbs. The man was now bent over in what looked like pain, his right hand clutching his side. He wrapped his other hand around a liveried kneecap.

"You rang so early," he began, still panting but standing at attention again, his hands behind his back. "I wasn't prepared. I thought there was an emergency. Are you all right?"

Charles glanced at the clock on his bedside table, then turned back to Gibbs, narrowing his eyes at the valet. He supposed eight in the morning *was* early for him. He typically remained in bed until noon most days.

"Of course I'm all right," Charles said, doing little to hide his annoyance as he tore the bedclothes away from his frame and moved his legs over the edge of the bed. He stood, completely naked, and Gibbs scrambled to place his slippers before his feet. Gibbs was not usually so scatterbrained.

"Is an earl rising early on a weekday to finish some work before breakfast truly all that unusual to you? I am sure my father did the same all the time." Charles stepped into the slippers one by one. Gibbs then grabbed his velvet banyan from a nearby hook, moving behind Charles and holding it out for him. "I will have my bath and then go downstairs to my study until Mother rises for breakfast."

Charles turned after he shrugged on the banyan, expecting Gibbs to start buttoning it closed. Instead, the valet stood there practically trembling, the color drained from his formerly ruddy cheeks. Gibbs mumbled something Charles couldn't hear. "What did you say, Gibbs?"

"It's about the dowager countess, my lord," Gibbs replied, louder this time so Charles could hear him. "She left yesterday evening—while you were out."

Charles furrowed his brow, confused. To be sure, his mother was upset with him, but she hadn't said anything about leaving town. "What do you mean she left? Has she returned to Linfield without me?"

Linfield Hall was the Earl of Bolton's country seat in Kent. It had belonged to Charles ever since his father died earlier that spring.

"Not exactly," Gibbs replied sheepishly, pulling a folded and sealed letter from his jacket pocket. He handed it to Charles, who looked at it, immediately recognizing his mother's handwriting. She had scrawled his name in artful strokes on the front.

Quickly, Charles tore the letter open. He scanned its contents, then looked at Gibbs, frowning. "She is deserting me for the Haddingtons and their house in the Lake District."

Gibbs nodded as if he already knew, and Charles sighed, handing the missive back to his valet. "Fine," Charles muttered. "I was growing tired of her company anyway."

His mother blamed him, of course, for what happened with Rosamund, his younger sister. His *only* sister, as far as he was concerned. The other one—the bastard—didn't count, even if she did try to offer him her inheritance to pay off his debts to the duke. Rutley was quick to foil that plan, anyway, as was the girl's husband, his former friend and solicitor Samuel Brooks.

His father had revealed his half sister August's existence on his deathbed earlier that year, along with his intention to leave her twelve thousand pounds. He also insisted that she be made part of the family. Obviously Charles objected. He would not be made the laughingstock of London by introducing *Lady* August to the ton, as his father insisted upon calling her.

The late earl sent Brooks to inform her of her inheritance and true family. After his father died, Charles sent August to live with their aunt, Lady Ramsbury. He thought if anyone could handle such a scandal, it was the dowager duchess. But somewhere along the way August fell in love with Brooks, and they were married soon after that, much to Charles's chagrin. He wanted August to marry his cousin on his mother's side, Edward Swinton. But Brooks uncovered Charles's plan to have Edward give back August's inheritance to him once they were married. Brooks was furious with him.

Charles sighed. He was running out of friends now that Brooks wasn't speaking to him. He could always find someone to drink or gamble or whore with, but a true friend? Those were in short supply.

Meanwhile, his sister was having second thoughts about her intended, the duke. And now she had finally called off the wedding to the man Charles owed twenty thousand pounds to.

To put it simply, Charles was in terrible trouble.

He glanced at his valet. "You won't leave me, right, Gibbs?" Charles asked.

The heavyset man shook his head right away. "Of course not, my lord."

Charles was relieved to hear it, but then again, what other choice did the man have? Charles frowned, and Gibbs headed to the sideboard where Charles kept brandy and glassware.

"Shall I pour you a drink?"

Charles hesitated. He must do this, he decided. If there was one thing he *must* do, he must avoid brandy. "That's all right, Gibbs. As of today, I am giving up all that."

His valet nearly dropped the bottle of liquor he was holding. "G-giving up b-brandy?" Gibbs practically sputtered. "Are you sure nothing is wrong, my lord?"

Charles's face fell. Did everyone think he was some sort of helpless drunkard? He sighed. Well, he supposed if they did, they had good reason to. "Why would there be something wrong, Gibbs?" He glanced back down at the bottle of brandy in Gibbs's hands. "You should clear the house of all of it."

"All of it?" His valet's brow rose comically high.

Charles sighed again. "That's right. All of it." He pointed to the collection of bottles. "Some of those unopened bottles might fetch hefty prices. You should try selling them."

Unfortunately, we might need the money, Charles thought to himself. Gibbs still seemed confused but eventually nodded slowly. When they were through talking, he helped Charles dress and bathe, and after having his very *sober* breakfast in the morning room, he went to his study.

Charles had an hour to pore through his estate's books before meeting the duke. He hoped to find some sort of resolution to his financial crisis that wasn't marrying off either of his sisters, seeing as how one was already married and the other refused to marry, but none of the numbers made sense, and his head still hurt from the night before, even after a hearty breakfast and a large cup of coffee.

He sighed, then sat back in his chair, admiring the ornate surroundings of his study—the floor-to-ceiling cherry bookshelves, the giant globe in the corner by the window. The house was quiet with no one but him there. He wondered if that was what it would be like from there on out, just him alone at home, where there were no temptations.

For a moment, he considered selling Finch Place, the London town house where he presently sat. Selling it would certainly solve his problems, and staying away from town would help him avoid temptation. But where would he stay in London if he ever decided to take his seat in the House of Lords? He intended to do just that one day, so selling their home in town was simply out of the question.

Other than selling the liquor—which would hardly be enough—Charles had no idea how he would come up with the twenty thousand pounds needed to pay back the duke. He hoped Rutley had a plan other than berating him when he called on him later that morning.

The duke's home in London was a short walk from Finch Place, only on the opposite end of Berkeley Square. Charles and Rutley had been best friends since childhood, which close proximity rather than a closeness to one another dictated. Their fathers' country homes were located on adjoining estates as well, but their difference in rank was drilled into them since they were children. Charles always felt he had something to prove as a result.

He anxiously waited in the entry hall while the butler informed the duke of his arrival. They had not seen each other since the earl's younger sister decided to break off her three-year engagement to the duke the previous day, and he did not know what to expect when he finally saw the man again. Rutley hadn't gone to the club with Charles the evening prior, preferring to be alone.

When Charles finally entered the duke's study, he was sitting behind his desk, watching Charles with careful eyes. He was just the type of man most society girls swooned over, tall and dark and handsome. Truthfully, Charles couldn't understand why Rosamund no longer wanted to marry him. There was the issue of his past infidelity while they were engaged, but what man was faithful? Charles's late father was not, which was how he ended up with a second sister he did not want and twelve thousand pounds missing from his estate coffers.

That thought gave him pause. Perhaps Rosamund had a point in breaking off her engagement.

"Charles," the duke said. He tried not to let it bother him when his family and Rutley all called him Charles instead of Bolton. He liked to think it wasn't a lack of respect, only that he did not command so much of it as, say, the duke.

"You seem different," he continued, observing him. Charles stared back at him. He was not wearing a jacket, only a shirt and waistcoat, and he had pushed his sleeves up to his elbows. A stack of papers, a half-empty pot of ink, and a pen rested on the desk between them. Rutley sniffed once. "You *smell* different."

Charles's lips twitched. "I took a bath this morning. Thank you for noticing."

"No," Rutley said, shaking his head. "It is not that. You do not smell of brandy."

Charles nodded once. "Ah. That is true. I have given up the stuff."

The duke nearly scoffed. "Truly? For how long?"

Charles pursed his lips. He did not blame the duke for not believing him. They had attended Oxford together, and the duke had seen Charles in all the different stages of intoxication, including facedown in the mud.

He did not want to admit it had been less than twenty-four hours, but Charles saw no other option. "Since this morning. I thought it was the least I could do after the mess I've made of the estate. Even my mother wants nothing to do with me. She's gone off to the Lake District with the Haddingtons."

"That sounds like a wonderfully quaint way to spend the summer."

"Quite." Charles cleared his throat with a single cough. "But we aren't here to talk about my mother."

"No, we aren't."

The duke stared at him, and Charles shifted uncomfortably in his armchair. The chairs in Rutley's studies, both in Kent, where they were neighbors, and in town, were always far too small for any grown man to sit in and be at ease. Charles swore the duke did it on purpose. After all, Rutley was one of the most powerful men in England. Why shouldn't his guests be uncomfortable?

"How are you feeling?" Charles asked, unable to bring himself to say something about his debt. "I *am* sorry about my sister, by the way. I know you cared for her, regardless of what she thought."

The duke glanced down, fiddling with the stack of papers on his desk, then looked back up at Charles. "I am fine," he said, smiling, though Charles could tell he was forcing himself to appear unperturbed. "I am more than fine. I no longer care. I have decided the end of our engagement is for the best."

Charles nodded, though he wasn't quite convinced the duke meant what he said. "I wish you would reconsider taking her dowry anyway and counting it against my debt. God knows she doesn't deserve it."

Rutley's eyes darkened, and Charles feared a furious put-down in exchange for his derisive comment about his sister. "We went over this yesterday in the carriage, Charles. I do not want Rosamund's dowry. Whoever her worthless husband turns out to be may have it."

Charles scoffed. "Why should I give anything to her

future husband? She has made her hatred of me well known. I rid myself of all responsibility for her. She is my aunt's problem now."

"Do you think it's wise to leave your sister in her care?" The duke shifted in his chair. "I hear she frequently receives late-night visits from Lord Ridlington."

Charles tried not to laugh. Rutley sounded like a concerned mama. "How scandalous."

The duke's jaw clenched. "Do not mock me."

"And you say you do not care." The duke's glare deepened, and Charles bit back peals of laughter. When he regained his composure, he continued. "But in all seriousness, Your Grace, you sound like Brooks. He protested when I sent August to live with my aunt, and look what happened. He married her."

Rutley cleared his throat. "Well, I apologize, but look what happened to force that marriage in the first place. The incident at Lord Ridlington's ball is a perfect example."

Charles cocked his head to the side. "Do you mean the incident with one of Lord Fitzgerald's sons?"

Rutley nodded. Charles supposed he had a point. If it weren't for that incident, August and Brooks might have never married. His cousin Swinton might have eventually wooed her and gained her hand instead. Her inheritance would have become Swinton's upon their marriage, and his cousin had agreed to give that money back to Charles.

But that didn't happen. Nothing had gone to plan—or so it would seem. Charles let out an angry huff.

"Well, she did end up married by going to my aunt's, and isn't that the goal for any young girl's season?" Charles shook his head. "But I digress. We should be discussing my debts—all twenty thousand pounds of it. If you will not take Rosamund's dowry or allow me to consider August's offer—"

"A very generous offer you do not deserve. Perhaps you ought to think twice before shunning your half sister."

Charles rolled his eyes. He didn't understand why everyone acted like August was some sort of saint. "Yes, yes, I know. But if you do not let me do either of those two things, I am unsure what my other options are. I have already decided I cannot part with Finch Place."

The duke shook his head. "I do not want you to sell Finch Place. I have another proposal for you." He took a piece of paper from his stack and slid it across the desk. Charles picked it up, squinting at the figures written on it. His gaze went back to Rutley.

"What is this?" he asked.

"A plan to pay off your debt—all twenty thousand pounds of it—within five years. You will probably have to economize to meet the monthly payments, which I am sure I can help you achieve if you allow me to look at your ledgers."

Charles sighed. "I suppose I do not have any other choice." He did not like the idea of Rutley controlling his spending, but Charles would have to bear it. He folded the piece of paper and placed it in his jacket pocket.

"There is one other option," Rutley said.

Charles raised his brow. "Oh? What is that?"

"You could marry someone wealthy."

Charles laughed. "The last thing I need right now is a wife, no matter how wealthy she may be. Besides, any respectable woman would not be interested in me after the way my family's name has been dragged through the mud this season. The daughter of a cit who wants the title of countess might have a different opinion, but I have no interest in social climbers, thank you very much."

Rutley pursed his lips, annoyed. "You do recall our neighbors to the north in Kent, don't you? The Stricklands?"

Charles grew very still. He hadn't thought about Louisa Strickland in a long time, but just the idea of her red hair was enough to make his heart skip a beat. He hoped Rutley would not hear the uncertainty in his voice. "Yes."

"The youngest daughter will debut next season. Her dowry is thirty thousand pounds. That is more than enough for you to pay off your debts."

Charles shook his head at Rutley as if the duke were mad for even making such a suggestion. "I cannot marry her."

"Why not?"

The image of Louisa Strickland's face walking in on him in his aunt's study while he mounted an opera singer from behind flashed in his mind. "You do not recall me courting the elder sister six years ago? Surely it would be in bad form to go after the younger sister now."

A look of recognition passed over the duke's face, then disappointment. "I had forgotten about that," he murmured.

But Charles hadn't forgotten. After Louisa left town, he decided to write to her, hoping they might leave on better terms after their argument. But his letter went unanswered, and his feelings of loneliness only grew for some perturbing reason. He even returned to Kent for a month during the summer. He attempted to call on her a few times, but she was always busy whenever he did.

The only time he managed to see her was at her father's funeral, but even then, she avoided him. She even had the nerve to use some distant cousin named William as a shield against him that day. Charles almost expected to find out she married him one day, but she never did, preferring to be an independent spinster, just as she'd always planned.

Charles was happy for her. Louisa had gotten what she always wanted. He wished he even *knew* what he wanted. Maybe then he could go about finally achieving it. For now he would just try to get out from underneath Rutley's thumb.

The duke sighed, interrupting Charles's tumultuous

thoughts. "Regardless of all that, Flora Strickland was still the best option I could find for you."

Charles couldn't disagree more, and he was sure his face showed that. "What do you mean?" he asked.

"Why should I have to explain it to you any further? She is *rich*. I don't care who her sister is. Since you have tried so hard to meddle in the affairs of your sisters in the past few months, I think it is only right that I try meddling in yours. If you do not want me watching your every move for the next five years while you pay off your debts to me, then you should marry Flora Strickland."

Charles shifted in his chair. He could not think of a worse idea. "The last time I saw Flora Strickland, she was twelve years old. She is far too young for me—not to mention her sister and mother hate me for what I did all those years ago."

The duke sighed. "What exactly did you do, Charles? To make them hate you so?"

"It doesn't matter," Charles said, shaking his head. It would take too long to explain, and the two women hated him for very different reasons. Louisa hated him for the truth, and Mrs. Strickland hated him for the ruse. Charles and Rutley sat in silence for a long moment while Charles considered his options. "Could I marry any heiress as long as her dowry was at least twenty thousand pounds?"

The duke considered this for a moment, then shrugged. "I suppose. Heiresses do not exactly grow on trees, though. Just remember that you are land rich and cash poor right now, Charles. You can use all the help you can get."

Charles rose. "Well, then, I accept your challenge. If I must marry to get myself out of this mess, then I will. In the meantime, you can take a look at my ledgers. I supposed living as a pauper will only motivate me to find that special woman as soon as possible."

Rutley smiled, then made an encouraging gesture with his

fist. "That's the spirit." He paused a moment. "You really ought to consider Flora Strickland, though. My mother tells me she is quite accomplished and far prettier than her older sister."

Charles almost defended Louisa but didn't want the duke suspecting him of anything untoward. He supposed Rutley's mother just didn't know Louisa like the earl did—or at least the way he used to know her. He sighed. "I will call on her at Strickland Manor when I return to Linfield if that pleases you, Your Grace. But do not think Flora Strickland will end up being my only option. I plan on returning to town next season a changed man. I'll be the most eligible bachelor in all of London. You'll see."

The duke snorted, turning back to the papers on his desk. "Yes, we most certainly shall."

Charles bristled at his friend's lack of confidence in him, but given what he owed, he was hardly in a position to say otherwise.

Chapter Two

Kent, England

LOUISA STRICKLAND FOUND herself tired of the party before it even began. Her younger sister had been chattering about it every day at breakfast, luncheon, and dinner for the past two weeks, so it was not surprising that Louisa felt that way. It would seem her stepmother had created some sort of tiny monster, one who could only talk of muslins, ribbons, and eligible bachelors.

As Louisa looked around the local inn's ballroom, she wondered what use eligible bachelors could be to them. Their estate, Strickland Manor, was not entailed, and their father had left it to Louisa upon his passing five years ago. The estate's income totaled ten thousand pounds per annum and was more than enough to sustain two girls and their mother.

*Step*mother, that is. Louisa's *actual* mother died when she was seven. The new Mrs. Strickland came into the picture not even two years later, only ten years her new stepdaughter's senior. Little Flora arrived within a year of her father and new stepmother being married. And Flora *was* little, just like her mother. They were both petite women, with dark-brown hair and eyes and delicate features that men admired. What wasn't little was Flora's thirty-thousand-pound dowry, but Louisa was sure they would admire that as well.

Unlike her sister, Louisa was tall rather than petite, with long, muscular limbs better suited for farming than dancing. Her fiery red hair and alabaster skin never gained her many admirers, either.

The crowd that evening was noisy and rambunctious. They were surrounded by members of the gentry but none with any titles as far as Louisa could tell, very different from the much more refined group of people at the last ball she attended in Mayfair six years ago. But she tried not to think of that night on Park Street too often. Thank goodness her neighbor, Charles, the new Earl of Bolton since his father died a few months ago, would never be caught dead at one of the local county balls.

"Isn't it wonderful, Louisa?" her sister asked before giggling. Flora was practically trembling with excitement. She pulled her silk fan from her velvet reticule and began wafting it in front of her face.

Louisa shot her a reproachful but teasing look, her brow arched and one corner of her lips slightly upturned into a smile. "Indeed, but you must try to control yourself, Flora. You would not want to frighten any potential husbands with such an overeager demeanor, would you?"

Her sister slowed her fan and frowned. "I am not overeager. Why would I be? I'm sure none of these men are my future husband. I have thirty thousand pounds, after all! They are only for practice, of course." Flora paused, then firmly nodded her head. "I will meet a nice man in town next spring instead." She turned to Mrs. Strickland. "Won't I, Mama?

Someone much more impressive than the men who find themselves here."

Mrs. Strickland smiled reassuringly. "That is the plan."

Louisa stifled a groan but still rolled her eyes, though she kept her opinion of the entire matter to herself. She and her sister Flora couldn't be any more different. Ever since she was a little girl, all Flora ever talked about was being a bride. But if Louisa ever married, her husband would become the new owner of Strickland Manor. Suddenly, the three independent women would become beholden to a man they barely knew thanks to the strict rules of courtship. Louisa couldn't think of anything worse than that.

Some might argue that two young women *needed* a man to run their estate, but Louisa refused to subscribe to such a belief. She was more than competent enough by herself, so much so that she didn't even employ a land steward. Flora would be just as capable as well if she were less interested in going to London the following spring and more interested in their tenant farmers.

"Come, girls," her stepmother said, interrupting Louisa's thoughts. "We must mingle with the other guests."

Mrs. Strickland and Flora set off into the throng of people in front of them, and Louisa reluctantly followed. When they found familiar faces with whom to speak, she half-heartedly partook in small talk, allowing Flora and her stepmother to handle the bulk of the socializing.

Of course, everyone was far more interested in Flora anyway, as expected. She was the one with the thirty-thousand-pound dowry, after all. Louisa already knew what the rest of the county called her behind her back. Spinster. Shrew. Snob. Her companions that evening were probably thankful she kept her mouth shut since she usually said one contrary thing after another. What they didn't seem to understand, though, was that any man who wanted to marry Flora would have to answer to Louisa. She, much to society's collective horror, was the one who held the purse strings.

As Flora and her stepmother spoke to some other guests, Louisa caught the eye of Mr. Hardy, Lord Bolton's land steward, from across the room. He smiled at her, and she reluctantly smiled back. He may have been the only man in Kent who didn't avoid her, but they both knew he only hoped Louisa would hire him to help manage her estate. He was also hopelessly infatuated with Louisa's younger sister, but Flora, fickle creature that she was, hadn't seemed to notice.

Although he did not manage Louisa's land, she occasionally invited him to dinner at the manor, where Flora politely tolerated him, though she made occasional comments that he was beneath them whenever he left. Louisa could only wonder how her younger sister became such a brat. Of course, she had her list of suspects. If her father had any failings when he was alive, it was spoiling his younger daughter.

As for Mr. Hardy, his cottage bordered their land, which would have made it easy for him to manage both Linfield and Strickland. But Louisa insisted on doing it herself, using the excuse that it was much more economical that way. It meant one less person to pay, but truthfully, she just wanted to prove a point. She was sure she could run her estate more profitably than any of her neighbors, all without the help of any man—and she wanted the whole county to know it.

Louisa waited for the earl's land steward to walk to her, turning away from her current group of acquaintances. "Mr. Hardy. How do you do? Lovely evening, isn't it?"

He chuckled. "Come, Miss Strickland. You and I both know you have no desire to be here."

"Are my true feelings so obvious?" she asked, frowning.

Mr. Hardy nodded. The land steward was a handsome young man of two-and-twenty with a full head of chestnut-colored hair, a strong jawline, and prominent cheekbones.

BECKY MICHAELS

Although he was handsome, Louisa saw him as a friend and nothing more, not to mention she was sure he preferred Flora to her in terms of looks.

As if he could read Louisa's mind, the land steward's eyes flickered in the direction of her younger sister. "Miss Flora seems to be enjoying herself."

"Indeed," Louisa said, giving him a sidelong look. "You ought to ask her to accompany you for at least one set while you still have the chance. We are to go to London for the next spring season, and I believe my sister expects to come home as an engaged woman."

As he was drinking his ale, listening to her, Hardy suddenly fell into a coughing fit. She watched him, concerned, until he finally regained his composure. "Why shouldn't she? She will be the talk of the town when she arrives." He paused, still appearing uncomfortable. Clearly Louisa had struck a nerve by mentioning her sister marrying another man.

"How is Strickland Manor?" Hardy continued, his voice becoming more and more strangled. He coughed once more.

Louisa arched her brow but allowed him to change the subject. "Strickland Manor is the same as when we last spoke about it, Mr. Hardy. How is Linfield Hall?"

After clearing his throat, Hardy started to speak much more confidently, seemingly more eager to discuss land than young ladies. "This weather we have been having hasn't done us any favors. I am sure you are dealing with the same issues at the manor."

"Yes, the damp and cold lasting this long into the spring has me concerned about the harvest this year."

"Perhaps I might look after Strickland while you are in town next season."

Louisa opened her mouth to protest, but he continued.

"Just for the season. Then I will leave you be."

34

Louisa doubted he would ever stop offering to be her land steward, but she reluctantly nodded. She would need someone to look after Strickland while they were away, after all. "I will consider it." She paused a moment, wondering about all the rumors she had heard about Charles recently. She glanced at Mr. Hardy beside her. "I heard the earl cannot afford the harvest to fail this year. Is that true?"

Hardy grinned without looking at her. "And where did you hear that?"

"You know how people like to talk," Louisa replied, shrugging. She would not say the rumors aloud—Louisa did not particularly care to gossip—but from the look Mr. Hardy gave her, what she had been hearing was accurate.

When the late earl died, everyone said he left twelve thousand pounds to his illegitimate daughter, even though his son, Charles, owed the Duke of Rutley from Sedgewick Park twenty thousand pounds in gambling debts. To make matters worse, the duke's engagement to the earl's sister had supposedly come to an end a week ago. Louisa imagined His Grace was enraged, leaving Charles in quite the conundrum. After all, he still owed Rutley twenty thousand pounds.

Truthfully, Louisa thought the entire story was delightful. She always knew Charles would fail, what with his love of drink and gambling and women. Coming across him with another woman in that library all those years ago felt like a blessing now. That incident had separated them irrevocably, saving her from any future association.

"I do not like to gossip about my employer," Hardy said, proving himself to be as loyal as Louisa should have suspected. She smiled at him.

"What will you do, Mr. Hardy, if Linfield Hall fails?" Louisa asked, her voice teasing. "Will you have to come and beg me for a position at Strickland? Well, let me remind you again that I don't need your help, and you should not expect me to take pity on you if you find yourself unemployed at the end of the year."

The man beside her raised his brow. "You speak as if you *hope* I become unemployed at the end of the year." He shook his head, appearing disappointed. "You do recall that the new Lord Bolton and I aren't the only ones who depend on Linfield's success, don't you?"

"Of course! Do you think that land will go to the duke when all is said and done? If you want my opinion, Rutley would be a far better owner for Linfield than the earl, and I'm sure he would let you stay on if you asked His Grace. As for the earl, the man is worthless. You will be thankful when you are finally rid of him."

Someone cleared his throat behind her. At first, Louisa froze. She had not meant to ramble on like that, disparaging the second-most powerful man in all of Kent, especially in such a public place. Slowly, she turned and looked over her shoulder, her eyes widening when she saw Charles Finch standing behind her.

Chapter Three

As it turned out, weaning himself off alcohol wasn't a pleasant affair for Charles. His mother was lucky she was staying with the Haddingtons up north. After returning to Linfield, he spent most of the day anxiously pacing the house and losing his temper at servants who dared to cross his path. At night, he barely slept due to the constant pounding in his head, not to mention the layer of sweat that coated his body at all hours of the day.

His valet, Gibbs, assured him he would feel better soon, but all Charles truly wanted was a drink. Brandy, wine, even gin. He would have accepted anything. However, it was all out of the question. He had a point to prove to Rutley, his mother, and even his sister Rosamund, so he demanded his valet hide every bottle of wine and liquor in some undisclosed location within the massive country house. And then Charles asked him to begin the process of selling it all, except this time more pleadingly.

The duke was the first to visit Charles at Linfield, leaving London and returning to Kent shortly after him. Rutley immediately inquired over his progress with the Strickland girl, only to discover none had been made, which was how Charles ended up at this dreadful country ball with Rutley, standing behind Louisa Strickland and his land steward, Hardy. A multitude of things irked him at that moment.

First, the apparent familiarity between Louisa and his steward surprised him. He'd had no idea they even knew each other, which irritated him. And second, her complete lack of faith in his ability to save Linfield, not to mention calling him worthless. That hurt. Hadn't they been friends before? Or had their ruse all those years ago fooled even him?

"Your Grace," Louisa said immediately to Rutley, dipping her head and curtseying for the taller of the two men. She turned to Charles next, doing the same. "Lord Bolton. I did not see you standing there."

"Clearly," he replied, sounding as unamused as he felt. Charles thought he saw the beginnings of a blush on Louisa's cheeks.

The duke began to bow, and Charles reluctantly did the same, though he pinched his features together with irritation. He had not seen Louisa in years, not since the night at his aunt's ball in London. At least Rutley knew now that Charles wasn't exaggerating when he said Louisa hated him.

Despite being six years older, Louisa seemed unchanged from that night so long ago. She was still tall, with the prettiest skin he had ever seen and bright red hair that sat curled on the top of her head.

"I should apologize for what I said earlier," she said.

"Perhaps—but will you?"

Her cheeks turned an even deeper shade of scarlet. "I was exaggerating, of course, only repeating some idle gossip I heard. I did not mean it."

Charles smiled slightly, still not hearing an apology—as was expected from what he knew about Louisa. He turned and looked at Hardy, who stood at Louisa's side looking as if he wanted to sink into the ground. "What do you think, Hardy? Did she mean it?"

Charles playfully tilted his head to the side, turning back toward Louisa. Louisa glared at him, her blush fading, and his smile broadened. There was the Louisa he knew, the one who always challenged him on everything, even when they were children.

Hardy didn't have a chance to answer the earl's question before Louisa spoke again. "I am surprised you are here, my lord. I thought gatherings such as this were beneath you."

"The duke was the one who suggested we come," Charles said, glancing at Rutley, who still stood beside him in his typical statuesque manner, surveying the room with cold eyes. He was a tall, imposing man, towering over the rest of the guests. "If a party such as this is good enough for a duke, surely it is good enough for an earl."

Louisa shot a sheepish look in Rutley's direction. "I am sorry, Your Grace. I did not mean to insinuate—"

"There is no need to apologize, Miss Strickland," the duke said, looking down at her. He cast a sidelong glance in his companion's direction. "I did have to drag him here."

Charles scowled at his friend while Louisa bit back a smile. The earl's and Louisa's eyes briefly met, and her pleased expression quickly faded before she abruptly turned away.

Meanwhile, Rutley addressed Hardy. "Will you join me at the refreshment table, sir? I would like to ask for your advice in regard to Sedgewick Park."

Louisa looked as if she was growing nervous at the thought of being left alone with Charles, which almost made him smile. She shot Hardy a desperate look, but he was focused on the duke. "Of course, Your Grace."

The duke turned toward Charles, who knew he shouldn't be anywhere near the refreshment table after only a week sober. "Why don't you keep Miss Strickland company until we return?"

Charles looked at Louisa just in time to catch a flash of unfettered panic on her face. She smiled nervously at the duke.

"Thank you, but I'm sure I'll be fine by myself, Your Grace." She glanced at Charles, her smile becoming bitter. "I do know how the earl enjoys his refreshments."

"Not anymore," the duke said matter-of-factly. Rutley looked at his friend as if he was waiting for him to agree, but Charles shot him an irritated look instead. He wasn't quite ready to announce his sobriety to anyone, especially when it had only been a week. There was still plenty of time to fail, especially when he had such a storied history of failure. "Isn't that right, Bolton?"

Louisa's jaw nearly dropped, and Charles forced himself to nod, if only because the duke hadn't embarrassed him by calling him Charles in front of a lady and his employee. "That's right."

Charles and Louisa stared at each other, her bitter smile slowly fading. Now she looked at him more curiously, her brow knitted together. He couldn't blame her. She didn't know a Charles who didn't love to drink. He forced himself to turn and look at Rutley. "I will stay with Miss Strickland."

After the duke and Hardy left, Charles and Louisa faced each other once more. Her curiosity from before remained the same, and she narrowed her eyes. "You no longer drink?" she asked, sounding somewhat incredulous as she did.

He tried not to glare at her, but it was difficult. "I am *trying* not to drink."

Louisa stared at him in awe, as if she did not quite believe what she was hearing.

He sighed. "Although that may sound surprising to you, I have not touched the stuff for a week now."

She shook her head. "But why?"

Why not? Charles thought.

"You made it clear earlier that you have heard all the rumors regarding my family's sad state of affairs over the past few months. You, out of all people, Louisa, should know how my drinking and gambling has been a detriment to all of us."

Now it was her turn to glare. "Do not call me by my Christian name. We are not friends anymore." She inched closer to him, her voice a low hiss. She looked around to make sure no one was listening to them. "And I do not wish to give anyone the wrong idea."

His mouth twitched, and his eyes fell on her pale-pink lips. He imagined that no one had ever kissed them, especially when their so-called courtship was the only one she probably ever experienced. Then again, there was her cousin. Had William ever kissed her?

The intrusive thought about kissing her alarmed him, and he forced himself to redirect his attention to her eyes. "Fine. Miss Strickland, then."

An awkward moment passed. Louisa looked away from him at the dancing couples on the ballroom floor. A small orchestra played a waltz at the far end of the room. "Why are you here?"

Charles shrugged. "The duke told you. He invited me."

"But why?"

What could he say? That Rutley wished him to marry her younger sister for her impressive dowry? Charles sighed. "I am in search of a wife. She will need to be someone wealthy if I am to save Linfield."

Louisa blinked. "Someone wealthy?" She crossed her arms, shaking her head. "If you think I will agree to marry you after all this time, you are sorely mistaken."

Charles couldn't help but grin at her mistake. She

assumed he'd come here for her, after all these years. "I do not mean *you*."

Her face fell, and her blush returned soon after. "Then who—" She looked around the room until her eyes landed on a petite brunette standing next to Mrs. Strickland. Charles squinted his eyes. Was that Flora? If she was, the girl had indeed grown up beautifully.

Perhaps she might make a good wife after all, just as Rutley said, and he did enjoy irritating Louisa. Marrying her little sister would drive the woman wild. As he grinned at the idea of it, Louisa turned back to him.

"You cannot marry my sister! I will not let you, and neither will Mrs. Strickland. She thinks you ruined my come-out."

Charles chuckled. "And who asked me to do that?" Her blush deepened, and he looked over her shoulder, his eyes landing on Flora once more. "Will you introduce me to her?"

"You have already met her," Louisa stubbornly replied. "When she was *twelve*."

He laughed. "She might as well be an entirely different person. Look at her! She's so much older than I remember. So much *shapelier*."

Louisa glared at him. "That is my *sister*, you insufferable —" She pursed her lips together, avoiding cursing him out completely. When she spoke again, she was firm and direct with him. "You cannot have her. Do you think I would let you marry my sister for her fortune alone?"

Charles shook his head. "Who said anything about marrying her for her fortune alone? Perhaps I might come to love and adore her." He tilted his head to the side, studying her sister's form. "She looks quite easy to love."

"I am sure you are not capable of love," Louisa snapped.

"I thought that was you, not me."

That seemed to unnerve her. She huffed and turned away.

Charles sighed. "If you must know, the duke was the one who suggested it. But until I find someone to marry, he is helping me economize so that I can pay him back slowly. So whether I take a wife or not, Linfield will remain mine as long as I pay off my debt within five years."

Her head snapped in his direction. "And what happens when you pay him back? Do you intend to start gambling again until Linfield is ruined once more?"

"Is it truly that hard to believe I am a changed man?" he asked, narrowing his eyes at her. "I do not drink or gamble anymore."

Louisa gave an unladylike snort. "And how long have you not gambled? Has it been only a week as well?

"It has been a year."

Surprise pulled her eyebrows upward. When she recollected herself, her gaze became much more discerning. "I do not believe you."

"Why not?"

She turned away. "Because I know you," she mumbled softly.

"Louisa—"

But he could not finish what he wanted to say. Mrs. Strickland and Flora suddenly appeared before them, their round eyes blinking like owls as their gazes traveled back and forth between Charles and Louisa.

"Lord Bolton," Mrs. Strickland said, curtseying. She eyed Louisa suspiciously. "I see you have begun reacquainting yourself with my eldest daughter." Charles thought he saw Louisa roll her eyes. He smiled. Her stepmother then gestured toward the young brown-haired woman standing beside her. "Do you remember Flora, my other daughter?"

Flora curtseyed as well, and Charles swiftly bowed. "Of course I remember, Mrs. Strickland." He smiled broadly, trying to be as charming as possible. "The better question is: Does Miss Flora remember me?"

He knew he should have stood there admiring Flora and Flora alone, but he kept stealing glances at Louisa, wondering what she was thinking now that her stepmother and sister caught them together. He saw the telltale signs of fury on Louisa's face—a crinkled nose and pinched-together lips—which made it difficult for Charles not to grin like a madman. Meanwhile, Flora flushed.

"Yes, I remember you, my lord," she murmured. The younger girl glanced at her older sister. "You came to my father's funeral, and you used to call on us that season we spent in London. I have always been sad our families didn't continue our acquaintance when we returned to Kent, even though we are neighbors."

Charles did not miss the glare that Louisa shot her younger sister. He nodded, frowning slightly. "I now find myself in Kent indefinitely without my father, mother, or sister to keep me company. Perhaps we might renew the acquaintance."

He looked at Mrs. Strickland, who watched him with narrowed eyes. He could tell she did not trust him either, but the Strickland family matriarch was far too polite to say anything about it, unlike her stepdaughter. "If it pleases you, my lord."

Charles didn't even have to look at Louisa to know she was radiating even more anger than before. He smiled to himself, hoping to push her even further by turning to Flora. "Have you danced yet this evening, Miss Flora?"

The girl shook her head, appearing almost enraptured by him.

"Well, that is a shame. Perhaps you might allow me the honor of being your first partner for the evening."

He offered her his arm, and she happily took it. As they

walked toward the dance floor together, he turned over his shoulder, taking one last look at Louisa. She stood beside her stepmother, her hands clenched into fists at her side. He faced forward again, trying not to take too much delight in her displeasure.

"You mustn't let him court her."

Mrs. Strickland looked at Louisa, surprised. "You would begrudge your sister the chance to become a countess simply because you do not like the man?"

Louisa blinked, unable to believe what she was hearing. "I do not like the man? You shouldn't like the man either!" She tried not to shout, but Louisa always did have a temper, regardless of where she found herself. She did her best not to let her eyes drift to where her sister and Charles danced. That would only make things worse.

He was just as she remembered him. Unjustifiably smug. A truly pompous asshole. Worst of all, her sister had encouraged him, despite being aware of their past. "Surely you know of his gambling debts to the Duke of Rutley, not to mention his love of drink. Regardless of his title, he is hardly a suitable match for Flora, and if they married, she would come to regret it. I am sure of it."

"He seems sober now," her stepmother observed with a shrug.

"But how long will that last?" Louisa asked. If she knew Charles at all, it wouldn't be much time at all before he turned to brandy or cards again, especially once he paid off his debt in five years. They hadn't even touched on his love of women! Surely the earl could not be faithful to one woman for long, even if she was his wife.

Louisa shook her head. She must protect Flora at all costs. "I'm thankful my father had enough foresight to prepare for a situation such as this. I hold the purse strings in this family, so I must approve of any man Flora wants to marry. You wouldn't want someone like the earl marrying her for her money alone, would you?"

"And what if she comes to like him? Will you let your jealousy break your poor sister's heart?"

Louisa felt her cheeks turn hot. "Jealousy?"

Her stepmother arched her brow but did not say anything else.

"I am not jealous," Louisa mumbled. She turned her head back in the direction of the dance floor, watching her sister and Charles once more. "Besides, it's only one dance. I'm sure it will amount to nothing."

Her stepmother sighed. "I have never quite been able to figure out what happened between the two of you six years ago. I know you believe yourself quite on the shelf, but if the earl is finally looking for a wealthy wife—and he must be, at his age and in his financial situation—then you are more than welcome to throw your cap at him as well. You have just as good a chance of winning his affections as your sister."

Louisa faltered. Was that a compliment? She couldn't deny that her stepmother had always been kind to her, even after Flora had been born, when it would have been easy to forget all about Louisa. But Louisa had always preferred to maintain a safe distance from her stepmother, even when she was a little girl, so she always met her kindness with distrust.

"Do not lie to me to make me feel better about myself. You know how I despise it." Her stepmother frowned at her. "Flora will be the talk of the ton next season, but I will not let fortune hunters anywhere near her. I will happily play the part of the shrewish older sister to protect her."

Louisa excused herself after that, heading to the refreshment table where she could distract herself with a cup of punch. She lurked in the shadows for the rest of the evening, spying on Charles, waiting for the right time to speak to him, to warn him away from Flora. Finally, she saw him slip out into the entry hall by himself, so she followed him.

"Lord Bolton," she called after him. The hall was empty, and the sound of her voice reverberated off the room's wood-paneled walls. Charles stopped, turning to face her. He did appear sober still, and she hadn't seen him drink at all that night. Perhaps he really was trying to change.

"May I help you, Miss Strickland?" He looked at her, puzzled.

Louisa realized she had been standing in front of him staring for longer than appropriate, lost in her thoughts. She cleared her throat. "Please do not call on my sister at the manor."

Charles sighed. "But Louisa—"

She did not bother scolding him for using her Christian name this time. If he listened to her about one thing, it would be this:

"If you can remain sober until the start of next season, I will fully support your courtship in town. But not before then. I need to know you can remain sober for more than a few days or weeks. And if I hear about you misbehaving—and you *know* I will—you can forget about me approving your courtship of my sister." Louisa paused, letting the weight of her words sink into Charles's thick skull. "Do not forget that you need me to like you, my lord. I can take away Flora's dowry just as you threatened to take away your sister's when she cancelled her wedding."

His face fell. "You must think I am a complete rogue."

Louisa knitted her brows together. "Are you not?"

Charles sighed. His eyes searched hers, and she thought she stopped breathing for a moment until he finally nodded his head. "Fine. I accept your challenge. I will see you in London in April."

Chapter Four

London, England
April 1817

"OH, look! Someone has already sent us flowers."

Louisa and her stepmother exchanged surprised looks. The Stricklands had just arrived at their rented town house in Mayfair that afternoon, ready to embark on Flora's first season, but Louisa wasn't prepared for her little sister to have admirers already. Who could have sent such a gift? Who even knew their address in town yet?

Louisa handed her bonnet and pelisse to one of the footmen, then walked with Mrs. Strickland to the drawing room. Flora was there, standing in front of the collection of flowers on one of the side tables, reading the note that came with it. Flora's face slowly fell, and she turned to her sister and her mother. "They are from the Earl of Bolton."

Louisa's face took on an expression similar to her sister's. She should have known better than to tell Mr. Hardy where they were staying that season. She'd reluctantly agreed to let him manage the manor while they were away for the next few months as she helped her sister find a worthy husband. He must have been the one who gave Charles their address.

"Why would he send me flowers in London when he couldn't even be bothered to call on me in Kent over the past year?" Flora wondered aloud.

Louisa did not answer, only shrugged, an innocent look on her face. She had not told Flora or Mrs. Strickland about her agreement with Charles. She stepped closer to the flowers, inspecting the massive bouquet, an artfully arranged monstrosity of pink roses accented with lilies and daisies. The gift felt as if it was a message to her as much as it was to her sister.

If that was the case, then there must have been some truth in the rumors circulating in the scandal sheets over the past week. Charles Finch, the Earl of Bolton, had returned to town a changed man. He no longer drank or gambled and was more handsome than ever. *And* he was apparently in want of a wife.

A *rich* wife.

Louisa turned back to Flora, searching for the note she'd been holding. But her sister had handed it to her mother while Louisa had been staring at the flowers, lost in thought. She waited for Mrs. Strickland to finish reading, and then their eyes met. "The earl wishes Flora good luck with her first season in town. He hopes she will accept these flowers as an apology for never visiting Strickland after the ball last summer. He says his estate kept him too busy for social calls."

Flora scoffed. "There was hardly a harvest last autumn. What could have kept him so busy?"

Louisa tried not to take her sister's comments personally, but she did. "Whether the harvest is good or bad, there is always plenty of work to do on an estate, though I wouldn't expect you to understand."

Flora rolled her eyes before walking toward the chaise in front of the room's bay windows and taking a seat, letting out a big sigh as she did. The room fell silent, and Louisa saw an opportunity to influence her sister's opinion of Charles. She turned back toward the flowers, walking toward them and taking one of the delicate petals between her fingertips. She looked back at her sister.

"I, for one, couldn't care less whether or not you forgive Lord Bolton," Louisa said, her tone breezy as she spoke. "Surely you can do much better than a man twenty thousand pounds in debt. There will be much better gentlemen to be had this season."

Louisa may have agreed to allow Charles to court Flora if he managed to stop drinking, but that didn't mean Louisa had to approve any match between them in the end. And with Flora now disliking the man, Louisa would have a much easier time keeping them apart.

"You need a man who brings as much to the table as you do," Louisa continued as she paced the room, tapping her chin with one finger. "Someone intelligent and wealthy. Handsome, too." She spun around, facing her sister and flashing a broad smile. "And who cares if he has a title?"

After all, most men with titles were far from intelligent, wealthy, or handsome. A self-made gentleman would be perfect for Flora and far better than a stuffy aristocrat. That was what Louisa thought, anyway.

"What about the Duke of Rutley?" Flora asked, suddenly taking an interest in her sister's musings from where she lounged on the yellow chaise. "Do you think he's looking for a wife like the earl is? Not only is Rutley intelligent, wealthy, and handsome, but he is titled as well."

Louisa and her stepmother exchanged a look. Everyone knew the duke was still in love with Lady Rosamund, Charles's younger sister, even after she called off their engagement last year. Flora didn't stand a chance in winning his affections. But Mrs. Strickland was never one to discourage her daughters.

"The two of you would make a lovely couple," she said encouragingly.

Louisa nearly spoke over Mrs. Strickland. "But perhaps it is best to keep your options open."

Flora waved a single nonchalant hand. "That goes without saying." But then she focused her attention on her mother. "Do you think he'll be at the Talbots' ball?"

Mr. Talbot was a friend of their late father's, and the invitation to their ball in a few days was one of the many Mrs. Strickland had already secured that season. Louisa expected neither the duke nor Charles would be there, as Mrs. Talbot was the mother of the earl's illegitimate sister. From what Louisa understood, Charles and his sisters weren't on good terms, and if the duke was loyal to Charles at all, Louisa could only assume the Talbots wouldn't invite either man to their ball.

"I'm not sure if the duke and Mr. Talbot are friends," Mrs. Strickland said, "but I'm sure there will be plenty of other eligible bachelors there."

Much more suitable ones, Louisa silently hoped.

THE FOLLOWING MORNING, Louisa and Flora walked through Mayfair to Hyde Park. They didn't bother bringing one of their maids. At eight-and-twenty, Louisa thought she was more than old enough to be her younger sister's chaperone, and her stepmother luckily agreed. While her sister walked along the Serpentine with the hopes of being seen by someone important, Louisa only wanted to enjoy some fresh air and exercise.

"Must you strut about like that?" Louisa asked her younger sister, who wore an outfit of head-to-toe purple. "You look like a peacock."

"I believe the females are called pea*hens*." Flora looked her sister up and down as Louisa laughed slightly. "Nevertheless, I will take that as a compliment. The males are much more colorful. And at least I don't look like a sad old spinster."

Louisa stopped laughing and gasped, offended. "I beg your pardon!"

But her sister had a point. The colors in Louisa's wardrobe were much more subdued than her younger sister's. After all, she had no interest in attracting a mate if it meant relinquishing her independence to him.

"Why haven't you ordered any new frocks?" Flora asked. The hour was still early, and they sauntered down the dirt pathway, nodding at other passersby as they did. A few ducks floated lazily down the Serpentine.

Louisa pinched her eyebrows together. "Why would I? I'm not the one in search of a husband."

Flora glanced at her sideways. "Why not, though? Surely since we're here, it wouldn't hurt for you to look for your one true love. Think of all the people we'll meet!"

Louisa rolled her eyes. "Not this conversation again," she muttered. Her sister was always going on and on about her one true love. Flora honestly thought there was someone out there for everyone—even for Louisa, who hadn't believed in love since she turned nine and her father decided to remarry only two years after her mother died. If love did exist, it certainly had nothing to do with marriage.

"I would hate to watch you grow old and regretful when I start a family of my own with the husband of my dreams," Flora continued anyway, ignoring her sister. "You know,

Louisa, you won't always have me and Mama. One day you'll find yourself alone in that big manor by yourself, wondering where your life has gone."

"As long as the manor remains successful through these trying times, I will be more than happy with my life."

And times *were* trying. Last summer had been cold and wet, and their yields that harvest had been much smaller than average. Luckily, Strickland Manor could withstand a poor harvest now and again. But maintaining their income was not the sure thing Flora thought it was, which was why Louisa knew she must work hard and make smart investments outside of tending to their land. That wasn't always as easy as Flora assumed.

"But don't you want a family?" Flora asked.

Louisa shrugged. "Surely you will provide me a few nieces and nephews to dote upon."

"But—"

Flora was interrupted by the sounds of a frenzied horse in the distance. A man on a black mount charged toward them, shouting at them to get out of the way. Louisa frantically reached for her sister, hoping to pull her to safety, but it was too late. The horse was upon them, and it came to an abrupt stop, nearly bucking its rider off its back as it stood up on its hind legs.

Even after the man finally managed to control his mount, Louisa still clutched her sister close to her. Flora must have been able to hear Louisa's heart, what with how wildly it pounded in her chest. Louisa took a deep breath, wishing she were a man so she could yell obscenities at the rider.

"Sir!" Louisa exclaimed. "What were you thinking? This beast of yours could have trampled me and my sister."

The man in question dismounted his horse, which Louisa suspected to be a Friesian. She eyed it suspiciously, though she knew she must blame its bad behavior squarely on its owner, not the poor animal. The man standing in front of them now couldn't have trained it properly. What was he thinking to take an untrained horse out to such a public place as Hyde Park?

"I apologize to you and your sister," the man said, though he seemed to be looking more at Flora than Louisa. That didn't come as a surprise, though. Petite Flora, with her doe eyes and chestnut-colored hair, always attracted more attention than Louisa, who narrowed her eyes at the stranger. "I am still training poor Fred. Something spooked him, and I wasn't able to stop him until he came upon the two of you. I meant no harm." He patted the horse's neck, laughing slightly. "Neither did Fred."

Louisa looked at the beast in question, a look of confusion creasing her face. What sort of name was *Fred* for such a beautiful horse? She pursed her lips together before turning her attention to Flora. Her little sister stood beside her quite transfixed, either by the giant horse or the very virile man standing in front of them. Louisa supposed the stranger was somewhat handsome, but that wasn't what concerned her, not when they'd just nearly died.

"Very well," Louisa said, taking her sister by the hand, practically dragging her away from the mysterious man. "You are forgiven. We will just be on our way, then."

One didn't talk to strangers at the Serpentine, after all. But this man was persistent, even as others watched them as they walked by. Louisa smiled as if nothing was wrong, but her smile quickly faded when the man called after them. "Wait! Surely you are willing to tell me your names so I can extend a more proper apology at a later date. Perhaps over afternoon tea?"

Louisa stopped, her nostrils flaring as she turned to face the man. This entire exchange would be plastered across all the society columns the following morning with the number of people now listening in, especially if this man was someone important. She knew she must choose her words carefully.

"I am Miss Louisa Strickland, and this is my sister, Miss—"

"Flora Strickland."

Louisa's eyes widened as her sister interrupted her. Flora bent at the knees, curtseying to the gentleman. She eyed him shyly through thick eyelashes, and he stared back at her, doing nothing to hide his grin. Louisa could have died from embarrassment.

"And I am Viscount Fitzgerald," he said, swiftly bowing his head. The viscount appeared to be in his early thirties. "Have you two ladies been in London long?"

"We only just arrived yesterday from Kent," Flora said.

Louisa cleared her throat before her sister could say anything else. The two of them exchanged equally irritated looks before Louisa turned back to the viscount.

"We really must be going, my lord," Louisa said. She gave a wary glance in the direction of Fred the Friesian. "Best of luck with your horse."

She quickly guided her giddy sister away from the viscount before the man could say anything else. When they were out of earshot, Louisa turned toward her sister, annoyed. "You mustn't turn into an insufferable ninny every time we come across a handsome man."

Flora's eyes widened with what appeared to be delight. "So you agree that he is handsome?"

Louisa tried not to groan. Flora looked over her shoulder, smiling when she spotted the viscount in the distance. He was still watching them. She turned back to her sister. "I think he is the most handsome man I have ever seen! And a viscount, no less! We must find out more about him." Flora grinned triumphantly. "I think I have just met my future husband."

Louisa tried not to tip over from shock. "But you don't even know him!"

Flora let out a dreamy sigh, then frowned at her sister. "Don't you believe in love at first sight?"

"Certainly not!" Louisa said, grimacing. When two men walked by them and tipped their hats at them, she forced a smile. When they passed, she shot her sister a pointed look. "See? That is how men and women who are strangers are supposed to interact in a public park."

Flora grimaced. "But that is so boring! The viscount seems much more exciting."

Louisa sighed, unable to try to reason with her younger sister any longer. Perhaps nineteen was too young for a girl's come-out, but Mrs. Strickland had insisted it be that year, no matter how silly Flora was. And she *was* silly. She didn't stop talking about the mysterious stranger from the park all the way home.

"I wonder if he has an invitation to the Talbots' ball," Flora mused aloud. "A viscount! I like the sound of it. I could be a viscountess. Oh, I do hope we see him again!"

Louisa hoped the opposite, especially if her doubts about his character turned out to be more than just a vague notion inside her head. As featherbrained as her sister was, Louisa did not want to see Flora hurt. But with the whole of the season in front of them and so many more men to meet— respectable and otherwise—Louisa was beginning to realize that might be easier said than done.

Chapter Five

CHARLES PACED his study at Finch Place, having yet to hear anything from the Stricklands or his family since he arrived in London. The Stricklands shouldn't have been a surprise. He'd spent his entire summer and winter holed up at Linfield, only receiving occasional visits from the duke and Mr. Hardy, ignoring all other forms of polite society. His mother had decided to stay on with the Haddingtons up north indefinitely.

Meanwhile, Rutley grew even more annoyed by Charles's inability to manage an estate effectively, not to mention his friend's complete lack of progress in engaging Flora Strickland's affections. But the earl's steward was the picture of patience when it came to estate affairs, even after the disastrous harvest that autumn. Hardy also provided occasional tidbits of information about the Stricklands, who apparently invited him over for dinner on occasion.

Charles thought Flora was a sweet and lively girl, very unlike her shrew of an older half sister, and after one dance with the younger Miss Strickland, he decided marrying her wouldn't be all that bad. Plenty of men had suffered much worse fates, but as Charles explained to Rutley, her older sister had to approve Flora's choice of husband, and Louisa asked him to stay away until the spring.

This development irritated the duke to no end, and so Rutley was the one who demanded Hardy give them the Stricklands' address in London so Charles could send flowers immediately upon their arrival in town that spring.

Hardy scoffed at such a plan. "Miss Flora won't be impressed with flowers after Lord Bolton failed to call on her at the manor last summer."

"Do you have a better idea?" the duke asked, clearly annoyed that the land steward would question his judgment.

Unfortunately, the steward did not. After Hardy finally gave Rutley the address, the duke and Charles departed for London and waited for the Stricklands to arrive as well. When the day finally came, Rutley insisted on choosing the flowers, and he even dictated the note that Charles included with them.

"It's a wonder I'm receiving romantic advice from you," Charles noted sourly as he sealed the short missive with red wax, imprinting it with the Bolton family's coat of arms. Rutley glared down at him from where he stood in front of Charles's desk at Finch Place. They both knew the duke still carried much pain from his failed engagement to the earl's younger sister, Rosamund, and that the duke preferred not to talk about it.

"You will thank me later," Rutley grumbled, quickly snatching the letter from Charles and handing it off to a servant who stood behind him holding a vase of roses, lilies, and daisies. But a day later, Charles had yet to receive any sort of response. Perhaps Hardy was right, but what else could he do?

Charles scowled, still pacing his study. This had probably

been Louisa's plan all along: to take him out of the running entirely. Why had he listened to her?

His next hope was seeing Flora at the Talbots' ball, but since Lady Sarah Talbot was his illegitimate sister's mother, receiving an invitation seemed unlikely, especially after his family ignored his invitations to join him for dinner that evening. And why wouldn't they? He hadn't reached out to them since they converged upon his aunt's Park Street mansion to watch the bitter end of Rutley and Rosamund's relationship almost one year ago.

So now he paced, feeling like a failure and wondering what the duke would demand of him next when his gaze suddenly fell on the empty sideboard in his study. He stopped for a moment, realizing he had succeeded in at least one way. Charles had stopped drinking, and although his finances may still be a mess, he had become an extremely eligible bachelor in every other way, what with his title and newfound good health.

There must be other wealthy women of marrying age in town besides Flora Strickland. Perhaps Rutley could help him come up with a list of eligible ladies, and there would be plenty of balls other than the Talbots' at which to woo them that season. He had survived almost a year without his family. He could go another if he must, and another after that.

"My lord."

The sound of Gibbs's voice behind him made Charles jump after being alone in his study all day. He turned, ready to scold the valet for startling him, but his eyes fell upon a letter the stout man held between his thick fingers.

"What is that?" Charles asked, pointing. Had Flora finally written him? Or perhaps it was from Rosamund.

"A letter from the Dowager Duchess of Ramsbury, my lord," Gibbs replied, handing the earl the letter.

Charles took it, then walked behind his desk and sat

down. He dug through one of the drawers, looking for his erasing knife. When Charles found it, he carefully removed the wax seal, then hastily unfolded the piece of paper. The note was short, but Charles sighed with relief. He looked up at Gibbs, who appeared nervous, beads of sweat forming at his brow.

Charles smiled. "Have no fear, Gibbs," he said. "It is good news. My aunt, sisters, and Mr. Brooks will be joining us for dinner this evening after all."

Gibbs let out an audible sigh of relief. But before the valet could scramble away to brief the cook belowstairs, Charles spoke again, this time more seriously. "Do make sure the duke stays away this evening, even if he pounds on the front door in one of his drunken stupors. I will not have him upsetting Rosamund when I'm only just beginning to repair my relationship with her. Let all the other servants know as well."

The valet nodded nervously, probably because he knew no one could stop Rutley when he was in one of his moods. But if he came that night, something would have to be done.

Charles watched as Gibbs swiftly left the room. He debated whether or not to use the time until dinner to tell the duke himself of his plans to mend his broken relationship with his family.

No, that was one area of his life he didn't care to have Rutley dictate, so he went upstairs to his bedroom instead, where he practiced a dozen different apology speeches in the mirror, hoping one of them might work.

His half sister August was the first to arrive that evening for dinner, joined by her husband, his former friend and solicitor Brooks. Brooks barely spoke, regarding Charles with a suspicious gaze as they sat in the drawing room waiting for the others to arrive.

August did most of the talking, and she was just as bright and cheery as Charles remembered her to be. Only her round belly was different, now that she was seven months pregnant with her and her husband's first child.

"I did not know I was about to become an uncle," Charles said with a nervous smile.

Brooks shot him a sour look. "That's not surprising. We have not heard from you in ten months. Funny—a month for each of my clients that you scared away."

Charles grimaced. He had done that, hadn't he? When Brooks and August first became engaged, the earl went to the solicitor, asking him to sign over his half sister's inheritance to him after the couple married. But Brooks refused, even when August agreed to it.

And rightfully so, Charles reminded himself. Brooks was only trying to protect his new wife. Charles had never treated August with any respect, too angry over his late father's secret indiscretion, not to mention his decision to leave her twelve thousand pounds. If he had those twelve thousand pounds, he would have been able to pay back over half his debts. The mountain he faced now would be more like a small hill.

But it wasn't meant to be, and before Charles could apologize, August spoke. "But you gained ten new ones in the past few months, haven't you?" she asked, shooting her husband a reproachful look.

He reluctantly nodded, and August turned back to Charles, offering an apologetic smile as she did, though Charles knew he didn't deserve it.

"And although it's been a long time, we are glad to hear from you now," August continued.

He shifted uncomfortably in his seat. Shouldn't she be angry at him? How could she be so gracious in her behavior?

"I always knew there might be an adjustment period

between our father telling you and Rosamund of my existence and when you might accept me as one of your own. My husband even warned me of it."

Charles thought he heard Brooks grunt disapprovingly beside her, but if August heard, she ignored him. "I only hope from now on that we might be more than just brother and sister in name only."

Charles smiled slightly. "I would like that."

He knew at once why Brooks had fallen in love with the girl. The man needed someone with a forgiving nature, especially when his old friend could be so stubborn. Charles turned to the solicitor. "Perhaps I might retain some of your services later this season."

Brooks blinked, appearing confused.

"I might as well be blunt," said Charles. "I am here in town to find a wife, and I will need someone to draw up some marriage papers when she finally reveals herself to me."

"I heard you sent flowers to Flora Strickland," a familiar feminine voice said from behind him. Charles whipped his head around, finding Rosamund standing in the doorway, flanked on her right side by their aunt. His sister looked the same as she always did: tall, elegant, blonde. When he rose to greet her properly, she looked at him with discerning eyes.

"Good evening, Charles," she said. His sister always brought an air of confidence with her wherever she went, but she seemed even more self-assured now, despite her broken engagement last year. Charles imagined that was their aunt's influence at work. "You look well. Along with the flowers, I also heard you gave up drinking. It certainly shows."

Charles quietly chuckled as they all sat down. "Do the scandal sheets report on everything I do and don't do?"

"Our family has been the talk of the town ever since Father died and Brooks brought August to Park Street," Rosamund replied, eyeing her brother suspiciously. "You have not tried to deny anything I said, though. I suppose you have called us here to help you find a wife since Miss Strickland wants nothing to do with you."

"I have called you here tonight because I would like to make amends."

Rosamund stared at him, and Charles knew right away that he would have a much more challenging time convincing her of his good intentions compared to their half sister.

"I am truly sorry for what happened last year, and I would like us to be a family again, which is how Father would have wanted it, regardless of what Mother thinks about August." He looked toward his younger sister, who smiled at him, then he turned back to Rosamund. "He wouldn't want us to quarrel."

Charles paused, waiting for Rosamund to say something, but she didn't. She only appeared unimpressed by his proclamation. He swallowed. "And the truth is I will need help from all of you if I'm to make Linfield—our family home—a success again."

Rosamund rolled her eyes as she folded her arms against her chest. "Where have I heard that before? Who do you need me to marry this time, Charles?" She glanced at August. "You are lucky you already have a husband, or else he might scheme up some wicked plan for you as well."

"My schemes have nothing to do with you, Rosamund—not this time."

His sister straightened, though she still gave him a wary look. He didn't blame her. He looked around the room at his family gathered there.

"I know I have used you all terribly at one point or another, but I hope you can forgive me. As it turns out, spending nearly a year by yourself gives you ample time to see the error of your ways."

"And how do we know we can trust you?" It was Brooks who interjected this time.

Charles frowned, knowing he had hurt his old friend as much as his sisters. "I can tell you that Rosamund's correct. It is true that I no longer drink, if that makes any sort of difference to you." Brooks seemed surprised by the earl's admission, though he was no doubt not entirely convinced it was the truth. Charles continued with his gaze fixated on his friend. "I think you and I both know how brandy had the power to turn me into quite the fool."

"Like most men," his friend muttered.

Charles nodded. He couldn't disagree after all that happened last year. "I like to think my character has much improved since I gave up the stuff. Perhaps you might agree if you were to give me another chance." Charles turned back to Rosamund. "And I am sure you will find my newfound dedication to saving Linfield as proof."

August stirred in her seat. "I could always—"

"I do not want your money," Charles interrupted her before even Brooks could. His sister's husband watched him closely. Charles tried to smile. "I appreciate the offer, truly, but Father desperately wanted you to have your inheritance. He told me as much before he died. I will find another way to restore Linfield to its former glory."

A bored sigh came from Rosamund's direction. "Yes, yes, you already said that. But how? What is your plan? And why do you need our help?"

"As I said when you first arrived. I must do what any impoverished earl would do: marry well. And having your recommendation as I court the ladies of the ton will be a tremendous help in my efforts."

Rosamund sat down in a nearby chair, shaking her head. "Well, if you want my opinion, you must give up this senseless pursuit of Flora Strickland."

August leaned toward her sister. "Who is Flora Strickland?"

"One of the wealthiest young ladies to make her come-out this season," Rosamund explained. "Her dowry is supposedly thirty thousand pounds. I imagine many gentlemen will be after her hand in marriage for that reason alone, though she's also very pretty."

Charles interjected before August could ask another question. "Why do you think my pursuit of Miss Strickland is senseless?"

"Miss Strickland," his aunt echoed, furrowing her brow before looking at him. "Where have I heard that name before?"

"Charles courted the elder Miss Strickland seven years ago," Rosamund explained before he could. He waited for Rosamund to say something—better yet, multiple things—less than flattering about his decision to pursue the much younger Flora now. "I believe Louisa attended one of your parties on Park Street that season. Everyone thought Charles would propose that night, but he did not—*of course*—preferring to remain entangled with that opera singer of his. And now he's going after her younger sister. Poor Louisa!"

Although expected, Charles bristled at Rosamund's accusations. "Well, she hardly meant anything." Charles exchanged glances with August, who frowned at such a brusque statement. "The opera singer, I mean." He turned back to his other sister, thinking back to his bargain with Louisa. "I assure you that the elder Miss Strickland doesn't mind my pursuit of her younger sister. Truthfully, she gave me her permission to court Miss Flora."

Rosamund arched her brow. The look immediately made Charles nervous, who feared his sister might suspect that he was taking liberties with the meaning of the word *permission*. "Is that so?" she asked.

August cut in before he could answer. "I believe the Stricklands are on my mother's guest list for her ball this Saturday evening." She turned to Charles. "Would you like to come? I'm sure I could procure you an invitation if you would like one."

"August—"

"I would love to come," Charles said before Rosamund could convince August to retract her offer.

Rosamund did not seem pleased.

"There will be other eligible ladies there as well," August said, shooting Rosamund an apologetic look. Turning back to her brother, she added, "Perhaps I might introduce you to some of them."

Rosamund looked as if she had just gotten a brilliant idea. "Yes, some of the wealthiest ladies are truly terrible this season. I will introduce you to them. You will get along very well."

August ignored her. "But do try to arrive early. I don't plan on staying very long on account of my condition."

"I would rather you not go at all," Brooks grumbled.

Charles fought back a smile. He wondered what it was like to feel so protective over someone, and the fact that it was his friend who once swore off matrimony made it all the more intriguing to Charles.

"I will arrive whenever you would like," Charles said.

"Splendid!" August excitedly clapped her hands together, apparently unbothered by her husband's and sister's mutual lack of enthusiasm. Both of them sat there with matching looks of irritation.

The party moved to the dining room soon after. While they ate, the conversation was primarily polite and tepid, except when Lady Ramsbury recounted the latest gossip for them with her usual flair for theatrics.

After dinner, the two men stayed at the dining table while the women stood up and went to the drawing room.

"Would you like another drink?" Charles asked, gesturing toward Brooks's empty glass across the table. "I'm afraid I no longer keep any snuff in the house. Truly a nasty habit, isn't it?"

Brooks blinked as if in shock. "You know I don't like the stuff either. You really have changed, haven't you?"

Charles chuckled slightly at his reaction. "I suppose you must find this all so surprising. If you are worried that I might have had nefarious intentions with this dinner, let me assure you that I truly have changed. I realize the pain I caused everyone with my love of excess. I do not want to do that anymore—to anyone."

He was about to say more when he heard a commotion coming from the drawing room. Brooks was the first to react, practically jumping out of his chair and running to the large wooden doors between the two rooms, hastily pulling them open. Charles quickly followed him, finding a very drunk Rutley wobbling in front of the drawing room's fireplace. Two footmen were trying to hold him steady while Gibbs, August, and Lady Ramsbury nervously watched, each with equally horrified looks on their faces. Rosamund looked positively furious. Charles's and his sister's eyes met from across the room, and right away, he knew Rosamund would blame him for Rutley's sudden appearance that evening.

"Your Grace!" Charles exclaimed, taking long strides to reach the duke in record time, helping the footmen steady him. The familiar stench of alcohol invaded his nostrils, and Charles suddenly felt sick. He forced himself to speak anyway, though the words were strained. "What are you doing here?"

But Rutley didn't seem to comprehend the question. "Why didn't you tell me you were having dinner with your sister?" he asked accusingly.

The duke's eyes fell on Rosamund, who turned away and walked toward the room's front bay windows, no longer facing the scene. Charles grimaced, but at least it didn't seem like he had planned this. He only hoped Rosamund wouldn't be too upset with him.

"I will call on you tomorrow morning, and we can discuss it then," Charles said firmly. He did not stand up to the duke very frequently, but for the sake of his relationship with Rosamund, he knew he must at that moment. "Shall one of my men find you a hack? Or perhaps you could borrow—"

"No," Rutley snapped as he clumsily placed his hat back on the top of his head. He spoke to Charles, but his eyes remained fixated on Rosamund, even as she continued to stare out the window, ignoring her former fiancé. "It's a short walk. I will see myself out."

He swept out of the drawing room, and Gibbs stood wide-eyed and motionless. "Make sure he finds the front door, won't you?" Charles said, irritated.

Gibbs nodded before dashing out of the room. Sighing angrily, Charles turned around and walked toward Rosamund. When he reached her, she was watching Rutley walk across Berkeley Square, away from Finch Place. Her expression unreadable, Charles swallowed nervously.

"I am so sorry, Rosamund," he said. "The duke sometimes likes to show up at my door unannounced. He did the same thing in Kent all winter. I should have told him I was hosting a dinner tonight, but—"

"It's all right, Charles," Rosamund said suddenly, turning around as she did. Her smile was forced. "But I think I should go now."

Charles protested, but it was no use. The night, as pleasant as it was, was over. The entire party made their way to the entry hall, where the footmen brought them their coats and hats before they departed for the evening. August lingered behind, Brooks close beside her. "You'll still come to my mother's ball, won't you? I'll have her send a footman with an invitation tomorrow if you say yes."

Slowly, Charles nodded. "Yes, I will come. Thank you, August."

His sister smiled brightly at him while Brooks offered him a pitying glance. But then they both left, and Charles was alone again. He wandered into his study, where he went to the sideboard that once held an array of liquor bottles and glassware. He stood there staring at its empty shelves, frowning as he did. The light from the full moon reflected through the window and onto his face, but everything still felt dark.

Sighing, Charles turned away, heading upstairs to bed.

Chapter Six

"STOP FIDGETING," Louisa said, shooting daggers at her sister beside her. Flora gave her a nasty look of her own in return, her brown eyes a picture of ferocity framed between glossy ringlets.

"I cannot help that I'm excited," Flora said in the carriage on their way to the Talbots' ball that evening, a defiant look on her face. "Perhaps you ought to try it. You would be more bearable to be around if you did."

Louisa rolled her eyes, practically doing so with her whole body. If anyone had been acting insufferable recently, it was her little sister. "Is that the best insult you could think of?"

Flora narrowed her eyes and spoke through gritted teeth. "Actually, I can think of much worse."

"*Girls!*" Louisa's and Flora's heads snapped in Mrs. Strickland's direction. She sat across from them in the carriage, her face pinched together in irritation. "Please, no more bickering. I have heard quite enough of it over the past few days." She glanced at Louisa. "This is your sister's first ball. You must allow her some degree of nervousness."

Louisa's look soured almost immediately, then she tilted

her chin upwards, pointing her nose high in the air. "I was only trying to remind her to act like a lady." Louisa turned to her sister, a saccharine smile plastered on her face. "*Ladies* do not fidget."

"What would you know about being a lady?" Flora asked. "You would much rather toil in muddy fields all day long than go to balls!"

"And you wouldn't be able to go to balls if it weren't for me toiling in muddy fields all day long! Perhaps you ought to show me some respect for actually giving a damn about the estate I inherited, the one that provides you such fine clothes and carriages."

"*Louisa May Strickland!*"

Louisa winced at her stepmother's bellowing, which was most impressive for a woman of her size and stature. Perhaps Louisa had taken it too far. She shot the older woman a contrite look. "My apologies, ma'am."

But that wasn't enough. Mrs. Strickland looked impatiently between Louisa and Flora until the former finally sighed. Louisa turned to her sister. "My apologies to you as well, Flora." She paused a moment before continuing, her countenance softening slightly. "You know, there's no reason to be so nervous. I'm sure it will be a lovely evening, and you'll be the talk of the town in all the best ways when morning comes."

Flora grinned. "Do you truly think so?" She turned to her mother, still smiling. "I wonder if the viscount will be there."

And with that, Louisa's pleasant attitude for the evening was gone forever. She couldn't help but groan, turning to look out the carriage window, watching the brick and stone town houses of Mayfair pass by. "What?" she heard Flora ask, but Louisa couldn't respond, not unless she wanted to continue quarreling.

That must have been the tenth time Flora mentioned the

viscount in only the past few days. It was exhausting listening to Flora speculate about Lord Fitzgerald, a man they barely knew and who almost ran them over with his horse named Fred. *Fred.* Yet, for some reason, Flora fancied him as the Man For Her.

Louisa wasn't quite so sure. She reminded her sister there were plenty of other men to meet, but Flora wouldn't let it rest. It was as if Cupid himself had struck her with one of his cursed arrows. Poisonous arrows, Louisa had decided. She usually got along well with Flora, ridiculous as she could be sometimes, but Louisa couldn't stand a complete ninny—and that was what Flora had become as of late.

When they finally arrived at the Talbots' ball, Flora took one look at the sparkling ballroom and gasped. Louisa couldn't blame her. Balls in London were nothing like the ones in the country. The rooms were much grander, with impressive paintings in gilded frames decorating the finely papered walls. Meanwhile, the guests walked and talked with the sort of dignity exclusive to members of the ton.

But the crowded room quickly began to feel suffocating to Louisa, and she started to blush as women and men slowly walked by them, watching her and her sister and stepmother with curious gazes. Some women even discreetly dipped their heads behind their fluttering fans, whispering to their companions, their eyes remaining locked on Louisa. She swallowed, frantically searching the room for a friendly face she recognized. Unfortunately, there was no one.

For once, Louisa was comforted by the fact that Mrs. Strickland was such a fastidious dresser. As her sister said earlier, Louisa may have preferred the mud, but at least her stepmother had finally convinced her to purchase a whole new wardrobe for the season. Louisa wanted to blend in, not stand out by wearing obsolete fashions. But as it turned out, her tall frame, broad shoulders, and bright red hair gave little hope of that.

"Mrs. Strickland!"

Louisa quickly looked in the direction of the voice, breathing a sigh of relief as she did. Louisa recognized Mr. and Mrs. Talbot as they walked toward them, despite not having seen either of them in a while. Mr. Talbot had traveled to Kent for her father's funeral, but the last time Louisa saw Lady Sarah was during her own come-out all those years ago. The woman had a few more wrinkles now, but they only seemed to make her more beautiful, perfectly framing her full lips and glittering eyes.

"Mr. and Mrs. Talbot," Louisa's stepmother said, smiling, appearing as relieved as Louisa felt upon finally recognizing old friends in the mass of people surrounding them. "What a beautiful home you have. You remember my daughters, Louisa and Flora, don't you?"

Once everyone had exchanged pleasantries, Louisa found herself scanning the room for more familiar faces. She froze for a moment when her eyes fell upon the dancers at the center of the room, one of them being Charles Finch, appearing pleasant and jolly and quite unlike himself. He looked healthy and trim and... Well, Charles looked attractive. She would even dare to say he looked *handsome*. Louisa immediately frowned at the thought.

"Is that Charles Finch?" Flora asked, sounding as surprised as Louisa felt. "My! He *does* look different."

Louisa's heart dropped into her stomach for some unspeakable reason as she looked back and forth between her sister and Charles. Maybe Fitzgerald and his runaway mount weren't so terrible after all, despite the fact that she suspected the viscount had done that on purpose to force an introduction between himself and two unsuspecting, well-to-do ladies.

"He has been waiting for you to arrive all evening," Lady

Sarah said with a mischievous smile, her eyes twinkling as she spoke.

As all good ladies did, Flora looked away shyly, her cheeks flushing. Louisa forced herself to bite her tongue.

"My daughter, August, insisted we invite him. After dining with him the other evening, she said it's as if he's a whole new man compared to last season. I must take you to him as soon as he's free."

So he had taken Louisa's challenge to heart. She bit her lip, considering how much trimmer he appeared now that he no longer drank. His complexion seemed brighter too, and his hair much less of a mess. Was he that desperate to marry an heiress like her sister? How long could his sobriety last? Louisa tried not to appear too angry as she watched him twirl about the room with a girl who appeared to be at least ten years younger than her.

"Lady Sarah," said Flora, "I hope you don't mind me asking, but did you extend an invitation to Viscount Fitzgerald? My sister and I met him in the park the other day, and..."

Flora's voice trailed off. She must have noticed the way Mr. and Mrs. Talbot froze like two statues at the mention of the viscount's name. Louisa watched them curiously, puzzled by their equally strange responses.

"Did I say something wrong?" Flora asked, frowning.

"Not at all," Lady Sarah said, forcing a smile. Louisa and her stepmother exchanged a discreet glance. There was something the Talbots weren't telling them. "I did not know Viscount Fitzgerald was in town. I heard his father only recently passed."

Flora's frown deepened. "Oh. I suppose that means I won't be seeing him at many parties this season if he's still in mourning."

Not wishing to talk of Viscount Fitzgerald any longer, Louisa quickly interjected. "Is Lady Rosamund here? I don't think I've seen her since my come-out, and we were such dear friends that season."

Charles's sister was three years her junior, but they had made their come-outs during the same season. If anyone knew why Mr. and Mrs. Talbot looked so uncomfortable at the mere mention of the viscount's name, it would be Rosamund. Not to mention, she might be able to help keep Charles far away from Flora. With the right quality of gossip from Rosamund, Louisa could possibly kill two birds with one stone.

"I believe I last saw her by the refreshment table," Lady Sarah said.

Louisa turned to her stepmother. "Do you mind if I go and find her?"

Mrs. Strickland sighed, knowing very well that Louisa was a wealthy spinster of a certain age and could very much do as she pleased at this point. And from what Louisa heard about the earl's sister, Rosamund was well on her way to the same fate after ending her engagement to the duke.

"Go ahead," Mrs. Strickland said.

Louisa shot her a thankful smile and began to turn.

"But Louisa!" Flora cried before she could go.

Louisa stopped, moving closer to her sister and leaning down to whisper in her ear. "I am going to ask about your viscount."

When Louisa backed away, her sister was grinning from ear to ear. Flora gave a single nod of approval, and Louisa was on her way once more. She wasn't quite sure where the refreshment table was, but she quickly moved to the perimeter of the ballroom, where she could traverse in the shadows without much notice.

Just as Louisa caught sight of the refreshment table—as well as Rosamund and a fair-haired pregnant woman she didn't recognize standing in front of it—she collided with something unexpected: the firm chest of a gentleman. She looked up at the man in question, blinking, and she knew at once what Flora must have felt like when she first saw the viscount.

She must have felt like *this*. Chest contracting. Heart pounding. Cheeks burning. Louisa swallowed. What was happening to her?

The man was in his forties, but he was the sort of male specimen that aged like a fine wine or brandy, the exact opposite of someone like Charles and his boyish good looks. His hair and eyes were dark, and Louisa had to fight back a sudden urge to reach out and touch the faint shadow of facial hair on his jawline.

Shaking her head, Louisa forced herself to return to reality and speak. "P-pardon me, sir," she said, her voice trembling despite herself. She glanced over his shoulder at Rosamund and her unknown companion, still standing by the refreshment table. He followed her gaze, then turned back to her, smiling slightly.

"Are those your friends?" he asked before she could take her leave. His voice was almost melodic, and she very nearly sighed at the sound of it. Even her heart seemed to flutter. Again she wondered what was happening to her.

"Well, Lady Rosamund is my friend, or at least she used to be," Louisa replied. She winced, hating the way she sounded so unsure of herself. She tried to steady her voice. "I do not recognize the other woman."

The man chuckled slightly, looking at her. "You must not come to town very often, then, nor know Lady Rosamund very well at all. That is her half sister, Mrs. Brooks, or Lady August, as some call her. She was the talk of the town last season before she married that solicitor husband of hers."

He turned back to Louisa, who flushed, feeling like he had

caught her in a lie. Clearly she and Rosamund did not know each other all that well anymore.

"And what, may I ask, is your name?" he asked, his voice very low.

She swallowed again, trying to find her nerve. Gentlemen weren't supposed to just go around asking young ladies their names, but this man didn't appear to be the polite sort of gentleman to which she was accustomed. And besides, she was eight-and-twenty! What was the harm in telling him her name? She was her own woman. "I am Louisa Strickland of Kent."

"And what are you doing, Louisa Strickland of Kent, lurking about in the shadows, not watching where you are going?"

The man smiled at her like a cat ready to pounce on its prey. Louisa knew right away he was teasing her. She frowned. "I was only trying to escape notice, and I wasn't watching where I was going. I apologize, sir. Now, if you'll excuse me—"

"And where is Mr. Strickland?" he asked, interrupting her. She blinked at him. Was he slyly trying to ask her if she was married? He was an impertinent one, this stranger. Handsome and impertinent.

"There is no Mr. Strickland, sir," she replied, shaking her head. "I am not married, and my father is dead. His estate was not entailed, you see, so he willed it to me when he passed. I am here with my stepmother chaperoning my younger sister's first season." This information seemed to surprise him, and Louisa smiled slightly. "If you'll excuse me, I must see to my friends before I lose sight of them. Good evening, sir."

"Aren't you going to ask me my name?" he playfully asked. She made a pained expression. How many times would she try to leave only to have him prevent her? Perhaps if she played along, he would lose interest. She sighed.

"What is your name, sir?"

He bowed to her. "Philip Hayward, at your service."

Louisa nodded once, trying to appear unimpressed, though Philip was a rather lovely name for a not-a-gentleman. "Well, Mr. Hayward, it's been very nice meeting you, but—"

"Would you like to dance?" he asked suddenly.

She pursed her lips, looking up at him, his gaze capturing hers and not letting go. "But I do not know you."

"Then get to know me," he said, his ingratiating smile making her heart thump. She nervously looked around the room before replying in a hushed tone.

"We should at least ask Mr. Talbot to introduce us properly before we dance."

Her eyes widened when he laughed at her. "Miss Strickland, you are, by your own account, an independent woman, and believe me when I say I am the opposite of the stuffy aristocrats to whom you find yourself accustomed. In this case, I think you would enjoy forgoing propriety if you only tried it." He offered her his hand. Louisa looked down at it, blinking, not sure what to do. "Consider it just this once. I swear I don't bite."

Her face warmed. "Oh, very well."

Louisa took his hand, and Mr. Hayward guided her to the dance floor.

NEVER HAD a night gone so well for Charles Finch, at least not in a very long time. Although Rosamund was still primarily cold toward him, August made good on her promise, introducing him to many eligible young ladies before the first dance had even taken place that night. And when Flora

Strickland arrived, August's mother brought her to him right away.

But that was the moment things started to sour for the earl. As he took the young and beautiful Flora out onto the dance floor, he noticed another couple joining them: Louisa Strickland and Philip Hayward.

"Do you know that man Louisa is dancing with?" Flora asked, looking in the same direction as Charles. Flora looked on with curiosity, but Charles felt his jaw involuntarily tighten. Louisa's entire body appeared to be a shade of pink as Hayward guided her through the dance steps. Meanwhile, Hayward looked at Louisa like he wanted to eat her up.

Charles forced himself to turn back to Flora. "That's Philip Hayward. He is a businessman here in London."

Charles didn't bother explaining what sort of business he ran. It wasn't appropriate conversation for the ears of a young lady like Flora.

"How nice of him to ask my sister to dance!" Flora said, flashing a charming smile at him. Charles ought to focus on that smile of hers, but he was too busy grimacing at the way Hayward seemed to be drinking up Louisa with his eyes. "Perhaps this might convince her she's not so on the shelf as she thinks after this."

Charles frowned. "Indeed."

"I have always thought my sister to be rather pretty, but she's always complaining about how tall she is or how red her hair is or some such nonsense. I'm sure she could find a nice gentleman who would want to run the manor with her if she only tried."

Charles didn't respond. Instead, they danced on in silence, though he knew he ought to be saying something that would woo Flora. After all, he *was* supposed to be trying to marry her, not her sister, even though Charles's eyes kept drifting toward Louisa and Hayward throughout the dance.

He wondered if Louisa knew that Hayward was the worst sort of rogue, not to mention the owner of one of the most notorious gaming hells in London. Charles had lost most of his money at that man's tables. So much of it, in fact, that Hayward probably would have had him killed if it weren't for Rutley paying him off. That was how Charles had come to owe the duke twenty thousand pounds.

Someone ought to warn Louisa about the man, Charles thought. Then again, it was only a dance. Hayward knew better than to pursue anything more than that, so he was probably only having a spot of fun. Louisa may have been a wealthy landowner, but as far as Charles was concerned, she was still an innocent young lady, not to mention the daughter of a gentleman. An eccentric gentleman, but a gentleman, nonetheless. Men like Hayward should not trifle with someone like her.

When the set was over, Charles walked with Flora to the refreshment table, as was customary. He watched Hayward do the same with Louisa and purposefully made it so that they were standing next to each other when they reached the table, practically dragging Flora with him so they arrived at the same time.

"Lord Bolton!" she exclaimed. "You are hurting my arm."

Charles loosened his grip, though he was too focused on Louisa and Hayward to notice any harm done. Flora huffed behind him. "Hayward," Charles said, ignoring her. Louisa and her new friend faced them just as they were reaching for silver cups of punch. Louisa's eyes widened when she saw Charles standing there. He forced a smile.

"Lord Bolton!" Hayward said, grinning as though nothing was amiss. "How do you do? I have not seen you in London for at least a year."

Charles glanced at Louisa for a split second, who did not look at him, then turned back to Hayward. "I have been rusticating in Kent, believe it or not." Charles paused a moment, studying Hayward carefully, debating whether or not to ask the question he wanted. Charles took a sharp breath. *Oh, to Hell with it.* "Is Mrs. Hayward here this evening?"

Hayward's face fell for only a moment, then he shook his head. "I'm afraid not. You know how my dear wife prefers the country." He gestured toward Louisa. "I believe you know Miss Strickland? She says you're her neighbor."

Charles smiled at Louisa, who stared back at him with a menacing gaze. It did little to intimidate him. He looked back at Hayward. "That is true. And how did the two of you end up dancing together?"

"I'm afraid I accidentally ran into him while looking for Lady Rosamund," Louisa said before Hayward could answer. Louisa looked around, as did Charles, but he didn't see Rosamund anywhere. "She must have moved away from the refreshment table while we were dancing."

"I will help you find her," Charles offered. He would do anything to get Louisa far away from Hayward.

"What about me?" Flora asked, causing him to wince. He had forgotten she was standing there. He could almost hear Rutley's voice inside his head, scolding him for bending to the wrong sister's will.

"You will come with us," Louisa said quickly, reaching and looping her arm in the crook of her sister's elbow. She nodded at Hayward without looking at him. "Thank you for the dance."

Louisa walked away, leaving Charles to follow her. But before he did, he shot Hayward a sheepish look, then tried not to be too perturbed by the way the man ignored him and wistfully looked after her.

Chapter Seven

LOUISA WALKED AWAY from Philip Hayward feeling irritated and embarrassed, muttering a multitude of oaths against men under her breath. She had never received such individual attention from someone so handsome before, but then to find out he was married? From Charles Finch, of all people? She cursed her rotten luck. Charles was surely gloating inwardly at that very moment.

She discreetly checked over her shoulder to see if the earl was still following them. He was. Quietly huffing, Louisa stopped walking and turned to her sister. "Perhaps you ought to go find your mother. She will be wondering how your dance with Lord Bolton went."

Flora frowned. "But what about Lady Rosamund? You said she might know something about Viscount Fitzgerald."

By then, Charles had caught up to them, slowing as the two girls spoke furtively by one of the columns at the edge of the ballroom. Charles flashed a pleasant smile, but Louisa eyed him suspiciously before turning back to her sister, whispering, "I will report back what I learn in the carriage later this evening. Until then, you should allow your mother to show you off to other suitors." Despite whispering, Louisa wasn't really trying to be discreet. She shot a pointed look at Charles, who frowned. "You mustn't put all of your eggs in one basket, after all."

Flora let out an unladylike sound, but Louisa silenced her with a warning look. Even if Louisa didn't want Charles marrying her sister, Flora still must act like a lady around him. Men talked to other men, after all—especially men like Charles. Flora turned to him, offering a quick curtsey in his direction. "Thank you for the dance, Lord Bolton."

He bowed, then watched her go. When Flora was out of earshot, Louisa turned to him, finally free to speak what she was feeling. "You did that on purpose, didn't you?"

Charles looked at her, his brow furrowed as if he didn't quite understand, though Louisa suspected he did. "I'm not sure what you mean."

"Must you be so thick skulled?" Louisa asked. When Charles still did not give any sign of understanding, she felt her hands starting to curl into tiny fists at her side. "You asked him about his wife to embarrass me!"

His face fell. "That couldn't be further from the truth," he argued. Louisa shot him an unconvinced look. "I only brought it up because I doubted he told you himself. What were you thinking dancing with a man like that? Have you any care for your reputation? You are lucky I was there to rescue you."

Louisa wasn't sure what Charles meant. Hayward seemed no different from anyone else she might meet in a London ballroom: overly conceited and self-important. "And what sort of man is Mr. Hayward? I have never heard of him."

"He only owns the most notorious gaming hell in all of London," Charles said, his voice low. "I would not advise dancing with him again."

Louisa made a tiny sound of frustration, looking away. This was why she hated society. If a handsome gentleman asked one to dance, one could not say no for fear of being rude. But handsome gentlemen did not exactly come with warnings that they were married and owned a notorious gaming hell.

Oh, why must society dealings be so complicated?

Louisa sighed, finally meeting Charles's inquisitive gaze. "Who do you advise I dance with, then? Is anyone acceptable to you? Or is a spinster having a spot of fun with someone truly that shocking?"

"You could dance with me," Charles said with a shrug.

She laughed. "I highly doubt that would be enjoyable for either one of us."

Charles stared at her for a long moment, and then he leaned in to say something in her ear. Right away, Louisa could tell he smelled different. Gone was the odor of expensive brandy, since replaced with a mixture of fresh laundry and unoffensive cologne. She found herself so surprised by it she could hardly move, allowing his warm breath to assault her ear as he spoke.

"I am only looking out for you, Louisa," Charles said. He pulled away, their eyes meeting. For a brief moment, she softened toward him. The back of her mind told her she would regret it, but she stupidly ignored it. "You are far too innocent to understand what sort of *fun* Hayward enjoys."

Her face fell when she realized the back of her mind had been correct. "Innocent? *Innocent?*" She made a half-hearted attempt to mollify her anger but failed miserably. Her nostrils flared. "What do you know of my innocence? Need I remind you that I once caught you ravishing an opera singer in your aunt's library? Do you truly think I am so innocent that I do not understand what sort of *fun* a man truly wants?"

Louisa thought she saw the beginnings of a blush forming on the earl's cheeks. "I'd hoped you had forgotten about that," he mumbled.

She narrowed her eyes at him. She most certainly had not forgotten, though she wished she had. If she had, maybe it would have meant it hurt her less than it really did. Charles looked at her, his gaze seeming almost remorseful over what transpired.

"Louisa, I feel I must apologize for what happened between us all those years ago. I was young and immature and—"

"Spare me, Lord Bolton," she told him, practically shaking herself, refusing to fall for his tricks. "And do not call me Louisa."

He might have the appearance and scent of someone who was no longer young or immature, but he would not convince her of that with a mere apology, especially when she knew he was only saying these things because he had eyes for Flora and her fortune.

"Miss Strickland, I am sorry. But will you let me finish? Like I said, I was too young and immature to understand it at the time, but I know why you never returned my letter or allowed me to see you in Kent after that season."

She stiffened, hoping he wasn't about to say it was because she was secretly in love with him. "Before you continue, you must allow me to explain myself."

"By all means."

Louisa did her best to remain expressionless. She knew she must steel herself against him at all costs. "It was because our courtship was nothing more than a charade, and continuing the liaison would have served no purpose for either of us."

Charles appeared as if her words hurt him, which Louisa had a hard time comprehending since she always thought the earl wasn't capable of true feelings. "Do you truly believe that?" he asked, his voice sounding almost sad.

Louisa paused, inwardly telling herself to ignore his

sadness. She was impervious to those big blue eyes of his, or at least that was what she told herself. "Yes."

Charles appeared to stiffen. "And here I thought that I hurt you with my careless actions. But I see that is not the case. Nevertheless, I would like to apologize. I should not have done what I did." The corners of his lips turned slightly downward, his eyes glistening ever so faintly when he looked at her. "Perhaps we might still be friends if I hadn't, and what a blessing that would be right now. I have always thought a friendship between us might have prevented me from making such a mess of my life."

Louisa faltered for a moment, unnerved by the sincerity in the earl's voice. She cleared her throat, forcing herself to gather her wits before saying anything too sentimental. *Impervious*, she reminded herself.

"I am very much past what transpired between us and do not need any sort of forced apology." She paused a moment, looking around the ballroom. "But if you still feel you owe me something, you could help me find your sister as you said before."

His face remained still, and for a moment, she thought he might make some sort of excuse to get away from her. Not that it mattered if he helped her or not. Louisa could find Rosamund on her own quickly enough. The tall and beautiful blonde woman tended to stick out in a crowd, but Charles soon relented.

"I will help you," he said, offering her his arm.

She reluctantly took it, allowing him to walk her along the perimeter of the room as they looked for Rosamund. She tried to ignore his overwhelming presence beside her, but he could not stay silent for long.

"Why are you seeking out my sister anyway?" Charles asked. "You have avoided my family for so long—Rosamund included."

Louisa shot him a sidelong glance. "Can you blame me? I had to pretend I was some sort of scorned female after the end of our ruse all those years ago. It was the only way my stepmother would ever believe our courtship was real *and* that I made a valiant effort to find a husband that season." She paused a moment, waiting for him to say something, but he remained silent, so she continued. "As for your sister, she's always been a wealth of information when it comes to the ton. I mean to ask her about someone."

This seemed to pique Charles's interest. "Who?"

"Viscount Fitzgerald."

"Fitzgerald? What do you want to know about him?" Charles made an incredulous face. She frowned at him, and Charles shook his head. "A complete rogue, that one—worse than me and Rutley combined."

Louisa abruptly turned away, annoyance contorting her face. She should have known. Riding an untrained horse through Hyde Park and confronting ladies he'd never been appropriately introduced to... The man couldn't have been a *true* gentleman.

And yet Flora fancied herself in love with him. Louisa sighed, looking around the ballroom. She hoped some other man might catch her sister's eye that night. Love could be such a fickle emotion at Flora's age. There was no reason she couldn't fall for someone else if only she met the right person.

After searching the room for Rosamund again from where they stood, Louisa's gaze landed on Charles once more, who was studying her with a discerning look. She turned away, flushing. "You did not answer my question," she heard him say. "What do you want to know about Fitzgerald?"

Louisa sighed again, reluctantly turning to face him. "We met him briefly at the park the other day. I'm afraid Flora's quite taken with him."

"It must have been quite a meeting for her to be so infatuated already."

"Lord Bolton, you must take care to remember how young my sister is," Louisa warned, her voice serious. "She is only nineteen and knows very little of the world. I'm not surprised she became infatuated with the first man who showed her attention outside of Kent."

"I have an idea," Charles said, a mischievous grin playing at his lips. She narrowed her eyes at him, afraid of what might come out of his mouth next. "I could woo her away from the blackguard."

Louisa's eyes widened. "Certainly not! I'm sure neither one of you are appropriate for my sister."

Charles appeared slightly taken aback, which Louisa didn't understand. He obviously wasn't right for her sister— how could he be? Flora deserved someone who truly loved her and wasn't only seeking a hefty payment for marrying her.

"Did I not do what you asked of me?" Charles said. Louisa made a dismissive sound, and he bristled in response. "I locked myself away in my house and gave up my brandy and port, and I did not turn to cards or whores as a result, though I was very lonely. Sometimes I found myself wishing you might come check on me and my progress."

He looked at her as if expecting sympathy from her, but she only scowled at him, finding his insinuations distasteful. "Do you think because I'm a spinster that you don't have to be polite and proper around me?" she asked. Despite acting so high-and-mighty earlier, he was no better than Hayward.

Nevertheless, Charles grinned at her, and as he leaned closer, she felt that same alarming jolt from when he drew closer to her before. "You are the one who reminded me of the time you caught me with an opera singer."

Charles slowly backed away. Louisa couldn't help but gape at him, and when he winked at her, she felt her heart leap into her throat. She forced herself to swallow it back down, then made her face as expressionless as possible, though she was sure her cheeks were flushed bright pink. The way he laughed at her told her that very well may have been the case.

"What?" he asked. "You said it yourself. You understand what a man truly wants."

Louisa's throat went dry, and for a moment, she was at a loss for words. Then, that familiar feeling of anger bubbled up inside her. "Yes, well, I suppose what *you* want are light skirts, so I hope you can understand why I want you nowhere near my sister, regardless of whether or not you have given up drink. Surely there is some other heiress you can marry!"

"The only other heiress I know is you."

She glowered at him. "Do not tease me."

"No, I'm serious," he said, frowning. "You and your sister are the only wealthy women I truly know, so unless you have some sort of secret list of women like you, I'm afraid you must suffer through my attentions. You and I both know the harvest was terrible last autumn, and Rutley will not rest until I pay him back."

Charles continued, but Louisa wasn't listening. "That's it!" she exclaimed suddenly. "If I help you find another heiress to torment, do you promise to leave my sister alone?"

"Torment?" he asked, appearing offended. "Is that what comes to mind when you think of marriage to me? Torment?"

Louisa shook her head. "Who cares what I think? I am not the one you are after; it's also beside the point. If I make a list for you, will you leave my sister alone?"

"A list of what?"

The familiar feminine voice startled Louisa. She and Charles turned to find Lady Rosamund and her half sister, Mrs. Brooks, staring at them. Rosamund's inquisitive gaze darted from Louisa to her brother and back again. Rosamund appeared as elegant and fashionable as ever, with her hair decorated with feathers, ribbons, and jewels. Despite the awkwardness of being discovered in the midst of conversation with Charles, Louisa forced herself to smile, then curtsey.

"How lovely to see you again, Lady Rosamund." She paused for a moment before deciding honesty was the best path to take in this situation. "I was only telling your brother that I would make him a list of heiresses to pursue so that he may focus his marriage efforts on someone other than my sister."

Rosamund looked at her brother with a triumphant smile. "Then it is as I predicted the other evening. Flora Strickland is out of the question."

Charles scowled at his sister, then turned back to Louisa. "I will take you up on your offer. I'll come round tomorrow morning for that list if you don't mind."

"Tomorrow morning?" Louisa asked, wringing her hands as she did. "I'm not sure I could prepare something in such a short amount of time, especially after being away from town so long—"

"I'll come round to call on your sister whether you have the list or not," Charles said sternly, causing Louisa's expression to harden toward him. He moved to leave, then paused, turning to speak to her once more. "Try to stay away from any devious gaming hell owners, won't you? I would hate to feel the need to rescue you again. Good evening, Miss Strickland."

Louisa watched him go, bewildered and slightly slack-jawed. She nearly forgot that Rosamund and Mrs. Brooks were still standing next to her until Rosamund cleared her throat. Louisa turned, smiling. Rosamund gestured to her sister.

"Miss Strickland, allow me to introduce my sister, Lady August Brooks," Rosamund said, gesturing to the woman beside her. "August, this is Louisa Strickland. She owns Strickland Manor, a neighboring estate to Linfield. She also had a brief tendre with my brother seven years ago. I imagine that's why you want him to stay away from your sister, isn't it?"

Louisa blinked, feeling her entire body go warm with embarrassment after Rosamund had spoken so bluntly. She had forgotten that Rosamund had a habit of saying whatever she wanted, wherever she wanted, regardless of propriety. "I only want my sister to marry someone who truly loves her, not someone who is only after her money."

Louisa paused a moment, recalling what she had heard about Rosamund and her former fiancé, the Duke of Rutley. Apparently the duke had been unfaithful to Rosamund at some point during their engagement. "Surely you understand that desire, my lady."

Rosamund smiled slightly. "I do understand, though I'm not sure a man who does not consider the size of a girl's dowry when choosing a bride exists. You may end up disappointed in all of Flora's suitors, not only my brother."

Louisa realized it was the perfect time to ask about Viscount Fitzgerald. Although Charles called the man a complete rogue, she wanted confirmation from Rosamund, who always seemed to know everything about everyone. "What do you make of Viscount Fitzgerald? He is at the top of Flora's list, but I'm not sure I approve."

The pleasant expressions on Rosamund's and August's faces quickly vanished. The color drained from their cheeks, and the two girls exchanged a look. It did not escape Louisa's notice that Lady Sarah had had a similar reaction to the mention of the viscount's name. When Rosamund and August turned back to Louisa, Rosamund was the first to speak.

"We do not know the new viscount—his father only

recently died—but we do know one of his younger brothers," she said before glancing at her sister.

August sighed. "One of his brothers used me very poorly before I married my husband," she explained. Louisa carefully watched her, frowning, unsure of what she meant. "It would be unfair to judge the viscount on his younger brother's behavior, but I could not recommend him to your sister on account of their relation."

Louisa nodded, wondering what had happened, but it would be impolite to ask for any further detail. "I appreciate your honesty."

She looked out onto the dance floor, searching for familiar faces. She saw Flora dancing with an unknown gentleman. Her sister wore a broad smile, which gave Louisa hope that her little sister had heeded her warning about hanging her hopes on one man in particular.

"Perhaps we might help you with this list of yours if you should like my brother to stay away from you and your poor sister," Rosamund said.

Louisa turned away from the dance floor to face her. Rosamund wore a devious look on her face. "I know of more than a few disagreeable heiresses for whom my brother might be the perfect match."

Louisa bit back a grin, but August was quick to scold her older sister. "You must give your brother a chance." August shot Louisa a sidelong glance, one that made her smile fade and the hair on the back of her neck stand up. "He will choose the heiress he prefers, regardless of any list, but I'm happy to help nevertheless."

"As long as he does not choose my sister, the earl can have any woman he likes," Louisa grumbled.

Chapter Eight

CHARLES GREW tired of the ball within minutes of leaving Louisa with his sisters. He watched them from across the room, speaking furtively to each other. Rosamund laughed at something Louisa said. Meanwhile, his other sister frowned. He wondered what they were discussing.

The three girls eventually walked away together, most likely headed for the retiring room. His eyes lingered on Louisa's retreating figure for longer than he would have liked until a servant walked by with a tray of champagne, finally distracting him. Charles reached for his cravat and tugged at the knot, suddenly feeling warm.

He ought to go home. He had done what he had set out to do—dance with Flora Strickland and meet a few of August's single friends—and staying any longer would only tempt him into having some sort of alcoholic beverage before long. The incident with Louisa and Hayward had soured his mood, not to mention her insistence that he not even try to court her sister. As far as he was concerned, she could take her bloody list and—

"Lord Bolton."

Startled, Charles jumped. Philip Hayward, the blasted man himself, stood behind him, appearing as menacing as ever. The man was nearly twenty years his senior and, as much as Charles hated to admit it, extremely handsome. Although he had been married recently, Hayward was still very active in town, running his exclusive gaming hell out of Covent Garden. As for his wife, Charles had heard he deposited her at some house he bought for her in the country. Charles had no idea why Hayward married her in the first place, nor did he much care.

"Hayward," he said, forcing a smile, knowing he must have wanted to discuss Louisa with him, though Charles couldn't think of anything he wanted to do *less*. Hayward didn't appear any more thrilled than Charles did.

"Did you have to tell the country chit I was married?" Hayward asked, moving to stand beside Charles. They both turned away from each other, looking out onto the ballroom. Smiling couples waltzed across the sparkling floors, and Charles noticed Flora Strickland in the arms of another man. It should have bothered him, but it didn't. Perhaps it was better that way, since Louisa would never allow them to marry.

"She would have discovered it eventually," Charles said. He glanced at Hayward out of the corner of his eye. The older man wore a pensive look, his irritation seeming to fade. Charles wondered what he was thinking.

"Do you think it matters to her?"

Charles's head snapped in Hayward's direction. Clearly, he was not thinking. His nostrils flared. "Mr. Hayward, need I remind you that Louisa Strickland is a gentleman's daughter?"

Hayward chuckled, and Charles quickly turned his head, fearing if he looked at the man much longer, he might pummel him. When Charles finally felt it was safe to turn back, Hayward gave a little shrug. "But her father is dead.

Now she's a wealthy landowner. Who is protecting her?" Hayward leaned closer. "And does she want to be protected?"

Charles glared at Hayward, who remained smiling. The man always wore a self-assured, smug look. Charles never liked the way Hayward carried himself, though he hadn't been so keenly aware of that fact until then. "Be careful, Hayward. I have known Louisa Strickland since we were in leading strings. She is like a little sister to me."

But as soon as he said it, such a description felt false to him. He wondered if Hayward noticed the way his mouth twitched, rebelling against his lie. "But someone told me you courted her once before," Hayward said.

Charles grimaced. It appeared that farcical courtship would haunt him forever. "Why are you interested in her in the first place?" Charles leaned in closer, his voice dropping to a whisper so no one else would hear. "You realize she is a virgin."

The earl leaned back as Hayward's shoulders moved up and down in laughter. Charles's face twisted with disgust, and he immediately regretted saying anything at all. Still, he felt the need to continue with his argument. "Surely you would prefer some elegant courtesan from one of those exclusive brothels in Covent Garden that you frequent."

"I suppose I have grown tired of those girls," Hayward replied with a shrug.

"And what about your wife? Have you grown tired of her as well?"

Hayward's gaze darkened. "I would have had to be interested in her in the first place to grow tired of her." Charles nervously swallowed, realizing Hayward was crueler than he initially suspected. "Miss Strickland feels like just the challenge I need to reinvigorate me. Besides, my friend Fitzgerald intends to court her younger sister this season. I plan on accompanying him on their outings. Perhaps her sister might want to come along with us."

"Fitzgerald intends to court Miss Flora?" Charles echoed incredulously, surprised the viscount was looking to settle down. That must have been some meeting in the park.

Then again, Fitzgerald had just inherited from his father like Charles had. Perhaps he was looking to replenish his coffers as well. If Charles could gather some information about Fitzgerald, perhaps Louisa might not hate him so much. "Is the viscount seriously considering settling down?"

Hayward laughed. "I wouldn't say that, but he is in desperate need of money. When his father died, he discovered the estate's coffers to be quite empty. Miss Flora has a thirty-thousand-pound dowry, more than enough to remedy the problem."

So it was as Charles expected. He grew quiet, wishing there was some way to warn Hayward and Fitzgerald against such a plan. Louisa would sniff them out with ease, hastily foiling their plans, just as she did to him. But there was no dissuading either man when they wanted something. Charles only hoped Louisa was smart enough to ignore Hayward's imprudent advances. Even as the independently wealthy daughter of a gentleman, Louisa wasn't immune to temptation—or ruination by scandal. Any negative gossip about Louisa would put Flora in a less-than-desirable light as well. And unlike Louisa, her sister *wanted* to marry.

"You must tell me everything about her," Hayward continued, interrupting Charles's thoughts. Charles looked at him as if he had gone mad. The man beside him sighed. "You *did* court her, didn't you? Surely you must know something about what might capture her attention."

Judging by how she'd been looking at him with dreamy eyes while they danced, he already seemed to have done that without Charles's help. Charles was about to tell Hayward to go to the devil when he paused and thought a moment, slowly realizing he could use this situation to his advantage. He would tell Hayward lies that would only drive Louisa further away, thus protecting her from any sort of inappropriate liaison. She'd already seemed slightly disgusted by him when she discovered he was married, so it shouldn't take much. Charles cleared his throat.

"I did," he said, offering what he felt was an extremely convincing nod. Hayward narrowed his eyes anyway, so Charles desperately tried to maintain his serious demeanor. "I mean, I do know some things about her."

He searched for something to say about Louisa—something untrue. "She adores flowers," Charles suddenly blurted.

Hayward furrowed his brow. "Flowers?"

Charles nodded vigorously. "Especially red roses. You ought to send her a dozen tomorrow morning with a personal note thanking her for the dance."

"You are joking," Hayward said after a moment, scowling at the earl. Charles did his best to maintain a straight face. "Isn't she in town with her stepmother? Wouldn't the woman have a fit if I—a married man—sent her daughter a dozen roses?"

"Need I remind you that Miss Strickland answers to no one—not even her stepmother?" Hayward still did not look convinced. Charles clapped him on the shoulder. "Trust me. She will love them."

LOUISA'S FACE turned as red as the dozen roses one of the servants presented to her. Up until that moment, all the deliveries of bouquets that morning had been for her sister. The footmen had placed them in vases of varying shapes and sizes, and they now covered all the possible surfaces in the drawing room. The Strickland family was expecting more than one gentleman caller that afternoon, all for Flora.

But these flowers were for Louisa. Hesitantly, Louisa put down her embroidery and took the bouquet of roses, resting them on her lap and reaching for the note attached. Louisa, very much aware of the curious eyes fixed on her, not only by her stepmother and sister but the footman as well, carefully opened the note. Her heart pounded as she read the message inside.

Louisa's eyes flitted toward Mrs. Strickland and Flora. "They are from Mr. Hayward, the gentleman I danced with last evening."

Louisa quickly crumpled the note with her hand, giving it along with the roses back to the servant.

"Didn't you say he was married?" Mrs. Strickland asked, furrowing her brow. Flora nodded beside her.

"Lord Bolton asked him how his wife was last night," Flora said.

Ignoring her sister, Louisa spoke directly to the footman. "Send them back. I do not want them."

He nodded, then took the flowers and left. Louisa avoided looking at her stepmother and sister, picking up her embroidery once more. She was sure her face was still as red as a tomato, and she had no desire to speculate over why a married man had sent her flowers. If her father had been alive, Hayward would have never made such a gesture. The nerve of him! But she would not sit there wishing for masculine protection in her life now.

Still, Louisa shook her head, dropping her embroidery to her lap, unable to control her anger. She looked toward the ceiling, considering for a moment that this was the first time a man had ever shown her genuine interest. Her much-talked-about courtship with Charles during her first season prevented such a thing from ever happening. Not that she was complaining, as that was the goal of the entire ordeal.

She let out a huff, looking down and focusing on her embroidery once more. Why was she even surprised that Hayward was married? That was just her luck. Not that it would be any different if he weren't. She had no desire to marry. The idea of giving up her independence and impressive income in exchange for lifelong obedience to some man she hardly knew did not sound appealing to her.

Realizing Mrs. Strickland and Flora were still staring at her, Louisa glanced up at them, hopeful her face had returned to its regular pale shade. "What is it?" she asked, looking back down at her embroidery. "You are acting as if you have never seen a gentleman act without propriety toward a young woman."

"Did you perhaps give him the wrong idea as to what sort of young woman you were last night?" her stepmother asked gently.

Louisa's head shot up. "Of course not! How could you even ask me such a thing?"

When she turned back to her stitches, her companions thankfully did the same. Mrs. Strickland and Flora eventually forgot the roses from Hayward, and they then happily chattered back and forth, wondering which gentlemen from last night's ball would call on Flora that afternoon. So many had promised, but Flora kept mentioning Viscount Fitzgerald, even after Louisa shared what she learned from Rosamund and August in the carriage home last night.

"Why should I be concerned over something his younger brother did?" Flora had asked, still not entirely convinced she should avoid the viscount, too blinded by lust thanks to Cupid's dratted poisonous arrows. "The viscount cannot be blamed for the actions of any of his siblings."

She had a fair point, so Louisa couldn't exactly argue with

her. Instead, she would have to hope that Viscount Fitzgerald wouldn't show up that afternoon or any other afternoon after it.

When the clock finally struck three in the afternoon, Viscount Fitzgerald did not appear in their drawing room, but plenty of other men did, all there to see Flora. At one point, it all became so overwhelming, being surrounded by gentlemen on all ends, that Louisa abruptly excused herself, heading out into the hallway.

There, she ran straight into Charles. When she realized who it was, Louisa looked up and scowled, not in the mood to bother with him that afternoon. "You came," she said after he begged her pardon.

He smiled at her, smoothing his jacket where she just collided with him. "I came," he said, peering around the doorway into the crowded drawing room. His eyes widened, and he turned back to Louisa. "My! Every eligible bachelor in London is here. Is that why I caught you scurrying out of there like a frightened baby rabbit?"

He said it with a grin, but Louisa was less amused. Then she remembered the list of eligible women she made with his sisters last night. "Wait," Louisa said, holding up her finger. "I have something for you. I will be right back. Wait here. Don't go in yet. *Don't!*"

"But Louisa—"

"Miss Strickland," she corrected.

Then she walked away, waving her hand over her shoulder, ignoring any further protests coming from his direction. She turned the corner and dashed up the stairs, quickly retrieving the list from her bedside table. When she went back downstairs, Charles stood stiffly in the doorway of the drawing room, seemingly intimidated by the crowd.

Louisa paused for a moment behind him, her lips forming a sad smile. His lack of confidence—the cracks in his once shiny veneer—were almost comforting to her. For a moment she felt connected to him, as she was all too familiar with feelings of inadequacy in social settings. They often made life difficult, and for a moment, she felt sorry for him.

She, Louisa Strickland, felt sorry for Charles Finch.

Because she had been there before.

She shook her head, moving to stand beside him. He glanced down at her.

"I did not expect so much competition for your sister's hand," he grumbled.

Louisa glanced at Flora, who always looked beautiful no matter what frock she wore or how she styled her hair. She would make the perfect wife, so unlike Louisa, with her petite frame and delicate features.

Effectively silencing her own feelings of inadequacy, Louisa turned back to Charles and handed him the list. Charles reluctantly tore his eyes away from the beautiful Flora long enough to look at it. He furrowed his brow, grabbing the list from her. "Why are some of the names crossed out?"

"Those were the names Lady Rosamund suggested with a tad too much glee," Louisa said, her eyes meeting his. She quickly looked away, blushing for some unknowable reason. She scolded herself for being ridiculous and forced herself to look at him again. "I thought you might want to stay away from those women, lest you wind up with a wife you will end up hating in the end."

Slowly, he started to grin at her.

Her face fell. "What?" she asked sheepishly.

He shook his head. "Nothing," he said as he folded the list up and held it behind his back before turning to look at the various men surrounding her sister. "I will share your list with Rutley for his opinion as well. He is, after all, somewhat of my keeper these days."

Louisa raised her brow. For a moment, she almost felt bad for him again, but then she quickly reminded herself that he was the one who'd gotten himself into this position. Why should she care if Charles married someone he ended up hating so long as Flora could find true love instead of someone who only wanted her for her money? Louisa looked at the five men her sister was presently entertaining all at once. She did it with impressive ease, and the men all seemed awestruck—as they should be.

"And what is your opinion of the men standing in my drawing room right now?" She surreptitiously eyed Charles, who tilted his head to the side, carefully regarding each of Flora's suitors. "Are there any she should be warned against?"

Charles turned to her, a sheepish look on his face. "All of them are far wealthier men than me. If that's what concerns you, then any of them would make a fine husband."

"But what about their character?"

"I think you and I can both agree that I am not qualified to judge anyone's character." Louisa frowned. He moved to leave, then stopped himself. "There is something I wanted to tell you."

Louisa's frown only deepened at his grave tone. "What is it?"

"I spoke to Mr. Hayward last night after you and I parted ways."

Louisa groaned. "He sent me a dozen roses this morning. If you see him again, you must tell him that I'm not that sort of woman, and I find even just the suggestion to be impossibly rude."

The earl's lips twitched as if he was about to smile. She didn't understand why. It wasn't funny. "I will make sure to share the message with him. But that's not what I wanted to tell you."

Louisa grew nervous, unsure of what Charles might say.

"Apparently, Mr. Hayward is friends with your sister's beloved viscount." Louisa made a face. She didn't like it when Charles called him that. "When Fitzgerald inherited his estate, he found there was no money left. I am afraid to report he is a fortune hunter, just as I am."

"I knew it," Louisa muttered. She looked back at her sister and stepmother, surrounded by gentleman callers. She would have to tell them once everyone had gone for the day.

"There is something else." Louisa turned back to Charles, eyes wide, afraid of what he might say next. "Hayward plans to join Fitzgerald when he calls on your sister so that you may all go on outings together. Louisa—" He stopped himself for a moment, correcting himself before she could. "Miss Strickland, I would be careful. I wouldn't want anything to happen to you."

Louisa's face softened. What an unusually kind thing for Charles to say. "I will be careful," she said. "Thank you for warning me."

Charles nodded once. Their eyes met, and for what felt like a long moment, they stared at each other. Somehow unable to move, Louisa allowed Charles to reach for her hand. "I would never want anything bad to happen for you." Before she could protest, Charles brought her gloved hand to his lips, pressing a kiss to her knuckles. "Good day, Miss Strickland. Thank you for the list."

Dumbfounded, Louisa stood and watched him go. She wondered if she would see him again now that he had options other than her sister. She then questioned herself as to why she was wondering about him at all. A few encounters with Charles Finch and she was already under his spell again. She shook her head. *Insufferable ninny*, she thought to herself. He did not want her. And she did not want him.

But what if he did want her? What would that be like? She sighed. Hopeless. She was absolutely hopeless.

Returning to the drawing room, Louisa wondered why she even cared one way or the other whether she saw Charles again or not, or whether or not he would ever want her. Even if he had shown her kindness by warning her about Fitzgerald and Hayward's plan, Charles Finch was a thing of her past. He would safely return there now that he had his list, and she would happily forget about him again.

It was for the best.

Chapter Nine

CHARLES WALKED SWIFTLY down the street toward the coffeehouse where the duke was drinking that evening, Louisa's list in hand, still smiling over some of the little things she said that afternoon. From her horror over Hayward sending her flowers to the way she crossed out names she thought might be unsuitable for him, Louisa was just the way he remembered her. Despite her somewhat hard exterior, Louisa was still the same sweet, innocent girl he knew seven years ago. Looking at the list, he wondered if she even realized she was looking out for him like a friend might—like the friends they used to be.

When he reached the coffeehouse, Charles immediately looked for Rutley, hoping the duke wasn't too far into his cups already. Charles didn't plan on staying for long, and their conversation would be much easier if Rutley were at least somewhat sober. Charles found the man sitting at a small table by himself, nursing a glass of brandy and looking as dark and broody as ever.

They had not spoken in a while, not since the morning after Charles's dinner party with his family. Although Charles apologized for not telling Rutley about the party ahead of time, the duke would hear nothing of it, preferring to pretend it hadn't happened at all. After all, Rutley was the one who had shown up at Finch Place acting like a drunken fool. He only had himself to blame for Rosamund's increasingly low opinion of him.

"If it makes you feel any better, she still thinks no more highly of me," Charles begrudgingly told him at the time. Not much had changed since then. Even after attending the Talbot ball and behaving admirably, Rosamund still wasn't impressed with her brother. She would probably be even less impressed if she knew Charles was sitting down with the duke that evening, but Charles didn't have much of a choice when he owed Rutley so much money.

The duke seemed to have his wits about him because he shot Charles a suspicious look, knowing he did not come to places like this anymore. "Charles," he said, leaning back in his chair and finishing his drink in one gulp. He placed the empty glass on the table, and Charles looked at it, feeling envious for a brief moment. "What brings you here? Shouldn't you be at a ball or dinner party wooing a certain young lady?"

Instead of answering him, Charles sat down and placed the list that Louisa and his sisters had drawn up for him on the table. Rutley looked down at it, confused, just as one of the serving girls dropped another brandy on their table. She turned to Charles, waiting for him to order something, but the earl only shook his head. Looking around the coffee-house, he knew he wasn't wholly immune to the temptations of his old life. He wondered if he knew any of the blokes playing cards in one of the secret back rooms.

"What is this?" the duke asked. He picked up the list, turning it over as he waited for Charles's response.

"A list of eligible heiresses other than Flora Strickland," Charles said.

Rutley appeared confused. "Why are some of the names crossed out?"

Charles hesitated. "Miss Strickland didn't think they were as suitable as the others," he said, not wishing to mention Rosamund's name. The earl never knew how it might set Rutley off when he did. Nevertheless, the duke's eyebrows shot upwards.

"Miss Strickland?" he asked incredulously. "As in Miss Louisa Strickland? This was her idea, wasn't it?"

After a moment of hesitation, Charles nodded. The duke appeared dismayed by the discovery. "She still doesn't want me courting her sister, so she presented a list of alternatives. Do you know any of them?"

Rutley furrowed his brow, reaching inside his jacket as he did so and procuring a pair of spectacles. He gingerly placed them on the bridge of his nose after putting the list back down on the table. When he picked it up again, Rutley peered at it carefully.

"I have heard of some of their fathers," the duke said as his eyes scanned the list. "They have generous dowries, no doubt. Any one of them would be more than suitable for your needs."

Rutley handed the list back to Charles and then removed his spectacles, replacing them in his jacket pocket. He watched Charles closely, and the earl became more and more nervous under Rutley's penetrative gaze. Rutley always had a way of making Charles feel unworthy of his company, which was why Charles had always tried to impress him, whether by a ludicrous bet at a card table or always staying at the club or coffeehouse for one more drink.

"And has Miss Strickland agreed to introduce you to them as well?" Rutley asked.

Charles hadn't considered it. "I believe Miss Strickland gave me the list so I would stop pestering her and her sister, so her obligation ends with this sheet of paper."

Rutley sighed and ran his hands through his hair. "You can't run about London making yourself known to every wealthy heiress without a proper introduction first." The duke paused a moment, appearing deep in thought as he rubbed his jaw with his thumb and forefinger. He took his first sip from the fresh glass of brandy the serving girl had just delivered before he finally spoke again. "Are you sure your mother has no desire to come to London for the season? She would be quite helpful."

Charles grimaced. He wrote to his mother occasionally, but most of his letters went unanswered. The dowager countess seemed content to stay with the Haddingtons until Charles sorted out the estate's financial difficulties. After Charles and his mother's selfish insistence that Rosamund marry the duke as a partial payment of her brother's debts, Lady Bolton blamed her son for driving Rosamund, hurt and angry, away from her and to Lady Ramsbury. Charles wouldn't have been surprised if she asked him to open the dowager house for her rather than returning to Linfield Hall once he had the money.

"Perhaps my aunt might help me," Charles suggested.

"Would she?"

But before Charles could answer, he heard a familiar voice call his name. He did nothing to hide his annoyance in front of Rutley, who shot his friend a curious look as Philip Hayward came to stand beside their table. "Mr. Hayward," Charles said, forcing a smile at the older gentleman, whose handsomeness rivaled even the duke's. "How do you do? I am surprised you are not at your own establishment this evening."

"Someone told me I might find you here," Hayward replied, flashing a menacing smile as he did.

Charles and Rutley exchanged nervous looks.

"Is something the matter?" Charles asked hesitantly.

"Yes. Miss Strickland returned my flowers." Charles remained silent, waiting for Hayward to say something else. He couldn't possibly believe it was Charles's fault Louisa had returned his flowers, but the man's jaw remained set and angry. "The ones I sent to her upon your advice."

Charles felt his face warm as the duke shot him a suspicious look. "Did she?" Charles innocently asked, turning toward Hayward. "You can hardly blame her for returning them. A married man sending an unmarried woman a dozen roses? Very inappropriate."

Hayward looked as if he might strangle him, but Charles knew he wouldn't. After all, Charles was an earl, and Hayward was nothing but a businessman. They were also in the middle of Mayfair, not Covent Garden. Since Charles owed him nothing, and he had no plans on going back to his card tables anytime soon, Hayward could not touch him. And if the earl was the only one who cared enough to protect Louisa's good name, he would do everything in his power to do so—even if it meant lying to Hayward about Louisa's preferences and perhaps embarrassing him in the process.

Hayward's voice fell to a low hiss. "You said she would like them."

Charles shrugged. "I suppose I am not the expert on Louisa Strickland that you thought me to be. I did court her a long time ago. Sorry, old chap."

Hayward scowled at him before walking away from the table, leaving Rutley to stare at Charles over his brandy. "What is it?" Charles asked, though he thought he might already know the answer to that question.

"You should be careful in your dealings with Miss Strickland. Everyone knows she has no desire to marry. Do not become distracted. Or even worse—*hurt*."

Rutley said the last word with such seriousness that Charles scoffed. "Hurt? Distracted? I do not think of Louisa Strickland that way. She is an old friend, and she deserves protection from the likes of Philip Hayward. Who better to provide it than me, her neighbor?"

"I am her neighbor as well, yet *I* have no desire to provide her any protection."

"I suppose that makes me a better neighbor." Charles served a glare with his retort, not wishing to speak of Louisa Strickland any longer.

Rutley shook his head. "You *were* quite smitten with her seven years ago," he said thoughtfully, as if he suddenly recalled something important. While the duke carefully studied his friend's reaction to his words, Charles struggled to remain expressionless. "Or at least you pretended to be whenever you were around her. Whatever happened?"

Charles was surprised the duke didn't remember but didn't feel like reliving the incident with Miss Coppola for the third time that week. "Nothing happened. We were so young. As you said, everyone knows Miss Strickland has no desire to marry. I gather she used me to avoid other suitors during her season."

The duke did not look convinced, even though Charles had just told him the truth. Louisa *had* used him to avoid other suitors during her season. Charles had even agreed to it so he might evade marriage-minded mamas as well.

"Well, then," Rutley said after a pregnant pause. "If the Strickland girls are out of the question, then I recommend you call on your aunt tomorrow. You should ask her to help you meet all these women on your list." Charles nodded, but the duke's look grew darker. "And stay out of Miss Strickland's business with Philip Hayward. I do not think she is as innocent as you might believe. Surely she can take care of herself."

Charles furrowed his brow. "What do you mean?"

Rutley shrugged. "I have heard talk amongst our neighbors."

"And?" Charles asked, his heart pounding. He did not know why, but it was awfully uncomfortable.

The duke only shrugged again. "I have heard she is friendly with your land steward, Mr. Hardy," he explained. "Rather *too* friendly, that is."

Charles blanched, not liking what Rutley was implying. Louisa and Mr. Hardy? Charles supposed such assumptions weren't all that shocking; she had entrusted Strickland Manor to Hardy's supervision while in London for the season, a task she did not delegate lightly. But surely Louisa knew better than to embark on an affair with the help. Charles swiftly stood.

"If she *is* too friendly, that's none of my business—or yours," he said, ignoring the intrusive thoughts inside his head. "As are her dealings with Mr. Hayward. So I appreciate your advice, Rutley. I will gladly heed your warning and no longer involve myself in Miss Strickland's affairs. That should please you, shouldn't it? Good evening."

AFTER FLORA STRICKLAND was dubbed that season's incomparable, a flurry of new invitations and gentleman callers arrived almost every day at their house in Mayfair. As Louisa had suspected, they saw nothing more of Lord Bolton, who Louisa imagined was making his way through the list of potential brides she had given him. But Charles Finch seemed to be the only problem that Louisa managed to solve with efficiency and ease.

Lord Fitzgerald and Mr. Hayward were different stories.

Louisa had tried to tell her stepmother and sister what Lord Bolton told her about the viscount, but they were unconvinced by his story. Flora believed the earl was only jealous that she preferred Fitzgerald to him. Mrs. Strickland decided to reserve her judgment until meeting both gentlemen, though she admitted Hayward had gotten off on the wrong foot.

They eventually arrived together one afternoon, outside of regular calling hours at their town house, and if the viscount hadn't been a viscount, their butler probably would have turned them away at the door. But Mrs. Strickland was eager to meet the younger of the two gentlemen, especially when her youngest daughter wouldn't stop talking about him.

As for Hayward, Louisa watched him with suspicious eyes for the entire duration of their call. When Flora rose to play the pianoforte for the viscount, Mrs. Strickland joined her to help turn her pages of music, and Hayward took the opportunity to sit next to Louisa when no one was paying much attention to them. Louisa froze, unable to look at him. She did not want to become mesmerized by his handsomeness once more; she had worked very hard to forget the way he looked over the past few days with only moderate success.

Flora began to play, and Louisa felt the cushions beneath them shift. Hayward leaned toward her. "You returned my flowers," he said simply. Her breathing hitched, but somehow she managed to turn and look at him.

"I could not very well accept them," she forced out. Hayward watched her carefully, his gaze impenetrable. Louisa grew very warm under it, and she quickly turned away.

"Why not?" he asked.

Louisa huffed with frustration. "If I accepted them, you might think I welcome your attention even though you are married."

"You do not, then?"

Louisa's head quickly spun in his direction. He was smiling, which only served to make her feel even more flabbergasted. "*No*, I do *not*," she resolutely replied before turning away from him once more and shaking her head slightly. "Not only are you married, but I'm not entirely sure if the nature of your business is legal."

"That is why I am so lucky powerful men like your friend Lord Bolton love my business so much."

"Lord Bolton is not my friend."

Hayward didn't say anything for a while. Louisa tried to focus on the music instead, carefully watching the viscount as he admired her younger sister. He seemed like a pleasant enough fellow, despite their conspicuous first meeting, but there was something about him that Louisa didn't quite like; she just couldn't quite place her finger on what.

"Well, I gather we might be seeing more of each other in the coming days," Hayward said.

Louisa turned and looked at him. "And why do you say that, sir?"

Hayward eyed the viscount and Flora, then looked back at Louisa with a slight smile on his face. "We will be the best suited to chaperone the budding courtship of my friend and your sister."

Louisa frowned. She had no desire to spend any more time with Hayward. What sort of man pursued a much younger female while his wife remained in the country? Surely Mrs. Hayward would have liked to be with her husband in London. Louisa imagined the poor woman wasn't even allowed. She swallowed nervously.

"If the viscount wants even a chance of winning my sister's hand in marriage, then he must earn my approval," she said, mustering as much courage as she could. She took a deep breath. "And if he wants my approval, then you would do well to tell him to find another friend to accompany him when he calls on my sister."

Flora finished her piece, and the viscount burst into a round of applause. Louisa turned to face her sister, joining the viscount in clapping. Hayward did the same, but Louisa thought she saw his shoulders shaking slightly out of the corner of her eye as if he was holding back laughter.

"Has anyone told you that you are very amusing, Miss Strickland?" he said, his lips much too close to her ear. Louisa ignored him, refusing to be cowed by the man.

She was happy when they left, though she hated how her sister and stepmother fawned over the viscount.

"Isn't he wonderful?" Flora asked when the three women were alone again.

"Simply splendid!" Mrs. Strickland agreed.

Louisa, however, remained unsure. "Remember what I said, Flora."

Her sister rolled her eyes. "Yes, yes, I know. The viscount is a fortune hunter."

"And?"

"Do not put all my eggs in one basket."

Louisa nodded once, smiling and picking up her embroidery, doing her best to forget the feel of Philip Hayward sitting beside her.

Chapter Ten

LORD FITZGERALD and Hayward haunted each of their outings over the next week. Every party the Stricklands attended, so did Fitzgerald and Hayward. Fitzgerald and Flora did nothing to hide their attraction to one another, dancing at least two times together every evening, which was as much as propriety allowed. Louisa grew more and more concerned with every passing evening.

"Do you always look so serious?" Hayward asked. His voice startled Louisa, and she spun around to face him. She had been standing alone watching the couples twirl about the ballroom.

Louisa glanced back at Flora, presently giggling at the center of the dance floor. "One of us has to be the serious one," Louisa remarked bitterly.

Hayward chuckled at that, stepping beside her. She nearly froze when his elbow grazed her. When she regained her composure, she turned to him. Louisa supposed she might as well *try* to talk to him, seeing as how he was her only option for conversation. "Tell me about your gaming hell."

Hayward looked surprised she wanted to know anything

about it. "I gathered you found my business to be despicable from one of our earlier conversations."

Louisa sighed. That much was true. Gaming hells could ruin men, even ones as powerful as Charles Finch. And when men like Charles were ruined, entire estates crumbled. Tenant farmers, the backbone of an estate's success, dealt with leaky roofs and old equipment due to lack of funding. Everyone suffered. But Louisa doubted Hayward cared about any of that. With an expressionless face, she turned to Hayward. "I heard the viscount's estate is in ruin, which is why he is interested in my sister."

Hayward appeared taken aback, and Louisa guessed he wasn't used to ladies such as her being so blunt with him. But there was no point dancing around the truth when she knew it very well. She smiled sweetly at Hayward. "Your friend is a fortune hunter."

Louisa turned away, taking a sip of punch and waiting for Hayward to say something. He finally cleared his throat. "You ought to give him a chance. Yes, my friend's estate has fallen on hard times, but he is quite fond of Flora. He is not just a fortune hunter."

Louisa studied him carefully. "How did the two of you come to be friends? In fact, I often wonder how you manage to receive invitations to all these parties. I would expect most of the ton to disapprove of a man like you."

Hayward smiled slightly. "They do disapprove of me, but the majority of them also owe me money. The house always wins, after all."

"That makes sense," Louisa said, nodding slightly as she did. She shot him a curious glance. "Did Lord Bolton ever owe you any money?"

Hayward's face grew dark, then he nodded. "At one point, he did, yes. There were going to be serious repercussions if he couldn't pay his debts, but the Duke of Rutley intervened just in time." He huffed slightly, shaking his head as he seemed to recall some long-ago memory. "I wish I would have said no. Now the duke has Bolton by the bollocks instead of me."

Louisa looked away, blushing furiously. "Mr. Hayward!"

He laughed. "You care for him, don't you?" he asked, growing serious.

"Who? Lord Bolton?" Hayward nodded, and Louisa laughed once. "Don't be ridiculous. Didn't I just tell you the other day that we are not friends?"

"You sounded much too defensive to be convincing."

But Louisa shook her head. "We are nothing more than neighbors, Mr. Hayward. Believe me." When Hayward grew silent, Louisa looked around the room, and she realized she no longer saw Flora or the viscount anywhere. "Do you see my sister anywhere?"

He made a show of looking about the room. "I am afraid I do not see them anywhere."

Louisa turned and scowled at him. "You did that on purpose. You distracted me from watching them, and now I have lost them in the crowd."

Hayward laughed. "I am sure they are fine. Shall we dance this next set?"

It would have been rude to say no without some sort of excuse, and she had none, other than he made her wildly uncomfortable due to her undeniable attraction to him, a married man, but she couldn't very well say that aloud. At least by the time Flora finally reappeared in the ballroom, Hayward had told Louisa all about his gaming hell. It sounded like a vulgar place, and for some odd reason, Louisa found herself glad Charles no longer went there.

When they arrived at home that evening, Louisa scolded Flora for disappearing before they went to sleep. "You must be more careful, Flora," Louisa warned. Flora sat at her dressing table, brushing her hair and humming a tune from that evening's ball. "You must hope no one else noticed you were missing at the same time, unless you should like to see your names in the scandal sheets tomorrow morning. He hasn't tried to kiss you, has he?"

Flora stopped brushing her brunette hair, looking over her shoulder and winking at her sister. "What do you presume?" Flora asked in a suggestive tone.

This only served to enrage Louisa even more. Her head spinning, she sat down on her sister's bed. "You haven't made him any promises, have you?" Louisa asked, her lips trembling. If Fitzgerald had proposed to Flora, Louisa would have to forbid the match, even if that meant losing Flora's confidence forever. But Louisa knew Fitzgerald wasn't the one for her sister. She knew it with her entire heart and soul.

Flora grinned. "Of course not," she said, turning back to the mirror. "You mustn't say yes the first time they ask."

Louisa turned pink. *Ask for what?* She didn't want to know.

"You ought to make him work for it," Flora continued. She put down her hairbrush and looked back at her sister. "That's how you know they're true."

Louisa had never heard of something so ridiculous. "He knows he must come to me for permission, doesn't he?"

Flora furrowed her brow. She still held the hairbrush in one of her hands. "Why would he need to ask you for permission?"

Louisa blinked. She thought it was obvious why he might ask her. "He is clearly after your dowry. He must know I am not going to give it to just anyone."

Flora made a disgusted face. "Louisa! You are acting like some sort of tyrannical older brother." Flora turned away, muttering to herself. "You and Lord Bolton have more in common than you think."

Louisa abruptly stood. "I am only trying to protect you

from a bad match. I do not trust the viscount, and all I am asking is that you please be careful. Ensure his affections are true before you give yourself completely to him. Please."

Flora looked at Louisa in the large mirror sitting atop Flora's dressing table. They held each other's gazes for a moment until finally Flora slowly nodded. Louisa clasped her hands together and smiled, then nodded. "Good," she said, heading to the doorway. "Thank you. I will see you in the morning."

Chapter Eleven

AFTER TAKING a few days to gather the courage to call on her, Charles found himself in his aunt's drawing room. Lady Ramsbury and his sister rose to greet him as he entered, both of them with unreadable expressions on their faces. He would have liked to know what they were thinking, but their visages were quite impenetrable. Perhaps it was only that an invitation to dinner at Finch Place plus his excellent behavior at the Talbot ball weren't enough to convince them that they might be on good terms again.

"Charles," the dowager duchess said as she strode toward him. She always walked with such dignified grace, so much so that Charles sometimes had a hard time believing that he and his aunt were related. Then again, judging by the way his sister seemed to float toward him as well, perhaps it was only the Finch women who inherited what he considered to be the mysterious trait of easy dignity. "What brings you to Park Street?"

Park Street was where his aunt resided in a large mansion her late husband left her after his untimely death. Along with the magnificent house located between Grosvenor Square and Hyde Park, her late husband also left her a sizeable fortune after his death, making Lady Ramsbury one of the wealthiest widows in England. She wanted for absolutely nothing, and though many young, penniless but titled gentlemen would have loved to entrap her into marriage over the years, she remained single.

But that didn't mean she was ever lonely—at least that was what the scandal sheets said time after time. The dowager duchess had taken plenty of lovers over the last ten years, with no one batting so much as an eye at her many conquests thanks to her title, wealth, and impressive address. All three things made his aunt's assistance in finding a wife particularly valuable—if she would grant it.

"Seeing as how my mother insists on staying away from town this season, I thought I might ask for your help instead," Charles said.

While the dowager duchess arched her brow with interest, Rosamund turned away and shook her head. Charles did his best to ignore her, as all brothers must do with sisters from time to time. He focused on his aunt instead.

"What sort of help?" she asked.

Charles began to speak, but Rosamund cut him off before he had a chance to say anything at all. "He means to ask you to help him find a wealthy wife now that neither of the Strickland girls want him," she said as she turned back to him, wearing a bored expression on her face.

Lady Ramsbury appeared perplexed by such an admission from Rosamund. "*Neither* of them wants him? Do they know he's an earl, and that the girl who marries him would become a countess?"

At least his aunt was sticking up for him. Meanwhile, Rosamund rolled her eyes. "I heard Miss Flora would rather be a *vis*countess, and the elder Miss Strickland would rather dance with married men." She paused, laughing slightly, while

Charles bristled at the insinuation that Louisa might prefer Philip Hayward to him. "I always did think Louisa was the more interesting of the two."

Charles found he could no longer hold his tongue in front of his sister. "If you are referring to Mr. Hayward, I believe she only danced with him one time."

His sister smiled at him, though there was no sweetness in it. It was a smile of self-satisfaction, the sort that came with the knowledge that she knew something he didn't. "Then I suppose you have not been invited to any balls this week to witness it the four additional times."

Something inside Charles sank. It was probably his heart —no, it was most certainly his heart—but he didn't care to admit to that, especially not to Rosamund. Instead, he roughly shook his head, ignoring his sister and forcing himself to remember the task at hand. He reached into his jacket, procuring the list Louisa had given him earlier that week.

"Well," he said simply, waving the list about in front of him, "I am not here to talk about Louisa Strickland. That being said, I cannot deny I am here to talk about finding a wife, one who can help pay off my debts and restore Linfield to its former glory. The duke has been very patient with me, but I should not like to depend on his kindness for too long."

Although the payment plan was working well, Charles did not like that Rutley had so much control over his life—or his pocketbook. Rosamund, however, didn't seem concerned. "The duke will never call in his debts. He likes you far too much for that."

Charles did his best not to lose his temper. Yes, he and Rutley were friends—no thanks to Rosamund, who'd rejected him—but the duke now tracked every purchase Charles made. He was already paying his debt back slowly through various economies, such as shuttering the dowager house instead of allowing his mother to live there. That was part of the reason she decided to stay on with the Haddingtons. But being under the thumb of another man all the time was not the way Charles wanted to live his life, and a wealthy wife would only pave his way to freedom much more quickly.

Rosamund, of course, could never understand. She could not comprehend what it meant to have actual responsibilities. All she wanted was to wear pretty dresses and marry for love or some such nonsense that Charles didn't have time for, especially not after he'd spent all of his early twenties gambling whatever allowance his father gave him. He supposed that was his penance for being a complete and utter idiot.

"Nevertheless," Charles said in a firm tone, "I shouldn't like to be in debt to the man for any longer than I must. Surely you can relate." He shot Rosamund a pointed look, and she glared at him in response. He turned to his aunt. "I have this list of wealthy debutantes. I wondered if you might introduce them to me somehow, perhaps by throwing a ball."

"Let me see," Lady Ramsbury said. Charles handed her the sheet of paper, and she immediately made a face upon inspecting it. "Why are so many of the names crossed out?"

Rosamund frowned, snatching the list out of her aunt's hand. The younger woman gasped when she confirmed Lady Ramsbury's comment for herself. She looked up at her brother. "I made a list of at least thirteen names with August and Miss Strickland at the Talbot ball! Now there are only seven. What was wrong with these other six ladies?"

Charles tried not to smile. "Miss Strickland thought you gave their names with a little too much devious glee that she felt she must shield me from them. I suppose even though I have disappointed her in the past, she does not wish to see me suffer—unlike some people."

His sister and aunt exchanged a look, which Charles didn't bother trying to decipher or understand. Women could

BECKY MICHAELS

be so confounding sometimes, and it wasn't worth trying to make sense of the knowing glances they sometimes shared. Lady Ramsbury took the list back from Rosamund. She looked over it once more, then nodded.

"Very well," she said, handing the sheet of paper back to Charles. "I see no problem in hosting a ball with those ladies on the guest list. You can pick your favorite at the end of the night and begin courting her for the rest of the season. You will be engaged by June."

Charles folded the list back up and placed it in his pocket, then smiled. He was glad someone believed in him. "Thank you, Lady Ramsbury." He glanced at Rosamund. "My marrying well will be a good thing for all of us. I promise you won't regret helping me."

Rosamund didn't look convinced, but then her face suddenly brightened. Her eyes fell on something far past her brother's shoulder, so he turned his head, following her gaze. He quickly rose from his chair when he saw who it was, his heart thumping.

"Miss Strickland!" Rosamund exclaimed, rising as well and walking toward their visitor at the entrance of the drawing room. "You came."

Louisa seemed unsure of stepping any further into the room when her eyes met his, and Rosamund practically had to drag the girl toward him and her aunt at the center of the massive drawing room. Charles could tell Louisa was surprised to see him, just as he was to see her. He looked toward his sister, hopeful for some sort of explanation.

"We invited Miss Strickland to tea," Rosamund finally said, her eyes darting between her new guest and her brother. Charles bowed slightly, and Louisa quickly curtseyed. They spoke practically at the same time.

"Lovely to see you, Miss Strickland," he said.

"How do you do, my lord?" she asked. He should have

replied that he was fine, thank you very much, but he suddenly remembered his sister's earlier comments about Louisa and Hayward. When Charles found himself awkwardly tongue-tied at Louisa's sudden presence, Rosamund kindly intervened.

"My brother stopped by quite unexpectedly," she said before offering one long, graceful arm to him. "I was just showing him out. Isn't that right, Charles?"

Charles nodded, then took his sister's arm and forced himself to smile at Louisa. "Good afternoon, Miss Strickland."

After they left the drawing room and entered the hall, Rosamund turned to him. She almost looked concerned, which surprised him. It wasn't like Rosamund to be worried about him at all, especially after all that had happened last year. "Are you all right?"

"What do you mean?" he asked, sounding innocent enough.

Rosamund bit her lip. "You acted very peculiarly in front of Miss Strickland. From what I have heard and witnessed in the past, it's unlike you to act shy and uncertain around a female."

"I think you have me confused for your former fiancé," Charles replied coldly. The remark must have stung, for his sister quickly turned away, frowning. Charles immediately regretted the barb and relented, his voice growing soft. "I'm sorry." He almost said something about Miss Strickland, about how being around her had made him nervous and anxious for some unspeakable reason. However, Charles wasn't quite ready to confess that to anyone. "I shouldn't have said that. I have a terrible habit of speaking without thinking first. I know you cared for him."

They stopped underneath the giant crystal chandelier in the circular entry hall at the front of Lady Ramsbury's house.

Two servants stood at either side of the front double doors before opening them for Charles. "Why did you never stop him?" Rosamund asked, her voice soft.

"Stop him from what?"

Rosamund blushed and looked away. "You know," she said. After a moment, she turned and looked at him directly. "From taking lovers even though he was engaged to me."

Charles hesitated, then sighed. There was no use hiding it from her. "One doesn't tell a duke what he can and cannot do. Besides, I think I always wanted to impress him, and I couldn't do that by censuring him."

Rosamund was watching him with large, curious eyes, which were a bluish green, just as his were. He tried to smile. "He was like an older brother to me, and I never had the courage to say anything to him about his bad behavior, especially as my luck started to run out, but his never did." Charles paused a moment, thinking. "Well, I suppose his luck eventually did run out, didn't it?"

Rosamund tilted her head, appearing confused. "What do you mean?"

"Well, he lost you, didn't he?" He smiled more broadly at his sister, even when she seemed a bit taken aback by his observation. He was telling the truth, though. The duke was a miserable wretch now that Rosamund had called off their engagement. She must have known it, too, especially after seeing him at Finch Place.

Charles looked around the spacious entry hall, then back at Rosamund. "You know, you are welcome to return to Finch Place anytime. I will be honest and say it's been easier not having to worry about paying for your many clothes, but I am rather lonely there. I would be willing to take on the bills for some company."

When she realized her brother was teasing her, Rosamund slowly smiled, just as he hoped she would. "I think I would rather stay here—that way my former fiancé does not have to scold you over how many pairs of stockings I buy."

They both laughed, and when they finally quieted, Charles turned to leave. He was halfway out the door when his sister called after him. He turned to find her standing directly behind him. "I hear Louisa Strickland has ten thousand pounds a year. Is she wealthy enough to be considered as one of your potential brides?"

Charles paused, not sure what to say at first. "I am afraid it does not matter if I would consider her or not. Miss Strickland has no interest in me, and she does not want to marry."

Rosamund frowned. "But what of your earlier courtship? The scandal sheets would have one believe you left her heartbroken."

Charles sighed, taking off his hat and running his hand through his unruly hair. "I am afraid it was all a ruse. She never had any interest in marrying me, or anyone, knowing she did not have to with what her father would eventually leave her. Her future has always been most secure, with or without a husband."

But Rosamund didn't seem convinced. She waved her hand as if none of what Charles said mattered. "But all that aside, would you consider Miss Strickland if I could change her opinion of you?"

Charles's first reaction was to laugh, for he doubted Miss Strickland would ever change her opinion of marriage, even less her opinion of him, but his sister continued to stare at him with wide eyes, waiting for a genuine answer. He forced himself to think of Louisa, his old friend who happened to be quite beautiful and seemingly still cared for his happiness, at least somewhat.

"I would consider her, yes," Charles finally said, his voice coming out more strangled than he would have liked. He knew he would come to regret his admission judging by the delighted look on his sister's face. She clapped her hands together.

"Splendid!" Rosamund exclaimed before placing her hands on his shoulders. She stood on her tiptoes and pressed a kiss to his cheek. "Goodbye, Charles."

Rosamund was gone before Charles could warn her against whatever scheme she currently had in mind. Shaking his head, he replaced his hat and left Park Street.

LOUISA AWKWARDLY SAT across from Lady Ramsbury and Rosamund, sipping her tea as her eyes anxiously darted back and forth between them. They smiled pleasantly at her, but Louisa was still thinking of her chance encounter with Lord Bolton. Although it wasn't so odd that she would run into him at his aunt's house, she did wonder what they had been discussing before she entered the room.

Although Rosamund told Charles they had asked Louisa to tea, Louisa had invited herself to Park Street to discuss the troubling situation she presently faced: Flora's infatuation with the viscount. The Stricklands had already seen him at four separate balls since his initial call—and then he'd called on Flora at least three other times at home. Mr. Hayward always accompanied him, much to Louisa's chagrin, but that was beside the point. She could handle him herself.

Flora and the viscount were another story.

There was something about the viscount that Louisa just didn't like, and she defended this by telling herself she had plenty of reasons as to why. But the many warnings about his poor character weren't enough to discourage her sister or her stepmother, who had grown quite fond of the viscount in such a short period of time. His overt charm was proving to be quite the disadvantage to Louisa, which was why she had written a desperate note to Rosamund, hopeful that she might have even more gossip or ideas to deter Flora from Fitzgerald.

"You will have to excuse my brother," Rosamund said as she returned to the drawing room. "He has been unlike himself since he returned to town. It must be the complete lack of social interaction he had over the winter. He has forgotten how to act in front of a lady!"

"It's no bother," Louisa said, putting her teacup on a porcelain saucer that rested on the table. She was suddenly very aware of Rosamund's exacting gaze and forced a smile. "He was probably only surprised to see me here. We have not exactly been the friendliest of neighbors over the past seven years."

Rosamund leaned closer. "And whose fault is that?"

Louisa bit her lip, recalling her brief—and fraudulent—courtship with Charles.

"I was so disappointed when he did not propose to you that season," Rosamund continued, sitting back in her chair. "I was so fond of you. But I don't blame your family for avoiding us afterward. He used you very badly, as my brother often does with people."

Louisa never knew how to act when someone mentioned her brief tendre with Charles. As far as she knew, no one but them knew it was a ruse. But Rosamund looked at Louisa so expectantly that Louisa suspected the earl's sister might be in on the secret as well. Louisa sighed. "Truthfully, Charles was doing me a favor that season. I never wanted to marry, but my stepmother insisted that I have a proper come-out in town. He helped me deter all the serious suitors, not to mention please my stepmother with his attentions."

Rosamund did not look surprised. She only smiled broadly, as if she were happy Louisa had admitted the truth to her.

Meanwhile, Lady Ramsbury shook her head, sighing. "I

should have known," the dowager duchess said. "Charles was much too immature to be courting anyone seven years ago."

Louisa suddenly recalled that it was in the dowager duchess's library where she'd discovered Charles with that opera singer. Louisa still remembered her name very clearly: Miss Coppola. She also remembered the shame and utter mortification when she and Charles locked gazes while he partook in such a vulgar act.

"Indeed," Louisa hastily agreed, eager to steer the conversation in another direction. "But I was wondering if we could discuss my sister's suitor, Lord Fitzgerald."

Rosamund nodded, thankfully dropping the subject of her brother right away. "Yes, that is why you requested an audience, isn't it? The scandal sheets are predicting an engagement between him and Miss Flora by the end of the season!"

"That is what I fear," Louisa grumbled. She reached for her teacup, taking another sip of the warm liquid. Her eyes darted toward Rosamund. "I already told you what your brother mentioned to me, but you wrote that you might know something that confirms my suspicions about his poor character even further."

Rosamund nodded, glancing at her aunt and then back at Louisa. "We have also heard he has been carrying on with Miss Coppola, the opera singer."

Louisa nearly dropped her teacup. "W-what?" she stammered, unable to believe that Fitzgerald's lover was also the woman she saw Charles tupping in the library on the red settee. It was too much of a coincidence, but then again, Louisa had never found herself much surprised by the little ways life could be cruel before. "Are you sure?"

Rosamund nodded again, a look of concern growing on her face. "Yes," she replied, "but you are acting as if you have heard of Miss Coppola. Have you seen her perform?"

"Something like that," she murmured, placing her teacup

back down on the table, where it wouldn't be in danger of accidentally spilling. "But what shall we do? My sister already knows I have a low opinion of Fitzgerald. If I simply tell her the viscount has a lover, she won't believe me. And if she dares to ask him about it afterward, you know he will pretend as if it's nothing more than idle gossip. There must be some way I can prove it to her."

Rosamund glanced at her aunt, who smiled as if she had the answer to all of their problems. "I'll be hosting a ball here soon. I could ask Miss Coppola to perform that evening. She has done it for me in the past."

Lady Ramsbury shot Louisa a knowing glance as if she remembered what happened in her library all those years ago. Louisa swallowed, preferring to forget. "And you will invite Lord Fitzgerald here, even after what his brother did to your other niece?"

The dowager duchess and Rosamund exchanged a rueful glance. "We will have to tell August first, of course," Lady Ramsbury said.

Rosamund waved her hand. "She will not mind if we tell her it is for the greater good. We need to show Flora what sort of men the Fitzgerald brothers are. August will understand." Rosamund's eyes mischievously twinkled as she studied Louisa. "And *you* will understand, of course, if we use this ball to accomplish two tasks."

"Two tasks?"

"My brother asked my aunt to introduce him to the women on that list we made him at the Talbot ball. It was very curious that some of the suggestions were crossed out when I saw it again this afternoon."

Louisa flushed, realizing what Rosamund suspected—that Louisa cared for Charles and might grow jealous at the sight of him entertaining other women. Louisa looked at Lady Ramsbury, ignoring Rosamund's comment about the list. "I cannot stop you from inviting your nephew to your ball and introducing him to eligible ladies. But if you could leave Mr. Hayward off the guest list, I would appreciate it greatly."

Lady Ramsbury's and her niece's eyebrows shot up together. After exchanging a brief look, they turned back to Louisa, both of them smiling broadly. "Of course, Miss Strickland," the dowager duchess said, reaching again for her teacup.

Louisa should have felt reassured, but there was something about the way Lady Ramsbury spoke that made her feel quite the opposite.

"Very good," Louisa replied with a smile. "It will be a most enjoyable evening, then."

Chapter Twelve

LOUISA SPENT the following afternoons at Park Street, which gave her a much-needed respite from the daily outings with Lord Fitzgerald and Hayward. Flora became annoyed that her sister was always conveniently missing whenever the two men called, but Louisa preferred the company of the dowager duchess and Lady Rosamund. The two women were planning the viscount's downfall, and Louisa didn't want to miss a second of it.

She wondered if Charles would make another appearance at Park Street one of the days she was there, but he never did. Louisa decided it was for the better. As she already decided before, there was no point in growing their renewed acquaintance any further. After all, their goals in life were vastly different from one another. Charles wished to marry a wealthy wife to pay off his debt, and Louisa wanted to maintain her independence and manage Strickland Manor without interference from a man.

But although Louisa was determined to be rid of Fitzgerald, Lady Ramsbury's ball wasn't for another fortnight. She still had to deal with Fitzgerald's and Hayward's incessant attention at dinner parties and balls until then. Louisa didn't understand why Hayward seemed so interested in her, especially when she made it clear she would dance once or twice with him every evening—but that was it. There must have been plenty of widows or wives who would have been willing to start an adulterous affair with him.

Not that Louisa knew the first thing about adulterous affairs. She didn't even know the first thing about *regular* ones. Charles had never tried to steal a kiss from her, not even during their months-long pretend courtship, and neither did Cousin William when he stayed for an extended time at Strickland after Papa's death. She always assumed it was because she was unattractive.

But now Hayward was showering her with *genuine* attention, and Louisa didn't always know how to react. Who had ever treated her like she was desirable? Certainly not Charles, who ran off with an opera singer the first chance he got.

But Hayward was married. Louisa tried to remember that, even when she politely agreed to dance with him, if only to keep him from pestering her for the rest of the evening. Usually one dance was enough to satiate his appetite, so she hesitantly agreed every time. She could ignore the way it felt to be in his strong, capable arms for a few moments, as well as the way his dark eyes bore down on her with a hungry look whenever she dared to glance up at him.

That particular night, Louisa focused her attention on the room around them, doing her absolute best to avoid Hayward's gaze. What felt like a sea of people watched them with discerning looks. They were dancing a waltz, and she instinctively put some space between her and Hayward, hoping the scandal sheets didn't say anything too nefarious about them the following day. But Hayward only gently pulled her back toward him. Louisa finally dared to look at him.

"People are staring, sir," she said. "We should not be so close."

"Is that not the point of a waltz—to hold one's partner close? I believe that's why so many meddling mamas forbid their daughters from dancing it."

Louisa wished Mrs. Strickland would have forbidden her. But Mrs. Strickland never did anything that might upset Lord Fitzgerald, seeing how fond Flora was of him. And Hayward was supposedly Lord Fitzgerald's dearest friend. Louisa had called that fact into question, seeing the age difference between the two men, not to mention Hayward was a businessman and Fitzgerald a young lordling. But Hayward insisted the two men became friends through the viscount's patronage at Hayward's exclusive club.

Louisa sighed. How convenient that her stepmother forgot Hayward's improperness when Flora's happiness could be put at risk.

When the dance finished, Hayward led Louisa to the refreshment table. She had not seen Charles Finch at a ball or party since the Talbots', but she would have liked him to interrupt them now as he did before.

"You are quiet tonight, Miss Strickland," Hayward said after handing her a glass of champagne. The bubbly beverage did nothing to calm her growing nerves.

"I no longer know how to act around you," Louisa admitted. "You are incorrigible with your impolite advances, yet I cannot seem to rid myself of you since your friend is courting my sister." She looked at him critically, but he only smiled.

It was a handsome smile. Louisa hated it. "Have you no care for what your wife might read in the scandal sheets?" she asked.

Hayward made a face. "I'm sure she does not get them in Hertfordshire."

Louisa's mouth briefly hung open. "And what of your conscience? You made your vows in front of—"

"It was an arranged marriage." Hayward sounded more solemn now. His mouth made a firm, hard line. "Some of us do not have a choice in remaining single."

He shot her a pointed look, and Louisa briefly relented. She was curious as to how the owner of a gaming hell ended up in an arranged marriage, but she didn't dare ask. "Surely you would prefer a..." Louisa hesitated briefly. There was no delicate way to put it, so she took a deep breath before she spoke again. "Surely you would prefer a more experienced woman to keep you company if you do not plan on remaining faithful to your wife."

Louisa flushed furiously as soon as the words left her mouth, and Hayward's eyebrows shot up. "On the contrary" —he leaned closer, whispering in her ear—"I look forward to teaching you all the devious things a man and a woman might do with each other—if you'll have me, that is."

Hayward leaned back to capture her gaze, and Louisa swallowed. "You'd have to teach me everything, I'm afraid. It will be a lot of trouble." She briefly turned away, then met Hayward's dark-brown eyes once more. Louisa immediately thought about how different they were from Charles's—what a strange, intrusive thought to have about him. She wondered if memories of the earl would always haunt her. "I have never even been kissed."

Hayward squinted. "What did you say?" he asked. He mustn't have heard her over the sounds of the orchestra readying their instruments for another set. Louisa quickly looked around, making sure no one was in earshot of their private corner near the refreshment table.

"I said I have never been kissed," Louisa practically hissed, her face even warmer than before. She hated having to say it a second time.

Hayward appeared surprised for a moment but then dismissively waved his hand while stepping even closer. "Then that will be the first thing I teach you."

Louisa had no idea a man's smile could look so devilish. Something inside her stomach stirred uncomfortably, so she could only return his roguish look with a blank stare.

"You are not put off by my confession?" she asked.

He shook his head. "No."

She chewed her lip. "But what if I'm bad at it?"

Hayward laughed. "I very much doubt that. Perhaps we might find a dark room—"

"No!" Louisa practically shouted, jerking away from him. He watched her, looking confused. She doubted anyone had ever resisted him for this long. How could they? Even she found her morals crumbling whenever he was around, yet a pressing voice inside her head urged her to remember his wife. "I would not dare offend Mrs. Hayward in such a way."

Hayward sighed and placed a hand on his hip. "Our marriage is not like that. She has had her lovers, and I have had mine. Be my mistress, Louisa."

Louisa stared at him, unable to say anything. She must have opened and closed her mouth at least three times, yet no words came out, appearing more fish-like than human. When Louisa said nothing, Hayward took both of her gloved hands into his. She stared down at them, thinking how she'd once wished Charles might treat her the same way. Even if she did not desire marriage, that didn't mean she did not crave the touch or love of a man. But Charles had always treated her like some sort of joke instead.

"You do not have to answer now," Hayward said, bringing one hand to his lips and kissing her knuckles. She suppressed a shudder of excitement, and he winked. "I will leave you to think about it."

He let go of her hand, and Louisa watched him go until

she lost him in the crowd. She stood unmoving for a long moment, unable to think of what to do next. She could not deny that Hayward was attractive, but something inside her told her any liaison between them couldn't possibly be right. He was *married*.

She was about to go and find her stepmother, but then a new gentleman staring at her caught her eye. Louisa recognized the Duke of Rutley right away. They were neighbors, though she didn't know the duke as well as Charles. Rutley was a very tall man with dark hair and a face that looked like someone chiseled it from marble. Truthfully, Louisa wondered how Rosamund ever gathered the nerve to reject someone like him. Not only was he intimidating, but he was incredibly handsome.

When Rutley approached her, she curtseyed. "Good evening, Your Grace."

"Miss Strickland," he said, bowing slightly.

"Are you here alone?" Louisa asked, wondering if Charles was somewhere nearby. If he was, she would be very disappointed in him for not intervening when she and Hayward were together earlier.

"My mother's come to town," Rutley explained.

Louisa wondered what that meant. As far as she knew, the dowager duchess never came to town.

"She heard the situation was dire and is encouraging me to find a new female to court." He briefly looked out into the crowd, then back at Louisa, his gaze sharp. The duke always appeared to be brooding. "But there is no one here tonight who could tempt me into marriage."

Louisa sighed, looking out to where he once did. Lady Ramsbury and Rosamund were not there that night. She turned back to him, gently smiling. "I feel much the same, Your Grace."

He seemed skeptical. "I saw you speaking to Mr. Hayward

earlier."

She frowned at him. "And you did not come to save me?" Louisa asked, disappointed.

Rutley looked at her as if surprised she needed saving. "You disapprove of Hayward's attentions, but you accept them so willingly." He paused a moment, narrowing his eyes at Louisa. Her face grew warm under the scrutiny. "Why?"

Louisa glared at him. She knew she shouldn't argue with a duke, but she couldn't help herself. "I do not accept them *willingly*. He asks me to dance every time I see him. I accept once out of politeness—nothing more, nothing less. Do you expect me to feign a sprained ankle every time he approaches me? Do you not realize how hard it is to be a single woman with no interest in marriage at one of these balls?"

He blinked at her, and she half expected him to scold her for her tirade against him. When he didn't, she slightly softened toward him. "May I ask why you were watching us in the first place, Your Grace?"

The duke tilted his head to the side. "I was asked to watch you."

Louisa's eyes widened, surprised. "By whom?"

"Lord Bolton," Rutley explained.

Louisa furrowed her brow. "But why?"

The duke shrugged. "We have all read the scandal sheets. Philip Hayward is quite mad for one Miss Louisa Strickland of Kent by the sounds of it. I can confirm as much by the looks of it as well."

Louisa ignored the fact that she must have been blushing and shook her head. "But why does Charles care to know my business?"

The duke shrugged again. "I cannot pretend to know how the earl's mind works."

Louisa glared at him. Worthless, dukes were. "Well, next time you see him, you can tell him that Miss Strickland spent the entire night flirting and dancing with Mr. Hayward." She was breathing heavily now, her chest rising and falling with annoyance.

Rutley arched his brow suggestively once more. "I was already planning to tell him just that," he replied matter-of-factly.

Louisa's nostrils flared. "I believe I see my mother," she said, though she was still looking at the duke. She quickly curtseyed, eager to be free of the man. "Good evening, Your Grace."

She turned away, but Rutley called out to her. "Wait!" he said.

Reluctantly, she looked over her shoulder to face him.

"How is Lady Rosamund?"

Louisa noticed right away that the duke's typically severe look softened when he spoke her friend's name. "The scandal sheets also say you have been calling on her and Lady Ramsbury at Park Street quite frequently."

Louisa sighed. These men were obsessed with their scandal sheets, weren't they? This was only her second time in town, yet these broadsheet writers seemed to love reporting her comings and goings whenever she was there. "Lady Rosamund is fine, Your Grace." Louisa shot him a pitying glance when his face seemed to brighten. "But perhaps your mother is right. You *should* find a new female to court."

And with that, Louisa turned and walked away, leaving the characteristically glum-looking duke behind.

THE WAIT for Lady Ramsbury's ball was long and arduous. Charles spent most of his evenings walking the halls of Finch Place alone, wishing someone other than the duke might call. His half sister August had dragged Mr. Brooks along on a few occasions, but Brooks never seemed happy about it. Their conversations still felt forced and awkward.

Occasionally he went to the coffeehouse down the street, but only upon Rutley's request. Otherwise, there wasn't much there for him, as he no longer drank or gambled.

But that night, he received a short missive from his friend, asking Charles to join him at Hayward's in Covent Garden right away. Reluctantly, the earl did as Rutley commanded, though he didn't particularly enjoy the idea of going to that den of sin. There were far too many temptations within those four walls, and he told himself he would stay for an hour at most. When Charles finally found Rutley that evening, it was at one of the card tables.

"There you are," Rutley said, looking over his shoulder. Charles glanced at the cards he held in his hand, then winced. Perhaps Rutley's luck *had* run out.

"You said you had something urgent to tell me," Charles said, irritated when Rutley simply turned and went back to playing. But before Charles could hear the duke answer, he saw Philip Hayward looking at him from across the room. The older man wore a satisfied smile, causing Charles to frown.

The earl had read the scandal sheets. They said the married Hayward, owner of the most notorious gaming hell in all of London, had enchanted the older Strickland girl. The skin on the back of Charles's neck prickled at the thought. He always thought Louisa was more intelligent than that. He thought she wouldn't fall for the devious man's charms, so he assumed the broadsheets mustn't have known the entire story.

"He is what I mean to speak to you about," Rutley said, standing up and following his friend's gaze at the same time. Together, they walked away from the card table. Charles wondered how much the duke had already lost that night—he had been on a losing streak, or so he said—but Charles didn't dare ask how bad things were. "I have just come from the Colborne ball, where I watched Hayward and Miss Strickland together, just as you asked."

Charles raised his brow, anxious. He had hoped the gossip wasn't true. "And?" he quietly asked.

The duke wore a somber look. "They flirted and danced. If she did not like him before, Hayward has certainly done a marvelous job wearing down whatever resistance she did have."

"Quiet," Charles practically hissed. "He is headed this way."

Rutley turned. Hayward was making his way across the room toward them. The two men stood at attention, waiting for Hayward to address them. When he finally stood directly in front of them, he bowed to each of them. "Your Grace. My lord."

Charles stoically nodded his head, pretending that he didn't want to strangle Hayward until he agreed to leave Louisa alone. "How do you do, Hayward?" Charles asked.

"Splendid!" Hayward exclaimed, wearing the same satisfied look from before. "I have just come from Lord and Lady Colborne's ball. I saw His Grace there, but not you, my lord. Were you not invited?"

"I am afraid not," Charles replied flippantly. He vaguely recalled being part of a drunken scene that involved a potted fern the last time he attended a ball hosted by the Colbornes. No wonder he didn't receive an invitation. Charles forced a smile, glancing from the duke to Hayward. "Did you have an enjoyable evening?"

Hayward nodded, then looked over his shoulder and pointed to a tall brown-haired man sitting at one of the tables across the room. Two serving girls sat on his lap, one on each knee. Charles scowled. "My friend Fitzgerald is having much success courting the younger Strickland girl. I have gotten to know your neighbors particularly well over the past fortnight. I even think Miss Strickland has come to enjoy my company."

Charles glanced at Rutley, who stood expressionless beside him. Charles turned back to Hayward, silently cursing his friend. He could be rather unhelpful at times. "Is that so?" Charles said as brightly as possible. He even tried to smile. "I have always enjoyed Louisa's company myself. I cannot say she feels the same about me."

Charles tried to sound jovial, but truthfully, he was irritated. What could have possibly come over Louisa, entangling herself with such a man? She seemed so adamantly against it that afternoon in her drawing room after she received the flowers.

"She said as much herself," Hayward said.

The forced contentment on Charles's face faded as he wondered if that was true. He thought they had last parted on good terms.

"I imagine it has to do with your previous courtship."

Charles shrugged. He did not want to say he left Louisa disappointed, as that certainly wasn't the case, but Louisa had always behaved more coldly to him after she caught him with that opera singer. Charles still struggled to come up with her name.

"I just can't believe you never tried to steal a kiss," Hayward said with a laugh.

The earl's head snapped in Hayward's direction. "Did Louisa tell you that?" Charles asked. His face must have been bright red, as Hayward nodded, still laughing. Charles pursed his lips, inwardly telling himself to pull it together. "Well, some of us do not kiss innocent girls unless we intend to marry them, and I never intend to marry Miss Strickland. Good evening, sir."

Charles turned to Rutley. "Is there anything else you need from me? Otherwise, I'm returning to Finch Place."

But the duke shook his head. "Charles, do you—"

"Pardon me, Your Grace," Charles said, bowing before he left. He did not care to answer the duke's questions that night, and he was too upset with Louisa not to be tempted by the footmen carrying around trays of champagne. He needed to return to Finch Place and await Lady Ramsbury's ball, where he might finally meet a girl who appreciated all he had to offer.

At least, he hoped to.

Chapter Thirteen

LOUISA DID NOT SEE Hayward for seven days after the Colborne ball. He was absent from the other social events they attended, despite the viscount being present. Fitzgerald said sudden business at home took Hayward to Hertfordshire.

"Have no fear, Miss Strickland," the viscount told her in that smooth voice of his, an easy smile playing at his lips. Flora stood at his side, fawning over him as she usually did. They were all attending the same dinner party; Louisa had already forgotten the name of their host and hostess. Mrs. Strickland's impressive list of friends and acquaintances in town that season were hard to keep straight. "He will not be gone long. He can never stay away from his business for very long."

Louisa had politely smiled back at him at the time, but as the days passed, she suspected Hayward was only playing a game with her, giving her more time to stew over his indecent proposition or perhaps even miss him. The truth was, she did miss his attention; balls were lonely without him there, especially when she had to watch Flora and Fitzgerald exchange coy looks all evening instead. She almost hated herself for such feelings.

But in the end, Louisa decided she would not be manipulated by him or her silly desires. While yes, she often imagined what it would be like to kiss or even make love to Hayward—she wasn't blind, he was an attractive man—Louisa knew any liaison with him would lead to nothing but trouble.

She couldn't trust him to be discreet, and although she did not care what the scandal sheets said about her, Louisa had her sister's reputation to consider. Once Louisa revealed Fitzgerald to be the rake that he was, Flora would need a new suitor. If the broadsheets labeled Louisa as some sort of hussy, her sister would have a much harder time finding a respectable husband.

By the time the night of Lady Ramsbury's ball arrived, Louisa was quite ready to be rid of the viscount, and she had high expectations for the evening. Fashionable guests crowded Park Street for the first time in over a year, as Lady Ramsbury had stopped entertaining when her niece August briefly lived with her last year. However, now that August was married and Rosamund did not need as much shielding from society as her father's illegitimate daughter did, Park Street easily became one of the centers of London society once more.

When they first entered Lady Ramsbury's mansion, Louisa saw Rosamund standing at the bottom of her aunt's curved staircase right away, talking to two finely dressed gentlemen beside her. Louisa smiled as she watched her, wondering what it was like to have that much confidence, and to have it so easily, too. Rosamund acted as much like a hostess as her aunt, the notorious dowager duchess.

When their eyes met, Rosamund held a single hand up to the gentlemen, motioned as if she was politely excusing herself, then hurried across the room to greet Louisa. Rosamund seemed nervous for some reason, and Louisa carefully watched her as she spoke to Flora, looking for some hint of trouble. They couldn't afford for their plan to go awry that night.

"Is the viscount here?" Flora asked Rosamund in a hushed tone. Rosamund smiled, her eyes darting apprehensively toward Louisa, who raised her brow, confused. Rosamund turned back to Flora.

"Yes, he arrived just moments ago." Rosamund looked at Louisa once more. "He even brought a companion with him."

"Oh?" Louisa asked, trying not to sound too alarmed. Who else could it be besides Hayward? She had requested Lady Ramsbury not invite him, but if the viscount brought him anyway... Well, the dowager duchess couldn't very well turn him away unless she wanted to cause a scene.

"Yes," Rosamund replied, looping her arm underneath Flora's. Mrs. Strickland smiled obliviously at the other guests as they walked down the hall and into the ballroom. Rosamund glanced back at Louisa, offering an apologetic look. "The viscount was sure my aunt forgot to send Mr. Hayward an invitation by accident."

Flora giggled, looking from her sister back to Rosamund. Louisa shot her a warning look, hoping she wouldn't say anything inappropriate. But Flora never quite knew when to hold her tongue. "It is a good thing he came anyway," Flora said with a mischievous grin.

Louisa groaned inwardly, briefly closing her eyes and praying for patience.

"Although she will never admit it, I suspect my sister's missed him terribly over the past week while he was away in Hertfordshire. I'm sure she's anxious to see him, and I'm surprised she let such an oversight happen, seeing as how she's helped you and your aunt plan this ball for the last fortnight."

"Perhaps it wasn't an oversight," Louisa said coldly, though Flora only continued to giggle. Louisa rolled her eyes; her sister could be so ridiculous sometimes. "What I do know is that I certainly did not miss him."

The four women came to a halt at the edge of the ballroom. It was still early in the evening, so people had not filled the room to the brim quite yet. Louisa looked around, hoping to find the viscount and Hayward, but her eyes landed on two other familiar figures instead. Lady Ramsbury was standing next to Charles at the other side of the ballroom, introducing him to some young lady and her mother. Their eyes met, but only for a moment. Louisa immediately turned away, her heart suddenly pounding. She had already vowed not to be jealous if Charles found his bride that night, so she ought not to look at all.

"You did your best not to miss him, but I'm not sure you succeeded," Flora said, not even noticing her sister had her eyes on another man altogether. But perhaps it was better that way.

"Let your sister be, Flora," Mrs. Strickland warned in a hushed tone. "She is only being polite to Mr. Hayward to better your chances with the viscount; you should be thanking her instead of teasing her. I have heard he's a very powerful man." Flora demurred slightly, and Louisa's heart warmed at her stepmother finally defending her. "Now stand up straight. The men are headed this way."

As Fitzgerald and Hayward made their approach, Louisa thought she saw Charles lean over and murmur something in his aunt's ear. The dowager duchess gave a knowing smile in response, but soon the viscount and his troubling friend required all of Louisa's attention. Hayward looked the same as ever: devilishly handsome. Louisa couldn't help but wonder if his wife was sad to see him return to town. Louisa knew she would be.

"I'm glad your business in Hertfordshire didn't keep you away from town too long, Mr. Hayward," Flora said, batting her eyelashes as she looked from him to her sister. "Louisa hasn't had anyone to dance with all week!"

Louisa glared at Flora. Even Mrs. Strickland looked disappointed in her.

"That's a shame," Hayward said before glancing at the viscount. "I thought Fitzgerald would have offered at least once or twice."

"I insisted he didn't," Louisa interjected before his friend could reply.

"Oh?" Hayward asked.

Louisa nodded. "Truthfully, I abhor dancing. Lord Fitzgerald was doing me a favor by not asking, as it would have been impolite of me to reject him."

Hayward arched a brow. "Are you saying you do not enjoy dancing with me, and you have only ever said yes out of politeness?"

Their eyes met, and Louisa gave him a defiant shrug. "Yes, I suppose that is what I'm saying, Mr. Hayward. It shouldn't come as a surprise, as I seem to remember telling you just that to your face."

Hayward chuckled. "I'm afraid you'll have to tell me at least one more time, for I was hoping you would grant me the first set this evening," he said.

Louisa sighed. "Well, if I have no other choice." She took his hand, letting him lead her out onto the dance floor, where other couples were lining up together. When the orchestra started playing, Louisa noticed Charles and his first potential bride a few couples down the row from them. Her partner followed her gaze.

"I see Lord Bolton is here tonight," he observed. The tone

of his voice was noticeably chilly.

"Is he?" Louisa said, her voice more high-pitched than she would have liked. She cleared her throat and inwardly urged herself to remain calm. She could talk about the earl without becoming nervous, couldn't she? "That would make sense, though. The dowager duchess is his aunt."

"I am surprised she invited him at all after that happened last year," Hayward muttered, more to himself than to Louisa. Of course, everyone who read the scandal sheets had some understanding of the friction within the Finch family.

"He seems like a changed man to me," Louisa said, not disingenuously. Perhaps even tenderheartedly, longing for the days when Charles was once her dance partner. She hoped Hayward didn't notice. She'd rather him not comment on it. "I imagine his family has forgiven him by now."

"And what of you, Miss Strickland? Have you forgiven him?"

Louisa tittered. "I'm not sure what you mean, Mr. Hayward."

The dance had them briefly switch partners, and Louisa was thankful for the respite from talking, however brief it was. She kindly smiled at the young gentleman who took her hand, and for a moment, she felt safe from Hayward's prying questions. Louisa had always preferred not to speak about Charles, not even to her sister or mother. But Louisa and Hayward were joined together in dance again soon enough, and she could not ignore him any longer.

"Did Bolton not court you the last time you came to town?" Hayward asked, his dark eyes capturing hers as they came toward each other. Louisa tried to focus on the steps of the dance but felt quite flustered. "And did he not fail to come up to scratch at the end of the season?"

"All that is true," Louisa admitted before pausing a moment. There was no use lying about it any longer. If her stepmother found out, then so be it. She had already told the truth to Lady Ramsbury and Rosamund a fortnight ago. "But that was seven years ago, and I never intended to marry him. Charles—I mean Lord Bolton—was only helping me avoid other suitors."

Hayward gave her a puzzled expression. "But why?"

"Why would a woman marry if she does not need to? My father always promised to entrust his manor to me when he died—no marriage required. My season all those years ago was only to appease my stepmother. I'm very happily a spinster now—a landed, *wealthy* spinster."

"But what about love?"

They switched partners before Louisa could answer. The question startled her. There was a time when she may have fancied herself in love with Charles, but it was a youthful, silly sort of love. Recovering from her broken heart was easy once she remembered what she truly wanted in life: her independence.

When Louisa and Hayward were reunited, she shot him a shrewd look. "I'm not familiar with the emotion. And even if I were, I'm sure I would still value my freedom more."

Eventually the dance ended, and Hayward escorted her to the refreshment table, where they found themselves alone. Charles did not follow them that time. Disappointed, she had almost forgotten Hayward was standing beside her when he dipped his head beside her ear.

"And what of lust?" he suddenly whispered.

Louisa jumped, turning to stare at him, eyes wide. "What of it?" she asked, her face warming as she did. A smile played at Hayward's lips, and his dark eyes gleamed with devilish intent.

"Have you given any more thought to my offer?" he asked.

Louisa shook her head. "Only that it's a bad idea."

Hayward frowned, clearly in disagreement. "And what has

driven you to that conclusion?"

"People will talk." Her eyes found her stepmother and Flora, still standing with the viscount and Rosamund in a corner of the room. Lady Ramsbury had joined them, and it appeared she was introducing that night's entertainment to the group: Miss Coppola. Louisa would have recognized her anywhere after what happened with Charles. She turned back to Hayward, suppressing nervous excitement over what was to come. "And I do not wish to embarrass my stepmother or sister."

"You do not have to worry about any of that." He said it so sincerely that she nearly believed him. His dark eyes bewitched her, but her stubbornness would not allow her to give in to him. She worried far too much about what people would say, or how his wife would feel, or even ending up with child. She certainly could not risk that. "I will protect you."

Louisa suppressed a shiver at Hayward's bold statement. No man could protect a woman from everything, not even someone so magnetic as Hayward. She looked down. "We should return to the others," she murmured.

When she looked back up, he nodded reluctantly. They returned to their group, where Miss Coppola still stood amongst them. Lady Ramsbury was quick to introduce the opera singer to Louisa and Hayward, her dark hair and olive skin the exact opposite of Louisa's. It was a sad reminder of what Charles preferred. Worst of all, Miss Coppola seemed to remember the incident in the library as well.

"Ah, yes, Miss Strickland," she said, baring straight white teeth. Even her teeth were perfect. Louisa tried not to sigh. "I seem to remember meeting before."

Everyone turned to Louisa, who tried not to flush at the sudden attention.

"You have met Miss Coppola before?" her stepmother asked.

"Yes," Louisa replied, looking from Mrs. Strickland back to the opera singer. "She sang at a ball we attended here seven years ago. Don't you remember?"

A look of recognition passed through her stepmother's eyes as she looked upon Miss Coppola once more. "Oh, I do recall!" Mrs. Strickland exclaimed with a smile.

The rest of the night was nothing but arduous small talk. Hayward always lingered close by wherever Louisa went, and in her peripheral, she saw Lady Ramsbury introduce Charles to woman after woman. Louisa felt her steely resolve toward Hayward start to waver, especially when Miss Coppola began her performance. The notes of her passionate aria filled the room, and all of the guests stood watching her, enraptured by her talent. Hayward stood at Louisa's side, listening intently as well, but she could only think of the scene she saw in the library all those years ago.

She doubted Miss Coppola ever said no to a man who wanted her, especially when she wanted him in return. Louisa glanced over at Hayward. Perhaps he might just kiss her so she would finally know how such a thing felt. Surely they could make some sort of bargain. After all, a single kiss from Louisa would probably make Hayward forget his plan to bed her. She was sure she couldn't be very good at it. And no one would ever have to find out.

With the rout still entranced by Miss Coppola's melodious voice, Louisa leaned over toward Hayward and discreetly whispered in his ear, "Do you know where the library is?"

Hayward turned to her, surprised. "I believe so," he replied with some uncertainty. She did not expect to change her mind so quickly either, but then again, she wasn't changing her mind. She was only asking for a single kiss.

Louisa nodded once, determined. "Meet me there."

And then she quietly slipped away.

Chapter Fourteen

WHEN THE NIGHT of Lady Ramsbury's ball finally arrived, Charles felt determined. Four out of the seven young ladies on Louisa's list had agreed to attend that evening with their chaperones, and Charles intended on making one of them his bride before the season was through. He would dance with each of them at least once and then bestow the offer of a second dance to the girl he preferred.

Charles felt quite confident in his plan until the Stricklands appeared in the ballroom, led by Rosamund. The cut and color of Louisa's gown drew his gaze immediately, as she wasn't wearing the typical virginal white that all the other single female guests did. Her frock was emerald green, the bodice embroidered with gold stitching. The cut of it was very daring and showed off her shapely bosom, much to his chagrin. When their eyes met, he forced himself to look away, only to see Hayward and Lord Fitzgerald walking toward the four women. Charles scowled.

"Lord Bolton?"

His head snapped back in the direction of the mother of the young woman his aunt had just introduced him to. He smiled sheepishly. "My apologies, ma'am. I have only just seen someone who shouldn't be here." The woman and her daughter's heads pivoted back and forth on their necks in a desperate search for whoever Charles meant. Meanwhile, Charles dipped his head to whisper in his aunt's ear. "What is Hayward doing here?"

Lady Ramsbury smiled, speaking through her teeth. "Lord Fitzgerald brought him. I couldn't very well turn him away."

"But it's *your* ball," Charles argued in a hushed tone. "And he's a hardly respectable man."

"He is more powerful than you presume. Most of the people here owe him money. You should know something about that. Besides, what does it matter to you?" She turned back to the woman and her daughter, who looked puzzled by the entire exchange. Lady Ramsbury smiled broadly and grabbed her nephew by his upper arm, squeezing tightly. He nearly winced. "Charles, why don't you dance the first set with Miss Campbell?"

Charles forced himself to smile at the unremarkable female in front of him. He knew beggars couldn't be choosers, but he had hoped at least one of the heiresses that night would be ravishing enough to make him forget about Louisa Strickland. Still, he'd vowed to dance with all the women at least once that evening. Miss Campbell would just have to be the first.

While they danced, he could think of nothing to say, too distracted by Louisa, who had partnered with Hayward for the same set. They seemed to have grown much more intimate since he last saw them together at the Talbot ball, just as the duke claimed. Perhaps there was some truth to what Hayward said about Louisa—maybe she did like his company.

The idea of Louisa falling for Hayward put Charles in terrible spirits for the rest of the evening. He could forgive her for Hardy if the rumors Rutley told him were true—his land steward was a clever, upstart sort of gentleman like his old friend Brooks—but he could not abide watching Hayward work his slimy charms on her. Charles had watched it too many times before, each affair ending with disastrous consequences for the lady but never for Hayward.

Charles fell into even more profound despair when his aunt carted out his former lover as that evening's entertainment. When he tried to ask the dowager duchess what she was thinking when she made that decision, she ignored him, so he was left alone to fend with the regrets that tormented him to that day. He still lamented the night Louisa found him with Miss Coppola in this very same house. Charles had done many stupid things in his youth, but he hadn't intended to act in such a way that she felt the need to sever their friendship. Honestly, Charles had believed it wouldn't bother her, as she never was interested in him that way.

Or was she?

The intrusive thought made his eyebrows shoot up. Perhaps there was something more there, something he hadn't noticed at the time of their faux courtship. His eyes searched the ballroom for Louisa as Miss Coppola performed at the front of the room. When he finally found her, she was standing next to Hayward. Charles grimaced.

He would have to approach her later and ask for a private word. But then he saw Louisa dip her head in Hayward's direction. A pang of jealousy hit Charles when Hayward turned and looked at her. Their faces were mere inches apart. Louisa said something to him, then turned away, leaving the ballroom.

Hayward soon followed her. From the other side of the room, Charles's stomach dropped, and for a brief moment, he felt paralyzed by indecision. He had no business interfering in Louisa's life. If she wanted to embark upon an affair with

Hayward, that was her prerogative. But really, someone ought to be looking out for her.

Charles decided he would approach it as if he were her older brother. It wasn't that Charles was jealous or anything. He was only looking out for her.

He quickly followed Hayward out of the ballroom. Upon turning the corner into the hall, he saw Hayward in the distance, opening the door to his aunt's library. Charles looked around to find no one else nearby; everyone was still gathered in the other room listening to Miss Coppola sing. Charles himself could still hear the faint notes of the aria she was performing as he wandered down the deserted hall.

Charles stopped for a moment at the door of the library, debating once again if he should enter. But seeing as how Louisa had interrupted one of his trysts all those years ago, it made perfect sense that he do the same to her. It was only fair, after all.

So he swung open the door, hearing Louisa's yelp before he saw them. They stood together in front of the fireplace, still a few feet apart. Charles guessed that nothing had happened—not yet, anyway. Louisa backed even further away from Hayward as he spun around to face Charles. Hayward's gaze darkened when he saw who interrupted them.

"Lord Bolton!" Louisa exclaimed, bobbing a quick curtsey, though she did not look him in the eye. Charles guessed her face had turned scarlet. He tried to look as surprised to see them there as they did him.

"Miss Strickland! Mr. Hayward!" Charles looked back and forth between them, then furrowed his brow. "What are you doing in my aunt's private library? I am sure she does not want guests in this part of the house, especially with Miss Coppola performing in the ballroom at the moment. You should be listening to her sing."

Louisa was immediately contrite. "I apologize, Lord Bolton—"

But Hayward held up his hand, effectively silencing her, then focused his attention on Charles, who shifted his weight awkwardly from foot to foot. "Did you follow us here, Bolton?" Hayward asked.

Charles pointed to himself, feigning surprise. "Did *I* follow you?" The earl shook his head. "Of course not, Hayward." He looked around the room, trying to find something he might want. He gestured abruptly toward the sideboard, where his aunt always kept her best brandy. "My aunt asked me to fetch her a drink. She has some of the finest liquor in the world hidden in this room."

Hayward did not look so convinced, but Charles remained firm in his stance. He was an earl, for Christ's sake. If Charles wanted the man to leave his aunt's library, he could very well demand it. The earl's face grew serious. "Why don't you return to the party, Mr. Hayward? I would like a word alone with Miss Strickland."

"But, my lord—"

"Now, Hayward." The two men stood staring at each other for a long moment before Hayward finally relented.

"Very well," he said, taking one quick look at Louisa over his shoulder before sulkily leaving the room. After Charles watched him go and the library door shut behind him, he turned back to Louisa in front of the fire. She now looked directly at him, wearing that typical defiant look of hers. Something about it made him smile, which Louisa did not take kindly to.

"What do you want, Charles?" she asked.

"Ah," he said, smiling slightly. "Not bothering with formalities now, are we?"

She glared at him, clenching her fists at her side. "Out with it, *Lord Bolton*."

Charles placed his hands on his hips, looking her up and down. She was rather delectable when she was angry. "I only want to know why you're sneaking off to the library during a ball with that sorry excuse for a man—"

"So you *did* follow us," Louisa exclaimed, shaking her finger at him. "Why do you care what I do with Mr. Hayward? You are not my father or my brother."

Charles was thankful he wasn't either of those things. He hesitated for a moment, then dropped his hands at his side. "Yes, well, that might be true, but I *am* your friend, and—"

"You are not my friend!"

"—someone needs to look out for you! Someone needs to *protect* you from doing something truly foolish, or who will? Have you no care for your reputation?"

Louisa's nostrils flared. Charles noticed that her hands had balled up into tiny fists at her side again, and for a moment, he worried she might punch him clear across the face. If he ended up in fisticuffs with any woman, it would be Louisa Strickland. He'd already felt the sting of those hands twice.

"My reputation as a shrewd old spinster?" she asked.

He looked up from her fists and found that her eyes were beginning to water. Charles frowned. "No one thinks of you that way."

Louisa laughed once, shaking her head. "I try to have *some* fun while forced to be in town with all these terrible people, but *you* are there to stop me—of course!"

Charles sighed. "Whatever Hayward might have told you, he is not someone you want to have *fun* with, Louisa." He looked down and pinched the bridge of his nose, feeling the beginnings of a headache. He shook his head. When Charles looked back at her, he spoke as calmly and convincingly as possible. "Philip Hayward is the worst sort of scoundrel. He has a new lover every season, all the while sequestering his wife at their country estate so she can do nothing about his bad behavior!"

His voice rose with every word. Meanwhile, Louisa's face fell. Charles sighed again, stepping closer to her so that he was in front of the fire as well. "But that's not what he told you, is it?" he asked.

Louisa spun around, turning toward the fire. Her body began to tremble, and then he heard a soft sob. His shoulders drooped. "Louisa—"

"Why must you ruin everything?" she asked, turning back to look at him, her bright blue eyes rimmed with tears. Then, she looked around the library, gesturing to her surroundings. "And why must it always happen *here*?"

Charles stiffened.

Eventually, Louisa's sad look turned into a glare. "Why is it that men can partake in whatever pleasureful act they desire without shame, while women such as I must always must consider their reputation?"

Charles tilted his head to the side, thinking carefully. "There is always marriage."

Louisa let out an unladylike snort. "Marriage? *Marriage?* No pleasure in the world could ever convince me to marry and give up my independence. Besides, most husbands and wives grow to hate each other, especially when the husbands most always turn out to be treacherous rats. Take, for instance, our very own Mr. Hayward. That lying weasel!"

"Louisa," Charles said, reaching for her. But she didn't seem to see or hear him; she was too enraged. He stepped close enough to put his hands on her shoulders, steadying her. Louisa slowly looked at each of his hands, then at his face. Her mouth opened slightly, and her gaze lowered, falling on his lips. He smiled. "What if I could convince you?"

She backed away quickly, and his hands dropped to his sides. "W-what?" she asked.

He stepped toward her, and she stepped back until she couldn't anymore. He had backed her into a bookcase, and he was sure he was staring at her like the hungriest man alive. For so long, Charles had been alone. He couldn't even remember the last time he'd kissed a woman, but it had been a while. His eyes flickered toward her lips.

"Think about it," he said, his voice low. Charles raised one arm over her, gripping one of the shelves so that he boxed one side of her in. "Our two estates combined would become the largest in all of Kent—even larger than Rutley's." He paused a moment, and she carefully watched him. Charles lowered his head even further, so his lips were right beside her ear. "And I think I could teach you a thing or two about pleasure."

She shoved him away, escaping across the room. He grimaced, remembering why he'd never tried to seduce Louisa before. She hated him. But at one point, she hadn't, or at least that was what he was attempting to tell himself as he tried to woo her. He spun around. "We were good friends at one point, Louisa. We would make a good match."

Louisa blinked. "Are you mad? Or only desperate? We haven't been friends in a long time; we are completely different people now. Besides, you have never been interested in me this way."

Charles furrowed his brow. "Why do you say that?"

Louisa looked at him as if he was stupid. "You never tried anything when you were pretending to court me, not to mention you kept a mistress while doing so. If you were attracted to me—"

But Charles held up a finger. "You gave me explicit instructions that our courtship was to be in name only. I never tried anything out of *respect* for you, but if I had known—"

"Respect! Respect!" Louisa huffed. "Like the respect that

you are showing me right now?" She gestured toward the bookshelves behind him. "You just had me pinned to a bookshelf in the same room I once caught you making love to another woman in!"

"Louisa..." He looked down, hesitating. How could he even begin to apologize? All of his excuses felt hollow. Nevertheless, he had to try. Charles looked back up at her, capturing her gaze with his.

"I am sorry," he said finally, taking a few slow steps toward her. To his surprise, she did not move, only stared at him with wide eyes. "I do not know what I was thinking. Well, I do know somewhat what I was thinking, but I am not sure you would appreciate any of those excuses spoken aloud."

Louisa made a face. He continued before she had a chance to interject. "All I know is that suddenly, I have realized I would like to spend the rest of my life making it up to you. Because I have seen what else is out there, but my mind and my eyes keep coming back to you. It is you I search for at parties and balls, not anyone else. It is you I think about when I'm home alone at Finch Place with no one to keep me company. And truthfully, that has *nothing* to do with how much property you own, though I won't lie, it does sweeten the deal and will make my life a whole hell of a lot easier." She scowled at him. Perhaps he should have left that part out. "But mostly—and I swear this to you—it has to do with *you*."

He tried to think of more he could say, but his mind went blank, standing so close to her in the quiet library. Her scowl began to soften, and at that point, Charles could only try to show her what he meant. He closed the distance between them in three meaningful strides and took her up in his arms, kissing Louisa Strickland full on the mouth. His hand cupped her cheek, and she raised her arm. For a moment, he suspected she might slap him—and perhaps that was what he deserved. But instead, she gently placed her hand over his, molding her body toward his. He wrapped his free arm around her waist, pulling her closer to him.

Who would have thought Louisa Strickland's body would have felt so glorious against his? But for a brief moment, the world felt utterly brilliant. One kiss, and Louisa had him hooked. Did she even know? Would she ever understand?

Unfortunately, it could not last forever. Charles heard the library door swing open, and they pulled away from each other. His heart pounded as they turned at the same time to see who had found them.

"Charles?"

Chapter Fifteen

IF there ever was a moment Louisa wished to disappear, this was it. Charles Finch, the Earl of Bolton, had kissed her—and she had let him. She hadn't tried to slap him, or push him away, even though she probably should have. After all, she had no intention of agreeing to his marriage proposal. But before she could tell him that, Miss Coppola and Lord Fitzgerald had burst into the dimly lit library and caught them. Never had a night gone so wrong!

In her lust-induced haze, Louisa had invited Hayward to follow her to the library. She had been in the middle of offering him a single kiss when Charles interrupted them. It was a surprise that he followed them there, let alone noticed they even left the ballroom at all. It was even *more* of a surprise when he proposed marriage to her.

And that kiss. That *kiss*! It was everything she had hoped and dreamed her first kiss would be and more. Immediately, she forgot all about Hayward, and all she could recall were fond memories of Charles Finch and his pretend courtship of her all those seasons ago.

But she hated him! And he certainly didn't think of her

that way. She discreetly peered over at him beside her, looking for some sort of sign that he'd kissed her only to find out she truly did disgust him. They were standing far apart, and he had his brow furrowed, but he was probably only trying to discern why Miss Coppola and Fitzgerald were there, together, in the library with them. He mustn't have known they were lovers. Why would he?

Louisa winced. That had been her and Rosamund's plan all along. Rosamund had offered her aunt's private library as a place for Miss Coppola to relax before and after her performance. Rosamund suspected that at some point, after properly diverting Flora, Miss Coppola would ask Fitzgerald to join her there alone. After which, Rosamund would lead Flora to the library under some pretense, where they would discover her suitor in the arms of another woman.

But Louisa had ruined it all—not to mention there wasn't much good that could come from them standing around, gawking at each other. Louisa grew serious. "We should leave," she said, starting for the door. But Fitzgerald held out his arm, blocking her.

"Wait a moment," he said in a menacing tone, and Louisa nervously edged away from him until she backed into Charles. She nearly stumbled, but Charles gently grabbed her by the waist with both hands, steadying her. Seeing Fitzgerald's suspicious look, she slapped one of the earl's hands away, then stepped a good three feet away from him.

Meanwhile, Fitzgerald pointed from her to Charles, then back again. "Does Hayward know about this?" he asked.

"Know about what?" Louisa was the picture of innocence, speaking as if the viscount and the opera singer hadn't just caught Charles kissing her. She didn't dare look at Lord Bolton's face. Knowing him, he was probably holding back laughter. She was ruined! Not unless she married Charles, much to his advantage. This was probably his plan all along.

But then she remembered the viscount's financial problems and the fact that Miss Coppola was there as well. Louisa smiled sweetly, suddenly realizing her advantage. "My lord. I apologize, but"—she pointed from him to Miss Coppola, then back again, just as the viscount had done to her—"does my sister know about *this?*"

Fitzgerald's face blanched as he straightened his back. "It would appear we both know the other's secrets."

Louisa clasped her hands in front of her. She held her chin high so as not to appear intimidated. "So it would seem."

The room fell silent. Louisa didn't want the viscount telling the whole of London society that he'd caught her in a compromising position with Charles. Still, she was sure the viscount didn't wish for Louisa to tell Flora that she saw him sneaking away with Miss Coppola, either. The opera singer stepped out from behind Fitzgerald, crossing her arms and grinning at Charles.

"I always thought you cared for Miss Strickland more than you ever dared to admit," she said with a slight shake of the head, her melodious voice sounding coy as she spoke. "I see I was right."

Before the earl could respond, the library door swung open once more, and in entered Rosamund and Flora. The latter's eyes went wide when she saw the viscount standing there with Miss Coppola. At the same time, Rosamund's brow knitted together in apparent confusion over Louisa and her brother being there as well.

"Lord Fitzgerald," Flora said, looking back and forth between her favorite suitor and the opera singer who'd just performed for the entire ballroom. "What are you doing here?"

"I was only pouring him a glass of my aunt's best brandy," Charles said without missing a beat, taking long strides over to the sideboard on the other side of the room. For once,

Louisa was thankful for Charles and his quick thinking. With his back turned to them, he began pouring a glass of the amber liquid for the viscount.

But Flora was still suspicious. She looked at Louisa. "But why are you here?" She turned to Miss Coppola. "And *you?*"

The opera singer shrugged. "We were talking with the gentlemen when Charles began boasting about his aunt's collection of cognac. We decided to join them for their drink." Miss Coppola looked over her shoulder. "Won't you pour me a glass as well, my lord?"

"But the earl no longer drinks," Flora protested.

Louisa could tell her little sister didn't quite believe their excuses. It would have been perfect if Louisa only wanted Fitzgerald to lose favor with her sister, but now she had a secret of her own to protect as well. Louisa glanced at Charles, who spun around, a glass of brandy in each hand.

"Miss Flora is correct," Charles said, handing one glass to the viscount and another to Miss Coppola. Louisa would have liked one herself, but it would have been unladylike to ask for one—not that her reasons for being in the library were ladylike in the first place. "But that's no reason for my aunt's guests not to enjoy good cognac."

When he finished handing out the drinks, Charles returned to Louisa's side. Her back involuntarily straightened when he came closer to her. His nearness only reminded her of what it felt like to have his hands and lips on her, and she didn't wish to give anything away, especially not to her sister. Not yet, anyway. From the way Flora was looking at her, Louisa knew it was only a matter of time before she discovered the truth.

After finishing his drink in two mere gulps, the viscount smiled and handed his glass back to Charles. "Delicious, my lord."

"Isn't it?" Charles said. His smile appeared forced as he took the empty glass back.

Fitzgerald turned back to Flora, offering her his arm. "Shall we return to the party, my dear? I believe you owe me at least one more set this evening."

For the first time, Flora looked at the viscount and his arm with trepidation. She gave Louisa and Charles the same look, and Louisa felt her heart squeeze. The last thing she wanted was to be doomed to a lifetime with Charles, even if kissing him was the most delightful thing she had ever experienced.

"Very well," Flora finally said, letting Fitzgerald escort her out of the room. With an impatient wave of her hand, Rosamund gestured to her brother and Louisa.

"Come, Charles, Miss Strickland. Let us give Miss Coppola her privacy. My aunt and I did offer her the library as a private retreat for the evening."

Louisa inwardly cursed, heading toward the exit of the library. She knew she had ruined their plan by inviting Hayward there and then lingering with Charles for far too long afterward. When they were all safely out in the hall with the library door firmly closed behind them, Rosamund and her brother spoke simultaneously.

"Miss Strickland—"

"Louisa—"

Rosamund arched her brow at Charles's usage of Louisa's Christian name. Even Louisa winced. They couldn't be any more obvious if they tried! Louisa looked up at the earl, speaking as firmly as she could. "Please, my lord. Allow me a moment alone with your sister." When Charles did not budge, she tried to sound more menacing, speaking through gritted teeth. "I will come and find you later."

Reluctantly, Charles nodded and walked away, leaving the two women alone. Louisa loudly exhaled as Rosamund linked their arms. As they slowly walked down the hall back toward the ballroom, Rosamund turned and looked at Louisa. "None of that was part of the plan," Rosamund muttered, though she said it as if she found the situation funny. Louisa shot her a glum look in response. "Do you truly plan on going and finding him later? What happened?"

"Nothing happened," Louisa said. Rosamund shot her a look of disbelief. "And I plan on avoiding your brother, the same as I always have."

And until she could forget those lips of his, Louisa knew she *must* avoid the earl, lest something genuinely awful happen, such as her ending up married to him.

CHARLES DID NOT SEE Louisa for the rest of the night. He paced the ballroom looking for her, ignoring the ladies his aunt had gathered there for him. He had more than an inkling now that none of them could ever compare to Louisa, so why should he even bother?

She was everything he wanted, wrapped in the prettiest package with the softest lips. He was a damned fool for taking so long to kiss her; Charles knew now he should have done it ages ago. He would have liked to drag her back into that library again and do much more than kissing, but the woman was nowhere to be found.

He had so much to tell her. Certain plans that needed to be established. They could build a life together, him and Louisa. And although he had come to this conclusion quite suddenly, he had never been so sure of anything in his life.

When the rout was over and guests began to vacate the premises, Charles desperately searched for her, but the only person he found was his sister, standing by his aunt's massive front door and bidding good evening to some guests. He waited for her to notice him by the staircase.

When she did, Rosamund slinked over to him, a knowing smile on her face.

"Have you seen Miss Strickland?" Charles asked after a moment of hesitation. He didn't want his sister causing a fuss, but there wasn't much hope of that judging by her coy smile.

"The Stricklands left a while ago," she drawled, pulling her delicately embroidered silk fan from her reticule and wafting it in front of her face. "What *were* you doing in that library, Charles?"

Charles turned and looked at her, realizing that Louisa hadn't confessed anything to her. "I was preventing Miss Strickland from committing a horrible mistake... amongst other things." His sister momentarily stopped fanning herself, and he tilted his head to the side. "Rosamund, did you mean it when you said you would try and change Miss Strickland's opinion of me?"

Rosamund sighed. "I did, but it's not going as well as I hoped. Even after your *mysterious* meeting in the library, she said she hoped to avoid you."

The earl's lips curled downward. Indeed, that kiss should have made her realize that there was something special between them. Charles barely heard what his sister said next, what with his mind suddenly fixated on the memory. "Your past behavior does make you rather unlovable, though the other young ladies you danced with tonight didn't seem to mind your notorious reputation. Who was the lucky girl you chose to partner with twice?"

Charles didn't answer for a long while, still thinking of Louisa. His sister elbowed him in the rib cage. "Charles?"

He looked down at her. "Hm?" He shook his head once. "There was no lucky girl. I didn't dance twice with any of them."

"Charles!" Rosamund exclaimed, snapping her fan shut and whacking him with it.

"Ow!" He flinched, rubbing his shoulder.

"Have you no care for Linfield anymore? What happened to no longer wanting to be under Rutley's thumb? Or have you developed some new evil plan to auction me off to the highest bidder so that you may finally repay him that way?"

Charles scoffed, crossing his arms against his chest. "Of course not! I have chosen an heiress, just none of the ones from the list." He paused a moment, then shot her a devious smile. Rosamund took a deep breath.

"Oh no... Do not say it."

"I have chosen Louisa Strickland."

"Charles!" Rosamund exclaimed again, viciously swatting him with her fan again. He yelped even louder this time. "What happened in that library?"

"I cannot tell you." Rosamund swatted him a third time. He groaned. "Will you stop doing that?"

"Not until you tell me what happened."

Charles sighed.

"Come on, now. Out with it."

He shot his sister a sheepish grin. "Can you keep a secret?"

AFTER HER MAID helped Louisa get ready for bed, she sat at her dressing table, staring at her reflection in the small mirror on top of it. She lifted her fingertips to her lips, gingerly touching them. So many hours had passed, yet she could still feel the earl's lips on hers.

A light rapping at the door startled her, causing her to jump. She dropped her hands, gripping the edge of the dressing table. She hoped the piece of furniture might provide her some stability. "Who is it?" Louisa asked.

"It is Flora. May I come in?"

Sighing, Louisa stood up, walking toward the door in her

shift and floral-patterned wrapper. Louisa's maid had plaited her red hair so that it hung down the side of her neck, and she wore a white lace nightcap on her head. Louisa opened the door, revealing her sister on the other side, similarly dressed.

"What is it?" Louisa asked.

Flora scooted around her and dashed across the room, jumping and landing on Louisa's bed with a loud thump. Giggling, she turned over to face her sister, who still stood with her hand on the open door. Flora patted the empty bed beside her. "Come sit with me," she said.

"All right, but we cannot stay up much later," Louisa warned before she turned and shut the door. "If your mother hears us, she will scold me in the morning."

Flora sighed. "Why must you always call her *my* mother? Don't you think she is as much our mama as she is *my* mama?"

Louisa sat down beside her. "No, I don't." Flora frowned, but as if reading her sister's mind, Louisa shook her head, continuing. "It's not that I do not *like* Mrs. Strickland. I like her very much. She made my father happy, and she has always treated me with respect, regardless of my decision to remain unmarried. But I was seven when my mother died. *She* is who I remember as my mama."

Flora frowned. "Do you ever wish you could talk to her?" she asked.

Louisa lifted her knees to her chest, resting her chin in the crevice they made. "Sometimes."

All the time, if she was being honest.

Flora shot Louisa a sly look. "Perhaps you might wish to speak to her now so that you could reveal some sort of secret to her, something that might have happened in a library this evening with a certain earl..."

Flora's voice trailed off, and Louisa snapped her head in her sister's direction. Louisa lips formed a thin straight line.

She was already growing annoyed. "What exactly is this about, Flora?"

Her sister narrowed her eyes. "What exactly were you doing in the library this evening with Lord Bolton?"

"He told you!" Louisa waved her hand as if the answer was simple, though her voice was much more shrill than necessary. "He was showing off his aunt's expensive brandy."

Flora sighed. "Do you genuinely believe I am that stupid, Louisa?"

"Sometimes," Louisa muttered.

Flora glared at her. "You know, I am more intelligent than you think. I saw Lord Fitzgerald and Miss Coppola leave the ballroom. Rosamund told me what she suspected, so we followed them. The only surprise was finding you and Lord Bolton there with them."

Louisa flattened her legs and dangled her feet over the edge of the bed. She looked down at her lap, fiddling with the hem of her wrapper. "If... if you must know, Lord Bolton offered marriage to me."

Flora gasped loudly, clapping her hand over her mouth.

"And then he kissed me."

Flora nearly screamed, though her hand muffled her sounds of excitement. Still, Louisa hushed her, afraid Mrs. Strickland might hear them. When Flora dropped her hand, her eyes were wide with excitement. "But what about Hayward?" Flora asked.

Louisa made a look of disgust. "What *about* Hayward? He is *married*, Flora, and apparently he takes a new lover every season. I was meant to be next, but I refuse. And you wonder why I think you are stupid."

Flora shrugged. "Sometimes love must overcome all sorts of odds."

Louisa shook her head. She always knew her sister was a hopeless romantic, but this was too much. "My dear Flora, some odds are just too unsurmountable. Besides, Charles told me the most horrid things about him."

Louisa hadn't seen Charles for the rest of the evening after the incident in the library. She had only managed to avoid him and Hayward for the rest of the ball by hiding in Rosamund's private sitting room upstairs. She had no desire to see either of them, especially Hayward. When her step-mother and sister were ready to leave, Rosamund somehow managed to sneak her downstairs and out the door without much notice.

"Oh." Flora raised her brow and nodded slightly. She crossed her arms against her chest. It was a very skeptical look. "*Charles* did. I wonder why he would do that."

Louisa glared at her. "I'm sure he is telling the truth. I have always been skeptical of Hayward myself. He is married, after all. I'm glad Lord Bolton confirmed my suspicions."

Flora shook her head. "Well, forget about him. Did Lord Bolton truly offer marriage to you?"

"He... he said he would convince me that I wanted marriage. And he said we both have something the other wants. And he said we would make a good match." Louisa paused a moment, chewing her lower lip.

Her sister stared at her, clearly eager for more information. "And?" Flora asked, her voice impatient.

"And that was when he kissed me," Louisa admitted, turning away as her cheeks turned pink. Her sister squealed with glee once more. Louisa clapped a hand over her mouth, hushing her again. When Louisa released her sister, Flora was still grinning wildly.

"What was it like?"

Magnificent.

Louisa shrugged. "It was fine."

Her sister's shoulders drooped. "You don't mean that. You were head over heels in love with the man at one time!" Eyes wide, Louisa turned and looked at her sister. "He is why you rejected Cousin William and have spent the past seven years moping around Strickland Manor by yourself!"

"Firstly, I was not head over heels in love with Lord Bolton."

Flora snorted as a way of showing her skepticism. Louisa glared at her but continued. "Secondly, I rejected Cousin William because I had no desire to marry him, regardless of Lord Bolton. And thirdly, I have not spent the past seven years moping, and I was hardly alone. You and Mrs. Strickland were there to irritate me every step of the way."

Still, Flora did not look convinced. Louisa sighed. "There is something I must tell you to make it all make sense, but you must swear not to tell Mrs. Strickland. I fear she'll be furious with me if she learns the truth."

Flora inched closer to her sister on the bed. "What is it? I swear I won't tell."

"The courtship between me and Charles was a ruse. I hoped his attentions would deter other gentlemen from trying to pursue me. You see, I had no interest in marriage, and I feared Mrs. Strickland might force me into something if the right opportunity came along. I knew Charles would never propose, which was why I asked him to help me. I have only pretended to be disappointed all these years."

Her sister appeared taken back. "No interest in marriage? *Pretended?* But I don't understand. You have never wanted to fall in love and marry?"

"I'm afraid that is not how marriage usually works."

But Flora wouldn't listen. "What about now? You said he kissed you. You must have felt *something.*"

Louisa couldn't exactly say no, but oh, how she wanted to. Kissing Charles had been a terrible mistake. She could not marry him. Marrying him would mean entrusting Strickland Manor to him. Marrying him would come with so much debt and a morose duke constantly looming over her and her husband. Besides, Louisa had no desire to become a countess, so attaching herself to the earl couldn't possibly benefit her. Why should she sign her life away to him?

Pleasure.

The evasive thought—a single word—wracked her mind. But Louisa couldn't very well tell Flora that. "I didn't feel a thing," Louisa said with a noncommittal shrug. Before Flora could say anything else about Charles, Louisa quickly changed the subject. "But never mind me. We haven't spoken yet of you. The viscount has a lover. How does that make you feel?"

Flora sighed, falling backward onto the bed. "Terrible," she admitted in a sad voice. "I do not want to share him with anyone." Flora sat back up, her eyes becoming less pained and more determined. "Once he officially proposes, though, I will make my terms known."

Louisa's eyes widened. "Flora! You can't possibly still hope that he proposes after what you discovered tonight. That man does not deserve you."

"But he met her before he ever met me. How can I be angry?"

Louisa shook her head, unable to believe what she was hearing. "Flora, if a man truly wanted you, he would not be able to touch another woman after meeting you."

"Is that why you won't give Lord Bolton a chance? Did he realize he loved you too late?"

Louisa's heart dropped. She shook her head and forced herself to smile at her sister. "Don't be silly. Lord Bolton doesn't love me. He only sees me as a way out of his problems."

"But—"

"It's time for you to go back to your room, Flora," Louisa interrupted, shooing her sister off her bed. Flora reluctantly stood up. "Your mother has most certainly heard us by now, and now I will have to face her wrath in the morning."

Flora rolled her eyes. "I am sure no such nonsense will occur. But very well, I will leave. Good night, Louisa."

As she started walking toward the door, Louisa called out for her. Flora stopped, turning to face her sister. Louisa swallowed. "You mustn't tell anyone about what Charles said or that we kissed—especially not your mother."

Flora smiled. "Your secret is safe with me."

Chapter Sixteen

"SOMETHING WONDERFUL HAPPENED LAST NIGHT."

The Duke of Rutley lowered his newspaper, shooting a blank stare at Charles. He was standing in the duke's morning room, where Rutley was taking his breakfast. It was so early that the duke's mother had yet to come down, but Charles couldn't wait to see his friend and had called as early as possible that morning after a restless night.

"Oh?" the duke asked.

Charles nodded eagerly.

Rutley folded his newspaper, placing it beside his place at the table. "Then the ball was a success?"

It was *more* than a success, Charles wanted to say. She may have called him mad and desperate, but Charles now saw Louisa Strickland in a new light. She was more than just his awkward neighbor. Louisa was a fiery temptress, with lips he wanted to kiss again and again. Now all he had to do was make her his wife, and he would have the extra income to pay off his debt to Rutley in record time. Charles would finally solve his problems.

And he would have the most delectable wife in his bed at Linfield Hall.

"It was more than a success," Charles told Rutley. The earl was practically buzzing with excitement, unable to stand still. "I have chosen a wife."

For a brief moment, the duke appeared pleased. "Is that so? Who is the lucky lady?"

Charles grinned. "Louisa Strickland."

Rutley's face fell. "Have you lost your mind? I have heard you call that woman a cantankerous shrew on more than one occasion, and I believe she feels no more fondly for you in return. And now you intend to marry her? Have you said anything to her about this?"

Charles felt his face become warm. Rutley always did a splendid job of making him feel like a complete and utter dullard. Refusing to let the duke cow him this time, Charles squared his shoulders and spoke firmly. "I may have mentioned something about it before kissing her last evening in my aunt's library."

The duke stirred in his seat, surprised. "Then she's accepted you?"

Charles grimaced. "Not quite."

Rutley's budding excitement died instantly. Charles was quick to defend himself.

"But I can tell when a woman enjoys a kiss!"

"A pleasant kiss seems hardly enough to tempt Louisa Strickland into marriage." The duke turned away, clearly irritated. Charles's heart sank, refusing to believe it was impossible to convince Louisa that marriage to him wouldn't be so bad. Rutley turned back and furrowed his brow. "And why should it? She is a woman of independent means." The duke leaned back in his chair, crossing his arms against his chest and shaking his head. "She will never marry you. You must choose someone else."

Charles blinked. The duke said nothing more, only uncrossed his arms and picked up his paper once more. A growing resentment brewed inside Charles. "Give me a month to court her properly. If she does not agree to marry me within a month, I will move on to someone else."

"The season will almost be over in a month." Rutley did not look up from his newspaper when he spoke. "Any lady worth having will have a fiancé by then. You must choose someone else now."

"*Please*, Robert."

The duke finally looked over at him. Charles thought he must have appeared highly pathetic, like a dog begging for scraps. He never called the duke by his Christian name. Rutley sighed and lowered his paper.

"Fine. One month, but not a day more!" The duke wagged one of his fingers for emphasis, and Charles happily nodded in agreement. Truthfully, he hoped it would take much less than a month to convince Louisa Strickland to marry him. "When will you see her next?"

"I am hosting another dinner party at Finch Place next week. I plan on inviting the Stricklands and reaffirming my desires to Louisa."

Rutley looked unimpressed. "Is that all?"

Charles frowned. "For now. I'm sure I'll think of other things as well, and I do plan on calling on her in the meantime, but—"

"When should my mother and I expect our invitations to dinner?" Rutley asked, cutting Charles off. The earl froze for a moment. He should have mentioned Rosamund was helping him host the dinner party. Having the duke there would be a terrible idea. Rutley mistook his friend's silence for not understanding the question. "Charles?"

The earl shook his head. "Rosamund is helping me host the party. I will have to ask her."

Rutley narrowed his eyes. "When you do, make sure you tell her that your success with Miss Strickland is of the utmost importance to me, so it is important that I attend in order to supervise the proceedings." He paused for a moment. Charles blinked at him, waiting for him to say something and trying not to be too offended in the meantime. "And tell your sister I am more than fine without her now. I can certainly sit through one dinner party and behave."

The duke paused again, and Charles nodded his head in agreement with Rutley's statement. He then quickly added, "Mother's been taking me around at parties and introducing me to all sorts of young ladies. You might not be the only one who becomes engaged by the end of the season."

Charles did his best not to laugh in disbelief. It was always best not to do such things to dukes, especially dukes scorned by love.

THERE WAS no sign of Lord Fitzgerald the day after Lady Ramsbury's ball, nor the day after that. Flora was beginning to grow worried, and Louisa could not decide if she should rejoice over his absence or begin to worry as well. After all, the viscount knew something very private about her. He could have been telling anyone what he saw occur between her and Charles, not to mention Fitzgerald was friends with Hayward, who had written her a note she decided not to open. She safely tucked it beneath her mattress instead.

All was quiet—including the broadsheets, thank goodness—until Flora received a missive from the man in question. As soon as the servant handed it to her, Flora took the note and hastily tore it open. Mrs. Strickland and Louisa sat across from her in their small drawing room, each working on separate embroidery pieces. They exchanged a glance as Flora's eyes scanned the letter. When she looked up, her round brown eyes were wet with unshed tears.

"It's from the viscount. He's returned to his estate in Cumbria to take care of some business. He's not sure if he'll be back in town before the end of the season."

Flora's lower lip began to quiver with the last statement, and when she finished speaking, she threw the letter down beside her and dropped her face into her hands. Mrs. Strickland and Louisa quickly stood, moving to sit at either side of Flora. Her shoulders shook with each full-bodied sob. Mrs. Strickland rubbed her back while Louisa reached for one of her sister's hands.

"There, there, my dear," Mrs. Strickland said kindly. Louisa remained silent. She was much too relieved to provide her crying sister any comfort other than to hold her hand. "Perhaps it's for the best. You have spent so much time fixated on Lord Fitzgerald. Maybe you should consider another young gentleman for the time being? There's still so much of the season left."

Flora squeezed her sister's hand so hard that Louisa nearly yelped. Flora stopped crying long enough to turn to her mother and practically shout, "I do not *want* to consider any other gentlemen!"

Flora abruptly stood, freeing herself from what her family hoped would be a comforting embrace, and ran out of the room. Louisa looked after her for a moment, then turned to her stepmother, biting her lip. "What shall we do?" Louisa asked.

Mrs. Strickland sighed, stood up, and returned to her chair where her embroidery awaited her. She took up her thread and needle once more. "There is nothing we *can* do. Give her time. She will forget the viscount eventually and move on to some other lordling." Mrs. Strickland's eyes flicked upward. "Hopefully you will like the next one better than Fitzgerald."

Louisa flushed. "I wonder what took him back to Cumbria so suddenly. As I have told you both before, his father left Fitzgerald an estate in disarray. Perhaps we should be giving thanks that he's returned there without much explanation."

Mrs. Strickland did not reply at first, seemingly focused on her embroidery. Louisa eventually stood up and returned to her project as well. When her stepmother finally spoke, it wasn't about Flora. "I saw you and Hayward disappear while Miss Coppola was performing at Lady Ramsbury's ball."

Louisa froze, her needle and thread suspended in the air by her thumb and forefinger.

"Is there anything you would like to tell me?"

Think, Louisa, think. Louisa resumed her embroidery but didn't dare look at Mrs. Strickland. "Mr. Hayward heard Lady Ramsbury had an impressive collection of first editions in her library. I agreed to show him." Louisa nearly winced at her unconvincing lie.

"Is that so?" her stepmother asked. "Does Lady Ramsbury often let you use her library when you call on her at Park Street?"

"All the time," Louisa insisted, perhaps too excitedly. She stood up suddenly, still holding her embroidery hoop and the fine cloth it framed. "Now that you mention it, I think I'll call on Lady Ramsbury and Lady Rosamund today. Perhaps they might have some gossip about what took the viscount from town so suddenly."

Louisa began to leave, but Mrs. Strickland called after her. Louisa froze in the doorway, turning over her shoulder to find the woman still embroidering. She hadn't even bothered looking up.

"Do be careful, my dear."

· · ·

ROSAMUND STOOD in her aunt's massive drawing room, loudly guffawing, sounding more like a sailor than the daughter of an earl. "His mother's come to town? I have done a number on the poor man, haven't I?"

If she had, Rosamund didn't appear to regret it. Charles forced a smile, not wanting to comment on the state of the duke's happiness. "May we please invite him and the dowager? He is the reason I am in search of a wife in the first place. He should like to be involved in my wooing of Miss Strickland."

Rosamund sighed, moving to sit down in front of the fireplace. "Very well. If he promises to behave, we can invite him and his mother to dinner." Rosamund held up one finger and wagged it. "That goes for his mother as well. I will not have her complaining about me calling off our nuptials all evening long in my family's own house."

"I will make sure to share that message with the dowager duchess right away."

His sister didn't miss her brother's pointed sarcasm and glared at him.

Charles gave her an exasperated look in return. "Rosie, you must learn to deal with the consequences of your actions. Rutley may not be your fiancé any longer, but he is still our neighbor, not to mention my friend as well."

Rosamund's glare only deepened when he used his childhood nickname for her. He hadn't called her Rosie in a long while. He first started saying it as a little boy when he couldn't quite pronounce Rosamund. But then his sister saw someone over his shoulder, and she smiled brightly, rising to her feet.

"Miss Strickland!" she exclaimed.

"Oh no," he thought he heard Louisa mutter under her breath. He smiled to himself, then turned to see her standing near the entrance of the drawing room. She looked horrified to see him there.

"Miss Strickland," Charles said, trying not to let her expression deter him.

His sister looped her arm underneath Louisa's, bringing her toward him. Rosamund blinked at her brother as if expecting him to say something else.

"How lovely to see you," he said. "You never did come to find me after we parted ways at my aunt's ball the other evening."

Louisa glanced uncertainly at Rosamund, probably trying to decide if his sister was on her side or not. Charles tilted his head at Louisa as if to say, *My sister wants us married as much as I do.* But Louisa didn't look all that convinced.

"I apologize," she finally said. "I developed quite the headache, but I didn't want to spoil my stepmother and sister's fun, so Rosamund let me rest in her bedroom until they were ready to leave."

Charles glanced at his sister, pretending he was just hearing this for the first time. "How kind of her." He turned back to Louisa. "I hope you are feeling better now."

"Yes, my lord."

Charles grimaced. He didn't particularly like when Louisa addressed him that way. It made her seem like an unfamiliar stranger to him, but Charles thought he must know Louisa better than anyone else. They had been the best of friends during that season. Surely they could pick up right where they left off? So he tried to make a joke.

"I hope it was nothing I did that caused your headache," he said with an easy laugh.

Louisa flushed and turned away. "No, my lord."

Well, that didn't work. Charles turned to Rosamund, desperate for help. She cleared her throat and looked at Louisa. "If he did, I wouldn't blame you. My brother has always given me *plenty* of headaches."

Rosamund shot him a playful smile, but Charles scowled at her. That wasn't exactly what he had in mind. He'd hoped, for once, someone might give Louisa a glowing review of him, but that didn't look like it would be happening anytime soon.

Rosamund turned back to Louisa. "What brings you to Park Street?" Rosamund asked. "I can call for tea if you would like."

Louisa glanced at Charles before addressing Rosamund. "There is something I would like to ask you about." She glanced at Charles again. "A private matter that has been bothering me."

His stomach did a flip. Did Louisa mean to ask Rosamund for advice about him? He shot a hopeful glance at his sister, who somehow urged him to say his goodbyes with a single sharp look. "Then you'll be pleased to know I was just about to leave," Charles said. He bowed his head slightly. "Good day, Miss Strickland."

"Good day, my lord."

After he walked past Louisa, he stopped and briefly looked over his shoulder. Louisa and his sister were making themselves comfortable in the chairs in front of the fireplace, and for a moment, his gaze captured Louisa's. She stared back at him with uncertainty, and as he turned away, Charles wondered what he could do to make her see that he was serious about her this time.

He decided to wait in the entry hall for her. When Louisa came out of the drawing room twenty minutes later, her eyes widened when she noticed him standing by the front door. "Lord Bolton," she said. "What are you still doing here?"

"I thought I might walk you home," he said, motioning for one of the footmen to gather his hat and walking stick.

"Oh, but that's too kind of you, especially since we live in opposite directions. I couldn't possibly ask you to waste your time."

Charles shrugged. "I have nowhere else to be. Come, I believe there was a time when you enjoyed taking walks with me."

With his hat and walking stick returned to him, Charles turned to leave. Louisa followed him, coming to walk beside him on the street below. He offered her his arm, and after some trepidation, she hesitantly took it. Although she looked straight ahead, he briefly stole a look down at her, smiling to himself. Did she know how beautiful she was?

"Did my sister help you solve this personal matter of yours?" he asked. She looked over at him, appearing startled after being lost in thoughts of her own. Charles silently wished she would tell him her secrets.

"She is going to try," Louisa said before turning away. "It's nothing serious, if that's what you are wondering. Lord Fitzgerald sent my sister a letter this afternoon. He claims he must return to his family estate in Cumbria to attend to some business. He is not sure when he'll be back in town. Naturally, my sister is distraught."

Charles frowned. "But isn't that a good thing? I thought you disapproved of a match between the viscount and your sister."

Louisa turned back to him, nodding. Charles rather liked when she didn't refuse to look at him. He much preferred having a full view of her charming face. "I do disapprove of their match, but I would like to know why he had to return to Cumbria so suddenly. If something nefarious is afoot, my sister deserves to know. Perhaps if it's something truly terrible, she might finally consider someone else, someone more suitable."

Charles nodded. "I will ask around to see if anyone has heard anything. Perhaps Hayward might know." Charles paused a moment, almost afraid to ask the question. "He hasn't bothered you since the ball, has he?"

Louisa turned scarlet, quickly shaking her head. "No. But there is an assembly at Almack's the evening after next." Louisa frowned. Charles could see the worry lines on her usually perfectly smooth face. "I'm sure I'll see him there."

Charles scowled. How Hayward had a voucher to Almack's and Charles did not was beyond his comprehension. A husband of one of the matrons must owe the man money. It seemed Hayward had the entirety of the Mayfair elite by the bollocks with the amount of invitations he received. Still, there had to be some way that Charles could protect her from Hayward's advances, regardless of the number of friends he held in such lofty places. "Do you think he knows what happened?"

Louisa sighed. "I doubt very much that Fitzgerald did not tell Hayward what he saw. But I am prepared to live with the consequences, should Hayward decide to take his revenge and tell everyone in London about us."

The earl's heart threatened to leap out of his chest and onto the pavement below. "And what consequences are those?" he managed to ask.

Louisa looked at him. "You and I will have to marry, of course, and I have no one to blame but myself. Stupid, foolish girl. I never should have been in that library. I do not care what the ton thinks of me, so long as I still have a successful estate, but I have decided I will not ruin my sister's dreams of matrimony to maintain my independence."

Charles stared at her. The statement troubled him, as he did not want Louisa to feel forced into marriage with him. He wanted her to see the same possibilities that he did. Charles stopped walking for a moment, turning to face Louisa. He grabbed her by the hands. "Why must we wait until the broadsheets start printing gossip about us? Why can't we become engaged now?"

Louisa quickly pulled her hands away, turning to continue walking down the road. He sighed and followed her, disappointed. "You mustn't touch me that way in public," she told him.

He chuckled. "I won't be able to keep my hands off you much longer, my dear, certainly not after that kiss."

Her head snapped in his direction. "So... you liked it, then?"

"I liked it very much, Louisa."

He spoke in earnest, so why did she look surprised? Charles would have pulled her into a darkened alley and kissed her all over right then and there if he thought she wanted it. But her hesitation toward even holding hands with him made him rethink everything. "I have not slept much since the ball," he admitted suddenly.

"Why?" she asked.

"If you must know, I have been in fear that my actions seven years ago have made you hate me forever. If I could take them back, I would. And if I had known kissing you would awaken such feelings in me, I would have done it a long time ago."

Charles thought he heard Louisa's breathing hitch beside him. She did not say anything at first, but when they turned the corner onto her street, she finally turned and looked at him. "Do you know what I don't like about marriage?" Charles waited for her to explain. "Whomever I marry will own both my estate and me. That is a fact." She turned away, her expression unreadable, but he thought he spotted a hint of sadness in her eyes. "Perhaps if it were set up more like a business partnership, I would be interested."

They came to a stop in front of the house that the Stricklands were renting that season. Charles looked at the front door, then back at Louisa. He did not want her to leave just yet, as that meant their conversation would have to end.

BECKY MICHAELS

"What if I could promise you this partnership you so desire? I would let you have a say in how Linfield Hall and Strickland Manor are run."

Louisa shook her head. "Charles, you could promise me the world, but what if you change your mind? The law is not written in a woman's favor. There is nothing to protect me when you inevitably grow tired of me."

"I would not change my mind, nor would I grow tired of you," Charles murmured. He reached for a loose strand of soft hair that had become untucked from underneath her straw bonnet. He gently pushed it back behind her ear, and she closed her eyes. When she opened them again, she pursed her lips.

"I'm sorry, Charles," she said. "But..." Her voice trailed off.

He sighed. "But you do not trust me."

She nodded, a sad look in her eyes. She began to turn away, but he still reached for her.

"Louisa."

She stopped, looking over her shoulder at him. Although he felt discouraged, he knew he mustn't give up hope. "I am hosting a dinner party next week. I wanted to ask you and your family to attend. If you would like, I could invite some eligible bachelors for Flora as well. I will let you look over the guest list first, of course, to make sure they are suitable."

Louisa hesitated for a moment, then sighed. "Very well," she said, "but they must be very good men. If my sister hasn't fallen in love with someone new by dessert, I shall be very disappointed in you."

Charles smiled. "I hope you never have a reason to be disappointed in me again. Good day, Miss Strickland."

Chapter Seventeen

IT WAS late in the evening when Charles arrived at Hayward's. He hadn't stepped one foot inside the building since Hayward taunted him before his aunt's ball, but Charles could no longer avoid it. He needed to speak to the man.

The smoke-filled room was dimly lit, not to mention crowded, which made navigating it difficult. He pushed through a mass of people to the main dining room, where Rutley immediately caught his eye. The duke waved him over to his table.

"What are you doing here?" he asked, sounding confused. "I thought you had given up on this place. I would have saved you a seat for supper if I had known you were coming."

Charles smiled and politely nodded at Rutley's three companions, then turned back to the duke. "Don't trouble yourself, as I don't plan on staying long. I only need a quick word with Hayward. Have you seen him?"

Rutley's shoulders tensed, a look of concern forming on his face. "What business do you have with Hayward? This isn't about Miss Strickland, is it?" The duke sighed, his gaze sharpening as he looked over Charles. "No good will come from a public feud, especially at the gaming hell the man in question owns. You are in his territory now, not some upscale coffeehouse or gilded ballroom in Mayfair."

But Charles had no intention of fighting with Hayward. After all, there was nothing to fight over. He had only helped Louisa see Hayward for what he was: a rotten scoundrel. Louisa was bound to discover the truth about Mrs. Hayward and the other women at some point; Charles only helped speed up the process—and without anything terrible happening, either. He was a downright hero for it if anyone asked him.

As for Charles and Louisa's kiss? Well, there was no chance he would apologize to Hayward for that.

"I only mean to ask him a question about his friend Fitzgerald," Charles said, hoping to assuage some of Rutley's concern. But the duke only furrowed his brow deeper. "He departed very suddenly from town. I should like to know why."

Rutley sighed. "So it *is* about Miss Strickland."

Charles frowned. "No. It is about the viscount—"

"Who is Flora Strickland's favorite suitor," Rutley finished for him. "And Miss Flora is Miss Strickland's younger sister. I am not stupid, Charles. And even if I were, I'm sure I could make the connection."

Charles pursed his lips, then eventually sighed. Perhaps he might be able to play to the duke's more sensitive side—if he even had one of those. "The girl is distraught. Further explanation—good *or* bad—might help her recover."

Rutley rolled his eyes, still not convinced. But then one of his companions, a portly, ruddy-faced fellow on the other side of the table, spoke. "Did you say Lord Fitzgerald?" the stranger asked.

Charles turned and looked at him. He nodded once. "Yes, that's right."

"I heard it was his brother who called him home. Not the youngest, who—if I recall correctly—is a vicar in Hampshire, but the middle son. The navy officer who won all that prize money and is now richer than the viscount himself. He was still sorting through his late father's documents when Lord Fitzgerald arrived in town. I wonder if he found something."

Charles frowned. He was hoping for something more sinister-sounding, something that would finally encourage Flora to move on from Fitzgerald after nothing else had worked. But what could the middle brother have found?

"Any idea what?" Charles asked.

The gentleman shrugged. "I haven't the foggiest, but I did see Hayward earlier."

Charles looked around the room but saw no sign of the fiend in question.

"He knows the viscount best," the man continued, "but he has been in a foul temper all evening. You ought to be careful, as His Grace suggests."

Charles and Rutley exchanged a look. "I wonder why he's in a foul temper," the duke mused, still eyeing Charles, who shook his head and turned away. "You ought to leave before there is a scene."

"I am not afraid of Hayward," Charles muttered. If anyone had acted dishonorably, it was Hayward, not him. But as much as he would be willing to come to blows over Louisa, he couldn't marry her if he ended up beaten to death by one of the burly men Hayward employed. As Rutley said, Charles was in Hayward's territory now. It didn't very much matter that he was an earl. "But I suppose there are other ways I might collect the information I need. Good evening, gentlemen."

But as Charles walked away, he felt a hand on his shoulder. He closed his eyes and took a deep breath, realizing right away to whom the viselike grip belonged. When Charles turned to look, Hayward was standing behind him. Although Rutley and his friends remained seated at the table, they all pivoted in their seats to watch the scene unfold.

"Hayward," Charles said, trying to recall the cocky attitude he once had whenever he entered his gaming hell before. Taking a deep breath, he told himself he did not need brandy to put the insufferable man standing before him in his place. He smiled brightly. "How do you do this evening? Did you enjoy the rest of my aunt's ball? I must say, it was rather forward of you to arrive without an invitation."

Hayward's expression only grew darker than it already was. Someone groaned behind him, and Charles could only assume Rutley had made the noise, but the earl went on smiling anyway.

"I think you know how I enjoyed it," Hayward said. His eyes flickered in the direction of Rutley and the others sitting behind Charles. The duke continued watching, but the other men turned back to their suppers, knowing it was best not to risk angering Hayward by staring. "Perhaps we should go somewhere more private to speak."

Charles looked over his shoulder. The duke shook his head once, as if to forbid it, but Charles turned back toward Hayward. "As you wish."

Hayward, his jaw set, guided Charles away from the spectators. He thought he heard Rutley curse under his breath as they walked away.

Hayward took Charles to one of the back rooms. Two men sat in leather armchairs in front of the fire, nursing glasses of amber-colored liquor. But after one look from Hayward, they scurried out of the room, muttering apologies. When they were gone, Hayward closed the large wooden door behind them. Suddenly the cravat around Charles's neck felt very tight. He took another deep breath, trying to remember the last time he fought anyone, let alone a man with professional bodyguards on staff.

"What sort of game are you playing, Bolton?" Hayward asked from behind Charles.

The earl turned, arching his brow. "I'm not sure what you mean," he replied as he smoothed the sleeves of his jacket. He knew his nonchalant attitude would bother Hayward, but Charles decided he rather liked bothering Hayward, especially as he watched the man's jaw tighten beneath his skin. Hayward had an impressively sculpted jawline. Charles would take great pleasure in punching it if given the opportunity.

"You know what I mean," Hayward snapped. He paced the room, holding his hands behind his back. His shadow from the fire seemed to loom over the entire room, but Charles remained smiling, unintimidated by the other man. "I saw you watching Louisa Strickland and me for the whole evening, even as you danced with other ladies. Then you followed us to the library, even though you had no business doing so. Why?"

Charles shrugged. "Miss Strickland has no male relative to watch out for her while she's in town. As her neighbor and someone who once knew her father well, I see it as my duty to prevent her from doing anything she might regret."

Hayward's nostrils flared, and he stopped pacing for a moment, turning to scowl directly at Charles. "I believe you did more than your duty after I left."

The earl's lips involuntarily curled into a smug smile; he just couldn't help it.

Naturally, that only further incensed Hayward. "I thought you were only out to embarrass me after the incident with the flowers. Perhaps you were still angry after you lost all that money at my card tables." Charles did his best to remain smiling, but the comment bothered him. He felt his jaw involuntarily start to clench. "And when you came upon us in the library, I thought the same thing as well. After all, Miss Strickland told me your previous courtship was nothing more than a ruse."

He couldn't control it any longer. The earl's smile started to fade, and Hayward laughed once, his shoulders shaking with the sudden sound. "The look on your face!" His laughter faded, and his gaze grew serious again. "Fitzgerald told me the scene he came upon in the library after I left. You kissed her, which, if I'm to believe what you told me the last time you were here, is as good as a marriage proposal according to you —yet I know for certain that Louisa has no desire to marry."

"You will refer to her as Miss Strickland in my presence," Charles snapped. Judging by the twinkle in Hayward's eye, he enjoyed pushing Charles as much as Charles did him. "I suppose there's no use denying anything, as I'm sure Fitzgerald has already told you everything. To be frank, the viscount is why I'm here tonight. Do you know why he's left town so suddenly? Miss Flora is distressed over his sudden departure."

Hayward snorted, then resumed his pacing once more, practically leaving a visible path across the plush red carpet. "Do not try to change the subject, Bolton. Tell me at once. Did you always intend to steal Miss Strickland out from underneath me?"

Charles tilted his head to the side, then laughed slightly. "Miss Strickland is not for either of us to *steal*. But I have decided Miss Strickland would make an ideal wife. She is intelligent and pretty, not to mention very, very wealthy."

"So you are after her money. She will not like that."

No, I am after her heart.

But Charles wouldn't dare say that aloud, so he shook his head instead. "I only think she would make a far better countess to a young and lively earl like myself than a mistress to a practically decaying owner of a gaming hell like you."

Charles thought he probably deserved what happened next. Hayward charged at him like an angry bull, knocking him to the ground. Charles landed with a thud, intensely aware that this would hurt tomorrow. Hayward pulled him up by the cravat, drew back his fist, then pounded it across his face.

Once the initial shock of being attacked wore off, Charles refused to let Hayward pummel him into oblivion without putting up a fight first. If there was anything useful that Rutley taught Charles in his youth, it was how to throw a punch. As Hayward drew back his arm again, Charles took him by surprise, landing a swinging blow just underneath his chin. Hayward fell backward, and Charles scrambled to his feet just as the duke himself burst into the room.

"Charles!" he barked. "We are leaving."

Realizing the duke was right—no good could come from a public feud—Charles followed him out of the room. "Bolton!" Hayward shouted after him, somehow pulling himself to his feet. "I am not done with you!"

But Rutley quickly led Charles through a door at the end of the hall, and soon they were in a dark alley behind the building. All was quiet except for the earl's breathing, which was rather frantic after engaging in fisticuffs.

"Have you lost your mind?" the duke asked. "Or have you only started drinking again?"

Charles immediately drew back, offended by the accusation. "What? No! He was the one who punched *me*. I do not think he appreciates the fact that Miss Strickland would be better off marrying me than becoming his mistress."

Rutley groaned, running his hands through his hair. "Your sudden obsession with this woman is troubling. I hope you remember that paying off your debt to me comes first. If she does not accept you..."

Charles scowled. Must he be so negative? Even Rosamund

was doing her best to support his pursuit of Louisa, though she admittedly found her unlikely to marry her brother. "Yes, Your Grace. I'm aware I only have a month to make her accept my proposal."

The duke looked back at the closed door behind them, the one that led back into Hayward's. He then turned to Charles. "Are you sure she would not prefer to be Hayward's mistress? As long as they are discreet, her sister's reputation would be well-protected."

Charles's shoulders drooped. The truth was he wasn't sure what Louisa wanted. When he held her, she seemed to give herself willingly to him. But even he couldn't deny that she had been cold that morning with him, acting nothing like a woman in love—or even lust. Would she ever follow him willingly into a darkened library like she had Hayward? Charles frowned when he realized he couldn't be sure.

"That's why I need your help, Rutley," Charles said, clapping his friend on the shoulder and forcing a smile. "You must help me woo her."

Rutley shook his head. "You'll need more than my help to do that," he muttered with a frown. "Besides, I am not sure I am any good at wooing."

And then Charles remembered something. Louisa said the next time she would see Hayward would be at Almack's for an assembly the evening after next. If Charles wanted to attend, he would need a voucher from one of the matrons. He had lost his two seasons ago after an unfortunate incident with a potted plant. Those damn ferns were always getting him in trouble.

"I need a voucher for Almack's," Charles told Rutley.

"A voucher for Almack's? Whatever for?"

"Miss Strickland and Hayward will both be at the assembly the evening after next. I cannot miss it."

Rutley huffed. "Fine. My mother knows one of the

matrons. I'm sure I'll be able to procure a new voucher for you."

Charles grinned broadly. "I can always depend on you."

"But if you cause another scene," Rutley was quick to warn, "I will never do another favor for you again."

LOUISA STOOD in a corner of the ballroom at Almack's, wafting her fan in front of her face as she lazily watched her sister dance. After only a month in town, Louisa was exhausted. She had not slept for days, her mind too muddled with conflicting thoughts about Charles and Hayward. She had expected to see the latter there tonight, but he had yet to make an appearance.

Surprisingly, Louisa's lack of sleep made her appear much worse for wear than her sister that evening, even though Flora was nursing a broken heart. Her sister refused to speak of Fitzgerald anymore, and any man within arm's length that night was fair game for flirting. No gentleman at Almack's was immune to her sister's charms that evening, and Louisa wondered if they were silently thanking their lucky stars that Fitzgerald left town. She knew she was.

"You look deep in thought, Miss Strickland."

The voice startled her, but she recognized it right away. Hayward came to stand beside her, and she forced herself to smile at him, wishing to appear as unaffected as possible. "Good evening, Mr. Hayward," she said. "I was wondering when you might appear this evening. I am surprised you come to Almack's. I would think these sort of affairs would be too boring for you."

Hayward did not respond right away, choosing to study her carefully instead, and she momentarily forgot that she was supposed to be disgusted by him. His brown eyes were much too seductive for her to be completely unaffected by him. She shifted her weight from foot to foot, feeling uncomfortable. "You do not look or sound pleased to see me," he said.

"On the contrary, Mr. Hayward," Louisa said, only just beginning to gather her nerve to tell him off, "I am very pleased to see you. There is something we must discuss."

"Perhaps we might find somewhere private, or—"

"I would prefer others to be near," Louisa said, snapping her fan shut. She took great pleasure in watching the sound make him jump slightly, then stuffed the fan into the velvet reticule hanging from her wrist.

"What is the matter, my dear?"

Louisa scowled. "Do not call me that. You lied to me about your wife. You told me she is allowed just as many lovers as you are, but how could that be when you leave her sequestered in the country? Why, I gather she is nothing more than an innocent bystander to your bad behavior! How could I have been so foolish?" She shook her head, taking a deep breath as she did. "I can no longer stand to be polite. If and when Fitzgerald returns to town, the two of you ought not call on us anymore. *I* run my household. *I* control my sister's dowry. And *I* forbid a match between the two of them. It will serve you well to see that information communicated to him before he calls on my sister again."

Hayward's expression turned dark, the playful look in his eyes gone. "You would be wise not to forget what Fitzgerald and I know about you and Lord Bolton. You wouldn't want to end up married to that awful bloke, would you?"

Louisa laughed, but it was mostly at herself. She had gotten herself into this mess. She would face the consequences if she must. "I can think of worse fates. For one, becoming your mistress. If I have to marry him, so be it. Just so long as you and your friend stay away from me and my family."

"Louisa—"

Her nostrils flared at the use of her Christian name. "I have made up my mind, Mr. Hayward. I will not be your mistress—not now or ever. I would rather die!"

She turned to leave, but Hayward latched onto her wrist. He squeezed tightly, and she spun her head around, glaring at him. "Unhand me, sir!" she exclaimed.

When he did not let go, she yanked her hand away even harder, hurting her shoulder in the process. She reached up and rubbed it, wincing, but Hayward did not seem to care about the physical pain he caused. "You are making a terrible mistake," he said.

Louisa looked up at him, glaring. If she could punch him, she would. But they were at Almack's, where ladies weren't allowed to punch the men—unfortunately. They were lucky they had gotten away with as much as they already had without causing a scene. "How dare you," she hissed. "You, sir, are not as charming as you think you are."

She spun around, hoping to get away from Hayward for good this time, but a tall figure with broad shoulders blocked her way. She looked up to find Charles standing there, his serious gaze locked on Hayward. "Is everything all right here?" Charles asked.

With an irritated expression, Louisa looked back and forth between the two men. "Everything is marvelous," she muttered, going around Charles and finally walking away.

Louisa wanted to find somewhere quiet to sit, where the men couldn't bother her, so she headed to the retiring room. After finding a comfortable sofa, Louisa mainly sat in silence, only exchanging pleasantries with other women in the room when she had to. But for the most part, she sat there thinking.

Hayward didn't seem like the sort of person to make idle threats, but she couldn't rush into marriage with Charles on

BECKY MICHAELS

threats alone. She hadn't been lying, though. She knew she would much prefer marriage to Charles than becoming Hayward's mistress. Sure, one situation would most likely be temporary, the other permanent. But at least becoming Charles's wife wouldn't make her feel cheap.

She sighed. Oh, how could she have made such a horrible mistake? Louisa rued the day she first laid eyes on Hayward. If it weren't for him, Charles never would have cornered her in that library alone. How he concluded that they should marry was beyond her. Charles was undoubtedly handsome, and she would be lying if she said she didn't enjoy their kiss. And at one point, they *had* been friends.

They had been friends, yet they had always been complete opposites in temperament. Neither could deny that. And there was no way she could trust him after what happened with Miss Coppola. At least she didn't think she could. Not to mention they had spent most of this season arguing or bickering. That being said, he had offered to help her find Flora a suitable husband. And he did stop her from making a terrible mistake with Hayward.

But that had only led to her making a terrible mistake with Charles. She groaned inwardly, still unsure of what to do. Louisa asked one of the attendants for the time, hoping the night was almost over, only to be informed it was still quite early. Knowing she couldn't spend the entire evening hiding in the retiring room, Louisa reluctantly stood and headed outside into the hall.

Charles was there waiting for her. She tried not to be too touched by the concern on his face, for she knew he wasn't playing any less of a game than Hayward was. Charles had his motivations for wanting to marry her, just as Hayward had his motivations for wanting to bed her, and she knew she must be wary of both of them. Could any man be trusted?

"Have you been waiting for me?" she asked, walking right

by him instead of joining him where he stood. He shuffled behind her, eventually coming to walk beside her.

"Yes," he said, his voice soft. Louisa dared not look at him. "I wanted to make sure you were all right."

When she finally did look at him, Louisa noticed a bruise along his cheekbone. She gasped, stopping to reach for it with gloved fingertips. "Charles! What happened?" Then she snorted. "I am surprised the matrons allowed you entry with *that* on your face."

He glared at her. "And here I was thinking you were being sweet."

Suppressing a giggle, she tried to appear contrite. "I apologize. What happened?"

Realizing that acting too familiar with the earl at Almack's could only lead to further disaster, she quickly pulled her hand away, and her giggles faded. Charles almost looked disappointed. "I ran into Hayward at his club last night while searching for more information about Fitzgerald," he explained. He smiled as if he were about to laugh. "He thinks I stole you from him."

Louisa's expression soured. "I am not anyone's to steal."

Charles only grinned more broadly. "That's what I told him."

"Then I suppose you know me better than Hayward," she said reluctantly.

Charles laughed. "I should like that in writing."

"Do not count on it," Louisa replied before heading toward the ballroom once more. She hoped he wouldn't join her, but he did, as if the only natural place for him was by her side. She shot him a sidelong glance. "I did not think you had a voucher for Almack's."

"I was worried what Hayward might do to you, so I had Rutley procure one for me. His mother is friends with one of the matrons. They even permitted me to ask you to accompany me for a waltz this evening."

Louisa came to a stop again, this time her heart pounding. "What?" She looked around, waiting until the hall was clear of people. Her voice dropped to a whisper. "That is almost worse than Hayward threatening to tell everyone about our liaison in the library."

Charles frowned. "Why?"

She sighed. "If we waltz together, our names will be linked together in every society column in London tomorrow morning." Her shoulders drooped. "Not to mention it will anger Hayward. He's already threatening to tell everyone about us."

"And if he does, then we will be forced to marry—I know. I was only hoping to show you how that might not be so terrible."

Louisa furrowed her brow, not quite understanding. "With a waltz?"

He stepped closer to her, dipping his head beside hers. "Amongst other things," he murmured in her ear.

She looked up at him, her eyes falling on his lips.

Do not fall for it. The evasive thought shook her from her reverie. Louisa took a careful step back from him, willing her pulse to return to a less frenzied beat. She cleared her throat. "I will waltz with you if only to avoid upsetting the matrons —but nothing more. Do you understand?"

But he must have known that she didn't quite mean it, that she was still very curious about him, for the devious look on his face remained the same even as he quietly agreed.

Chapter Eighteen

As soon as Charles took Louisa up into his arms for that evening's waltz, he knew he must convince her to marry him sooner rather than later. He wasn't sure how much longer he could stand not being her husband, when he would be allowed to explore every inch of her lithe body. The kiss had awakened something inside him that must have been lying dormant for years, a long-ago secret feeling that he never even knew he felt.

They hadn't waltzed together before, not even seven years ago when Charles first pretended to court her. He suddenly felt nervous, holding her so closely, especially in public. It was as if his heart were on his sleeve for all to see. But had it always been that way? Was that why the broadsheets were always reporting on their courtship all those years ago?

His eyes darted around the room, and he wondered if anyone was whispering about them as they danced together. Perhaps even after all this time, their reunion was a foregone conclusion by everyone except them. At least now he saw it. All he had to do was convince Louisa of it as well. It would be an uphill battle, but an uphill battle worth fighting.

"You have suddenly become quiet," Louisa observed softly, interrupting his tangled web of thoughts. Her blue eyes almost looked concerned as she studied him, and her hair was a vibrant shade of red underneath the glow of the ballroom's candlelight. Charles considered her carefully, then decided it was best to be out with what troubled him.

"I am only trying to discern how I might finally win your affection," he said. Their gazes remained locked on each other, but Charles thought he saw Louisa flinch.

"Are you capable of turning back time?" she asked. Oh, how he wished he was. For a moment, she looked fragile, but then her face grew taut, as if she was stoning herself against him. "But even that is no use. I do not wish to marry, yet you have put me in a position where I might have to if the gossip becomes too much to bear. For some, that might be reason enough to despise you."

"And do you despise me?" Charles asked. His heart pounded like a drum in his chest awaiting her answer.

Louisa looked away, then slowly shook her head. "No." She sighed, turning back to face him. "Against my better judgment, I cannot."

Charles tried not to smile. "Do you ever wonder if things could have been different between us?"

If things could have been real, he wanted to add, but he resisted the urge. He knew it was an impossible question already. He was who he was back then, and there was no changing that, no way to turn back time like Louisa requested.

"How so?"

"If I'd proposed to you at my aunt's ball all those years ago, for example. What would you have done?"

Louisa laughed, almost too loudly to be polite. "That never would have happened."

"But if it had, what would you have said? Would you have accepted me?"

Louisa's face momentarily stilled. She looked up at him through her eyelashes. "I don't know," she said so softly that he almost didn't hear. He was glad he did, though, for it was a much preferable answer to hearing her say no outright.

But then she quickly shook her head. "But if I had said yes, surely we would be estranged and hate each other by now."

Charles frowned. Now that answer he didn't like. "Louisa Strickland, you managed to make me behave for three whole months when I was only three-and-twenty. If anyone could have saved me from the destruction I caused, it would have been you. We would have been fine together as husband and wife. You would have kept me from going down the wrong path."

Charles thought he saw the beginnings of a flush spreading across her cheeks. For a moment, they danced on in silence with his arm wrapped tightly around her waist. She seemed to be deep in thought, so much so that she didn't even protest when he pulled her a little closer.

When she finally spoke, Louisa was looking up at him through her lashes again. "It is not my responsibility to save you," she murmured.

Charles furrowed his brow. "I know, but you have always made me want to be a better man. If you had looked at me seven years ago the way you looked at Hayward, perhaps things could have been different. Perhaps I would have taken the risk and..." His voice trailed off. Such things shouldn't be spoken aloud in Almack's.

She shook her head, laughing slightly. "But you are still forgetting one crucial detail. I have no desire to be married. Nothing can change that. Even if I eventually give in to you, my resistance to the whole idea of it will drive a wedge between us, and you know it."

"Not even if I could promise you that Strickland Manor would remain in your control after we married?"

"Yes." Her eyes challenged him to try to push her further. Her face remained still and impassive, seemingly unresponsive to his touch and his words.

He leaned in closer. "Not even if I kiss you senseless again?"

"Especially not that," Louisa hissed, careful that no one else would hear the nature of their conversation. When the dance was over, Charles offered to take her to the refreshment table, as was customary, but Louisa shook her head.

"Spare me the annoyance of partaking in any more performative acts with you for the sake of other people's pleasure," she said, abruptly curtseying. He bowed in return, about to say something to stop her from leaving, but she had turned and started walking away before he even lifted his head. He frowned as he watched her go.

THE STRICKLANDS' invitation to dinner at Finch Place came the next day. Charles also enclosed a list of the gentlemen attending for Louisa to review. That interested Flora the most, and she quickly snatched it from her sister, wandering out of the room while she read it to herself.

"I should like to see that when you are finished!" Louisa called after her. But Flora raised her hand over her shoulder and waved it before disappearing into the hall. Louisa sighed.

"What is the meaning of this?" Mrs. Strickland asked, still holding the invitation.

Louisa faltered at her tone. Her stepmother had become all the more suspicious of her behavior after Louisa ignored Hayward at Almack's in favor of dancing with Charles, and she had heard about very little else since the carriage ride home the previous night. "Is the earl courting you again?"

"Of course not!" Louisa exclaimed, perhaps too quickly. Her denial was all the more unbelievable after Charles and Louisa's names were linked together in every broadsheet that morning, just as Louisa predicted the evening before. She regretted ever agreeing to the dance. Offending the matrons would have been preferable to her stepmother's incessant questioning.

Mrs. Strickland narrowed her eyes. "You danced the waltz with him at Almack's. Of all the places! To certain people, that means something."

Louisa groaned, but Mrs. Strickland held up her hand, wanting to continue anyway. Louisa reluctantly listened.

"Everyone knows Lord Bolton is looking for a wife. Has he spoken to you about such a topic?"

"How many times must I tell you that I am not interested in marriage?" Louisa snapped, quickly losing her temper. "If you must know, Lord Bolton only offered to help me find Flora a more suitable suitor than Fitzgerald. Those names enclosed with the invitation are the gentlemen he would like to invite to dinner."

Louisa looked over her shoulder, searching for her sister, who was still missing from the drawing room. She turned back to Mrs. Strickland, who appeared entirely unconvinced. "You really ought to call her back into the room. I must review the list and send my opinion back to Charles."

Her stepmother immediately appeared skeptical at Louisa's usage of Lord Bolton's Christian name. Louisa winced, only realizing what she had done when it was too late. "Lord Bolton, I mean," she murmured, embarrassed by her mistake.

Before Mrs. Strickland could say anything, Flora returned to the drawing room, handing the list to her sister. Louisa took it, quickly scanning it. She was surprised to see the Duke of Rutley as one of the attendees. As far as Louisa knew, Rosamund was hosting the dinner with Charles. Already, Louisa was questioning his judgment to put those two in the same room for an extended period of time. How could anyone think a marriage between Louisa and Charles would be successful? She would annoy him by constantly disagreeing with his decisions.

"Well, I think it is quite sweet that Lord Bolton has finally come to realize his feelings for you after all these years," Flora said.

Louisa looked up from the list of names, blinking at her sister. "Were you out in the hall listening to us the entire time?"

Flora grinned coyly, then nodded.

Louisa shook her head, turning back to the piece of paper she held. "Unbelievable."

"I think you will be pleased with the list he has curated," Flora said, taking a seat beside her sister. Flora slid even closer to Louisa, resting her chin on top of her sister's shoulder. Louisa glared at her out of the corner of her eye. "I am sure one of them will help me forget the scoundrel who shall not be named."

Except for his initial communication, Flora had received no letters from the viscount since he left town. Louisa was pleasantly surprised by her sister's determination to move on from him. Louisa had yet to discover the real reason behind Fitzgerald's sudden departure, but she secretly hoped it was something truly sinister. Louisa wanted the viscount out of Flora's life for good.

"You are right," Louisa told her sister as she passed the list to Mrs. Strickland. As far as Louisa knew, no one Charles had included had a bad reputation or a mountain of debt. Unlike him.

Louisa chewed her lip. If she knew she didn't want to marry, why, then, could she not stop thinking about him? Never had Charles been so outrageously flirtatious with her, and never had Louisa expected to enjoy it so much. When she left him on the dance floor after their waltz, she almost wished he would have followed her. She half wondered what would have happened if she'd let him pull her into a dark room and have his wicked way with her.

Disaster, she silently reminded herself. Disaster would be what happened. And she couldn't allow it. Although she lived in fear that Hayward would spread gossip about her and Charles, Louisa was determined to see her sister engaged before that happened. Then, Louisa thought, she wouldn't have to worry about a thing. She could return to Strickland Manor and live out the rest of her days in peaceful ruination.

Louisa thought that was what she wanted, but if that was truly the case, she didn't understand why her heart fluttered every time someone mentioned Charles's name. Or why she found herself so terribly nervous to see him again, this time in his house, where he probably knew all the best places to seduce a lady.

But not Louisa. Louisa would resist. She was sure of it.

CHARLES WAS in desperate need of a drink. The pressure to host a perfect evening was mounting as the start of the dinner party drew closer. All he wanted was for Louisa Strickland to see that he was the ideal husband for her, and that she should marry him right away. The lure of liquid courage called to him.

But he knew even touching a bottle of brandy would have the opposite effect, no matter how much he craved the amber liquid.

The drawing room at Finch Place had started to become

crowded as guests arrived for the dinner party. His sister Rosamund stood beside him, trying not to glower at the scene in front of them but failing miserably. To even out the number of men and women guests, Charles had invited a few single women and their mothers along with the eligible bachelors he had chosen for Flora. While the men flocked to the younger Miss Strickland, the women eagerly surrounded the Duke of Rutley and his mother.

Rosamund took out her fan, wafting it nervously by her neck. "Must you have invited so many people, Charles?"

Charles glanced at her. He had already noticed earlier that evening that his sister was dressed much more provocatively than usual. Her frock was low cut, red, and showed off her slim shoulders, not to mention the color was quite striking against her pale skin. But if she was trying to attract the attention of a certain duke, she seemed to be failing miserably. Perhaps that was why she looked so glum.

"You and I know the only way I could convince Miss Strickland to attend this evening was if she believed there was something in it for her," Charles said after sighing. "I needed more women here to even out the large number of male guests I invited for Miss Flora."

Rosamund glared at him out of the corner of her eye. "But did they all need to be so beautiful and wealthy? You have certainly collected quite the group of people here tonight. It is a wonder any of them will socialize with us at all, considering how far we have fallen beneath them in just the past year."

Charles furrowed his brow. "Firstly, you forget that I am an earl, not a mere mister like the majority of the men here. Secondly, I thought you didn't care about our family's reputation?" He glanced at their heavily pregnant half sister, August, who had come with her husband, Mr. Brooks, as well as her mother-in-law. They stood on the other side of the room, speaking to Louisa, her stepmother, and Lady Ramsbury. He turned to face Rosamund once more. "Thirdly, you told me you didn't mind if Rutley came."

Rosamund laughed slightly, waving her fan as she did. "Of course I don't mind. I only wish some of Miss Flora's gentlemen might pay me some attention this evening, seeing as how last time I checked, I am still the sister of an earl."

Charles shot his sister a skeptical glance. The way her eyes kept drifting in Rutley's direction told a different story. "Do not worry," Charles said. "I made sure to seat you next to the two best gentlemen I could find, and Rutley will be far away from you."

Charles expected his sister to rejoice, but she said nothing. Instead, she turned back to him, tilting her head to the side as she did. "And what of Miss Strickland? Where will she sit?"

"Next to me, of course."

"A distinction that won't go unnoticed by the rest of the party." Rosamund arched her brow, turning to her brother. "I only hope it doesn't upset her."

Charles looked at Louisa from across the room. Light-blue ribbons that matched her dress were woven through her hair that evening, and a pair of sparkling pearl earrings framed her angular face. She had barely looked at him when her family arrived, and if she was nervous, Charles was willing to wager he was even more so.

As Louisa laughed at something August said, Charles hoped she remained at ease when eating dinner next to him. He turned to his sister. "Why would it upset her?" he asked.

Rosamund sighed. "I'm not entirely sure if you have noticed, but Miss Strickland is much less keen on matrimony than you are." Charles turned away, rolling his eyes. Of course he had noticed. Rosamund snapped her fan shut, waved it once at her brother, and smiled. "But I suppose if anyone could convince her otherwise, it would be you. And she was rather good at pretending to be in love with you all those years ago." Rosamund thoughtfully tapped the tip of her fan against her chin. "It was so good that sometimes I wondered if she was pretending at all."

Charles furrowed his brow, looking at his sister. "Do you mean that?"

She shrugged. "You will have to ask her yourself."

Rosamund walked away, joining Flora and her many admirers. Charles couldn't help but notice that his sister and the duke kept exchanging discreet looks across the room even as they spoke to other people. He wondered how much longer it would take for the two of them to find their way back to one another.

"It would appear there is more than one pretender in the room this evening," he murmured to himself before his eyes fell on Louisa, who remained in the same place as before. Charles approached her slowly, so as not to startle her.

"Pardon me, Miss Strickland," he said from behind her.

Louisa turned to face him. Her expression revealed nothing, certainly no secret feelings from seven years ago. His sister must have suspected incorrectly.

"I was hoping I might escort you into the dining room for this evening's meal."

Charles half expected her to reject him by the way she paled. Instead, she nodded politely and took his proffered arm. "Thank you, my lord," she said.

Louisa did not look at him as he guided her into the dining room, which was attached to the drawing room by a set of double doors that a pair of footmen now opened. The others filed in behind them, and when Charles led Louisa to the seat beside his at the head of the table, she did not flinch. Louisa seemed so unbothered by the honor that even Rutley shot the earl a hopeful glance from across the table.

When everyone was seated, Charles turned to Louisa to speak, but she beat him to it. "Your sister August is lovelier every time I meet her," she said, reaching for the wineglass one of the footmen just filled. "Are you looking forward to becoming an uncle?"

Charles watched her take a sip of the red beverage, narrowing his eyes as he began to suspect she wasn't as calm as she pretended to be. "Yes," he replied, wishing he had a glass of wine to nurse as well. "I believe the babe is due next month."

Louisa seemed surprised he even knew such a detail. "That's right. Do you see your sister and her husband often now that you are in town?"

Charles smiled slightly. If he didn't know any better, he would think Louisa was trying to get to know him better. "My sister insists I have dinner at Dover Street at least once a week. I am lucky that Mr. Brooks allows it at all."

"Has Mr. Brooks not yet forgiven you for all that happened last year?"

He was surprised she even cared enough to ask the question at all. Charles shook his head. "He tolerates me because his wife has the most forgiving heart in all of England."

Louisa smiled at that. August *was* a sweet girl. He regretted not realizing it earlier. "But the cracks in our personal relationship will take more time to heal."

"Yet you are putting in the work."

Charles nodded once. "I am trying." Louisa grew silent, so he decided to change the subject, glancing toward Flora and the two gentlemen on either side of her. "Are you pleased with the selection of young men for Miss Flora?"

Louisa immediately brightened. "Very much so, thank you. I hope at least one of them makes her forget Fitzgerald."

Charles grimaced, remembering what Rutley told him about Fitzgerald when he arrived that evening. Charles would have to tell Louisa what he learned at some point that evening.

"Have you learned something about him, my lord? You have an awful look on your face."

He glanced at his aunt, who sat at his other side. She was in conversation with her dinner partner, paying no mind to Charles or Louisa. Still, he spoke as discreetly as possible. "The rumor is that one of the daughters of his tenants is pregnant. Her father claims that the viscount is the father, which is why his brother called him home."

Louisa's face fell. "Oh dear. How will I ever tell my sister?"

Charles reached for her hand. "Perhaps you won't have to tell her." He looked across the dining room table, where people laughed and talked, especially Flora. The footmen scurried about the perimeter of the room, pouring wine and distributing bowls of white soup. Charles turned back to Louisa, but she was not looking at him, too busy fixating on his hand holding hers. "She seems to be enjoying herself tonight."

Louisa nodded, gently pulling her hand away from his. "Flora enjoys herself wherever she goes. I wish we shared the same disposition."

"Have you grown tired of town?" he asked.

Louisa nodded again, then looked around the table before her eyes landed on him, as if to make sure no one was listening to them. "I know it is hardly fashionable to say, but I much prefer the country."

"I find myself missing Linfield as well."

Louisa didn't appear convinced. "Truly? But I thought you loved London."

Charles chuckled. "I wonder when you will realize how much I have changed since we last knew each other."

Louisa flushed, reaching for her spoon. Charles suspected she would eat the rest of the meal in silence, but suddenly she turned to him. "I am surprised that both Lady Rosamund and the duke are here. I thought she despised him."

Charles bit back a smile. "Do not let her words fool you. She far from despises him, no matter how much she would like it to be so."

"What do you mean?" Louisa asked in between spoonfuls of soup.

"Surely you have noticed the way she has been staring at him all evening and he at her."

Louisa tilted her head to the side as she watched the two in question. She turned back to Charles. "They both look at each other frequently, him more so than her. But he seems rather taken with the young lady sitting beside him."

"Yes, much to Rosamund's displeasure," Charles observed.

"Do you truly mean that?"

Charles shrugged. "Those two will find their way back to each other again, whether they like it or not." His steady gaze fell on Louisa, who peered back at him with what seemed to be uncertainty. Her mouth was slightly open, listening to Charles speak. "Once love ties you to someone, it is rather hard to untangle yourself, no matter how hard you try."

Louisa narrowed her eyes at him. "Is that why you were so determined to make them marry last year?"

Charles grimaced. "I have noticed you seem rather well versed in all my moral failings as of late."

Louisa fell silent for a moment. "I suppose I am only trying to discern your true character now that you no longer have your façade of being a rake to hide behind."

Charles grinned at her. "And why would you want to do that?" He suddenly felt quite pleased with how things were progressing, watching her bite her lower lip as she watched him. He would have liked to lean over and take that lower lip for his own.

But Louisa admitted to nothing. "I am only trying to get

to know my neighbor better after not speaking for such a long time."

"Is that so?" Charles asked, still grinning. "And how do you find him? Has your opinion of him improved at all?"

Louisa began to laugh. "You may be an earl, but I do not think it's right to ask your dinner guests such forward questions, my lord."

"I suppose so." He paused. "If only I had a wife to temper me."

Louisa glanced at the young ladies sitting beside Rutley. "Well, if what you say about your sister and the duke is true, there will be more than a few broken hearts that will need mending after this evening. Perhaps you might offer your assistance."

"There is only one heart I'm interested in mending," Charles murmured.

Louisa arched her brow. "My heart is in excellent condition already, my lord."

Charles leaned back in his chair, studying her carefully. "Rosamund was speculating earlier this evening that perhaps you were not pretending all those years ago. Do you care to defend yourself against such accusations?"

Louisa did not answer, choosing to change the subject to something more mundane instead: the quality of the soup. They continued in such a way until the end of dinner, though Louisa's sharp wit was enough to make any conversation entertaining. Suddenly, Charles understood Rosamund's lack of faith in his ability to win Louisa's affections. But he couldn't simply give up.

When the men and women came together again in the drawing room, Louisa was nowhere in sight. Charles quietly slipped out of the room, walking down the hall until he found her in the library. She had her back turned toward him.

"Louisa?" he asked, causing her to jump.

She spun around, facing him, her hand on her breast. "Goodness! You startled me."

"I apologize." Charles stepped into the library, drawing closer to her. Upon further inspection, she seemed to be trembling. "Is something the matter?"

Louisa sighed, turning her back on him once more. "I couldn't sit in the drawing room listening to the other ladies plan our wedding." She spun around again, no longer trembling. In fact, her blue eyes appeared quite vicious instead. "Was it entirely necessary to have me sit next to you at dinner?"

Charles nodded once. "Yes."

"Why?" Louisa appeared flabbergasted.

He half smiled. "I wanted to be near you. Is that so bad?"

Louisa rapidly shook her head, turning away again. She balled her hands into fists at her sides. "And what if I had no income? Would you still want to be near me then?"

Charles didn't hesitate. "Yes."

She looked over her shoulder at him. "Do you mean that?"

Slowly, he reached for her waist, gently pulling her toward him. "I would give Linfield to Rutley if it meant I could have you."

"But... but why?"

Charles paused, searching for the right words. "I have been so lonely, Louisa. Even when I first came to town and held a dinner party for my family, I felt lonely. No one I cared about wanted to be near me. I do not really blame them." He paused again, searching for signs of fear in her eyes. But he only saw concern, which comforted him enough to continue. "There has been something missing in my life, but I could never quite discern what. So I tried to fill it with brandy and women and cards, but they were never enough. You, on the other hand... you make me feel whole again."

He'd barely finished his sentence when Louisa wrapped

her hands around the back of his head, forcing his lips down to hers. She kissed him with such hunger that all he could do was try to match it. But just as his hands started to roam across her supple body, she quickly pulled away from him. They both breathed heavily, staring at one another.

"Marry me, Louisa."

But she shook her head. "I can't."

And then she ran from the room, leaving him to stare after her, wondering what he'd done wrong.

Chapter Nineteen

LOUISA QUICKLY RETURNED to the drawing room, grateful that Charles didn't chase after her, especially after she'd gone and done something so stupid, so dangerous! Again! Luckily, no one seemed to notice her absence, what with the boisterous game of charades taking place at the center of the room. Flora stood in the middle of it all, reading a riddle for the others to solve.

Louisa joined in watching the gentlemen of the party try to guess the answer, happy for the distraction after her unnerving encounter with Charles in the library. She thought she saw her stepmother's eyes flicker in her direction when she sat down, and Louisa felt herself flush under Mrs. Strickland's penetrative gaze. Flora had managed to keep quiet about the earl's proposal, but Louisa somehow suspected she would have to tell Mrs. Strickland the truth soon.

Of course, it would all be much simpler if Louisa just agreed to marry him. Part of her had dreamed of Charles confessing to such feelings seven years ago. Although she valued her independence, she wasn't entirely immune to feeling affection toward a man. There was no other explanation for kissing him like that. But now that he'd finally uttered such precious words, she wasn't quite sure if his feelings were genuine or if he had only spotted a weakness in her character. For years, she *wanted* to hear him say he was sorry. And now he finally had. But perhaps he was only trying to take advantage of her because he needed something in return.

But oh, how she wanted him. That much Louisa knew. And she had something he wanted as well, an impressive income, enough to pay off his debts in a few short years if he continued to avoid card tables and expensive bottles of brandy. But really, how long could his good behavior last? It had been less than a year since she first saw him again at that country ball. And how long would he enjoy kissing her as much as she enjoyed kissing him? Surely he would grow tired of her. And did she really want any of her income going to the cold and calculating Duke of Rutley?

Regardless of her lustful feelings, any marriage would be a disaster, and Louisa knew she must do everything in her power to prevent any word of their liaison from appearing in the broadsheets—at least until Flora found a proper suitor to marry. The men Charles had collected there tonight were impressive—she had to give him that—and the news he passed along about Lord Fitzgerald would surely be enough to make Flora forget that rogue forever.

When the evening finally, thankfully, came to a close, Charles personally escorted the Stricklands to the front door. Flora giggled uncontrollably as she watched Lord Bolton bring Louisa's gloved knuckles to his lips. Louisa resisted the urge to turn and glare at Flora, regretting not paying attention to how many glasses of table wine her younger sister drank at dinner.

"Perhaps I might take you driving in Hyde Park tomorrow afternoon, Miss Strickland," he said.

Mrs. Strickland spoke before Louisa could answer herself. "That would be wonderful, my lord."

Louisa winced, displeased her stepmother would speak for her. Mrs. Strickland only shrugged in response, so Louisa reluctantly turned back to Charles. She forced a smile, but not before her eyes fluttered down to the earl's lips. A blush started to form on her cheeks. "Yes, that would be... nice," she managed to say, her voice sounding strangled.

Suspecting Charles might laugh at her and her weakness for his touch, Louisa quickly headed out the front door, not daring to look back at him. A footman helped her into their carriage, and Louisa took a deep breath when all the Stricklands were safely inside. But a figure soon caught her eye outside the carriage window. The earl stood at the open front door, watching her as the Stricklands' carriage pulled away. She quickly faced the other direction, once again regretting kissing him that evening. Now he thought he stood a chance, that he could whittle her down until she finally gave in and married him.

Determined to think of something else, Louisa looked at her sister. "What did you think of the young men Lord Bolton gathered for dinner this evening?" Louisa asked. "Have any of them captured your attention?"

Flora hiccupped and sighed, leaning her head against the cushioned side of the carriage. "None of them were quite as handsome as Lord Fitzgerald."

Louisa furrowed her brow. "Surely there is more to a man than his looks, Flora." Her sister rolled her eyes, but Louisa persisted. "And you seemed to have had a marvelous time playing charades. You must have found at least one of the men this evening charming."

Flora shrugged, and Louisa felt her temper rising. "Do you know how much money a season costs?" Louisa asked. Her sister did not respond, closing her eyes instead. Louisa suspected it was the wine. "You will not be having another one if you do not find a husband this year, so I suggest you stop wasting your time pining for a rogue of a man who left town without making you any promises!"

"Louisa!" Mrs. Strickland exclaimed.

Flora's lower lip began to quiver, and her eyes opened, appearing glossy. The carriage rolled to a stop.

"What do you know?" Flora asked, pushing the carriage door open before one of the footmen could help. "How could you possibly understand anything about love or devotion with the way you have been treating the earl?"

Louisa scowled. What did Charles have to do with anything? "Flora—"

But she had already quitted the carriage and was stumbling toward the front door of their rented town house. Louisa and her stepmother exchanged a brief look.

"What did she mean by that?" Mrs. Strickland asked.

"I haven't the slightest idea," Louisa said, her voice sounding more high-pitched than usual, a telltale sign that she was lying.

"Louisa—"

But Louisa quitted the carriage too, following her sister into the house and leaving the confused Mrs. Strickland behind. Louisa saw a ruffle of skirts at the top of the stairs, but then Flora turned the corner and was gone. Louisa shouted after her sister and was ready to ascend the stairs herself when her stepmother stepped into the entry hall.

"Let her be and come with me to the drawing room," Mrs. Strickland said with a sigh as she walked down the hall.

Louisa stood motionless at the bottom of the staircase, staring upward and biting her lip.

Her stepmother impatiently waved her hand. "Come!"

Sighing, Louisa reluctantly followed her. Mrs. Strickland took a seat in one of the upholstered armchairs and motioned for Louisa to join her. Louisa would have preferred to remain standing so she could make a hasty escape if needed, but somehow she knew there was no avoiding her stepmother's interrogation that evening.

"Is there something you would like to tell me, Louisa?" Mrs. Strickland asked.

Louisa grew very still. Perhaps if she made no sudden movements, her stepmother wouldn't see straight through her. "No," Louisa murmured, sounding more mouselike than human.

"No?" Mrs. Strickland echoed.

Louisa placed her hands in her lap, nervously grabbing at her skirts.

Her stepmother sighed. "Then there's no reason why Lord Bolton asked you to waltz at Almack's and invited you to dinner at his home?"

"Plenty of women were invited this evening," Louisa countered softly, still clutching at her skirts. Although Mrs. Strickland was only ten years older than Louisa, the woman certainly had a way of making her feel like a little girl.

"Yet the earl paid them no mind and gave all his attention to you. *And* he only offered to take one young lady driving the next day in the park."

Louisa laughed, though it sounded more bitter than happy. "I am hardly a young lady anymore, Mrs. Strickland."

"Clearly," her stepmother snapped, causing Louisa to jump slightly. "You may not think I noticed, but I saw you and the earl sneak away from the party at the same time. What were you doing?"

Louisa bit her lip. She supposed there was no reason to hide it from Mrs. Strickland any longer. Plenty of men proposed to women who rejected them. Louisa was hardly mad or anything like that. It was a lousy match, after all, what with Charles's debts and sordid past. She let out a huff of air. "If you must know, the earl has proposed to me."

Multiple times now, Louisa added in her head, a fact that managed to thrill and trouble her at the same time.

Mrs. Strickland gasped, covering her mouth with her hands. Louisa nearly groaned at the evident delight in her stepmother's brown eyes. Mrs. Strickland slowly lowered her hands. "And did you give him an answer?" she asked breathlessly.

"I said no, of course!" Louisa exclaimed. "Twice, actually. It actually might have been three or four times at this point, but I have quickly lost track."

Her stepmother's face fell.

Louisa grew serious. "Please, Mrs. Strickland. How could I entrust the manor to *him*?" She shook her head, standing up to pace the room, her stepmother carefully watching her. "Not to mention, he could easily gamble away Flora's dowry by the end of the year if I accept."

"Surely you don't believe that," her stepmother protested. "You and I both know the earl is much changed over the past year. He just hosted such a lovely dinner party. I would think you would be happy with this news, especially after you insisted he end his pursuit of Flora."

Louisa stopped pacing and crossed her arms against her chest, growing more frustrated with each passing moment. "You still think I did that out of jealousy, don't you?"

Her stepmother huffed. "Well, it seems obvious that it is the truth now that you have ensnared him for yourself, just as you always wanted."

Louisa groaned. She could take it no longer. She must tell Mrs. Strickland the truth about her courtship with Charles all those years ago. Louisa sat back down and looked at her stepmother with an intent gaze, speaking carefully. "But it's not what I always wanted. What I always wanted was to remain unmarried and run Strickland Manor by myself. But when you insisted on giving me a season, and Papa eventually gave in, I approached Lord Bolton with a plan. We would pretend to be courting so that I could avoid other suitors. It would make you happy, and then when he never came up to scratch, I could use the excuse of heartbreak as to why I wanted to remain a spinster forever. Such an excuse seemed much more acceptable to females than the other one."

Her stepmother stared blankly at her. Then, she shook her head as if she didn't quite believe what she was hearing. "But you and Lord Bolton were always so happy together! I truly thought you were in love, which was why..." Her voice trailed off.

Louisa frowned. She had no idea they had put on such a convincing show all those years ago. Slowly, Louisa rose from the chair. "I am sorry to disappoint you, but please believe me when I tell you it was nothing more than an act, and the earl and I will not be getting married."

"But you would be a countess! Think of the honor you would bring to your father."

Louisa furrowed her brow. "Papa is dead! What does he care whether I am a countess or not?" Louisa gestured wildly at her stepmother. "Am I not doing a fine job at taking care of you and Flora, with your fancy dresses and your season in town? You want for nothing! And you have no idea what I do to keep a roof over our heads."

Louisa shook her head, laughing bitterly as she did. "Inheriting a successful estate is one thing; maintaining its success is another, especially as a woman. I should think that's all Papa would care about if he were still alive, not whether I were a countess or some such nonsense. Now, if you will excuse me, I must speak to my sister before she goes to bed. Good night, Mrs. Strickland."

Louisa spun around and walked out of the room, ignoring

her stepmother's calls for her to return. Louisa no longer wished to debate an unmarried woman's worth or her ability to manage an estate without a man. She was tired of such arguments. She had heard them from all sorts of people who knew nothing about anything ever since her father died and left her the manor.

When she reached Flora's bedroom door, she knocked lightly. Her sister's muffled voice came from the other side. "Come in."

Louisa opened the door, finding Flora already in bed, propped up on a pile of pillows, her chestnut hair done up in cloth curlers. She had her arms crossed against her chest, and she studied Louisa with a harsh gaze. "What is it?" Flora asked.

Louisa gently shut the door behind her and walked over to Flora's bedside, sitting on top of the plain cream-colored quilt, just beside her sister's legs. Louisa sighed, realizing there was no easy way to say what she needed to say. "There is something I must tell you about the viscount. Something the earl told me about him."

Flora sat further up in bed, uncrossing her arms and looking at her sister intently. "I am listening."

Louisa chewed on her lower lip nervously before finally telling her sister the truth. "He said the viscount's brother called Fitzgerald home because one of his tenants..." Louisa paused, taking a breath. She feared her sister's reaction. She did not want to hurt the poor girl; she only wanted to help her move on. "One of his tenants is claiming his daughter is with child." Flora stared blankly. Louisa swallowed. "The viscount's child."

Flora laughed. "Well, that is just ridiculous! It mustn't be true."

Louisa grew more and more worried. No, this wasn't the reaction Louisa wanted from her sister—not at all.

"It is probably only a vicious rumor started by someone who does not like him. It could even be the Earl of Bolton himself."

Sighing, Louisa's shoulders drooped. "I'll have you know it was the duke who informed Lord Bolton, but surely you don't believe the earl would do something like that. What reason would he have to do such a thing?"

"It would make you happy if I despised the viscount," Flora muttered, crossing her arms against her chest once more. Her lips formed an unhappy pout. "You have hated him from the moment you first laid eyes on him. I have always wondered why."

"I just had a feeling!" Louisa exclaimed. "He charged at us as if he had done it purposefully to startle us."

Flora rolled her eyes. "You are ridiculous."

That was when Louisa finally lost her temper. "For goodness' sake, Flora, he carried on with an opera singer at a ball while courting you! Do you honestly think he wouldn't carry on with farmers' daughters as well?"

Flora's lower lip began to quiver again. Louisa started to grimace as soon as she realized that tears would quickly follow. She began to apologize, but she couldn't even utter one word, for Flora grabbed one of the pillows beside her and vigorously tossed it at her sister. "Leave!" Flora shouted.

Louisa scrambled off the bed as Flora began to cry. Louisa stood a few feet away with her hands on her hips. "Get a hold of yourself!"

"He told me he loved me!" Flora wailed as she rocked back and forth in her bed.

Louisa sighed, thinking of Charles's confession earlier that evening.

You make me feel whole again. What a load of claptrap! "Men will tell you all sorts of things to get your money, Flora," Louisa said. "I tried to warn you."

Her sister glared at her, reaching for another pillow. "Didn't I tell you to leave?" she asked, looking as if she might assault Louisa with another pillow at any moment.

Louisa quickly scampered into the hallway. "I am only looking out for your best interests!" she shouted from the doorway.

"What is all this carrying on?"

Louisa turned. Mrs. Strickland stood there looking at her in shock. When she regained her bearings, she pointed to Flora's open bedroom door. "Ask your daughter. I, for one, am going to bed. Good night."

Chapter Twenty

LOUISA TOOK her breakfast in her bedroom the following day. She had no desire to join her stepmother and sister in the morning room after the incident last night. Mrs. Strickland would make her apologize to Flora, even though Louisa thought it ought to be the other way around. Her silly attachment to Fitzgerald was getting out of hand, especially when plenty of other eligible men were interested in her.

They filled the drawing room that afternoon, some from Lord Bolton's party the previous evening, others from Almack's. But Flora was despondent amongst the sea of gentlemen, hardly herself, and Louisa watched from the doorway, feeling disappointed and frustrated at her younger sister after she seemed to be making so much progress earlier that week.

"Miss Strickland."

Louisa froze. She had forgotten Charles was coming to take her driving that weekend. After gathering her bearings, she turned around and curtseyed. "Lord Bolton. How do you do?"

After bowing, he peeked over her shoulder into the drawing room. He whistled. "Quite the crush."

Louisa followed his gaze. "It is unfortunate she doesn't seem to like any of them. I suppose your efforts were for naught."

"My efforts weren't only for Flora." He spoke softly, and his breath warmed the back of her neck. Louisa stiffened, then she turned back to face him.

"If I am to go driving with you, I must first ask that you do not pester me with questions about marriage the entire time."

Despite her threatening tone, Charles smiled.

She pursed her lips. "I will send you away if you cannot promise me."

Charles sighed. "Oh, very well."

"Come," she said with a wave of her hand. She walked down the hall toward the stairs. Charles followed her. "I will fetch my bonnet, and then we will be off."

With her bonnet retrieved from upstairs, Louisa returned to the entry hall and followed Charles outside, where his curricle and tiger waited. Charles helped her into the seat closest to the front door, then walked around the back to climb up the other side. Louisa followed him with her eyes. Had he always looked so fine while wearing a topper?

When Charles sat down beside her, he had to position himself so that their thighs were touching, placing his walking stick on the other side of him. Louisa swallowed, their nearness to one another making her uneasy. She had never been on a curricle ride. She hadn't quite expected them to be so small, and when Charles reached for the reins of the horses, she laughed slightly in an effort to hide her nerves. "I do hope you know what you're doing."

He smiled at her wordlessly, then faced forward, making a sound with his mouth. The carriage lurched, and Louisa nearly tumbled forward. With one hand still on the reins, Charles placed his free arm around Louisa's waist. "Steady now."

Reaching for her bonnet, Louisa straightened herself, then promptly swatted his arm away. Her heart raced. "Both hands on the reins, my lord."

He smiled again, this time more broadly, but he did as she asked. And once Louisa became used to the curricle, she found herself smiling as well, relishing the breeze on her face as they made their way through Mayfair toward Hyde Park. Charles must have noticed, for he briefly turned to her and asked, "Are you enjoying yourself?"

Tempering her expression, she nodded slightly. "The weather is lovely today." Realizing that would bring more people to the park that day, she started to frown. "I do hope the park isn't too crowded."

"Why?" he asked, a coy look on his face. "Are you afraid of who might see us there?"

Louisa pouted slightly. "It was rather wicked of you to ask me to go driving in front of Mrs. Strickland. You knew she would force me into it, whether I wanted to or not."

Charles half smiled. "Sometimes mothers know best."

They had turned into Hyde Park by then and found it crowded with members of the ton, just as Louisa feared. Charles seemed to know everyone, smiling and tipping his cap at other couples passing them. Louisa felt awkward and uncomfortable beside him. All that people seemed to know about Miss Strickland was that she was a wealthy spinster from Kent. Meanwhile, society considered Charles to be in his prime, the perfect candidate for some well-to-do young girl in search of a husband—the exact opposite of Louisa. So much had changed in the past seven years that she wondered why Charles hadn't preferred any of the young ladies he met at his aunt's ball all those evenings ago when they first kissed.

"You appear deep in thought," Charles observed, shaking Louisa from her reverie.

She smiled nervously at him, trying to think of something to say. Louisa had no desire to tell him what she was truly feeling, lest he capitalize on such confused feelings and somehow convince her she was falling in love with him, which she was sure she wasn't. Or was she?

Oh, bother.

"And what does your mother think of all this?" Louisa abruptly asked, steering the conversation back to the earl's previous comment. "I seem to recall her not liking me very much."

Charles scoffed. "You exaggerate."

Louisa was unconvinced. She may be wealthy, but she was a mere miss, the daughter of an untitled landowner and successful investor. The closest Louisa came to nobility was a baron for a great-grandfather. Such lack of distinguishability made Louisa sorely lacking in Lady Bolton's eyes.

"My mother does not like anyone, so really, you shouldn't take her judgment to heart," Charles said.

Louisa laughed. "Do not worry, my lord. I never did."

Charles fell silent again. When he spoke again, he sounded upset. "Besides, my mother has abandoned me in my quest for a wife. That means she has no say in the matter, nor the final decision."

Realizing his mother was a touchy topic for the earl, Louisa decided to change the subject. "When are you due to have dinner at Dover Street next?"

"The day after next. Why?"

Louisa shrugged. "I am only making conversation."

Charles seemed to consider this for a moment, then spoke. "You should come with me. Brooks will be there, of course. Perhaps you might join forces and punish me with your harsh criticisms of my character together."

"And what harsh criticisms are those?" Louisa asked.

"That I am nothing but a ne'er-do-well fortune hunter from a slowly decaying class of people who will have no power in society by the turn of the next century."

Louisa nearly smiled. "Well, at least you will probably be dead then."

Charles couldn't help but laugh. "One can hope. But his prediction does not bode well for my children." He paused a moment, peering at Louisa thoughtfully. "And what do you think, Miss Strickland? Do you agree with my brother-in-law's assessment?"

"Some parts seem accurate. Others, not so much."

Charles raised his brow. "Oh?"

She looked at him sharply. "You are not the idle worthless person you once were, but that is the only concession I give."

Louisa noticed the way Charles grinned when she spoke and immediately regretted what she said. There was no use complimenting him and giving him the wrong idea. She shook her head. "As for you being a fortune hunter, I cannot disagree with that point, which is why you really must give up this senseless pursuit of me, my lord. Nothing will change my mind about marriage."

"Nothing at all?" he asked softly, sliding even closer to her, so close that their thighs felt like one. She swallowed, looking down at his lap and noticing the slight bulge there. She quickly looked up at him, their eyes briefly meeting before Charles had to turn away and focus on the crowded path ahead.

"Must you torture me this way?" she asked, her voice low.

His head turned sharply, capturing her gaze once more. "Must it be torture?"

Louisa turned away, unable to look into his blue eyes for very long without losing all restraint toward him. "How can I trust you won't ruin everything my father and I have worked for over the years?"

Charles sighed. "I acknowledge my behavior hasn't been perfect in the past—"

Louisa huffed loudly. "It's been *far* from perfect," she muttered under her breath.

Charles pursed his lips. "Yes, I have been far from perfect in the past. Even when we met again last summer, I teased you, and I danced with your sister against your wishes. But I will not deny my attraction to you any longer."

Louisa's breathing hitched. "W-what?"

The earl's expression grew pained. "Surely you must know, Louisa. You drive me mad with desire. Is it not written all over my face?"

Louisa fell silent, unable to speak for a long moment. Was she that blind? Or was he lying to her? She shifted uncomfortably until she found enough words to change the subject to something other than his attraction to her. "Nevertheless, your estate—"

Now Charles was the one to interrupt her. "I admit I cared very little for Linfield Hall when my father was still alive. You and I are opposites in that regard. But if you asked Mr. Hardy or even Rutley, they would tell you I have devoted myself to the running of the estate since I saw you at that assembly last summer. Why do you think that is?"

Louisa answered without hesitation. "You wanted to marry my sister."

Charles shook his head. "I wanted to impress you."

"Because you wanted to marry my sister."

Charles sighed with frustration. "Perhaps that was true on the surface, but I swear my true motivations were much different. I heard what you said about me, and I wanted to prove you wrong. And are you not impressed? After last autumn's disastrous harvest, I have still taken all the necessary economies. Linfield is still afloat, and I have even started paying back Rutley without the help of a rich wife."

Louisa scoffed. "But think of how much easier it would be if only you had one!"

"You're right," Charles snapped. Louisa shifted away from him. Noticing this, he more calmly added, "It would be easier. But I have realized I cannot marry a woman for her money alone."

"Which is why you insist on tormenting me," Louisa said.

Charles leaned over so that his lips were level with her ear. "You are tormenting yourself, Louisa. Not me." His hot breath tickled her neck, and she grew pale. He pulled away from her, turning back to the path ahead. "For once in your life, give in to what you want. I will be a good husband in more ways than one."

Louisa grew warm. Although he had pulled away from her, she could still feel his body heat radiating toward her.

"We will share equal responsibilities for both estates if that is what you truly want," he said. "Think about it. Linfield is much bigger than Strickland."

Louisa's mind began to wander with possibilities. Charles lacked disposable income at the moment, but Linfield was not a terrible property. He was what they called cash poor but land rich. The old earl kept Linfield well maintained when he was still alive, though he never managed to make it more efficient and profitable, not like the Stricklands had with their estate. The late Lord Bolton preferred to spend money on his children rather than invest in his land or industries outside of farming, which was why Charles was in his present predicament: dry coffers yet so many bills to pay.

Charles, as it turned out, was a bad investment. But with Louisa's help, he could pay back Rutley much more quickly and get back to growing his estate rather than being one more lousy harvest away from bankruptcy. Louisa's eyes flicked in his direction. "So I would get a say in how our money would be spent?" she asked.

"Of course!" Charles exclaimed, almost too readily.

She eyed him suspiciously, still not quite sure if he was being genuine.

He must have noticed, for he continued. "You and I both know that I would eventually run Linfield into the ground without you. I am not as inadequate as I used to be, but I am not near the level of genius you are if what Hardy says of you is to be believed."

She knew he was only playing to her egotistical side in the hopes of reaching an agreement, but she couldn't help but like what she heard. She always was the more responsible out of the two, and Charles did need a wife who could temper his more wild ways—if they even existed anymore. Louisa couldn't deny she hadn't seen him touch a drop of alcohol since he returned to London, nor had she read any stories in the broadsheets about him misbehaving at some social gathering.

Goodness! She was going around in circles. Louisa turned to him. "Enough," she said. "You promised we would not speak of marriage."

Charles frowned, disappointed. "Fine. Then what shall we talk about?"

Louisa paused a moment, blinking. "I don't know! See? Another reason we shouldn't marry. We have nothing to say to each other unless we are arguing."

Or kissing. Louisa sheepishly glanced over at Charles, who slowly began to smile as if he read her mind. "That's not true. I have a question."

"What is it?" She did not look at him while he spoke.

"Where did you learn to kiss as you do?"

Louisa's head spun in his direction, eyes wide. He must know he was her first. She had felt so clumsy and awkward kissing him for the first time. Surely he'd noticed! When she did not answer right away, Charles turned away, his gaze darkening. "Rutley told me there were rumors in Kent about you and Mr. Hardy."

Louisa's eyes widened even further, and then she burst out laughing. "Mr. Hardy?" she echoed in between loud guffaws, hardly believing the Duke of Rutley would spread such a preposterous rumor. "Please! Everyone knows he is in love with my sister. I am the furthest thing from his mind. Well, unless he is begging me to hire him to manage the manor. You really ought to pay him more so he stops pestering me."

Charles appeared uncertain, and for once, Louisa enjoyed the fact that *he* was jealous instead of the other way around. She suddenly felt very daring, leaning closer to Charles so that her bosom brushed against his forearm. His grip around the horses' reins tightened.

"And what if it was true?" she asked. "Would that bother you? That another man touched me before you had the chance?"

His Adam's apple bobbed in his neck. "No," he said firmly, not looking at her, his eyes focused straight ahead on the path. "I would still want you."

She sighed, leaning away from him. He seemed to take a breath as she did.

"It bothered me when I saw you with Miss Coppola," she admitted suddenly, speaking before her mind registered what she was doing. He looked at her for a split second before turning back to the path. "I know I said it didn't. But it did."

Charles looked at her again. "I'm sorry," he murmured.

She shook her head. "Do not apologize," she said with a sigh. "How could you have known I wished you would lose control around *me* for once?"

"Louisa—"

But she interrupted him. "I think I would like to go home now, my lord."

He frowned at her but didn't try to argue. "As you wish, Miss Strickland."

CHARLES WAS STANDING in the Duke of Rutley's study no less than thirty minutes later. Rutley sat at his desk, one leg propped up on the surface, eating an apple. "You are working hard," the earl observed.

"I am having an afternoon snack," Rutley said, removing his boot from the desk before leaning over it with his forearms. He still held the apple in his hand. "What is it?" The duke furrowed his brow as if concerned. "You look as if you're concocting some sort of evil plan, something the old Charles would have come up with."

"I have a favor to ask," Charles said after a moment of hesitation. The earl hated asking Rutley for anything, but he didn't see any other options. He was running out of ideas to woo Louisa, and this one was the best he had. Rutley stared at him, waiting. "I was wondering if you could throw a ball, like the ones you used to host before..." Charles trailed off, not wanting to mention the end of the duke's engagement to Rosamund.

Rutley glared at him, and Charles swallowed nervously. He went around one of the armchairs facing Rutley's desk and sat down. He started to wring his hands, not quite looking at the duke. "You see, in the past—"

The duke's face fell. "You wish to seduce Miss Strickland in the Red Room."

Charles responded by shrugging sheepishly. The duke sighed, standing up from his chair behind the desk and walking across the room to the sideboard. He opened the crystal decanter and poured himself a glass of brandy.

Whether Rutley was hosting a ball or a dinner party, both men utilized the Red Room, a small sitting room on the second floor, for their secret romantic rendezvous. Of course, they both agreed to stay away from innocents; widows and wives were fine, but never ladies in their first season. Louisa, though, was hardly a lady in her first season anymore. She was something else entirely.

"Are you sure this is the correct way to go about this?" Rutley asked, turning from the sideboard and squinting at his friend. He crossed his arms, holding his glass of brandy at his chest. "Louisa is not easily swayed. If you think sex will change her mind—"

"If it doesn't, then I will move on from her," Charles said suddenly. When the duke still appeared skeptical, Charles's countenance grew more serious. "I promise."

"Charles, I hesitate—"

"I do not know any other way to go about it at this point," Charles said, his voice sounding more desperate than he would have liked.

The duke raised his brow at his friend losing his composure.

"I have apologized over and over again. I have proposed on multiple occasions. I danced with her at Almack's. I have had her over for dinner and taken her on outings, all to no avail. So now I will pursue her the only way I know how."

The two grew silent.

"And that is?" the duke finally asked.

"By behaving like a selfish cad."

Rutley sighed, turning around and setting down his glass. He spread his arms, gripping the edges of the sideboard as he leaned over it. When Rutley finally turned around, Charles began to think he would say no, but the duke nodded once instead. "Very well. I will host a bloody ball."

Charles smiled with relief and bowed his head slightly. "Thank you, Your Grace."

The duke pointed a menacing finger at him, and Charles's smile faded slightly. "You will convince your sister to come as well. I want her to watch me flirt with every eligible lady in London. You see how it is bothering her, don't you? She was positively livid with me at your—"

Charles held up a hand. "If Rosamund's presence is required for you to host a ball, I am sure I could convince her to come. But I would rather stay out of your business with my sister if that is all right with you, so do spare me your rantings and ravings about her."

The duke nodded, albeit reluctantly.

Still, Charles drove to Lady Ramsbury's Park Street mansion to meet with his sister next. Rosamund saw him in the entry hall. It was the day of Lady Ramsbury's book club, and they had a strict no-gentlemen-allowed policy. As she was explaining this, Charles wondered if Louisa was inside.

"She is not here," Rosamund replied, as if reading his mind.

He frowned, forcing Miss Strickland from his mind. "That's not why I have called," he said, shaking his head. "The Duke of Rutley intends to host a ball. He wants to know if you will attend."

Rosamund snorted. "Does His Grace have you running errands for him now?"

Charles rolled his eyes, annoyed. "Just say you will go. For my sake."

"Well, now you have me even more intrigued." She narrowed her gaze. "What exactly are you planning?"

Charles forced a smile, not wanting to give anything away. "I am planning nothing. The duke is the one hosting the party, and he is the one who requested your presence."

Charles paused a moment, trying to think of a way to convince her.

Rosamund tilted her head to the side, watching him.

This led to Charles trying a different approach. "He claims to enjoy watching your reaction to seeing him flirt with other women."

Rosamund's nostrils flared. "What reaction? I couldn't care less if he flirts with other women." She crossed her arms. "You can tell him I will come to his ball just to prove it. He's the one who can crumble when he sees *me* flirt with other men!"

Her brother's mouth twitched. "Splendid."

Chapter Twenty-One

LOUISA DID NOT SEE Charles for a week after their drive in the park, and she never did join him for dinner at Dover Street. She wished it didn't bother her so, wondering what he might be doing—or scheming—if not pestering her. What made it worse was that Mrs. Strickland and Flora were barely speaking to her. They were sitting in the drawing room in silence when a servant appeared with an envelope.

Flora scrambled to take it, nearly shoving Louisa out of the way when she rose as well. She furrowed her brow, watching her sister open the missive. "What is it, Flora?" she asked. Even Mrs. Strickland sat at attention, her embroidery lowered to her lap. Flora tore open the letter, and her shoulders drooped soon after.

"The Duke of Rutley is hosting a ball next week," Flora said, sounding unimpressed.

She handed the invitation to her sister before sitting back down with a loud sigh. Flora had grown disinterested in parties and balls ever since Louisa told her the rumors about the viscount. Louisa frequently reminded Flora that they were due to return to Kent next month. She was running out of time to form any meaningful attachment if she wouldn't give any of the gentlemen currently pursuing her a chance.

Upon seeing the invitation, Louisa immediately wondered if the earl would be there, or whether he was behind the entire affair. She turned the thick piece of paper over in her hands.

Her stepmother spoke from behind her. "We do not have to go if you do not wish it," Mrs. Strickland murmured. "We could return to Kent tomorrow if that is what everyone prefers."

Flora huffed, crossing her arms against her chest. "That is what *I* certainly prefer," she said.

When Louisa turned and looked at her sister, Flora was glaring at her. Louisa narrowed her eyes. "We must go," Louisa said, her voice sharp. "The duke is our neighbor, and it would be rude to reject his invitation."

Flora perked up in her seat, as if her interests were suddenly engaged. "I wonder if Lord Bolton will be there. He has not called since your drive in the park." Her expression then grew cold. "What did you do to drive him away, Louisa?" She shook her head, her high-pitched laughter echoing throughout the room. "I'm sorry—what a silly question to ask —you probably only acted as you normally do."

Louisa glared at her sister, sitting back down and placing the cursed invitation on the table across from her. She didn't know why the insult bothered her after politely trying to reject Charles on multiple occasions, despite his determination to convince her otherwise. Louisa had gotten what she wanted, so why did she feel so ill at ease after not seeing him for a week?

She hated that feeling. Louisa didn't want to desire anyone. For years, she had been in complete control of her life and her funds, with no man to interfere. Papa had taught her everything she needed to know before he died, even when all his friends thought he was mad for leaving his estate to his eldest daughter instead of the nearest male relative. And they all thought Louisa was even madder when she refused to marry Cousin William upon inheriting.

But Charles was different than Cousin William. He left her wanting more than the life she had already chosen for herself. A life she had planned out long before they had even faked their first courtship. But Charles couldn't suddenly appear in her life again and expect everything to change, even if he did seem rather genuine from time to time.

But he stayed away another week, and by the evening of the duke's ball, Louisa found herself eagerly looking around the large ballroom, hoping to catch a glimpse of the earl. After such a long absence, she half expected to find him escorting another young lady out onto the dance floor, already recovered from his brief period of madness when he tried to convince Louisa to marry him.

Nevertheless, Louisa wore her most fashionable dress, a dark-pink frock with a detachable train made of netted silk. She thought she looked like a biscuit topped with cream and strawberries, what with her light-pink elbow-high gloves and matching ribbon in her hair. Louisa looked out into the crowd over top of her white silk fan.

There, across the room, she saw him. And much to her surprise, there was no other woman on his arm. Instead, he was looking back at her, smiling. He was too far away for her to make out too many of his features, but she could still imagine the dimple in his left cheek. When their eyes met, Louisa quickly turned away, snapping her fan shut as she lowered it. Although she did not watch, she could picture him walking toward her. Louisa's heart began to race.

Rosamund stood near her, observing the whole scene as it took place. "My brother is approaching us," she murmured into her cup of punch before taking a sip. She lowered it when she finished, smiling broadly. "Charles! You have arrived."

Reluctantly, Louisa turned around, offering a curtsey. "Lord Bolton," she said.

The earl, still smiling like before, bowed. "Miss Strickland," he said before turning to his sister. "Thank you for coming, Rosamund. The duke would have had my head if you didn't."

"I am enjoying myself immensely," Rosamund said without missing a beat, a coy smile playing at her lips. "I already have a partner for every dance."

Charles raised his brow. "Are any of those with the duke?"

Rosamund waved her hand. "Do not worry. I promised him the last one."

For a brief moment, Louisa and Charles exchanged a look. Louisa wondered if Charles was right. Could the duke and Rosamund find their way back to each other? Could Charles and Louisa do the same? Or had they already? He tilted his head toward her. "Do you have a partner for the first set?" he asked.

She shook her head. "No, my lord."

"Perhaps you might join me, then."

Louisa hesitated. The two siblings—Charles and Rosamund—carefully watched her. She glanced at Rosamund, who offered her an encouraging look. Louisa wondered to whose side she truly belonged before turning back to Charles. "As you wish, my lord."

When the set started, Louisa took the opportunity to question the earl. "I have not seen you since the park."

Charles raised his brow. "I thought you did not wish to see me."

Louisa paused. "Well, yes—yet that did not stop you from asking me to dance with you this evening."

"I thought we might dance as friends," Charles replied.

The dance movements brought them very close now, and Louisa thought she stopped breathing. When they separated, she gulped for air.

"Friends?" she asked when they joined hands again, furrowing her brow for a moment. Louisa looked him directly in the eye. "Then you promise you will make no mention of marriage for the entire evening?"

He cocked his head to the side. "I did not say that."

She turned away, smiling. "Then perhaps we might just enjoy the dance in silence."

They stepped toward each other, crossing arms. The earl's eyes captured hers. "Anything to be close to you."

She felt herself flush, and for a moment, she did not know what to say. "Charles," she murmured so that no one else on the dance floor could hear them. "What is the real reason behind you avoiding me for the past two weeks? You are never one without a plan. I only wonder what it is this time. Ambushing me in the library, a dance at Almack's, a dinner party at Finch Place, a ride in the park. Then complete avoidance. What is next?"

He smiled sheepishly. "Perhaps I only wanted to see if you missed me. I have a sneaking suspicion that you did, especially now that you've mentioned it. So, did you?"

Louisa's heartbeat quickened. "Only a little."

He laughed once. "Only a little?" he echoed.

Louisa shrugged. "I suppose some of my other companions aren't quite as interesting as you."

Louisa didn't know what brought her to flirt with him, especially when she knew it could lead nowhere. But there was something she enjoyed about making him smile. It was as if she had the power to make his entire face light up, and she rather liked making his face do that.

When the dance was over, Charles escorted Louisa to the refreshment table, where they intently stared at each other over their cups of punch. Eventually, Charles put his down and spoke. "There is something I should like to show you upstairs."

"What is it?"

"A painting that Rutley owns that I find quite impressive. I think you would like it too."

Louisa nearly spit out her punch before putting her cup down as well. "Is this how all ladies are lured away from crowded ballrooms and toward more hidden places? The promise of viewing an impressive painting?"

Charles stepped closer to her. "There are other impressive things I can show you."

Louisa's breathing hitched. She did her best to maintain her composure. "Are there?"

Charles nodded, then waited. Louisa looked at him, wondering how an affair with him was any different than an affair with Hayward. At least Charles wasn't married. And he could not force her to marry him, even if they did sleep together. She knew she was behaving recklessly, but she just couldn't help it. The punch had gone straight to her head. Her sister seemed less and less interested in marriage every day, and they would be returning to Kent soon, away from society's prying eyes.

"Show me," she said.

Charles reached for her hand, and she took it, following him through a door at the back of the ballroom. They entered a narrow hall intended for servants, and when she looked to her right, Louisa saw a set of service stairs. Still holding her hand, Charles led her up the staircase, then suddenly stopped on the landing halfway between the first and second floors. He let go of her hand, then reached for her waist, pulling her into the landing's corner so that they were out of sight from the floor below. Charles kissed her, and Louisa felt her body melt into his, all of her cares suddenly floating away. What was this power he had over her?

She broke away from him, trying to regain her senses. She blinked, observing how the freckles across the bridge of his nose were much more apparent when she was closer to him. He smiled at her, and she realized she must have been looking at him in a dazed sort of way.

"What is it?" he asked.

"I want to see the painting," she murmured. Smiling slightly, Charles nodded and took her hand once more, leading her the rest of the way up the stairs. The hall was much wider on the second floor, so they walked side by side, still holding hands. They didn't go very far before Charles pulled her into a room. Louisa yelped, surprised by the sudden change in direction.

As Charles closed the door behind them, Louisa stepped further into the small sitting room. Somehow the candles were already lit, even though she got the feeling guests weren't supposed to be in this part of the house. Everything in the room was red, from the carpet to the armchairs to the wallpaper.

Louisa, feeling bold, went to sit on the sofa. Charles still stood by the door, his eyes fixated on her movements. For a moment, she was terrified. She had never seen him look at her that way, as if she was something he wanted to devour. Slowly, she reached for the cushion beside her, patting it gently. Her gaze steadily held his, but all the while, her heart threatened to leap out of her chest. She worried he might laugh at her for inviting him to sit near her like she did.

But luckily, Charles did as she directed. He started to lunge for her, but Louisa quickly looked away, stopping him as she directed her gaze toward a painting above the unlit fireplace at the center of the room. "Is that the painting?" she asked.

An overbearing man in a red military jacket stared down at them. "That is the first Duke of Rutley," Charles explained. "He is the current duke's great-grandfather."

Louisa gave the portrait a thoughtful look. She saw the resemblance to the current duke right away, what with his strong jawline and dark brow. Louisa looked back at Charles, biting her lip. "It is a good thing I didn't come just for the painting."

The earl nearly smiled. "Why?"

"I mean no offense to Rutley, but I don't find his great-grandfather nearly as interesting as other things in the room. And really, if this is how you seduce the majority of your conquests, isn't it rather awkward having your closest friend's great-grandfather staring down at you as—"

Charles reached for her, resting his right hand on the side of her neck while his lips found hers. Effectively silencing her, Louisa kissed him eagerly, feeling a secret thrill down to her core as his hand slid down her neck toward her bosom. When his hand reached for her breast, she arched her head back, sighing happily. The earl's lips traced a pattern down her chin to her jaw, his mouth eventually finding the crook of her neck. He began to lower his hand, tracing a line from her breast to her bottom with his palm.

He roughly squeezed the flesh there, and she moaned just as he lifted her onto his lap. She yelped, finding herself facing forward while he sat beneath her, still peppering kisses up and down her neck. His hands frantically reached for her skirts, yanking and pulling them up toward her waist.

"Be careful, Charles," she murmured, knowing she would have to return downstairs at some point. She did not want to worry about a ripped dress.

With her bare legs now exposed across his lap, he traced the edges of her stockings with his fingertips. His right hand slowly moved up her thigh, and Louisa shivered at his touch.

She knew she could tell him to stop his ascent, and that he would if she asked, but she didn't want him to stop—not even in the slightest. Louisa wanted him to feel what he had done to her. Beneath her bottom, she could already feel what she had done to him.

After making his way through layers of netting, dress, and petticoats, Charles cupped her bare mound with his right hand, and she gasped. As he gently explored her tender folds with his deft fingertips, her legs began to quiver on his lap, yet even she knew he hadn't reached the spot where she would feel the most pleasure.

"So sensitive," he murmured before plunging a thick finger inside of her. She moaned loudly, bringing her gloved hand to her mouth and biting at the silk. Louisa glanced over his shoulder toward the door, but Charles quickly drew her attention back to him by sliding his finger in and out of her. "So wet."

He brought his fingertips, now damp with her arousal, to the crest of her sex, gently touching the bundle of nerves there. Louisa responded almost immediately, her hips bucking forward on his lap. He wrapped his free arm around her waist, securing her closer to him. He gently stroked, and all she could do was close her eyes and tilt her head back, resting it against his shoulder.

"Charles," she whispered beneath her palm, his fingers feeling better and better with each circular motion of his fingertips.

"You are exquisite," he murmured in her ear before kissing her where the fabric of her dress met her bare shoulder.

"It's too much," she said, her voice still muffled as she felt her insides becoming tight while he stroked her. Louisa squirmed against him, but he did not let her go. When her release finally came, she dropped her hand, crying out.

"That's a good girl," he said, continuing to stroke until he drew every last drop out of her. When he stopped, her cheeks felt flushed, and she panted heavily. Charles let go and slid out from underneath her, then carefully positioned her across the sofa so that he could be on top of her. Realizing what he wanted, Louisa reached for the bulge in his breeches, but he knocked her hand away.

She looked up at him, confused. He cupped the side of her cheek, smiling. It should have been gentle and reassuring, but she worried over what he might say next. "Tell me you will marry me, Louisa. Tell me you will marry me, and I will give you everything you have ever wanted."

Chapter Twenty-Two

Louisa pinched her brow together, then gave Charles a firm shove to his chest. She slid out from underneath him and sat as far away from him as possible. He eventually fell back onto his haunches on the opposite end of the sofa.

"You cannot be serious," she muttered, the lustful look in her eyes vanishing. The sleeves of her bodice were askew, revealing a generous amount of skin.

Charles swallowed. Unfortunately, his lust couldn't subside so quickly. "What?" he asked, not quite sure what he had done wrong. "You know I wish to marry you, and if we..."

His voice trailed off. With the look Louisa was giving him, Charles thought it best not to finish his sentence. She huffed angrily, pushing her skirts down and standing up. Without another word, she went to the mirror hanging opposite the fireplace, adjusting the bodice of her dress so that she was properly covered again.

While Louisa frowned at her mussed hair, Charles tried to determine where it had all gone wrong, but unfortunately, all the blood in his body had collected in his groin, which left very little for his brain. Then again, this ill-advised plan might not have started in his brain in the first place. "Louisa," he said, standing up and coming behind her. They looked at each other in the mirror. "Did I do something wrong? I thought you were enjoying yourself."

Louisa huffed again. She turned around, clenching her fists at her side. Despite their frequent bickering, Charles realized then he didn't particularly like disappointing Louisa. There was a sinking feeling in his stomach as it became more and more apparent just how displeased she was with him. How different it was from the feeling he had when they first came into the library, when he thought she might truly be falling for him. Would he have to settle for one of the forgettable debutantes he had danced with that season? Charles shuddered at the thought.

"You cannot propose to a woman while she's underneath you on a sofa at your best mate's ball, especially not while tempting her with... with that!" Louisa said, gesturing toward the obvious tent in his breeches.

Charles closed his eyes, bringing his thumb and forefinger to the bridge of his nose and pinching it. When he brought his hand down, he spoke sternly. "Louisa, I cannot just bed you and continue as we have. If we are to proceed any further, you *must* marry me." Charles grew exasperated at Louisa's blank look. "Did you not enjoy what just occurred? I, for one, did!"

Louisa flushed and looked away, and Charles knew her answer without her saying anything.

"Why must you still oppose a marriage between us?"

"Because I do not trust you with Strickland Manor!" She appeared pained as she said it, tears gathering in the inside corners of her eyes. "It was Papa's pride and glory. I cannot disappoint him."

Charles slowly came toward her, placing his hands on her shoulders. "And you will not disappoint him. You haven't after all these years. I promise you, Louisa, nothing will change in terms of how you run things if we marry."

Louisa stared up at him. Her eyes were desperately searching his, as if she wanted to believe him but couldn't quite. "I do not trust you with my heart either," she murmured. The sadness in her eyes was unmistakable. "You will grow tired of me. If you tupped me now, you would see. You would want to marry someone else by morning."

That made Charles laugh. "That couldn't be further from the truth," he said, bringing his hands from her shoulders to her face, cupping her cheeks. Her eyes became brighter, and for a moment, he thought he was making progress. "I will make you a deal. I will give you my heart for the time being. You can look after it and do whatever you very well please with it. And when you are ready—and only when you are ready—you can give me yours in return. And I promise to look after it, Louisa. I swear to you."

She did not look convinced. Instead, she still looked confused. "But how will I know when I'm ready?"

But then there was a knock on the door. Charles and Louisa both turned, her face still in his hands. Reluctantly, Charles released her and walked toward the door. When he opened it, the duke stood on the other end.

"What is it?" Charles nervously asked.

"I only thought you should know that people are beginning to notice your and Miss Strickland's absence from the party," the duke said in his usual unaffected tone. "Including the girl's stepmother. Unless you and Miss Strickland have reached some sort of agreement, I suggest you return to the ballroom immediately."

Louisa stepped forward. "Were you planning this all along?" she asked, looking from the duke to Charles. "Bringing me here and seducing me with the hopes of everyone noticing?" She moved so that she was standing beside Charles, facing the duke directly. "Well, nothing happened, and there will be no agreement." She curtseyed toward Rutley, ignoring Charles entirely. "Your Grace."

Louisa passed him, walking down the hall and back down-stairs. Charles moved to follow her, but the duke placed a hand on his chest, preventing him. "Remember our agreement," Rutley said. "Your plan did not work. It is time to move on."

Reluctantly, Charles nodded, though he wasn't quite sure how he was supposed to give up his pursuit, especially after what just occurred. Despite what Louisa claimed, something *did* happen that night. And now he wanted her more than ever.

WHEN LOUISA RETURNED to the ballroom, she was trying desperately not to cry. *Stupid, stupid girl*, she told herself. How could she not know that Charles would try to force her into marriage if she slept with him? That was all he wanted, after all.

She desperately wanted to believe his change of heart. That somehow, he *had* grown fonder of her than she ever expected. But he was the Earl of Bolton, and she was nothing more than a wealthy shrew from Kent. His eyes would begin to wander once he grew tired of her and their sham of a marriage, and then she would be trapped without any legal control over the estate her father left her.

Louisa's thoughts were interrupted by Mrs. Strickland, who approached her soon after she returned to the ballroom. "Where have you been?" her stepmother hissed.

Louisa tried to remain expressionless, as if her insides weren't all jumbled after everything that had happened. It was the most pleasure she had ever experienced, followed by the worst sort of disappointment. "And where is the earl?"

"I have no idea where the earl is," Louisa said, perhaps too defensively. Mrs. Strickland seemed unconvinced. "As for me, I was in the retiring room." Louisa looked around the ballroom, searching for her sister. "Where is Flora? I have grown quite tired. Perhaps we might all return home."

"No," her stepmother snapped. "It will look even worse if we leave now. Besides, this is the most I have seen Flora smile in weeks. I think she is actually enjoying herself."

When Louisa finally found Flora, she was in the middle of dancing a set with an attractive gentleman. Louisa sighed. "Very well."

"As for you, I better not lose sight of you again this evening," Mrs. Strickland said. "And you better pray tonight's gossip doesn't leave this ballroom, or else you and your sister will be ruined in the eyes of polite society, unless you finally agree to marry the earl."

Louisa was only half listening to her stepmother as she continued to look about the crowded room. "I think I will go find Lady Rosamund," she said suddenly. If anyone knew what sort of gossip the guests were whispering about, it would be Rosamund. Ignoring Mrs. Strickland's protests, Louisa took off into the crowd.

When Louisa finally found Rosamund, a group of men surrounded her. She said something, smiling brightly, and all the men laughed. But when Rosamund's eyes fell on Louisa standing on the outskirts of the circle, she quickly excused herself and approached her friend.

"People are saying the most curious things about you and my brother," Rosamund whispered as the two girls locked arms and began to promenade along the perimeter of the ballroom.

Louisa winced. "What sort of things?"

A coy smile played at Rosamund's lip. "That you and my brother are in the midst of a passionate affair, continuing right where you left off seven years ago. Everyone's expecting a betrothal announcement by the end of the ball."

Louisa frowned. "Well, then they will be disappointed. There is no passionate affair, and there will be no engagement."

Rosamund raised her brow. "I am afraid it is your word against everyone else's. People saw you and my brother leave the ballroom together. If something is not announced..."

Rosamund didn't have to finish her sentence for Louisa to understand what she meant. At the center of the room, Flora caught Louisa's eyes once more. As Mrs. Strickland had said, tonight was the happiest Louisa had seen Flora since the viscount quit town. A pang of guilt hit Louisa. If she ruined her sister's chance at happiness all because she gave in to her lust for Charles, Louisa wasn't sure how she would be able to live with herself.

Louisa squared her shoulders, knowing what she must do. "Has your brother returned from upstairs? I should like to speak to him, but perhaps you and the duke should be present this time."

Rosamund smiled. "I have already spotted them."

They started toward them. Upon seeing the two ladies approach, Charles appeared surprised, and Louisa didn't blame him, since she'd dashed from that red room so quickly less than fifteen minutes earlier. But if Flora's future was in danger, Louisa was determined to reverse the damage, no matter how much she didn't want to do what it would take.

Louisa also noticed that the duke and Rosamund seemed to exchange a knowing glance for the briefest of moments, and Louisa half wondered if they had something to do with the gossip spreading that evening. After all, the duke seemed to have known they would be in that room, and Rosamund was the one who had just convinced Louisa to marry her brother.

Louisa spoke before Charles had the chance to say anything. "I was wondering if we might speak somewhere private—with your sister and His Grace present, of course."

"We can use my private study," the duke said. Louisa, unable to look at Charles directly without thinking of their earlier passionate encounter, turned to Rutley. "Follow me."

Her arm still linked with Rosamund's, Louisa followed the duke and Charles out of the ballroom, walking down the hall until they reached a room with a large desk at one end. Rutley went to sit, opening one of his desk drawers and procuring a small tin of snuff. Rosamund made a tiny sound of disgust.

"Is something wrong, my lady?" Rutley asked.

Rosamund shrugged. "I only thought you had given up such disgusting habits."

He smiled slightly. "Perhaps I would if I had a wife to temper me."

Before Rosamund could reply, Charles interrupted. "Enough!"

He glanced at Louisa, who stood with her hands folded at her waist. The duke's study was massive, and she suddenly felt very tiny, despite her above-average height for a female. She tried to remind herself what she was bringing to this marriage, and that if Charles truly wanted her, he would agree to her terms.

"I do not think Miss Strickland asked for a private audience with me to listen to the two of you bicker as you always do," Charles said.

Rosamund scowled at her brother, taking a seat in one of the upholstered armchairs, facing away from the duke as much as she could.

Charles turned to Louisa. "What is it that you would like to discuss?"

Louisa noticed right away that Charles's tone had changed toward her. He had safely tucked the impassioned man from upstairs somewhere deep inside himself, far away from her or anyone else in the duke's study. She cleared her throat. "Lady Rosamund has been kind enough to inform me of the rumors swirling around the ballroom, and for the sake of my sister, I think it would be best if we..." She hesitated, the word getting caught in her throat. She swallowed, trying to find the strength. "I think it would be best if we marry."

The words came out all at once and very quietly. But judging by the way the earl's expression softened, Louisa knew Charles had heard her. "You do?"

There was a moment of hesitation, but she nodded. Charles's face broke into a smile, and he stepped toward her, taking her hands in his. She flinched at his touch, not wishing to deal with the emotions such loving gestures encouraged. He must have noticed, for he let go of her hands and grew serious once more. He glanced back at Rosamund and the duke, who both looked around the room, pretending not to notice the awkwardness of their exchange.

Charles turned back to Louisa. "I know marriage is not something you wanted, but I promise I will do everything I can to make you happy," he said.

Their eyes met, and Louisa searched his gaze, looking for some sort of sign that such a promise could be a lasting one. But with Charles, she could never be quite sure. Still, thinking of her sister, she nodded.

"Then I hope you will agree to my terms," she said, willing herself to speak as firmly as possible. Charles had to know he could not trample all over her just because he was an earl.

But Charles showed no resistance. Instead, he nodded once. "Of course."

Trying not to appear too surprised, Louisa continued. "I should like for both of us to meet at Dover Street tomorrow and have Mr. Brooks draw up a marriage contract for us."

"I had already told Mr. Brooks I was hoping to have some

papers drawn up by the end of the season. I will have a message carried over to him tonight so that we may meet with him early tomorrow morning."

Louisa nodded. Although Charles was being more than amenable, she remained firm in tone. She wouldn't let down her guard—not now or ever. "I am a wealthy woman, my lord, with plenty to offer you, but there are certain things I should like to protect should you one day decide you no longer wish to make me happy."

"I completely understand."

Louisa and Charles stared at each other for a long moment. Before either of them could say anything else, Rosamund clapped her hands together and rose from her chair. "Splendid!" she exclaimed. "May we return to the party now to share the good news with everyone?" She briefly glanced at the duke. "I am not sure how much longer I can stand sitting in this room with him."

Rutley said nothing, only glared at Rosamund. Meanwhile, Charles extended his arm toward Louisa, and soon she forgot all about the duke and Rosamund. Taking a deep breath, she took his arm. He dipped his head slightly, whispering in her ear, "It will be all right. I have you."

She nodded slightly, trying to believe him. After all, she didn't have much choice in the matter.

Chapter Twenty-Three

CHARLES KNEW he should have felt elated. Louisa had finally agreed to marry him, yet guilt ate away at his mind all evening, so much so that he barely slept that night. An engagement was what he wanted, but the knowledge that he had practically forced her into it made him feel much worse than he thought it would.

He held on to the knowledge that there was something inside Louisa that wanted him as much as he wanted her. Such knowledge was his only comfort. She'd followed him to the Red Room, despite her better judgment, and his gentle ministrations made her writhe with pleasure on his lap.

Charles smiled, thinking of her and her soft flesh while in bed the following morning. Surely she could grow to love him if he did everything right. And for some reason, Charles found himself wanting her love much more than her money. That fact was foremost in his mind when he met her at Dover Street that morning.

They arrived at the same time, meeting each other on the sidewalk outside. Louisa seemed to shrink when she saw him, so he quickly offered her a reassuring smile. "Good morning," he said, reaching for her gloved hands.

"Good morning," she murmured back, hardly looking at him. Without thinking, he leaned down and pressed a kiss to her cheek. Startled, she turned and blinked at him.

"You have nothing to fear," he said. "I am a fair man, and you certainly chose the right solicitor to draw up our marriage contract. As you know, I am not his favorite person, so I am sure you will get everything you want."

Louisa smiled slightly. Letting go of her hands, Charles offered his arm, and once she took it, they walked up the front steps of the house. Jenkins, the butler, greeted them and showed them to Brooks's study. He sat at his desk, holding a pen, with his nose buried in some papers. He only looked up when Jenkins cleared his throat.

"Lord Bolton and Miss Strickland are here to see you, sir," he said.

Brooks put down his pen and leaned back in his chair. He gestured to the two empty armchairs in front of his desk.

"Please, sit," Brooks said. The solicitor ran his hands through his hair, and Louisa noticed dark circles under his eyes.

She frowned. "Are you sure now is a good time, Mr. Brooks?" she asked. "You look dreadfully tired. Perhaps we should have given you more time to prepare for our meeting."

Brooks laughed slightly. "I am afraid this is only the beginning of my exhaustion. My wife is due any day now, and she grows increasingly uncomfortable in her present state. Neither of us are sleeping well, but especially her."

Charles glanced at Louisa, realizing that she would be in the same position as his half sister one day. Their eyes met, and Charles thought they might be thinking the same thing, for Louisa quickly turned back toward Brooks. She smiled, though her face was pale. "I can only imagine. I will keep you and Mrs. Brooks in my thoughts as you prepare for the birth."

"Thank you, Miss Strickland," Brooks said. He glanced at Charles. "But I know you have not come to ask after my health or my wife's. You wrote that the two of you are now engaged, and you would like to draw up a marriage contract."

Charles nodded. "Yes, that's right."

Brooks turned toward Louisa. "Congratulations, Miss Strickland. I, personally, am happy you finally agreed to the earl's scheme. He waxes poetic about you whenever my wife insists on having him over for dinner."

Charles glared at Brooks, but the solicitor only looked at him and winked. When Louisa turned toward her fiancé, it was with a look of surprise. "Is that so?" she asked, her voice playful.

"Brooks exaggerates," Charles said gruffly without sparing her an extra look, feeling embarrassed. "Now, we do not have all morning. I suggest we discuss the marriage contract as Miss Strickland requested."

Brooks nodded, opening one of his notebooks and taking up his pen once more. He glanced at Louisa. "And what are the terms you would like to discuss, Miss Strickland?"

Louisa fidgeted in her chair, clenching and unclenching her hands in her lap. Charles reached for one and squeezed it, offering her a reassuring smile as he did. Louisa smiled back at him, then turned to Brooks. "I should like to ensure my sister's thirty-thousand-pound dowry remains intact. As in, I want to make sure the earl cannot touch those investments or funds, no matter what happens in our marriage."

Charles expected her to make such a request, and it didn't bother him. He had no interest in stealing Flora's dowry. But Louisa still turned to him, waiting for some sort of reaction. "She is the reason we must marry, after all," she murmured.

The comment stung, but Charles nodded anyway. He

turned to Brooks, who watched them both carefully. "I can agree to that."

Brooks nodded, writing something down in his notebook. When he finished, he looked up at Louisa. "Anything else?" he asked.

Louisa swallowed, seeming even more nervous than before. He squeezed her hand once more, and she looked at him. "Go ahead, Louisa," Charles murmured.

Louisa nodded, turning back to Brooks. "Once we marry, Charles will become the owner of Strickland Manor and Linfield Hall." She paused a moment, glancing at Charles. He maintained a firm grip on her hand. "I know the temptation to create a new entailment will be strong, especially after what your father did when he gave so much money to your half sister, but I do not want our property to become entailed once we marry."

"Why?" Charles asked, doing his best to keep his voice level. Truthfully, he hadn't expected Louisa to be thinking so far ahead, but he knew he must hear all of Louisa's terms or risk losing her forever. "An entailment will be the best way to ensure the strength of our estate for my heir."

If Charles were to create a new entailment, it would ensure that all the property he owned, Linfield *and* Strickland, went to the next Earl of Bolton—his future son, hopefully—when Charles eventually died. He could set aside special funds for Louisa if she outlived him, as well as dowries or trusts for any daughters, but the bulk of his great fortune —his impressive property—would go to the next earl, thus strengthening the line for generations to come.

"Yes, but what if we have nothing but girls for children? Will they be driven away from their ancestral land to make way for some distant cousin we both barely know?"

Charles knew she was thinking of her cousin William,

whom everyone pressured her to marry after her father died. The idea of leaving an entire estate to a female was practically unheard of, but Mr. Strickland envisioned something different for his daughter. Her ownership of the manor was why she could reject William, and eventually, Charles suddenly realized, agree to marry him. Charles sighed, letting go of Louisa's hand and running his fingers through his unruly hair. "And what do you propose instead of an entailment?" he asked.

Louisa took a deep breath. "If we are lucky to have any children, then the first boy will become the next earl and inherit Linfield Hall."

Charles saw right away where she was heading with this. "And the first girl?" he asked.

"She will inherit Strickland Manor."

For a brief moment, Charles hesitated. It was one thing to hear about a man leaving such a large property to a daughter and quite another to be the man who actually agreed to it. Louisa had admired her father so much, but Charles wasn't sure if he could live up to such a man. But the late Mr. Strickland did seem to know what he was doing. Louisa had managed Strickland splendidly since he died, and any daughter of hers was bound to do the same. "And what if we have all girls?" Charles asked.

Louisa blinked. "Well, wouldn't you want all of your property going to your eldest daughter rather than some distant cousin whose name you probably don't even know?"

Charles sighed, considering this. His father had no brothers, but his grandfather did. And Louisa was right. Charles had hardly any knowledge of that part of the family. "And what if she marries a complete scoundrel?" he asked.

A coy smile played at Louisa's lips. "Then I suppose she's no different from her mother."

Charles bit back a laugh, turning to Brooks. "Very well. Write the contract as she wants, and I'll pray we have a boy, or else the next Earl of Bolton will be even unluckier than me."

"You are not so unlucky, are you?" Louisa asked, her voice soft.

Charles turned to her. Seeing her smile at him helped him realize that no, he wasn't.

"Not anymore," he said, bringing her hand to his lips and kissing her knuckles.

CHARLES AND LOUISA'S engagement was not a long one. Although Charles wanted to procure a special license, Louisa insisted they couldn't afford it, especially with how much money the earl still owed Rutley. Yet Charles was eager, and he proclaimed that as soon as the reading of the banns was complete, they would be married at St. George's.

Until then, Charles and Louisa spent little time together unchaperoned, mostly at the request of her stepmother, who demanded at least some propriety from her stepdaughter and future son-in-law. But the earl still called every afternoon, and he was the epitome of patience, even when Mrs. Strickland encumbered him with questions.

"Will your mother be coming to town for the wedding?" she asked.

Louisa glanced at Charles, wondering if he would tell the truth or not. He and his mother still weren't speaking after what happened last year with Rosamund and August, and she hadn't responded to his letter announcing his engagement— or any letter before that, either.

"We announced the date of the wedding on such short notice, so she won't be able to make it to London in time,"

Charles said. He glanced at Louisa. "I am sure she will visit Linfield when we are both settled."

Mrs. Strickland looked displeased by the dowager countess's lack of support. Luckily, Flora had come alive with all the talk of the upcoming wedding, and she was quick to fill in any awkward silences. "Do you think all of Mayfair will come? Everyone says they have been waiting for this wedding for seven years!"

Charles and Louisa exchanged a look. Truthfully, Louisa was dreading the festivities and all the pomp and circumstance of becoming a countess. But whether she liked it or not, Louisa would become the next Lady Bolton.

When the day finally came, Louisa found the whole affair to be a blur. She felt like another person in her white gown and veil, walking down the aisle at St. George's with everyone watching. Being a bride was never something Louisa envisioned for herself, let alone the bride of an aristocrat, but being the Lord of Bolton's bride somehow made sense. She'd decided that they'd sealed their fates the day they agreed to embark on a make-believe courtship.

After they had greeted all the guests who had come to the wedding breakfast, Charles leaned down and whispered in Louisa's ear, "I have a surprise for you."

Louisa arched her brow. "Is that so?"

He nodded. "I thought we might go away before returning to Linfield."

"Charles..."

They had already agreed there would be no honeymoon. Louisa was desperate to take a look at Linfield's ledgers, to which Charles said he would allow her access whenever she wanted. So far, he had made good on everything he promised her, and she truly felt they might be equal partners in this marriage after all. But she hadn't expected him to plan a honeymoon behind her back.

He cocked his head to the side. "Before you give me that look, allow me to explain. I have an old schoolmate from Eton who owns a cottage in the Wye Valley. I thought we might spend a couple of weeks there getting to know each other better before we return to Linfield."

"Do we not already know each other?"

He laughed. "I'm afraid there are still many things left to discover about one another. A lifetime of things, really." She flushed as he continued. "We could even visit Tintern Abbey. It's very close to the cottage. Haven't you ever wanted to see the inspiration behind all those paintings and poems?"

Louisa grew silent. It did sound tempting, the idea of being alone in a remote cottage with Charles for two weeks, no servants or tenants or meddling dukes to bother them. But it did feel slightly irresponsible taking a honeymoon when he —now *they*—still owed said meddling duke so much money. But she supposed if Charles's schoolmate was letting him use the cottage for free...

Suddenly, her husband grimaced. "You are thinking much too hard about this. Surely we are allowed *some* fun as newlyweds."

"Very well," she said with a sigh. "We will go."

After the wedding breakfast, a hired post chaise arrived to take the couple to Wales. The journey would take multiple days, but Louisa didn't mind. There was always plenty to discuss with Charles, from their plans for their new joint estate to which of Flora's many suitors they preferred. After a long day alone, Louisa decided she certainly favored this Charles, the one who didn't drink or gamble. He was much easier to converse with, and his eyes were far more alert, even after a long day of traveling.

When they stopped for the evening, Charles went into the coaching inn before her. She waited impatiently in the carriage, realizing their wedding night was fast approaching.

They had both behaved admirably in the weeks leading up to their wedding, much more admirably than the weeks leading up to their engagement. Of course, they never had much time to themselves until they stepped inside the post chaise earlier that day.

Charles returned to the carriage after he booked their rooms for the night. "Are you hungry?" he asked as he helped her out of the carriage.

Louisa nodded. They hadn't had anything to eat since they left London.

"Good. We will have supper while they prepare our room. They only had one available, unfortunately."

Louisa arched her brow at him. Had he expected a suite at a roadside inn? She tried to remind herself she was a countess now, not just a regular member of the landed gentry. "Is that so unfortunate, Lord Bolton?"

He smiled. "Perhaps not, Lady Bolton. But I thought you might enjoy some privacy after spending all day with me."

She shook her head. "Never."

Taking her by the hand, Charles led her inside. They sat down to supper, which was nothing more than cold bread, ham, and cheese, but Louisa could hardly eat anything despite her hunger—she was too nervous. She knew they had already done more together than most newlyweds, and she suspected there was nothing to fear in Charles's arms in terms of him being a capable lover... but what if something about her wasn't adequate?

When they went up to their sparsely furnished bedroom, Louisa's stomach felt tied up in knots. Charles reached for her, gently holding her by the waist. He furrowed his brow, studying her face. She couldn't hide anything when they were that close.

"Is something the matter?" he asked.

Louisa tried to smile. "Only slightly nervous, I suppose."

He kissed her on the forehead, and she closed her eyes. "There is nothing to fear, my darling. And if you aren't ready, we do not have to rush to do anything tonight." Looking around the spartan room, he smiled slightly, then tucked a piece of loose hair behind her ear. "I suppose this isn't the most romantic place to spend your wedding night. I should have done a better job thinking this through." Charles let go of her, running his hand through his hair as he shook his head. He shot her an apologetic look. "Perhaps we should have stayed in London this evening and left for Wales tomorrow."

But Louisa shook her head. "There is nothing wrong with the room. I only hope..." She paused, biting her lip. "I only hope I don't disappoint you."

He narrowed his gaze. "Louisa... you could never disappoint me."

His voice was so firm that she had no choice but to believe him. And when he leaned down to kiss her, she wondered why she was so nervous in the first place. There was something so wonderful about being in his arms, and by the time he guided her to the bed, she had no doubts at all.

Charles hovered over her, kissing her lips, then her jaw, and then finally her neck. She lifted her arms and wrapped them around his shoulders, pulling him closer to her. The hardness she felt all those weeks ago in the red room brushed against her inner thigh, and she gasped softly.

Charles must have heard her, for she felt him smile against her neck. "All of that is for you," he whispered before reaching around the back of her bodice. He deftly undid the buttons, and she raised her brow at how swiftly he could pull her frock off her prone body.

"You are rather good at this, aren't you?" Louisa observed, suddenly wearing nothing but her undergarments. He smiled at her, leaning down to explore the newly exposed parts of her body with his mouth. But she held a finger to his lips, stopping him. "If I am to lose one article of clothing, it is only right that you do as well."

He had already removed his jacket and cravat when they got to the room, so she reached for his waistcoat instead, clumsily unbuttoning it. "I am not quite as talented as you."

"Do not say that," he said, reaching to help her, then shrugging off the article of clothing before haphazardly discarding it somewhere on the floor. "You only have no idea how talented you are."

He reached for the laces of her stays next, undoing them so that nothing but her thin chemise covered her breasts. She had half a mind to cover herself with her arms, but she somehow found the nerve not to, allowing him to stare at her until he dipped his head, finding her left nipple with his lips. He rolled his tongue around the tip, and she gasped as he gently sucked.

"Charles," she managed to whisper. "You took off my stays. It is only fair that you take off your shirt now."

He grunted, pulling back from her and quickly tugging his shirt over his head. She stared at him for a long moment, reaching out to run her fingers through the dark matted hair on his chest.

"Are you happy now?" Charles asked.

Louisa nodded, taking back her hands and holding them by her chest.

"Good." He reached for the bottom of her chemise next, pulling it up and over her head. She wriggled underneath him as he did, realizing that she was now entirely naked except for her stockings. This time, she couldn't resist the urge to hide her body with her arms, but he quickly grabbed her by the wrists, pulling her hands over her head.

"Don't do that," he said with a smile. Slowly, Charles let go of her wrists, and she left her hands above her head, resting on the pillows. All she could hear was her breathing as he intently stared down at her, as if he was busy memorizing every inch of her naked body. He bent down so that their faces were level with one another. Charles gently touched her chin before kissing her. "You are perfect."

Slowly, he kissed her everywhere—from her neck to the undersides of her breasts to her navel. With each kiss, Louisa felt a pool of desire growing inside her core. All the while, her husband's mouth seemed to tease her, kissing the inside of her thighs, her kneecaps, her shins, but never where she wanted it most. He must know how much she yearned for it. Didn't he?

"Charles," she whispered.

"Mmm?" he asked in between peppering kisses down her thighs.

"Will you...?"

He paused, looking up at her. A slight smile played at his lips. "Will I what?" he asked teasingly.

Louisa swallowed nervously. "Will you kiss me there?" Her voice sounded hoarse. She needed him. She hated to admit it, but she *needed* him.

Still, Charles tortured her. "Where's there?" he asked. Louisa made an exasperated sound, but he took her by the hand. "Show me."

With some uncertainty, she closed her eyes and lowered her hand to where she ached the most. When her fingers grazed the peak of her sex, she opened her eyes again. Charles was grinning when her gaze found his face. "I am getting there," he said before leaning back down between her legs.

Charles continued to tease her, and she was about to tell him she could not take it any longer when his lips finally found the intimate folds of her sex. She cried out when his tongue lapped over her most sensitive spot. He wrapped his lips around it, gently sucking.

She couldn't believe it, but this was even better than the night at the duke's ball. Charles took his time with her, artfully exploring every inch of her sex. He discovered all the places that made her shiver and her toes curl. When Louisa finally hit the peak of her pleasure, she cried out his name, running her hands through his hair.

Eventually, he kneeled back, undoing his breeches and sliding them off. Louisa's eyes widened, and she sat up on her forearms. "That's supposed to go inside of me?" she asked, causing him to laugh. He leaned back over her, pressing a kiss to her lips.

"I'm afraid so," he said. He reached between them, positioning himself at Louisa's slick entrance. He inched forward, and she winced. Charles kissed her forehead. "I will go slowly, but I cannot promise it will not hurt. I'm sorry."

Louisa nodded, and he slid even further forward. She cried out, and Charles smoothed her hair back across her scalp. "That's it," he whispered, kissing her forehead. "The worst of it is over."

Charles started to slide himself in and out of her, and eventually, it became more pleasurable than painful. "Charles," she whispered, wrapping her legs around his hips and raking her fingertips down his back.

He groaned. "I'm not sure how much longer I will last," he muttered.

Louisa reached for his face, kissing him as he thrust in and out of her. "That's all right," she said with a smile. She wrapped her arms around him, enjoying this feeling of not only being one body, but one soul as well. Despite the earlier pain, Louisa didn't want it to end, but then there was one final thrust, and she felt his release inside of her.

For a moment, Charles panted as he hovered over her, his eyes closed. She looked up at him, watching him carefully. Slowly, he slid out of her before lying down beside her. She nuzzled against his body, resting her head on his chest as he wrapped his arms around her shoulders. Content to lie against him in silence, Louisa listened to his heartbeat until she fell asleep in his arms.

Chapter Twenty-Four

CHARLES COULDN'T REMEMBER a time when he had been happier. Louisa had tucked herself against his chest, and he had wrapped his arm around her shoulders, pulling her tight against him. She eventually fell asleep, but he remained awake for at least another hour. Tufts of red hair tickled his skin, and Charles smiled.

For someone who had spent most of his young adulthood avoiding marriage, Charles found himself reveling in it at that very moment. He never imagined marrying someone would make him feel so happy, despite knowing all along that he would have to eventually. But he had expected to feel shackled when it finally happened.

Except he certainly didn't feel shackled at the moment. Committed, but not shackled. Even his old friend Brooks commented on the peculiarity of his and Louisa's marriage contract, finally admitting his old friend might have actually changed over the past year. After all, it wasn't very often that the woman getting married was able to dictate how her husband's property might be split up between their children.

Louisa even ensured there would be trusts set aside for her stepmother and half sister if anything were to happen to her.

And Charles agreed to all her terms, though he was sure his mother would be furious when she found out what her son had done, what with preventing another entailment. She would accuse him of turning into his overly sentimental father, especially when she learned that he reconciled with August as well.

None of that seemed to matter as long as Louisa was happy, though. Looking down at her, Charles should have known this would have happened as soon as he met her again. He wondered if they would have married much earlier if she had answered his letters or granted him an audience at Strickland Manor in the year after their fake courtship.

But he supposed none of that mattered now. What mattered now was grasping onto this feeling of closeness and cultivating it for life. Charles only hoped he wouldn't disappoint her.

WHEN LOUISA WOKE the next day, she was alone in bed. Morning light streamed through the shabby curtains covering the windows, and when she looked across the room, she saw Charles standing there in a fresh set of clothes, making an awkward attempt to tie his cravat.

"Good morning," Louisa said, wrapping the bedclothes around herself before standing up in order to walk toward Charles. He looked over at her, smiling. "Why didn't you wake me?"

"You looked so peaceful sleeping that I couldn't disturb you," he replied, still fiddling with his cravat.

Louisa reached out, grabbing his hands. "Here, let me help you," she said. Biting her lip, she made quick work of the linen neckcloth, then patted her husband's chest. "There."

Raising her brow, she studied the rest of his outfit. He didn't look nearly as put together as he usually did. She chewed her lip. "Perhaps it was a mistake not bringing your valet on this trip."

"Can you blame me for wanting you to myself for a fortnight?" he asked, wrapping his arms around her waist and pulling her closer. "I didn't want any interruptions from bumbling Gibbs or your maid should I decide to make love to you in the middle of the floor of the cottage."

Louisa blushed. Never had she felt so wanted. She almost expected to wake up one day and discover it had all been a dream. But when he pressed a kiss to her lips, she realized that Charles was, in fact, very much real. He gently tugged the bedclothes out from underneath her arms, letting them pool on the floor at her feet.

"Charles!" she exclaimed.

"You are even more beautiful in the daylight," he said, using one of his hands to cup her left breast and the other to squeeze her buttocks. Louisa swatted his hands away.

"You will ruin your cravat, and right after I have just tied it," she weakly protested. "And I must get dressed."

Charles smiled. He must have sensed her weakness for him, especially his lips and his magnificent—

Louisa yelped. Charles had picked her up and quickly deposited her on the bed, where he loomed over her. "I will be quick—I promise."

He reached between her thighs, preparing her for him with great efficiency. She was still a little sore from the previous night, but not enough to reject his advances. There was no doubt that Charles was a very skilled lover, an observation that made Louisa slightly jealous. She wondered how many women he had bedded before her and how she could even begin to compare.

But she tried not think of that now, especially as he bent

down to kiss her breasts, taking her sensitive nipples into his mouth one at a time. Louisa arched her hips toward him, eager for more of him. Charles slipped a finger inside of her, and he moaned. "You want me, don't you?" he asked.

"Yes," Louisa managed to say, her voice a breathless whisper. When he withdrew his finger, she whimpered at the sudden feeling of emptiness.

Charles backed away from her for a moment, undoing just the top of his breeches, freeing his hard length. Louisa sat up on her forearms and watched as he entered her, filling her to the brim with his cock.

Charles grabbed hold of her hips, then thrust in and out of her. He was much less gentle than he was the previous night, tupping her with wild abandon. "Look at me," Charles said suddenly. Their gazes met, and she let out little gasps of pleasure with every thrust. "I want you to touch yourself."

"W-what?" Louisa breathlessly stammered.

"You heard me," he said, his voice demanding. "Touch yourself."

Hesitantly, she lowered her hand to where their bodies joined. Charles was taking much more shallow strokes now, allowing her to take her fingertips and circle the most sensitive point of her sex. "Yes," Charles said. "That's a good girl."

Louisa started to whimper, feeling the warmness in her core grow and expand. She felt herself tightening around him until she finally lost all control and saw stars when she closed her eyes.

"Charles!" she cried out, and he thrust into her harder and further. His release came soon after hers. When he finally spent all his seed inside her, Charles laid his clothed body over her naked one, panting.

He pressed kisses all across her face: her forehead, her nose, her lips. "I am the luckiest man in the world," he whispered.

Louisa smiled, the doubt in her mind fading with every sweet reassurance. But the moment quickly passed, interrupted by a loud banging on the door. Louisa gasped, especially since Charles was still inside her, and she was naked. He held her tightly, shielding her from the door, then looked over his shoulder.

"What is it?" he shouted.

It was one of their grooms. "Your carriage is ready to depart, my lord."

Louisa flushed, hoping the groom hadn't heard anything. But Charles didn't seem embarrassed at all. "We will be down in thirty minutes," he said.

"Very good, my lord."

Louisa heard the footsteps of the groom retreating. She looked at Charles with a terrified expression. "You don't think he heard anything, do you?"

Charles shrugged. "So what if he did? I wouldn't mind if the whole world knew how well loved my wife is."

She glared at him. "There is nothing wrong with some discretion. Now, release me so I can get dressed."

He chuckled, separating himself from her. She immediately regretted her request, though she didn't dare admit it. Some distance between them would be preferable, she thought. After all, Louisa hadn't wanted to marry him in the first place. Shouldn't at least some part of her be saddened by the death of her independence? Or had she changed completely? Part of her almost felt disappointed in herself.

Charles lay down on the bed, lazily watching her as she washed using a fresh towel from one of the cupboards and the small water basin at the corner of the room. She opened her trunk and found fresh undergarments, laying them out on the bed. Louisa managed to pull on her stockings and chemise by herself, but her stays were another story. Reluctantly, she turned to Charles.

"Will you help?" she asked.

He rose from the bed. "It would be my pleasure."

Charles came to stand behind her, lacing her stays with as much efficiency as a lady's maid. Turning to face him, she frowned. "I do wonder how you became so talented in the ways of women and their clothing."

"Would you rather I be a green lad with no knowledge of what pleases a woman?" He said it teasingly, but Louisa remained annoyed, moving across the room to put on her frock now that she had taken care of her undergarments. As if sensing this, Charles frowned. "Are you cross with me now?"

She turned to face him. It was hard to be mad at him after all the pleasure he'd brought her. Not to mention his eyes resembled that of a puppy when he studied her. She turned away, hoping he wouldn't see the way her face was pinched together in annoyance. "Only a little," she muttered.

Charles came around behind her again, helping her do the buttons on the back of her dress. "I cannot rewrite the past, Louisa," he said. Charles grabbed hold of her shoulders, turning her so that she was facing him. She bit her lip. "But I meant every word of my marriage vows. I could have had any wealthy woman I wanted."

Louisa furrowed her brow. "You do not have to remind me."

"But always remember that I chose you," he said, leaning down to kiss her.

Louisa felt her annoyance start to evaporate... and that was when she realized Charles already knew how to manage her. God help her!

"I chose you even when I knew it would be a challenge because I knew no one else could ever compare. Do you believe me?"

Louisa hesitated, and Charles grew impatient. "Louisa," he practically growled.

Quickly, she nodded. "I believe you," she said. Although her voice was meek and not altogether convincing, it seemed good enough for Charles.

He nodded once. "Good," he said, pressing a kiss to her forehead. "Shall we be on our way, then?"

Louisa nodded. There was, after all, no other choice but to move forward.

THE JOURNEY to Wye Valley was long, with multiple nights spent in coaching inns before they reached their final destination. Charles didn't mind the lengthy trip, especially when there was ample time every evening for him to teach Louisa all the different ways they could make love. But as much as she seemed to enjoy their more passionate encounters, Charles couldn't help but feel like there was still a wall around Louisa's inner being, one he couldn't quite penetrate.

It bothered him deeply, but he did his best to ignore his self-doubt. At least Louisa was always kind to him, and she laughed at his jokes, even when they weren't that funny. She trusted him enough to try anything he asked of her in bed, but there was still something guarded about her, as if she was doing her very best not to let them become too close.

Charles found this unfortunate, especially when he felt he was standing on the precipice of something grand. But Louisa wasn't there with him, which made the realization that he was falling in love with her very terrifying indeed.

When they finally arrived in Tintern, Charles did his best to push those fears to the back of his mind, determined to enjoy his honeymoon with his new wife. They ate at the local inn before taking the short walk to his friend's private cottage along the river. Charles reached for Louisa's hand as they walked, and she absentmindedly took it. She appeared too busy observing the natural beauty surrounding them to worry about their growing intimacy. He was thankful for that.

The rolling green hills and the soft sound of running water from the nearby river were a far cry from the noisy bustle of London. Their cottage, a small two-story brick home, sat just along the bank of the Wye. The housekeeper, an older woman with gray hair and a set of shrewd eyes, stood outside waiting for them. She curtseyed as they approached.

"My lord. My lady. Welcome to Potter Cottage."

Potter was his old school friend, the one who lent him the cottage for the entire fortnight for Charles and Louisa's honeymoon. The housekeeper, whose name was Mrs. White, showed them inside. The first floor was small and cramped, with a hearth at one end and a staircase at the other. There was a cabinet in the corner, filled with instruments for cooking, plates, bowls, and flatware.

"I can come round in the morning to fix your breakfasts," Mrs. White said. "I live right in town. I can prepare your suppers as well."

"That's quite all right, Mrs. White," Charles said. Although the housekeeper appeared offended, Charles didn't want anyone disturbing him and Louisa. "We will manage just fine on our own." Louisa shot him a skeptical look. "Or we will go to the inn when we are hungry."

Mrs. White huffed. "Suit yourselves. Is there anything else I can do for you, my lord?"

Charles shook his head. When Mrs. White left, he turned to Louisa.

"You didn't have to turn her away like that," she said, though she could have scolded him with her eyes alone.

He offered a sheepish shrug, stepping closer to her.

"I very much doubt you could cook either of us breakfast," she said.

"I do not want any interruptions when I make love to you in every corner of this tiny cottage," he said.

Louisa looked around the sparsely decorated room. "I doubt that will take very much time at all. It's very small."

Charles grinned, lunging for her and throwing her over his shoulder. Louisa screamed as she pounded at his back. "Put me down!"

"We shall start in the bedroom," Charles said, carrying her up the stairs. He playfully slapped her on the bum. "Stop squirming, or I might drop you."

"You are incorrigible!" she exclaimed.

But all was forgiven when he deposited her on the bed and climbed on top of her. He began planting kisses all over her neck and breasts, and she moaned happily, her protests long forgotten. Whether Louisa liked it or not, Charles always made quick work of her defenses against him. Now, if only he could make her love him too.

ALTHOUGH CHARLES WOULD HAVE LIKED to keep her in bed all day, Louisa demanded they go and see Tintern Abbey as soon as possible. She found an old wicker basket and blanket in one of the cabinets on the lower floor of the cottage, and together they set off to the village to buy enough food for a small picnic. Louisa also snuck a small bottle of wine for herself, hoping the sweet red liquid might alleviate some of her more unsettling feelings about Charles and his constant displays of affection.

It wasn't that Louisa disliked such displays. She only feared what would happen after the honeymoon, and she wanted to protect her heart as much as she could. Managing two estates was no easy task for any man, so Louisa hoped Charles would welcome her help. There were certain protections she could allow her sister and any children she and

Charles might have, but no contract could ever fully protect her heart—and that was what scared her.

They walked in silence toward the abbey, which was easily visible in the distance thanks to its massive size. There were no other revelers at the ruins when they arrived. Louisa entered the abbey and walked beside its enormous stone walls and pillars in awe. When she looked up, she saw nothing but open sky; the roof had been missing for at least three hundred years.

Louisa turned back and looked at Charles. "Isn't it magnificent?" she asked. She looked down, admiring the way the grass intertwined with the decaying stone pathways. "No wonder Mr. Wordsworth found himself so inspired."

"No wonder," Charles softly echoed, but when Louisa turned back and looked at him, he wasn't admiring the abbey. He was looking at her. She blushed slightly.

"Shall we find somewhere to sit and have our picnic?" Louisa asked.

Charles nodded his assent, and together they walked out from underneath the ruins and toward a grassy knoll where they could sit and look out onto the ruins and river. Louisa took the threadbare blanket from Charles, carefully spreading it on the ground, and they both sat down.

Charles placed the basket between them. Opening it, he pulled out the bottle of wine first and shot Louisa a suspicious look. "Where did this come from?"

She winced. "I hope you don't mind. I bought it from the shop in the village when you weren't looking."

He shook his head. "Not at all. I survived two months in town surrounded by the worst sort of lushes. Surely I can survive an afternoon with a wife who would like to enjoy herself on her honeymoon."

Charles made quick work of opening the bottle with a corkscrew that Louisa had stashed in the basket. She pulled out a tin cup, and he filled it to the brim. Her eyes widened. "Are you trying to get me foxed, my lord?" she asked.

"Perhaps," he said with a coy wiggle of his brow. As Louisa sipped her wine, Charles reached back into the basket, procuring wooden plates, bowls, and flatware, as well as fresh berries, cheeses, and slices of cold meat.

"What a beautiful presentation," Louisa playfully observed when he finished laying out all the food. She reached for a strawberry, biting into it. "I wonder if you should have been a cook instead of an earl."

"Unfortunately, I did not have much say in the matter," Charles replied ruefully, though more in jest than seriousness.

Louisa drank more of her wine while Charles sliced off bits of cheese with a knife. She watched him, looking for any signs of discontent, but Louisa found none. She furrowed her brow. "Don't you ever miss it?" she asked.

Charles appeared confused. "Miss what?"

"Drinking," she said, holding up her tin cup.

To her surprise, Charles did not hesitate. He immediately shook his head. "I certainly do not miss being a drunken fool. All liquor brought me was loneliness and an astronomical amount of debt. Perhaps if I were a different person, I might be able to enjoy a drink or two on occasion, but I much prefer the way I am now." He grinned, leaning in to kiss her on the cheek. She smiled back at him while he played with a strand of her hair that had fallen loose from her simple coiffure that day. "I would not risk my current happiness for one measly cup of wine, though I am quite curious to know what you are like when you are drunk."

She laughed. "You will have to remain curious, then. I do not plan on drinking the whole bottle in one sitting!" He reached for the bottle of wine, topping off her cup as if to challenge her. Louisa shook her head and laughed. "Do not do that! I do not want to waste it. Besides, I am not like you; I do not respond to every challenge thrown my way."

Charles gave her a thoughtful look. "What do you mean?"

Louisa laughed slightly, taking another sip of her wine. "Surely you remember the time you fell out of what was probably the tallest tree in all of Kent as you were trying to impress Robert." She cleared her throat. "I apologize—I mean His Grace, the Duke of Rutley."

Charles frowned. "You speak as if you do not like the duke."

Louisa shrugged. "He was the one who implemented the 'no girls allowed' rule at the forester's lodge when we were seven, and he wouldn't overturn it even after my mother died. I was dreadfully lonely when I was younger."

"You could have played with Rosamund."

Louisa shook her head. "I was far too much of a tomboy to play politely with your little sister and her dolls. I enjoy her company now, but we were very different as children." She paused a moment, already feeling the effects of the wine. For some reason, she wanted to continue talking. "I did appreciate it when you and your family called on us after Mama died." Looking down, Louisa smiled to herself. "I still remember that day. You brought me a bouquet of wildflowers."

When their eyes met again, Charles was shaking his head, laughing slightly. "I cannot believe you remember that. I had forgotten."

Louisa wasn't surprised. Once Louisa was no longer allowed to play with the boys, she only ever saw Charles and his family at church until he went off to Eton. It wasn't until they were both in town as young adults that Louisa approached him again, looking for help. He was far different than she remembered, so cocky and self-assured in his mannerisms. When he was just a boy, he was much less confident.

She took another sip of her wine. "Papa helped me press them. I put them in a glass frame and hung it above my bedside table."

There was that cocky grin of his. Louisa sighed, but he slid closer to her, lining up his body with hers on top of the blanket. He played with the loose ends of the ribbon tied about her waist. "I had no idea you were so fond of me when we were children," he said softly.

Louisa snorted, unable to admit what she somehow always knew. That she had always loved Charles, ever since she was a little girl. Louisa always knew if marriage were in the cards for her, it would have to be him or no one at all, though she would never dare admit it to anyone. That was why it was so easy to pretend she was heartbroken for the past seven years. She only hoped she didn't come to regret her weakness now that she had married him finally.

When she noticed Charles was about to speak, Louisa quickly waved her hand and took another swig of wine. "Let's talk of something else. Do you ever miss your father?"

It was an abrupt question, but it was something that Louisa had speculated over for a long time. Charles looked surprised she even brought the topic up at all, but she preferred that to discussing whether or not she was fond of him. He sat up, bending his knees and resting his forearms on them. "From time to time," he said.

Louisa sat up as well, their thighs touching as she took a similar position to him. She went to take another drink but found her cup empty. She pouted, turning to Charles and shoving the cup toward his face. "It's empty."

Charles laughed. "Should I pour you some more?"

Louisa cocked her head to the side, then nodded. "I think so."

"And I thought you said you wouldn't finish it all in one sitting."

"Hush."

Charles reached back into the picnic basket for the bottle of wine, uncorking it and filling Louisa's cup once more. "Try not to make yourself sick," he warned.

She giggled despite herself. "This wine *does* seem rather strong." Charles looked at the nondescript bottle, shrugged, then placed it back in the basket. Louisa wagged her finger at him, leaning close. "But let us return to the subject of your father. Are you still angry with him for leaving so much money to your half sister?"

Charles sighed, taking off his hat and running his hands through his hair. Louisa decided she would untie her bonnet as well but fumbled with unknotting the thick ribbon underneath her chin. "Here, let me help," Charles said, reaching for her.

When she was finally free of her bonnet, she pouted at him again. "You have not answered the question."

"I am no longer angry," Charles said, not looking at her. She repositioned herself so she could peer into his face. He wore a cross look on his face, and she frowned. "I only wish he'd prepared me better. I never expected him to have a secret such as August, nor did I expect him to die so suddenly. He never seemed interested in teaching me more about the management of Linfield, so I was rather naïve in regard to what it would be like. I always admired my father, but at the end of the day, he was nothing like yours."

Louisa leaned back, a rueful smile playing at her lips. "Papa truly was the best."

Charles grunted his assent. Louisa shook her head, placing her hand on his shoulder. "But just think of all you have learned in the past year alone. You mustn't be so hard on yourself, my dear. You aren't the first young gentleman to end up in your position, and I doubt you will be the last. But I do think we should raise our sons a little differently."

Charles laughed. "A stricter allowance for each of them, perhaps?"

"Much stricter," Louisa replied with a laugh.

Charles drew his body closer to hers. "But what is this talk of sons? How many children do you think we will have?"

"If you keep making love to me as you do, I gather we will have a bona fide litter of children on our hands within ten years."

"Are you not afraid?"

She grew silent, knowing Charles was referring to her mother's death. The first Mrs. Strickland had died during childbirth, her baby boy along with her. Louisa often wondered what it would have been like if either of them had survived. She might have never inherited Strickland Manor. Frowning, Louisa shrugged. "You will grow tired of me eventually. I doubt we will *actually* have a litter."

"Do not say that," Charles said softly, cupping her cheek with his palm and forcing her to look at him. "I already told you. I will *never* grow tired of you."

Louisa didn't say anything, so he kissed her instead. She would have liked to remain in that moment forever, sitting in the sun without a care in the world. But Charles pulled away. "You taste like wine," he said with a rueful look. "I should get you back to the cottage before you can no longer walk."

After packing up their things, they made their way back to the cottage. Louisa stumbled a few times, which only made Charles hold on to her more tightly as they walked. She kept telling him she was fine, but Louisa was feeling rather sleepy when they finally reached their cottage at the bank of the river—yet she had no desire to sleep.

Louisa turned, grabbing Charles by the hand and leading him up the stairs. He must have realized what she intended, for as soon as they reached the second floor, Charles reached out for her, forcing her against the wall and kissing her. As much as she liked the feel of his well-formed body against hers, Louisa pushed him away.

"No," she said.

Charles blinked, confused.

"I am seducing you this time."

Charles crossed his arms, chuckling slightly. "As you wish, Lady Bolton."

Louisa slowly stepped toward him, reaching for his shirt and pulling the hem from where it was tucked into his breeches. She leaned forward and kissed him as she clumsily continued to undress him. Charles reached out to do the same to her. Layers of cotton, silk, and lace fell to the ground around them, and when they were both finally naked, Louisa gently nudged him toward the bed until they were close enough that Louisa could push him into a sitting position. "Lie down with your head on the pillows," she said.

Charles arched his brow but did as Louisa told him. She felt powerful as she stood over him at the foot of the bed, completely naked and knowing he wanted her more than anything. She leaned down, putting her hands on either side of him before crawling over him. He inhaled sharply when her torso brushed the rigid shaft at his groin. Louisa smiled, leaning down to kiss where his jaw met his throat.

Out of the corner of her eye, she saw his hands reach for her waist, but she swatted them away. "No touching," she said. "Let me do all the work."

"But I want to—"

"Shhh." She placed a finger over his mouth. "You wouldn't want me to tie you up, would you?"

. . .

CHARLES LAY beneath Louisa in shock and awe. He had never seen this side of her, and he was beginning to wonder if there was something special about that wine. She nearly drank the whole bottle, yet she acted as alert as ever, ordering him about the bedroom.

He swallowed. "No, I wouldn't."

His hands itched to touch her, but he let Louisa have her way with him, trailing a line of kisses from his jawbone to his chest. When she started to approach his navel, he reached out and touched her shoulders without thinking. "Louisa, you don't have to—"

Lifting her head, she gently grabbed his wrists. Their eyes met, hers being more seductive than he ever remembered. "No touching. Now let me do this for you."

Louisa let go of his hands, and he placed them at his sides. She continued her descent, tracing a line with her tongue from his navel to his groin. Charles had been fully erect for some time, but now Louisa finally gave his stiff shaft a tentative lick from bottom to top. He closed his eyes and groaned. She swirled her tongue around the tip of his cock, and that was when Charles had enough.

"Please, Louisa," he said, raising himself up on his forearms. Louisa looked up at him, and Charles thought he might faint, seeing her in that position. He took a deep breath.

"I only want to give you the same sort of pleasure you always give me," Louisa said with a pout. "Show me how to make you happy."

Slowly, he nodded, taking a deep breath. "Do what you just did again... that's it... now take me into your mouth and... yes, just like that."

Charles lifted his hands over his head in utter contentment. When he realized he was close, he reached down to stop her. She looked up, her lips slick with moisture. He bit

BECKY MICHAELS

back a groan, pulling her toward him until her soft breasts were resting against his chest. "Sit up," he practically growled.

Louisa did as Charles told her, straddling him. When he started to lift himself from the waist, she slid downward until her soft bottom pressed against his rigid length. Charles reached between them, cupping her mound and dipping one finger into her. She threw her head back as he slid it in and out of her.

"I want more," she said when their eyes locked once more. Louisa put her arms around his shoulders and kissed him, and Charles placed his hands underneath her, gently lifting her and positioning her slick entrance over his cock. He slowly lowered her, letting her hot core envelop him. Charles moaned as Louisa began to move up and down.

She must have realized the reaction she was invoking, for she got the most devious look in her eyes. Louisa moved quickly at first, nearly bringing him to the brink, but then she slowed down, delaying his release. When she did it a second time, he inhaled sharply. "You are going to be the death of me," he said with a slight laugh.

Louisa smiled, and when she finally lost control of her senses and found her climax, he followed soon after. Gasping for air, Louisa climbed off and fell beside him on the bed. They leaned against the pillows and the bed's wooden headboard, holding each other. Louisa placed her head against his chest, and they sat in contented silence.

"Louisa," Charles said suddenly. "I think I'm falling in love with you."

She didn't answer, and when he looked down, she was sleeping. "Louisa," he said again, but her eyelids didn't even flutter. Sighing, he kissed the top of her head and gingerly stepped out of bed, careful not to wake her.

Chapter Twenty-Five

✤

WHEN LOUISA AWOKE LATER that evening, she half expected Charles to repeat his confession. He might not have known it, but she had heard his original proclamation, as she had been only pretending to sleep. The wine from earlier that afternoon may have loosened her lips, but that didn't mean she was any closer to discovering what was in her heart. She wasn't quite sure if she was ready to tell Charles she returned his feelings, and it would have ruined their honeymoon if she only mumbled *thank you very much* before going back to sleep.

She was extremely fond of Charles, of course, and he was an excellent lover—though she acknowledged she did not have much to compare him to—but what sort of *husband* would he be? Lover and husband were two very different roles, and she believed most men could never encompass both equally well. And considering her new husband's past, there was so much more trust to be built before she could ever call him a good one, much less confess she loved him.

Fortunately for Louisa, he didn't bring it up again for the rest of the honeymoon. But when the fortnight came to a close, Louisa found herself feeling sentimental, not wanting their stay at the cottage to end.

Sitting at the riverbank the afternoon before they were due to leave, Charles commented on her sullen mood that day. She turned and tried to smile at him. "I think I am only sad to leave this place. I wish we could be the way we are right now forever."

"Won't we, though?" Charles softly asked.

Louisa didn't answer him. Instead, she turned away, unsure.

They left for Kent the following morning. Although they spent many nights at poorly managed and hardly comfortable coaching inns, Louisa tried to enjoy those last few moments when there was no threat of possible arguments over the estate, and the only things that mattered were each other's happiness.

When they arrived at Linfield Hall, it was late at night, but Linfield's butler and housekeeper still greeted them in the massive entry hall. She hadn't been to Linfield since she was a child. The house was at least twice the size as Strickland, and she couldn't help but stare in awe at the enormous chandelier, the beautiful portraits hanging on the red walls, and the marble staircase that led upstairs. She had forgotten most of it as she had grown older.

After eating a late supper in the dining room, Louisa and Charles went upstairs, but not before Louisa promised Mrs. Hawkins, the housekeeper, that they could meet again early the following morning. "I want you to introduce me to the entire household staff, and I should like to review the household ledgers after that. Then you can take me on a tour of the house."

Charles spoke before Mrs. Hawkins could reply. "Why don't I give you the tour?"

Louisa looked back at him. There would be no "tour"

knowing how he behaved around her in private. He would just take her to some secluded corner of the house and have his wicked way with her. She looked down as she started to blush. "Thank you, but I think it best that Mrs. Hawkins do it."

Charles didn't try to argue, only nodded with a slight smile. He then led her to her bedroom on the second floor so they could retire for the evening. The room was more spacious than her room at Strickland, but the wallpaper and carpet were both shades of pink, and the bedclothes and curtains matched. Louisa must have let her disgust show on her face.

"You can redecorate it if you would like," Charles said. "I don't expect you to have the same taste as my mother."

Louisa forced a smile. "I'm not sure if we have the money for that. I don't mind keeping it this way."

Charles stepped toward her, wrapping his arms around her waist and pulling her toward him. "Do you plan on going through *my* ledgers tomorrow as well?" he asked, wiggling his brow.

Louisa unwrapped herself from his arms, moving toward the bed. She thought she heard him sigh behind her. "I had planned that, yes. I should like to see if there are any other opportunities for economizing the estate." She turned to face him. "I'll be doing the same with Strickland—I promise. I only wish to increase the monthly payment we are making to Rutley so that we might finish paying our debts to him sooner rather than later."

Charles smiled, then cornered her again, this time against the bedframe. She glanced down at his hands, which had slid down and settled on her hips. "What did I do to deserve such an intelligent wife?" he asked softly.

Louisa felt her heart pounding. Her mouth became dry. "I often ask myself the same question."

Charles laughed. "Must you always respond to every compliment I give you with some sort of sarcastic remark?" he asked. His tone was light and airy, and she knew he was teasing her as much as she was teasing him. But Louisa could also tell the walls she built around herself frustrated him. A small voice in her mind told her she could not hide behind them forever.

"Fine," Louisa began, her voice shaky as she spoke, "then I will tell you the truth. What did you do to deserve such an intelligent wife?" She sighed, half to calm herself as she searched her heart for a more truthful answer. "It has been a long uphill battle, one that started when we were children. There were many disappointments along the way, even times when I truly thought I hated you, but you always managed, time and time again, to surprise me in more ways than one."

This seemed to pique her husband's curiosity. "And what ways were those?"

Louisa half smiled. "When you kissed me, for one. And then when you kept pursuing me, even when I kept telling you it was a hopeless cause."

Charles gave a smug grin. "I always had a feeling it wasn't."

Louisa looked at him thoughtfully. "Perhaps not. But it was the concessions you so freely gave in our marriage contract that truly changed the tide of my feelings."

"Feelings?" Charles softly asked.

She looked up at him. "Yes, feelings."

Smiling, he gently brought his hand to her neck. Leaning forward, he kissed her, and Louisa started to melt into him. But she backed away, stopping herself. Their honeymoon was over. Surely things would change. Looking around them, she imagined they wouldn't even share a room anymore. Wasn't that custom for stuffy aristocrats?

"Where will you sleep?" Louisa asked suddenly. He

continued to smile at her, looking over her shoulder toward the corner of the room.

"That door leads to my bedroom."

She looked over her shoulder, then back at him.

"But I thought I might sleep here tonight." Charles leaned down to kiss her once more, this time much more vigorously, but Louisa broke away from him again.

"If you insist, but we cannot stay up all night. I have work to do tomorrow, and I should like to meet Mrs. Hawkins in the morning as I promised."

He nodded stoically. "I promise to be *mostly* good."

"Charles!" she exclaimed, wishing he would be serious for once. But then he forced her down on the bed and started to ravish her with his mouth. It didn't take long before she gave in to his lips and tongue and closed her eyes, allowing him to undress her and kiss her wherever he wanted. It amazed her how he already knew all her favorite places to be touched, all without her saying much at all.

She silently worried she was losing a part of herself, a part that Charles now owned, and that she could never get it back. Still, she let him love her that evening, and Louisa chose to enjoy it, even though it terrified her.

DESPITE WAKING UP SORE—AS it turned out, Charles *didn't* behave the night before—Louisa still rose early the next day, keeping her appointment with Mrs. Hawkins. Charles lounged in bed with his hands behind his head, watching as a maid helped Louisa wash and dress.

Irritated, she turned and glared at him. "Shouldn't you be returning to your room to bathe and dress as well?"

Charles shrugged, seeming content just to watch. "I am not in a hurry."

When the maid left, Louisa scolded him. "I wish you

wouldn't embarrass me like that. She will tell everyone below-stairs now."

Charles stood up, still naked from the previous night's activities. Louisa tried not to look at him, afraid she might be trapped in that room all day if her husband had his way. "And what do you think she will tell them? That the earl enjoys his new countess very, very much?"

He had come up behind her and whispered the last few words in her ear. Charles reached around her front, gently taking her clothed breasts in his hands. She nearly closed her eyes, let him bend her over her dressing table and have her again, but Louisa somehow managed to disentangle herself from his arms.

"I will see you later this afternoon after I finish my meeting with Mrs. Hawkins and take some time to visit Strickland." Charles started to protest, but Louisa quickly kissed him on the cheek. "Have a good day, dear."

She hurried out of the room, thankful when he didn't follow her, as that certainly would have caused a ruckus, given he was still naked. Louisa made her way belowstairs to Mrs. Hawkins's office, where the older woman introduced her to the cook and the rest of the servants. She then spent some time with the household ledgers, and Louisa was pleased to find that Mrs. Hawkins was a meticulous woman who kept her books well updated, not to mention there were detailed notes in the margins. There were a few opportunities to save more than they presently were, and Louisa wrote them down so she could discuss them with Charles later.

Mrs. Hawkins took Louisa around the house and grounds next, and thankfully there was nothing out of the ordinary. Everything was just slightly bigger than Strickland. The garden was well kept, and Louisa was pleased to see Charles hadn't sold off the collection in the library or any of the paintings. Many aristocrats chose to do so instead of economizing elsewhere, but Louisa always thought it was such a shame to part with things like art or literature.

When the tour was over, Louisa decided to walk to Strickland. The day was fine, sunny but not too warm, and it took less than an hour to visit Strickland on foot. She was halfway there when she came across Mr. Hardy, who looked surprised to see her.

"Mr. Hardy!" she exclaimed. "How do you do? I was only just thinking of you this morning."

They stopped along the dirt pathway. Mr. Hardy looked the same as always, with his golden hair, blue eyes, and dimpled smile. "Miss Strickland. I wasn't expecting you back for another few weeks." He looked over her shoulder, seemingly puzzled when he realized she was coming from the direction of Linfield. "What were you doing at Linfield Hall?"

Louisa put her hands behind her back, blushing slightly. "I suppose the news hasn't reached Kent yet, then. Lord Bolton and I are married."

Mr. Hardy nearly dropped his knapsack. "W-what?" he asked, his eyes widening. "You, a countess?"

Louisa couldn't tell if he was about to laugh or cry. "It is a very long story, one I shouldn't like to get into at the moment. I need to get to Strickland." She paused. "Are you going to see the earl now?"

Hardy, still flustered, somehow managed to nod his head. "Lord Bolton sent a note round this morning. He told me he had returned from town and had important news to share." Hardy looked her up and down, furrowing his brow and scratching the back of his head. "I suppose his marriage must have been part of that news."

Louisa forced a smile. "Well, do plan to stay awhile at Linfield. I should like an update on my tenants when I return from speaking to the housekeeper. Perhaps we might even have you over for dinner later this evening?"

"It would be my pleasure."

Louisa knew it wasn't common for aristocrats to dine with a man some might call the help, but she had invited Hardy over for dinner plenty of times at Strickland Manor. She saw no reason for their relationship to change now that she was a countess.

"How is Miss Flora?" Hardy asked before they parted ways. "Is she enjoying London?"

Louisa bit back a smile. How strange that the county gossip was always about *them* rather than her land steward's undying devotion for her younger half sister.

"She is enjoying it, yes, but she is not engaged yet, if that is what you are truly wondering," Louisa replied.

Hardy looked down, his cheeks turning red. "Well, I will see you at the house once you finish visiting Strickland. Good day, Lady Bolton."

Louisa faltered for a moment. How strange it was to hear someone call her that. She forced a smile. "Good day, Mr. Hardy."

"YOU MUST BE WONDERING what my important news is."

Charles sat across from his land steward. The man blinked at him. "If you mean your new wife, I happened upon her on my way here. Congratulations, my lord."

The earl stiffened. So Hardy and Louisa had already seen each other. An uncomfortable and unfamiliar feeling of jealousy struck him in his core. "Thank you, Hardy. So the countess was already off to Strickland?"

Hardy nodded, and Charles sighed. His wife was certainly much more productive than him. He must have lain in bed at least another hour just dreaming of her before ringing for Gibbs.

"I hope you don't mind me asking, my lord, but how did your marriage come about?" Hardy asked.

Charles shrugged, not entirely wanting to answer him. Charles didn't recognize any signs of disappointment in the young land steward, only confusion, which he supposed was normal. Charles and Louisa were a surprising match. "What always happens in situations like these? I was in desperate need of a wealthy wife, and somehow I convinced Lady Bolton she was the right woman for the job."

Hardy whistled. "Somehow, indeed."

Eager to change the subject, Charles asked after the tenants and the latest news from the village. Hardy was happy to supply him everything he wanted to know, but truthfully, Charles was only half listening, too busy wondering when his wife would return home. Eventually, she appeared in the study, the hem of her dress dirty from her long walk and her cheeks pink from fresh air and exercise.

In truth, she looked like a common country girl, not a countess. "Perhaps you might take the carriage next time," Charles gently observed.

She shot him a confused look as she sat in the armchair next to Hardy. She turned and smiled at the land steward, then looked back in the direction of her husband, who was admittedly growing impatient to be alone with her.

"Why?" Louisa asked. "It's such a beautiful day outside." She turned back to Hardy and smiled again. "Isn't it, Mr. Hardy?"

The land steward nodded, and Charles pursed his lips. He looked at his wife. "Perhaps we might take a turn about the garden later, just the two of us."

Louisa turned to him, appearing puzzled. "All right," she said with a slight nod before looking back at Hardy. "Now, you must tell me everything that I have missed since I was gone."

Charles watched the two of them speak as old friends would, and he was sure his expression grew more and more pressed as time passed and the two of them talked. If Louisa noticed her husband's souring expression, she didn't let on. When Louisa and Hardy finally finished their conversation, she turned to Charles. "I thought we might have Mr. Hardy over for dinner tonight. It's been just the two of us for so long that I think some different company might be an exciting change of pace."

Charles frowned, but Louisa stared back at him, expressionless. She was challenging him with only her eyes, daring him to say no. The idea of an earl dining with his land steward was absurd, but such stark divisions between the different classes weren't something Louisa or her family ever maintained.

The earl glanced at Hardy, who sat sheepishly in his chair. Hardy had already seemed so surprised by their marriage that Charles didn't want to prove him right by arguing with his wife in front of him, so Charles sighed and nodded his head.

"Of course you may come, Mr. Hardy," he said, rising from his chair. "We eat at six o'clock sharp. Try not to be late." Charles came around the desk, offering Louisa his arm. "Shall we take that turn about the garden now, dear?"

Louisa nodded and took his arm. Looking over her shoulder, she said, "Until this evening, Mr. Hardy."

Charles and Louisa walked through the hall in silence before reaching the back door to the garden. Neither had much to say as they traversed the walking paths through the flower beds and shrubbery in the garden, the only sound being the gravel crunching beneath their feet.

Eventually, Louisa sighed and turned to him. They came to a stop. "Are you going to tell me what's the matter, or do you plan on sulking about in silence for the rest of the afternoon?"

Charles made a face. "I am not sulking."

"You *are* sulking." Louisa pursed her lips as if waiting for Charles to just try disagreeing with her one more time. He sighed.

"Are you sure there is no truth to those rumors about you and Hardy? The two of you act very familiar with one another."

Louisa groaned. "Is that what is wrong? I happened to be friendly to another man? I told you before, Mr. Hardy only has eyes for my sister. She was the first thing he asked about when I came across him while walking to Strickland earlier."

Charles grew silent. "I see," he said after a moment. They began to walk again, and Charles sighed. "Now I feel foolish."

Louisa grinned at him. "It cannot be the first time, nor, I imagine, will it be the last."

"It's not nice to tease your husband, Lady Bolton."

She burst into laughter. "But I enjoy it so much, especially when I get to do it in the bedroom."

Charles arched his brow at her. "Can we go there now? I think we have both worked enough for one day."

"Hardly!" But that didn't stop Charles from picking her up by the waist and tossing her over his shoulder. She laughed, pounding his back with her tiny fists. "Put me down, Charles! You must stop doing this."

"Not until I show you what happens to ladies who tease their husbands."

He promptly carried her to her bedroom, where he made love to her for the rest of the afternoon. When she was thoroughly exhausted, Louisa curled up next to him, deciding to take a nap before dinner. Although she was asleep, he leaned down and whispered in her ear, "I wish we could be the way we are right now forever."

He kissed her on the top of her head before falling asleep as well.

Chapter Twenty-Six

THE TRANSITION from their honeymoon to their life at Linfield went much more smoothly than Louisa ever imagined. Charles never tried to manage her—at least not too much—and she had complete freedom over what she did every day. He didn't even become that upset when she came home with muddied skirts every afternoon, as long as she allowed him to help her "clean up" in her bedroom.

Charles was "helping" Louisa one afternoon when they heard the rattling wheels of a carriage coming down the drive. She patted her husband's shoulder as he kissed her. When Louisa tried to break away, he switched to peppering them down her neck.

"Did you hear that?" she asked.

Charles's response was incoherent.

Louisa looked toward the windows of her room. They were open, allowing the slight breeze to cool her warm bedroom. The curtains swayed back and forth, and then Louisa heard the opening of a carriage door. This time, she shoved Charles away from her.

He looked at her, confused, but Louisa was frantic.

"There is someone here!" she said, scrambling off the bed and gathering her undergarments, which her husband had strewn across the floor earlier. Finding one of her stockings ripped, she turned and shot him a menacing look. "This is why we shouldn't have marital relations in the middle of the day!"

Charles sighed, getting off the bed. He found his breeches, slipped them on, and walked toward the window. Louisa watched as his eyes widened and he tucked his entire body against the wall, out of view from any outside observers. "It is my mother," he said, his voice strangely calm though his expression wasn't at all.

"I should change my frock," Louisa said, looking down at her muddied hem. When their gazes met again, her husband was nodding. She frowned at him. She didn't want him to agree. "You get dressed and go down and greet her. I will be down shortly."

Thankfully, Charles did as she asked without much complaint. When he finished, he approached her at her dressing table. She was sitting, facing the mirror, and he leaned down and kissed her on the shoulder. "Don't be nervous."

Louisa nodded and tried to smile. When he left, she immediately reached for the bellpull by the bed, summoning her lady's maid. Louisa briefed her of the situation, and they got to work correcting her appearance. Louisa wore one of her newer gowns from that season, and the maid freshly curled her hair.

Before going downstairs, Louisa stood behind her bedroom door, took a deep breath, and closed her eyes. It was only her mother-in-law, she reminded herself. There was no reason for her to judge Louisa harshly. They had lived in the same neighborhood her entire life, and Louisa came from a respectable family. She may not have been the daughter of an aristocrat, but as far as Louisa was concerned, the Finches needed her much more than she ever needed them.

Louisa opened her eyes, nodded her head once, then went downstairs, wearing a look of determination. She heard the faint voices of a male and a female coming from the drawing room, so she headed down the marble staircase and turned right. Louisa saw them then, sitting at the center of the room. Charles faced away from her, so Lady Bolton noticed her first.

It was difficult to tell what Lady Bolton thought when their eyes first met. Her expression changed, and perhaps it was only in her head, but Louisa thought it was a look of disdain. Even Charles must have suspected Louisa had entered the room based on his mother's demeanor, for he turned right away.

"Louisa," he said, rising from the sofa and walking toward her with his arms outstretched. He winked at her as he offered her his arm. If he was trying to reassure her, it wasn't working. Her heart pounded in her chest as they approached the dowager countess standing at the center of the room.

In some ways, Louisa and her mother-in-law were similar. They both had red hair, though Louisa considered her own shade much less vibrant. And despite how tall Louisa already was, the dowager countess had at least two more inches on her. Even after traveling in a carriage, she was impeccably dressed, and seeing as they were both Lady Bolton, Louisa wondered how she could ever compare.

"You remember my mother, don't you?" Charles asked, looking down at his wife.

She forced a smile. "Yes, I remember," Louisa said, her voice sounding slightly breathless. She dropped into a curtsey. "How do you do, Lady Bolton?"

"I am better now that I have returned to Linfield Hall." She glanced at Charles, reaching up and gently tapping his cheek. "It would appear my son has started to make things right. He has gone about it in a slightly unorthodox way, but it is a start at least."

Lady Bolton turned, her skirts sweeping behind her as she went to sit down. Louisa and Charles exchanged a look. She had no idea what Lady Bolton's comment meant, but the look on his face begged her not to ask why. At least not at that moment.

Charles cleared his throat. "My mother told me she is here to discuss her living accommodations now that the family is in a better place financially."

Louisa nodded, going to sit down with Charles across from the dowager countess. The older woman studied her shrewdly, and Louisa did her best not to let it trouble her. "Yes, Charles and I have discussed this."

They had decided they would take on the extra cost of opening the dowager house if his mother wanted to return home. Although it was less expensive for them when Lady Bolton stayed with friends, Louisa understood she couldn't stay away forever.

"I have depended on the kindness of the Haddingtons for far too long," Lady Bolton said, looking back and forth between her son and new daughter-in-law. "I don't expect you to allow me to stay here; I'm sure two childless newlyweds such as yourselves would prefer their privacy."

Louisa wasn't sure how much longer she could hold her smile. She felt her cheeks turning pink, thinking of what was going on when the dowager countess first arrived.

"I was hoping I could take Strickland as my own. It's far better appointed for entertaining than the dowager house, and I should like to entertain from time to time, though I might be widowed."

The color drained from Louisa's face. She turned to Charles, searching for the same outrage in his eyes that she was feeling. But he appeared more nervous than angry. Louisa turned away, forcing her gaze back toward Lady Bolton. If Charles couldn't be firm, Louisa must do it for them. "I'm afraid that won't be possible. Where would my stepmother and sister live?"

Lady Bolton shrugged carelessly. "Your sister's a pretty girl. I'm sure she'll be married soon, and surely your stepmother won't mind living in the dowager house instead of me. It's much better suited for a woman of her character."

Louisa could feel her temper rising. She glanced at her husband, waiting for him to say something, do something—anything—but he remained silent. She gritted her teeth. "Strickland Manor is my stepmother's home. She will stay there as long as—"

"Well, we don't have to make a decision now," Charles said, interrupting her. Eyes wide, Louisa turned to him. He smiled at her, then looked at his mother. "How are the Haddingtons? I have not seen them in ages."

Louisa stared at him, unable to believe both his deftness in changing the subject and his complete inability to stand up to his mother. She half listened to them drone on about her time with her friends. One of the servants brought in a tray of tea, and Louisa served it with trembling hands.

When it was finally time to dress for dinner, Louisa went ahead of Charles and his mother. While Charles escorted Lady Bolton to the guest wing, Louisa sat at her dressing table, staring at herself in the mirror. This feeling of being trapped was precisely what she had dreaded if she ever married. Charles would give his mother whatever she wanted, no matter what Louisa said or argued, and there was nothing she could do about it.

She heard a knocking at her door. "Come in," Louisa said, still staring at herself in the mirror. She knew it was Charles without even looking. He padded across the carpet of her room, coming to stand behind her. He placed a hand on her shoulder, where he'd once traced kisses across her skin. She shrugged him off, and he sighed.

"Do not be like this, Louisa," he said.

She turned and glared at him. "Do not be like this, Louisa?" she echoed angrily. Her nostrils flared as she stared at him. She couldn't remember the last time she'd been this upset with him, and her heart physically ached in her chest as she watched him. "You would force my stepmother out of her home just to make your mother happy? How could you? You and I both know that's not right." She paused, turning to face the mirror once more. "Unless you don't know, in which case I suppose I have misjudged your character after all."

He kneeled beside her, and although she tried not to look at him, she recognized he was frowning at her. He took her hands into his. "Look at me," Charles said. When she didn't do what he asked at first, he repeated himself. Finally, Louisa turned. He tried to smile, but she could see the sadness in his eyes. "I have no intention of forcing your stepmother from her home. We will find a way to convince my mother that she would prefer the dowager house."

Louisa was unconvinced. "And what if you can't convince her? What will you do then?"

Charles sighed, then lifted her hands to his lips. He gently kissed her knuckles. "Then I will have to make my mother very unhappy, but it wouldn't be the first time, would it?"

That elicited a reluctant smile from Louisa's lips.

Charles reached up, pulling her face down to his and planting a soft kiss on her lips. "It will be fine, my love. Trust me."

Louisa froze at the mention of the word *love*. She was unsure of what to say, so she nervously smiled. "Thank you."

She thought she saw his shoulders sag, but he recovered

quickly, pressing another kiss to her lips and then standing up. "I will leave you to prepare for dinner, then."

Louisa smiled at him and thought about calling him back to her as he made his way to the door that connected their adjoining bedrooms. But she remained silent, still not trusting the secret feelings inside her heart.

Chapter Twenty-Seven

THE DOWAGER COUNTESS'S visit at Linfield was torturous. When they were all together, Louisa barely looked at Charles, and his mother somehow managed to criticize Louisa in every way possible. Her menus for dinner were never impressive enough, and she spent half her time speculating what Louisa did all morning with Mr. Hardy.

"They are calling on our tenants," Charles explained.

His mother made a face. They sat in the morning room, having just finished their breakfast, and now they were sipping tea before taking a walk together in the garden. Louisa had already left for the day, her first order of business a meeting with Hardy at one of the farms down the road.

"Isn't that Mr. Hardy's responsibility?" Lady Bolton asked as she shook her head and sighed. "I should have known you would pick her. You always were fond of her, even as a little boy. I should have come to town with you and helped you choose a proper wife."

Charles put down his tea, annoyed. "Louisa is a proper wife, and she came to the marriage with an estate valued at ten thousand pounds a year. She is the daughter of a gentleman, for God's sake. What is wrong with her?"

His mother shot him a look as if surprised he had gotten so defensive. She placed her teacup on its saucer as well. "So it is a love match," she said.

Charles grew silent. He hadn't even told Louisa he loved her yet, at least not while she was awake to hear it. "I chose her for many reasons. Her father was brilliant, and she is very bright in her own right. He taught her everything he knew about estate management. She will help me pay off the duke and restore Linfield to its former glory. Isn't that what you wanted?"

Lady Bolton laughed. "You speak of her as if she is part of the household staff, but I know that's not how you truly feel. You love her. That's why you won't let me have Strickland Manor. It upsets her."

"And rightfully so!" Charles exclaimed, losing his patience. His mother was purposefully needling him. "For the record, I do love her. I love her for a multitude of reasons, including all of the ones I just told you."

His mother sighed as she looked toward the window of the morning room. Charles followed her gaze, seeing Louisa and Mr. Hardy standing shoulder to shoulder in the distance as they walked back toward the house. They looked at each other and laughed about something.

Charles turned away, irritated at how it might look. "I wonder if it's a love match for her," his mother said. "She does seem close to your land steward, and there were those rumors I remember hearing about the last time the duchess had me over for tea. They say she rejected her cousin for his sake."

Charles abruptly stood, not wanting to listen to any more gossip. "You shouldn't believe everything you hear, Mama." He leaned down, kissing the top of her head. "I will be in my study if you need me."

Charles left the room, unable to think straight. Louisa had told him there was nothing between her and Hardy, that he preferred her sister, but sometimes his jealousy got the better of him. His mind wandered all day with thoughts of them together, but Charles didn't address his errant feelings until much later, after they made love and were preparing to go to sleep.

"My mother shared some gossip about you and Mr. Hardy this morning," he murmured in her ear.

She looked over at him, surprised. "I thought we already discussed this, Charles," she said, clearly annoyed.

"She said you rejected your cousin for his sake." Charles felt Louisa's body stiffen against his. "Is that true?"

"Of course not."

But she did not sound entirely convincing. He grabbed her by the shoulders and turned her to face him, capturing her gaze as he did. "Tell me the truth, then," he whispered, his eyes searching hers. "Why did you reject your cousin?"

Louisa sighed. "I couldn't marry someone who wasn't you. I didn't know it at the time, but now I do. My cousin was not the right man for me, no matter how much he wanted Strickland Manor. I couldn't be convinced, regardless of what everyone was telling me." She narrowed her eyes at him. "You, though, seemed to have always wanted both of us: me and the manor. And sometimes I even suspect you would have had me even if the manor wasn't part of the deal."

Louisa started to look away, but Charles caught her by the chin, gently forcing her to look at him. "You're right, Louisa. I would have."

He captured her mouth with his, dropping his hand and finding her breast, running his finger over her already-taut nipple. She gasped, and Charles began to grow erect once more. Breaking the kiss, he turned her away from him, so her bottom brushed against his groin. When he reached down and across her smooth stomach, finding her wet heat with his fingertips, he knew he must have her again that night. "Please, Louisa. Let me love you one more time."

She moaned as he moved his hand and rubbed the top of her sex. Still positioned behind her, Charles gently lifted her top leg and thrust his cock inside of her. She felt even tighter in that position, and he continued to use one hand to play with the bundle of nerves where their bodies met. As he stroked her, Charles whispered in her ear, "You're so wet and tight... Please, come for me... That's it..."

He felt her tighten around him, and she cried out, signaling her climax. He followed her not long after. He lay beside her afterward, bending his elbow and holding his head up with his hand so that he could study her face. Charles searched her eyes, looking for any sign that it was safe to tell her how he felt. "Louisa..."

She snuggled closer to him. "We should go to sleep," she said. "It's getting late."

Charles nodded, standing up and snuffing the candles. When he rejoined her in bed, she had turned over on her side and closed her eyes, facing away from him. He slid in behind her, shaping his body to hers and kissing her on the neck. "Good night, my love."

"A COURIER from London just arrived with a letter for Lady Bolton, my lord."

Charles sat in the drawing room with his mother. They both looked up, his mother resting her embroidery hoop in her lap. Louisa, like always, was calling on tenants at that time of day.

"Which one?" his mother asked.

"It comes from Mrs. Strickland, my lady," the footman said. Charles and his mother exchanged a look.

"Give it to me," Charles said, extending his hand. He flipped the missive over, recognizing Mrs. Strickland's handwriting.

"You aren't going to open it?" Lady Bolton asked when the servant left.

Charles furrowed his brow at his mother. "It's her business," he said.

His mother didn't look convinced. "What if it's urgent?"

Charles sighed. "Then she will be home soon."

"She really should stay home more often."

Charles refused to say anything, only grunted in response. It would be another couple of hours before Louisa returned, and Charles spent most of that time pacing the drawing room floor while he waited. He tried to play a few tunes on the pianoforte, but he was absolute rubbish at it after not practicing in years.

His mother would occasionally look up from her embroidery and carefully watch him as he moved about the room. "Your wife certainly has you wrapped around her finger," she observed.

Charles glared at her. "Indeed," he said before taking a deep breath. He couldn't take it any longer. For the sake of his marriage—hell, for the sake of his own well-being—he must finally stand up to her. "Mother, I think it's time for you to take up residence at the dowager house."

Lady Bolton's face fell.

"That was what Father intended for you after he died, and Strickland Manor is Mrs. Strickland's home. We won't be evicting her for your sake."

"But Charles—"

They both heard the front door open and close. Charles turned around and saw Louisa standing in the doorway. She must have sensed they had been having a tense conversation.

"Is everything all right?" she asked.

Charles walked over to the table, picking up the letter and bringing it to her. "This came for you earlier by courier."

Louisa took the missive from him. "It's from my stepmother," she said, recognizing the handwriting as Charles had before carefully opening it. Louisa scanned the pages, raising her hand to her mouth as she read. Charles thought he saw tears forming in her eyes.

"What is it?" Charles asked anxiously.

Louisa looked at him, then shoved the letter toward him. He took it before she walked around him, going to sit down.

"Flora's run off with Lord Fitzgerald," Louisa explained.

"What did you say?"

They all turned and saw Mr. Hardy standing in the doorway, holding his hat in his hands by his waist. Charles had never seen his features look so dark. The earl turned back to his wife, folding the letter and putting it in his pocket. "I will go after them," he said simply.

"What?" Lady Bolton and Louisa said at the same time. The two women exchanged surprised looks.

Lady Bolton shook her head, turning back to her son. "Do not be so foolish. What's done is done. The girl must have known the risk she was taking by doing something so thoughtless as running off with a man." She peered at Louisa. "You said he's a lord?"

Louisa nodded. "Yes, he's a viscount."

"Then what is the issue?" Lady Bolton asked. "Your sister will become a viscountess in exchange for her thirty thousand pounds." She shot her son a discreet glance. "Worse deals have been made amongst women and men."

"But I forbid it!" Louisa exclaimed, shaking her head. "The viscount is only marrying her for her money; I am sure of it. He will not have her dowry even if he succeeds in taking her to Gretna Green." Louisa turned back to Charles, rising again and walking toward him. She took his hands into his.

"You must go after her. Please. He will not marry her if he knows we will not give him her dowry."

"You would ruin the poor girl all so this man won't receive her dowry?" The dowager countess sounded enraged.

Louisa looked over her shoulder at Lady Bolton and nodded. "Yes. Lord Fitzgerald is a vile man, and I would prefer Flora be ruined than watch her marry him. I'm sure the latter outcome is a much worse fate than ruination could ever be." Louisa turned back to Charles. "You will go after her, won't you?"

Charles nodded. "I will have the grooms ready the horses." He looked over his shoulder at Hardy. "And you are coming with me."

RATHER THAN TAKE THE CARRIAGE, Charles and Mr. Hardy rode on horseback to London, where Flora and the viscount were last seen. The earl and his land steward started at the Stricklands' rented town house, where Louisa's stepmother was beside herself with grief. With shaking hands, she handed Charles the note that Flora left.

Mama,

I have gone off to Gretna Green with Viscount Fitzgerald. Louisa will never approve, so I thought I would save us all the trouble by eloping. We will return to town in a fortnight, when I hope you all can learn to accept me and my new husband.

F.S.

Charles studied the note carefully, then looked at Mrs. Strickland. "And you are sure this is her handwriting?" he asked.

Louisa's stepmother nodded, taking the handkerchief she was holding and dabbing her eyes with it. "I am certain," she said.

Hardy was standing over the earl's shoulder as well, looking at the note. The land steward sighed. "Yes, that is her handwriting."

Although the man did his best to hide it, Charles could tell Hardy was distraught over the situation, proving Louisa's point over which Strickland girl Hardy preferred. Charles despised himself for letting his mother make him doubt Louisa.

"Will you go after her?" Mrs. Strickland asked.

Charles nodded. "We must find her. Louisa has already made it clear that there will be no dowry without a proper betrothal and wedding."

Mrs. Strickland wept even harder. "But wouldn't it be easier if Louisa just approved of the match? Flora will be ruined, and we will never be able to come to town again!"

Charles and Hardy exchanged a look. Charles knelt beside his mother-in-law, speaking to her in a gentle tone. "The girl is only nineteen, and she will always be welcome at Linfield Hall and Finch Place. It may take some time, but I'm sure one day a gentleman will come along and not give a damn about her past."

Mrs. Strickland seemed skeptical. Charles was skeptical himself, but he wasn't about to say that. "Have the servants start packing your things here so you can return to Strickland immediately. When I recover Flora, I plan on taking her straight to her sister in Linfield. If you would like, you can stay there until we return so you do not have to be alone."

Mrs. Strickland nodded, and Charles looked at Hardy. "There is someone else I think we should see before we go after them."

. . .

If anyone knew what the viscount was planning, it would be his best friend, Philip Hayward. As they walked down the street toward his house, Charles glanced at Hardy. "Have you brought a pistol with you?" Charles asked.

His land steward furrowed his brow. "No. Should I have?"

"It's difficult to say," Charles replied thoughtfully. "The last time I saw Hayward, we ended up engaging in fisticuffs in the back room of his gaming establishment in Covent Garden."

Hardy's face fell. He looked at Charles as if the earl were mad. "Then why are we calling on him?"

"I don't want to ride to Gretna Green without confirming that is where they are heading first."

His companion still seemed confused. "Do you think Miss Flora would lie about where they were going?" Hardy shook his head, muttering to himself. "She is not like that."

"No, I do not think Miss Flora would lie. But I do believe the viscount may have misinformed her in regards to their final destination. He will not marry her if she does not come with thirty thousand pounds, and he knows her sister will never approve of the match." Charles shrugged. "And if he knows he will not get the dowry, perhaps he only means to have a spot of fun by bedding her and leaving her stranded at a coaching inn."

Hardy made a face of disgust. "What sort of man would do such a thing?"

"Men like Fitzgerald." Charles glanced at Hardy as they walked. He was a handsome chap, no more than three-and-twenty. Although he wasn't a gentleman, he had a respectable enough career. "You know, there is one way to save Flora from ruination."

Hardy raised his brow. "What is that?"

"*You* could marry her."

His land steward snorted. "You assume she would have me."

"Do you not get along?" Charles asked. He assumed they must have been somewhat friendly for him to develop an attachment to her.

Hardy sighed. "I know what you're thinking, but you should know that my affection for Miss Flora is very one-sided." He paused, clearing his throat as his cheeks turned pink. "I more admire her from afar, that is. I doubt she even realizes the depth of my affections toward her. Louisa—I beg your pardon, Lady Bolton—only proves how perceptive she is by noticing."

"And why do you assume it is Lady Bolton who told me?"

"Did she not?"

Charles paused. "Well, yes, she did. But you were extremely cross with me when I decided to send Miss Flora flowers in London, so I suppose it all makes sense. I was only too stupid to notice." He quickened his pace. "Come, Hayward's is just around the corner here."

When the two men finally reached Hayward's, it was closed, not set to open for another few hours. Charles pounded on the door until a stocky, fearsome-looking man answered.

"What is it?"

Charles handed him his card. "I need an audience with Mr. Hayward immediately."

The man took the small slip of paper, reading it. Then his eyes flickered back toward Charles. "Lord Bolton? Mr. Hayward has been expecting you."

Charles and Hardy exchanged a look, then followed the man inside. He showed them to a small office at the front of the building, before the dining or cardrooms, then left to fetch Hayward. Charles glanced at Hardy. "In case you were wondering, I did bring my pistol."

Charles grinned while his companion blanched. "Don't worry," Charles said. "I'm an adequate shot when I'm sober."

"That doesn't make me feel any better," Hardy muttered as the door separating the office from the hall opened.

Hayward appeared, wearing his signature cocky grin. "You are right on time," he said, glancing at the clock on the mantel.

Charles glared at Hayward. "Then you know why we are here. Where did Fitzgerald take my sister-in-law?"

Hayward arched his brow, sitting down at his desk and crossing one leg over the other. "Are you saying you do not believe they are on their way to Gretna Green? She's a beautiful girl; any chap would be lucky to marry her."

"Even without her dowry?"

Hayward lifted his hands and shrugged. "Well, that changes things. And I may have told him his plan was stupid due to that fact alone. You and I both know Miss Strickland would never hand over her sister's dowry if they eloped."

Charles disliked the way he said his wife's maiden name. "She is Lady Bolton now, and you shall address her as such."

Hayward chuckled. "Whatever you prefer, my lord." Hayward leaned forward, placing both feet on the floor. "But as I was saying, I may have suggested Fitzgerald convince the girl to elope with him regardless, then desert her at some faraway coaching inn the morning after bedding her. It's the least he deserves after he wasted an entire season courting her."

Hardy started to lunge for Hayward, but Charles reached out and grabbed him by the shoulders, pulling him backward and forcing him to sit. Hayward didn't even flinch. "You haven't introduced me to your friend."

"This is my land steward, Hardy," Charles explained. He only released him when he finally stopped huffing and puffing like a madman. Hardy brushed the arm of his mussed jacket with his hand, glaring at Hayward. "Don't mind him. Just give me the name of the coaching inn so we can fetch Flora. You wouldn't want any harm to come to the poor girl if she's left alone and frightened, would you?"

Hayward shrugged. "If I cared about the girl's well-being, do you truly think I would have suggested all this to Fitzgerald?"

Charles sensed Hardy tensing beside him again. Charles held out his arm, blocking him from charging at Hayward as a cautionary gesture. Something was amiss. Hayward had a look about him. "What do you want, Hayward?" Charles asked, dropping his arm once he knew Hardy wasn't about to do anything stupid.

Hayward's eyes became dark. "I should like to embarrass Louisa as she once embarrassed me," he said. "Her sister will be ruined after this, and everyone will question your sense in making the foolish girl's spinster sister your countess—not that anyone thought the better of you after what happened with your two sisters last season."

Charles breathed heavily, nearly lunging at the man himself. "For God's sake, just tell me the name of the coaching inn. You have already succeeded in achieving what you desired. Louisa is furious. Why withhold the name of the inn any longer?"

Hayward sighed. "I will tell you as long as you can agree to one condition."

"What is it?" Charles asked, his tone impatient.

"You mustn't take revenge on the viscount. I do not wish to be called as second to any ridiculous duel at dawn in the middle of Hyde Park."

"Neither do I," Hardy muttered.

Hayward glanced at him with a slight smile, then turned back to Charles. "You will fetch the girl," Hayward continued, "and we will forget this ever happened."

Charles didn't want to forget anything. Charles *wanted* to pull out his pistol and shoot Hayward dead right then and there. And perhaps the old Charles would have, as he was always quick to lose his temper whenever he was in a bind—especially while drunk. But if he shot Hayward, they would be no closer to finding Flora. There were also the bodyguards that were most likely standing outside he had to consider, and he had no desire to be arrested for murder, even if it was Hayward's. So Charles took a deep breath.

"Fine."

Hayward smiled. And then he told Charles the name of the inn.

Chapter Twenty-Eight

CHARLES HIRED a post chaise to take them to the small village of Stilton, where Hayward told him Fitzgerald planned to desert poor Flora at the Bell Inn the following morning. There was no chance they would arrive before the night was over, even if they hardly stopped for rest. Still, Charles hoped they might catch Fitzgerald on his way out.

Charles and Hardy arrived at dawn. When they opened the front door to the inn, Charles almost expected Fitzgerald to be traipsing down the main staircase, ready to make a speedy escape. Instead, the only man Charles saw was the innkeeper standing behind the front desk. He was a surly-looking fellow with white hair and bushy eyebrows. He looked up when he heard Charles and Hardy approach.

"Good morning," Charles said, nodding at the man. The innkeeper gazed at him critically through his spectacles. "Did a young man and woman stay here last night?"

"Who's asking?" the innkeeper said gruffly.

Charles sighed, pulling one of his cards out of his jacket pocket.

The innkeeper took it, glanced at it, then looked back up at Charles. The older man's gaze softened a bit. He handed the card back to Charles. "Pardon me, my lord. I did have a young married couple arrive last evening, except they quarreled in the middle of the night. The man left, but I imagine the lady is still abed. She wailed all night long; she is lucky I had no other guests last night, or else I would have had to put her out in the stables with the horses." The innkeeper huffed angrily. "Only I had to listen to her cries. Who are you, her brother?"

"Brother-in-law."

The innkeeper gave a knowing nod. Charles swallowed his disappointment that the viscount had already left; he would have liked to have Hardy hit him a few times before they let him go. After all, Charles only promised Hayward *he* wouldn't go after Fitzgerald after the earl finished this ordeal. Hardy made no such promise.

But then the innkeeper continued. "I believe the fellow slept outside in the stables. The post chaise he hired wouldn't travel through the night. The postboy had one too many run-ins with highwaymen, and the man couldn't offer him enough extra money to make it worth his while."

Charles and Hardy exchanged a look, and the earl started to grin. "Hardy, why don't you go awaken our friend in the stables? I will go fetch Flora upstairs." Charles turned back to the innkeeper. "Which room was it?"

"Up the stairs, third door on the left."

Charles turned to face Hardy. "I will see you—"

But Hardy was already gone. Charles smiled. At least someone might beat Fitzgerald to a pulp that day. Charles faced the innkeeper again, then reached into his jacket pocket and procured a half sovereign, placing it on the desk. The innkeeper smiled before taking the gold coin and pocketing it.

"Thank you for your help, sir," Charles said. "You have been most obliging."

Charles headed up the stairs, following the innkeeper's direction and knocking on the third door of the left. There was no answer on the other side. Charles repeated the motion, this time calling out as well. "Flora? Are you in there? It is your brother—"

The door swung open, and a small female with a tangled mess of brown hair sitting at the top of her head charged toward him. Charles held out his arms as she wrapped herself around his waist, burrowing her head against his chest. Not quite sure what to do, he gently patted her on the back. "This was not quite the reaction I was expecting."

Flora stepped back from him, looking up at him with those big brown eyes of hers, still swollen from her crying. "You came for me, which means Louisa told you to come for me, which means my sister does not intend to disown me— even though I have been a foolish, *foolish* girl!"

Charles laughed slightly. "Perhaps not total disownment— just a stern lecture. I doubt there will be any more seasons in town either."

Flora's shoulders sagged, and she dropped her face into her palms. "Oh, I am ruined! I should have listened to her." She looked back up at him. "Now *I* will be the spinster, and my sister will be the countess! No one will ever have me once word spreads."

Charles grew serious. "What exactly *did* happen, Flora? The innkeeper told me you and Fitzgerald quarreled, and he spent the night out in the stables."

Flora bit her lip. "I hadn't realized he slept in the stables." Then she sighed and pouted at the earl. "If you must know, nothing happened. When I would not give him what he wanted, he revealed the entirety of his dishonorable plan to me. That's when I locked him out of our room. I should have never trusted him!"

"If it makes you feel any better, I believe Mr. Hardy is giving the viscount a thrashing as we speak."

Flora's eyes widened. "Mr. Hardy? Your land steward? My family has always been friendly with him, but what is he doing here?"

Charles nearly laughed. "He happened to be there when your sister received the letter from your mother about you running away, so I asked him to come along with me. He didn't hesitate."

Flora chewed her lower lip. Charles almost said more, but he didn't think Hardy would appreciate the earl confessing the steward's feelings in his stead. "What about Mama?" Flora asked, already forgetting about Hardy. "Is she still in London? Is she very angry with me?"

Charles shook his head. "She's probably in Kent by now, waiting for you with your sister. Don't worry—you'll see both of them soon. For now, I would like to go and watch Hardy beat Fitzgerald to a pulp. He's a rather strapping fellow, isn't he? Have you ever noticed?"

Flora tilted her head to the side, as if considering his words. "I suppose he is, but the viscount is very strapping himself. Mr. Hardy ought to be careful."

Charles smiled to himself. At one time, he would have laughed at the idea of playing matchmaker, but he felt sorry for Hardy, fancying a girl who did not return his feelings. And if the earl could help sway her opinion at all, why shouldn't he? After all, everyone deserved an opportunity at what he had with Louisa.

"Why are you smiling, my lord?" Flora asked.

Charles shook his head. "No reason in particular—only eager to return home."

After Flora gathered her things, they went downstairs, where Charles thanked the innkeeper once more for his assistance. They headed outside, where the hired post chaise was waiting for them. The horses had already been switched out, so they could leave at any time, but Hardy was nowhere to be found.

Charles looked around, his eyes and ears drawn to a commotion coming from the direction of the stables. Hardy dragged the viscount across the ground, holding him by the collar, until they were out in the open. Both men were bloodied and bruised. Fitzgerald was soaked with water from head to toe and helplessly trying to free himself from Hardy's grip, but the viscount wasn't nearly as strong as Flora supposed him to be. Charles glanced at her now. She watched the whole scene with wide eyes.

"Unhand me this instant!" the viscount exclaimed. But Hardy did not listen, only held him up by the collar so their gazes were level. Fitzgerald's expression grew more and more frantic. "She came willingly, you know. I don't understand why you are thrashing me for taking something so freely given."

Hardy's eyes grew dark just before he punched Fitzgerald clear across the face. Charles winced, and from beside him, Flora gasped, bringing her hands to her mouth. The earl wrapped his arms around her, holding her tight to him, afraid she might bolt and try to help the viscount instead of the land steward defending her honor.

Much like Charles was at her age, Flora wasn't exactly keen of mind. But she did not try to break free of him, only stood there watching Hardy and her almost lover with wide eyes.

"If you ever come near Flora Strickland again, I will kill you," Hardy said. It was the most menacing Charles ever heard him. Quite frankly, he didn't know his land steward had it in him. "Do you understand me?"

Fitzgerald weakly nodded, which clearly wasn't a good enough response for the land steward.

"*Do you understand me?*" he asked, even more forcefully than before.

"Yes!" the viscount shouted.

Hardy nodded once. "Good."

And then he punched him across the face again, this time knocking him unconscious. The land steward loosened his grip on the man's collar, letting him fall to the ground with a loud thump. When Hardy straightened from his bent position, his eyes found Charles and Flora. His dark gaze wasn't so dark anymore, though Flora still trembled beside Charles.

Hardy rushed toward them. "Are you all right?" he asked Flora, stopping himself before he got too close to her. Charles released Flora and turned around, scratching the back of his head. He wondered if Hardy would go through with proposing to her in an attempt to protect her honor.

"I'm fine, t-thank you," she said. There was a long silence, and Charles closed his eyes, unable to turn and look at them. Hardy would surely boggle any attempt at asking Flora for her hand in marriage. The land steward cleared his throat.

"Lord Bolton and I were discussing your..." He paused as if he was searching for the least offensive word. "...your situation, and I should like to offer a solution."

Charles turned, watching them carefully now. Flora appeared as if she had no idea what Hardy meant. "Oh?" she asked.

"I will marry you, Flora," he said softly. "If you will have me, that is."

Flora blinked at him, speechless for a moment, before slowly shaking her head. Charles saw Hardy's shoulders sink out of the corner of his eye. The man looked as if all the wind had been knocked out of him with one turn of the head.

"No," she said, elevating her chin and holding her head

high. "I will not allow you to sacrifice your own happiness for the sake of protecting me from ruination."

Hardy blanched, and Charles knew he must say something. "Surely any man could find happiness with you, Flora. You mustn't think of Hardy. Think of yourself. Do you want to be completely ostracized by society?"

Flora turned so she faced Charles. "Neither of our families have ever acted how the ton would prefer over the years. I think I will be fine. Besides, any man worth having wouldn't give a damn if he truly wanted me." She briefly glanced over her shoulder at Hardy, who had turned the other way. When she looked back at Charles, she smiled. "Shall we go now?"

Charles nodded, and together they piled into the carriage. Although Flora chattered happily, Hardy didn't speak the entire way back to Linfield Hall. And when Flora offered him her handkerchief to clean his bloodied face, he refused.

Chapter Twenty-Nine

WAITING for Charles to return with Flora was terrible. Waiting while the dowager countess hovered over her was even worse, so Louisa was thankful when Mrs. Strickland arrived at Linfield Hall the day after Charles left. At least her stepmother could provide some sort of buffer between Louisa and her icy mother-in-law. But first, Louisa wanted to know if Mrs. Strickland had seen Charles in London.

"Yes, I have seen him," her stepmother replied as they took a seat in Linfield's drawing room. "He was the one who told me to return home. He plans on bringing Flora straight here when he finds her."

Louisa's brows pinched together. Finding Flora before she did something she regretted might be more challenging for Charles than it seemed. "Did he say where he was going after he left you?" Louisa asked.

Mrs. Strickland nodded. "He said he was going to see Mr. Hayward." Louisa flinched at the man's name. Thanks to Charles, she had mostly forgotten their brief flirtation. But what would Hayward have to do with Fitzgerald and Flora running away? Louisa grew even more concerned.

"I wonder why he went there?" Louisa murmured. But before her stepmother had a chance to say anything else, the dowager countess swept into the room. Mrs. Strickland rose, as did Louisa. Lady Bolton looked at her stepmother with a raised chin, a sign, Louisa believed, that the dowager countess thought Mrs. Strickland was beneath her.

"Lady Bolton," Louisa said. She gestured to her stepmother. "You remember my stepmother, Mrs. Strickland?"

Mrs. Strickland curtseyed.

The dowager countess continued to survey the woman with a harsh gaze. "Indeed," Lady Bolton said.

They all sat down, and Louisa tried to ignore the fact that her mother-in-law was impossible to like. Somehow she had become even colder since Charles left, and Louisa was starting to wonder if something had happened between them before he departed for London. Perhaps he'd finally told her moving into Strickland Manor was out of the question.

"Mrs. Strickland was just telling me what happened when she saw Charles in town," Louisa said to Lady Bolton before turning back to her stepmother. "Do you know why he went to find Mr. Hayward?"

Mrs. Strickland shrugged. "I believe he thought Hayward might have known where he took her. The road to Gretna Green is long; they would have had to stop somewhere for the evening."

Louisa nodded, growing more and more nervous by the minute. She looked pleadingly at her stepmother. "Will you stay here tonight?"

Lady Bolton stiffened. They both must have noticed, for Mrs. Strickland kindly smiled and shook her head. "I wouldn't want to impose."

"But I would prefer you here," Louisa said. She didn't give a damn what Lady Bolton thought or wanted. "It's terrible waiting alone." Louisa glanced at her mother-in-law. "I mean no offense, ma'am, but you don't know Flora. My stepmother and I, however..."

Louisa's voice trailed off, but she continued to look at her stepmother with pleading eyes, practically begging her to stay. Finally, Mrs. Strickland sighed and nodded. "Very well. Could you send a footman to collect some of my things?"

Louisa nodded. "Of course." She reached for the handbell on the table, and Lady Bolton abruptly rose, leaving the two women alone in the drawing room. When they were sure she was gone, they exchanged the same grave look.

"I suppose I am lucky that Mr. Strickland's mother had already passed by the time we met," the older woman said.

"Yes, you only had to contend with a bratty stepdaughter. Much better than an evil mother-in-law."

Mrs. Strickland laughed slightly. "Oh, you weren't so bad."

The two women grew silent. Louisa, suddenly feeling sentimental and realizing she wasn't always forthcoming with her feelings toward others, cleared her throat. "I hope you know I have always loved you, even if I did not always act like it. You were good for my father, and I adore Flora, no matter how frustrating she can be at times."

Mrs. Strickland smiled. "I know, my dear. I love you too. And I believe the earl does as well, based on what he's doing right now. I have only ever wanted you to be happy, whether you married or not. I am only glad you found someone who deserves you."

Louisa flushed. She already knew Charles loved her. How cowardly of her not to say it back when she knew very well that she returned his feelings. Still sitting, Louisa looked toward the drawing room window, hoping to see a carriage coming down the drive. But no one was there, and Louisa started to worry she might never get to tell him. What if Fitzgerald and Hayward were planning something truly horrendous?

Mrs. Strickland must have noticed the direction of her stepdaughter's gaze. The older woman reached out and patted Louisa's knee. "Don't worry, my dear. They will be home soon."

LOUISA HEARD the wheels of a carriage on the drive early the following morning. Half dressed, she ran to her bedroom window and looked out. She saw a yellow post chaise in the near distance and quickly turned back to her maid, who held Louisa's frock for the day.

"Hurry!" Louisa exclaimed, waving at the maid. "I think they are here!"

After frantically getting into her gown, Louisa took one last glance at her hair in the mirror and then dashed downstairs to the entry hall. As a pair of footmen opened the double doors leading outside, Louisa saw the post chaise pull up to the front of the house. One of the postboys climbed off his perch at the front of the carriage to put down the steps and open the door. Louisa waited, impatiently shifting from foot to foot as she did.

When the door opened, Flora was the first to appear. When her feet finally touched the ground, she ran to her sister, throwing herself into Louisa's open arms. She immediately began to cry.

"I am s-so s-sorry, Louisa," she said, her voice muffled against her sister's bosom. Louisa pressed a kiss to the top of Flora's head.

"For now, I am only glad you are safe. Now, where is my husband?" Releasing her sister, Louisa looked up. She saw Charles and Mr. Hardy standing there, and without thinking, she stepped toward Charles and threw her arms around him. "I was so worried."

Although Charles returned her embrace, he started to

laugh. "Worried about me? I am fine. Mr. Hardy is the one sporting a black eye."

Surprised, Louisa broke away from him, looking at Hardy over his shoulder. She gasped when she saw the discoloration around his right eye. Stepping away from Charles, Louisa looked at the land steward more closely. "What happened?" she asked.

"It's nothing," Hardy said with a shrug.

"He received it while defending my honor," Flora said from behind them. Louisa turned and looked at her sister, arching her brow as she did. Flora smiled coyly in response. "You will be happy to hear the viscount received a good thrashing."

Louisa faced Hardy again, her brow still raised. "Did he?"

The land steward shrugged. "It was nothing. If you'll excuse me, I think I'll return to my cottage. I haven't slept in days."

Frowning, Louisa nodded. "You should dine with us tomorrow evening, Mr. Hardy."

But the man had already turned away, waving his hand in the air. "Perhaps some other time."

Louisa looked after him, confused, before turning toward Charles. Her husband stepped toward her and whispered in her ear. "I will explain later."

THE STRICKLANDS GATHERED in the drawing room shortly after Flora returned. Charles went upstairs to take a nap, and Lady Bolton was outside in the garden, allowing the three women some time alone. Although she was happy Flora was safe, her sister had behaved extremely irrationally, and Louisa wasn't about to spare her an interrogation.

"What were you thinking?" Louisa asked as calmly as

possible, not wanting the conversation to devolve into a terrible argument.

Flora sighed, her shoulders sagging as she did. She was looking down at her hands clasped together in her lap. "I wanted to marry him. I really did, but I knew you would never approve."

"Surely you must understand why now!" Louisa said with a huff.

Flora nodded reluctantly, looking up at her sister for the first time. "You knew from the very beginning that the viscount wasn't a good man, but I never wanted to believe you. I was... I was so attracted to him, and I hadn't felt that way about anyone before. Logic suddenly carried much less weight than my heart."

Louisa frowned, thinking of her own situation. "Perhaps a balance of the two might be better moving forward. I will even join you in trying."

Flora blinked at her, clearly not understanding what her sister meant.

Louisa smiled. "Everyone knows I listen to my mind much more than my heart. But it's only when the two are in unison that one can truly live in peace. You might find it is the same for you if you try."

Flora's eyes suddenly appeared glassy, as if she were about to cry. "So you will not cast me out? You will not desert me?"

"I would never desert you, dear sister. I do hope you learned your lesson, and I must ask... Did anything...?"

Her sister shook her head once, and Louisa nodded. "Good." She couldn't help but smile with relief after preparing herself for the worst earlier. "I am glad."

Flora suddenly burst into tears, standing up and walking toward her sister, throwing her arms around her neck. "I have learned my lesson, Louisa. I promise. I have."

Smiling at her sister's typical burst of emotion, Louisa

gently patted her sister on the back. "Very well. I forgive you."

When Flora finally backed away from her sister, Mrs. Strickland came up behind her, handing her a handkerchief to dry her eyes. "Why don't you wait in the entry hall, Flora?" Mrs. Strickland suggested. "I should like a word alone with Louisa."

Flora nodded, and she took her handkerchief and headed toward the entry hall, leaving Louisa and her stepmother alone. She had an unreadable look on her face, one that Louisa didn't quite understand. She furrowed her brow. "What is it, Mrs. Strickland?"

"I only wanted to say thank you," her stepmother said.

Louisa blinked. "It was nothing. I—"

"When your father decided to entrust everything to you, I did fear that you would forget about me and your sister—especially me. But you did not, even though we are not related by blood. I always knew Flora was the reason—you would not have wanted to make her upset—and I—"

Louisa held up a hand. "Please, Mrs. Strickland. Whether Flora was here or not, I would have protected you. It is what my father would have wanted. In fact, it is what *I* want. You did raise me, after all."

Mrs. Strickland's eyes began to water, and then she pulled her stepdaughter into an awkward embrace. Louisa smiled into the nape of her neck, wrapping her arms tighter around the older woman. When they broke their embrace, Louisa placed her hands on Mrs. Strickland's shoulders.

"You should have dinner with us on Sunday. Perhaps we might start a new tradition, now that we will be living apart."

Mrs. Strickland nodded, smiling happily. "I would like that."

"As would I," Louisa said, smiling back at her.

· · ·

AFTER MRS. STRICKLAND and Flora left, Louisa quietly entered her husband's bedroom, where he was supposed to be resting. As expected, she found him in bed, and she took off her slippers and stealthily slipped under the bedclothes beside him. He started to stir as she slid up against him.

"Shhh," she said softly. "It's only me. Go back to sleep."

But he started to turn anyway, facing her in bed. As he became more alert, he smiled broadly at her, leaning toward her neck and planting a kiss there. He wrapped his arms around her, pulling her more tightly to his body. "I am so glad to be home," he whispered into her neck.

Louisa leaned her head back, smiling. "And I am glad to have you home. Will you tell me now how Mr. Hardy earned that black eye? Or are you too tired?"

Charles pulled back from her, shaking his head. "First, I feel I must apologize for ever doubting which Strickland girl Mr. Hardy preferred." Louisa shot him a pointed look, and he laughed. "But if you must know, Mr. Hardy received his black eye while engaging in fisticuffs on the dirt road outside the Bell Inn, where I found your sister at dawn this morning."

Louisa gasped, raising her hand to cover her mouth. She lowered it slightly. "I cannot believe it." She blinked. "What did Flora say?"

Charles knitted his brow together. "She didn't say much of anything, but I do think she will remember who Hardy is from now on. After all, he did propose marriage to her."

Louisa's eyes widened. "What?" She hit her husband on the chest. "And you waited this long to tell me? What did she say?"

Charles laughed. "She said no, of course. She told him there was no reason for him to spoil his potential future happiness with a bride of his choosing just to save her from ruination. Your sister does not know he is in love with her, does she?"

Louisa winced. "No, she doesn't. Flora has always been a little oblivious." She sighed. "Poor Mr. Hardy. No wonder he walked off so quickly this morning. He is probably embarrassed."

"He will recover," Charles reassured her, wrapping her in his arms once more and burying his face in her hair. "There is something else I want to tell you. It's about my mother."

Louisa stiffened.

He petted her hair, laughing slightly. "It is nothing bad, only that she is moving into the dowager house tomorrow."

She immediately relaxed, looking up at him with wide eyes. Part of her felt like she might cry. "Charles..."

"I should have demanded it as soon as she arrived," he admitted, turning his gaze away from her. "But I am tired of her trying to drive a wedge between us. I will not let anyone do that for as long as we are married—not even my mother. So I asked her to leave."

Charles looked back at her, and she smiled. "Thank you, Charles. And thank you for rescuing Flora. Mrs. Strickland told me you called on Hayward soon after you arrived in London. Please don't tell me he organized this entire ordeal."

"He certainly encouraged the scheme," Charles admitted.

Louisa sighed, letting herself fall into the pillows at the head of the bed.

"He said he wanted to embarrass you as you embarrassed him."

Louisa scowled. "Well, I am not embarrassed. The scandal sheets can say whatever they want about my sister—I do not care. Everyone will forget in three years, and perhaps she might have another season then... Or maybe she will fall in love with Mr. Hardy." She turned toward Charles. "We must have them both over for dinner."

Charles laughed. "Whatever you say, my love."

Louisa looked at him, realizing now was the perfect

moment to tell him how she felt. Suddenly, her hands felt very clammy. She swallowed nervously, turning away. "Have I ever told you how glad I am you stopped me from having an affair with Mr. Hayward? What a terrible mistake that would have been."

Charles looked at her, his mouth slightly open as he studied her face. He reached for her hand beside him, intertwining his fingers with hers. "You are glad even though it led you to marry me?" he asked.

Louisa flushed. That was what she was thinking precisely. She sat up on her elbows and looked over at him, carefully studying his face. Even though her mouth felt dry, Louisa tried to speak. "Yes. I am not sure why I was so afraid to say it before now, but I love you, Charles. I love you even though I have no idea what the future holds. And as much as that uncertainty scares me, it doesn't stop me from loving you with every ounce of my being." She turned away, unable to look at him any longer. He stared at her as if he could see through her. "I'm sorry it took me so long to realize it."

She felt Charles shifting in bed beside her. Soon he was sitting up with her, cupping the side of her cheek with his hand and gently turning her to look at him. "I think you and I have always cared for one other, Louisa. We might have felt it more strongly at certain times than others, and perhaps never at the same time, but things are different now."

With his free hand, he brought one of her palms to his lips, kissing it gently. His eyes met hers. Louisa already knew the answer, but she asked the question anyway, just because she wanted to hear him say it at least once a day for the rest of her days. She was nearly breathless when she spoke. "Why are things different?"

"Because I love you too," he said before pulling her in for another kiss.

Epilogue

Three years later

LINFIELD HALL WAS busy that morning. Servants scrambled through the hallways, going from room to room as they performed their last preparations for the house party. Charles was in his study, anxiously waiting for the duke to arrive. When he finally did show up, Rutley was fifteen minutes late.

"Apologies, Bolton," he muttered as he entered the room. The duke had bags under his eyes, and he seemed uncharacteristically agitated.

Charles hesitated to ask if something was wrong. He had heard rumors from London about Rutley and his sister, but Charles had vowed to stay out of their business a long time ago.

"You are hardly ever late," Charles said, forcing a smile. "I was beginning to grow worried."

Rutley only grunted in his response, so Charles opened his

top desk drawer, procuring a stack of crisp banknotes. He placed them on the desk. "I have your last payment here."

The duke reached forward, taking the money and placing it in his jacket. Charles exhaled deeply, as if someone had lifted a giant weight off his back. Even the duke, despite his tired look, cracked a smile. "Am I still invited to the house party even though you are no longer bound by money to be my friend?"

Charles laughed. "Of course you are! You were my friend long before I ever owed you any money." But then he grew serious, raising a single finger in warning. "You won't cause any problems with Rosamund, will you? I should probably warn you that we sent an invitation to her latest suitor. What was his name again?"

"Lord Branksome," Rutley said, his voice dropping an octave.

"Have you met him?"

"Perhaps at some occasion in town." Rutley abruptly stood, clumsily pushing the armchair out of place as he did. "I cannot recall. Excuse me, there are things I must attend to at home."

Charles stood as well. Even though Rosamund had broken off her engagement to the duke four years ago, she still seemed able to get under his skin. "When should we expect you for the party?"

Rutley sighed, and Charles had half a mind to tell the poor man to stay home. From what Louisa told Charles, Rosamund quite liked the viscount, who had a large family estate in Dorset. It was a great match for both parties. "I have never seen her write about any of her suitors this way," Louisa told him at the time with a small smile.

Charles only wanted his sister to be happy, and if Rutley was going to be a problem... but the duke interrupted his anxious thoughts before Charles could say something. "I will return later in the afternoon. Perhaps Swinton and Brooks would fancy a game of pool before we must dress for dinner."

Charles nodded at him, forcing a smile.

After the duke left, Charles went upstairs to the nursery, where he was sure he would find his wife. There, Louisa lay on one of the sofas with their two-year-old daughter pulled tightly against her chest. Louisa was holding a book and reading, and both still wore their nightclothes. That must have been one of the few night rails Louisa owned that Charles hadn't accidentally ripped at some point or another.

"Papa!" The little girl noticed him, climbing down from the sofa and running toward him as Louisa sat up, still holding the open book in her hands. Their daughter had the same fiery red hair as her mother.

"And how is my dear Lily today?" Charles asked, kneeling so that his eyes met his daughter's. He pulled her into an embrace, but the little girl wiggled against his chest, pulling back and frowning at him.

"Mama told me that Cousin Thomas is coming to stay. Is that true?"

Charles glanced at Louisa. Their daughter didn't particularly like Brooks and August's son, but that didn't stop Louisa from trying to force the two cousins to be friends. When Charles looked back at his daughter, he half smiled. "Yes, darling. Aren't you looking forward to seeing your cousin?"

Lily continued to pout, taking a step away from her father. "No. I hate boys."

Charles tried not to laugh. Louisa placed a hand over her stomach. The doctor said she was only three months along, and they hadn't told Lily yet, but they were hoping for a little boy. Charles worried how Lily might react to having a little brother.

Unfortunately, she would have to get over it.

"No more pouting, Lily," Louisa said, coming to kneel

beside her husband. "Your father and I must go now. Can you give Mummy and Daddy kisses?"

Lily reluctantly agreed, and somehow Charles managed to sneak in an extra hug, causing the girl to giggle uncontrollably before the nanny took her to go and get ready for the day. Charles and Louisa left the nursery side by side, sharing an illicit glance.

"Isn't it a bit late to be going around in your night rail still?" Charles asked teasingly when they were out in the hall. "Motherhood has changed you, Louisa."

Louisa huffed. "Is there something wrong with that?"

"You misunderstand," Charles replied, shaking his head. He pushed her up against the wall, and she yelped. He ran his hands up her torso until he was cupping both her breasts. "I am not complaining."

Charles leaned in to kiss her, and she returned the gesture twofold, wrapping her arms around his neck while he ran his hands over her thin night rail. Her body molded into his, and then he heard someone beside him clear his throat. Startled, Charles broke away from his wife, finding their butler standing in the hall. "What do you want, man?"

The butler was blushing red from head to toe. "I only wanted to tell you that Mrs. Strickland and Miss Flora have arrived."

Louisa and Charles exchanged a look. "They are here early," Louisa said before turning back toward the butler. "Tell them Lord Bolton will meet them in the drawing room shortly. I still have to go call on the Millers."

The butler nodded. When he'd left, Louisa started walking down the hall toward her bedroom, which was more like their bedroom since Charles hardly used his. Charles followed her, though he would have liked to continue kissing. "Perhaps I might go call on the Millers, and you can go and entertain your family."

Louisa looked over her shoulder, shooting him a sharp look. "But I always call on the Millers whenever there is a problem. They were my tenants long before you ever entertained the idea of making me your wife."

Charles sighed, running his hand through his hair. Although she was effectively telling him off, he continued to follow her. "I only worry about you overexerting yourself. You are pregnant—"

Louisa turned around and hushed him. They had agreed they wouldn't tell anyone about the baby quite yet. Nevertheless, he continued. "We should hire a new land steward. You cannot do it all, you know."

Louisa smiled. "But I would like to try."

Charles sighed. Mr. Hardy had left two years ago, off to God knew where to make his fortune. It was either Liverpool or Manchester; Charles couldn't remember. He was still quite bitter that working as an earl's land steward wasn't fulfilling enough for young Hardy. Or at least that was what the young man told Charles when he handed in his resignation. Privately, the earl wondered if Flora and her complete blindness to his affection had something to do with it.

Louisa had twiddled her thumbs over hiring a replacement ever since, and she wouldn't let Charles make a decision without her approval. He followed her into the bedroom, where she tugged the bellpull by the bed. "Let me get dressed in peace, please," she said. "You know how it embarrasses the maids when you watch."

Charles rolled his eyes. "It gives them something to gossip about belowstairs. They enjoy it. But Louisa, say you will consider hiring someone soon." He stalked toward her, wrapping his arms around her waist from behind. Albeit reluctantly, she seemed to melt into him. "You know, you always said you wanted any marriage we had to be a partnership. Shouldn't my wishes be taken into account sometimes?"

"I suppose so," Louisa murmured. Charles gently spun her around so that she was facing him. He recognized that look right away. It was the same one Lily gave him when he said Cousin Thomas was coming to stay. Charles tried not to smile, but it was impossible. Louisa furrowed her brow. "What is it?"

"Nothing," he said, smoothing her hair. Now was not the time to compare Louisa to a two-year-old. He was negotiating, not trying to make her angry. "But this is the first house party Linfield Hall has hosted in five years. I only want everyone to see you for the magnificent countess you are."

Louisa started to smile at him. "But what if I'm a magnificent countess because I can do three jobs at once? Mother, lady of the house, and land steward."

"You forgot one."

Louisa looked at him questioningly.

"Wife."

Louisa grinned, cupping the side of his face with her hand. He leaned into her soft palm, kissing the center. "Very well," she said. "You have convinced me with those charming words and pleading eyes of yours. I will go down to greet Mrs. Strickland and my sister, and you go call on the Millers. They say there is a leak in their roof."

Charles nodded at her. "And the land steward?"

She sighed. "We will look for someone once the house party is over."

He almost leaned down and kissed her, but then he realized he had forgotten to tell her something. "Rutley was here this morning. Just in from London. I don't expect he slept at all last night."

Louisa groaned. "I hope he doesn't cause too many problems. Rosamund sounds very pleased with this Lord Branksome fellow. I don't want the duke to muck it up. Why was he here so early, anyway?"

"I was giving him his final payment. We no longer carry any debt, Louisa."

She gasped, bringing her hands to her mouth. "What wonderful news!" She reached up to kiss him, and Charles fought the urge to push her back onto the bed and have his way with her. Fortunately for his wife, Louisa's maid entered the room, forcing them to part.

"I will let you get ready," he said, starting to back away.

Louisa smiled at him, leaning forward so she could whisper in his ear.

"I love you, Charles Finch, and this life we have created together."

He leaned in for one more kiss on the cheek, though one more kiss was never quite enough for Charles. "As do I."

Acknowledgments

Thank you, first and foremost, to my editors, Crystal Watanabe and Melinda Utendorf, who I would be absolutely lost without. I would also like to thank Leni Kauffman for illustrating and designing another beautiful cover for this series. I hope this story does it justice.

I would like to thank my friends and family for supporting me on this journey, especially the ones who buy and read my books. They know who they are. And I have to thank my partner Chris as well, as he's the one who lives with me and puts up with my furious typing day and night.

I'll admit part of me is afraid this novel is terrible because I wrote the majority of it with post-concussion syndrome, which has made writing and reading difficult for the past five months. I wouldn't have been able to do it without my wonderful physical therapists, Zak and Danielle, as well as my vision therapist, Kirsten. You guys are the real MVPs in my life at the moment, right up there with T. Swift and Carly Rae, and that's saying something.

I also would be nothing without the wonderful readers

who review, promote, or purchase my books. If you've read *The Land Steward's Daughter*, *Lady August*, and now *A Rake Like You*, thank you, thank you, thank you. You have no idea how much it means to me.

About the Author

Becky Michaels is a historical romance author and self-proclaimed Anglophile. After graduating from Boston University with a degree in English, she reluctantly decided to get a day job but never stopped writing—or dreaming. *THE LAND STEWARD'S DAUGHTER*, a Regency romance set in 1815 England, is her debut novel. Despite the cold winters and high rent, she still lives in the Boston area with her boyfriend and cat.

Also by Becky Michaels

Winters Series

THE LAND STEWARD'S DAUGHTER

Linfield Hall Series

LADY AUGUST

A RAKE LIKE YOU

Want news about future releases delivered straight to your mailbox?
Visit www.BeckyMichaels.com and sign up for Becky's newsletter.

CPSIA information can be obtained
at www.ICGtesting.com
Printed in the USA
BVHW082242020921
615904BV00003B/606